DESTRUCTION

GEORGINA FATSEAS

Destruction by Georgina Fatseas

ISBN 978-1-955136-47-1 (Paperback)
ISBN 978-1-955136-48-8 (Hardback)

Printed in the United States of America.

New Leaf Media, LLC
175 S. 3rd Street, Suite 200
Columbus, OH 43215
www.thenewleafmedia.com

CHAPTER 1

Stefan walked into the dining room of his house and slammed down three newspapers in front of his twenty-three-year-old son's face. Casually, Ivan looked up from his mobile phone. "What now?" he asked annoyed at the disturbance. Stefan leaned over the table and pointed to the overlapping newspapers. "This!" He pointed to the headline of the top newspaper. "How dare you carry on like this in public? Three newspapers, three different women in one night! Well explain!"

Ivan dragged the newspapers closer and read the headlines and then pushed them away. "Yep. All false but it was a fantastic night. Two parties, a night club and the thing is, I can't recall any of these girls."

"Fucking hell!" roared his father. "You didn't have to propose to all three!"

"So I was drunk. And I don't recall proposing to any bird. And do you mind not shouting. My head…"

"It won't be the only thing that will hurt. Sort this out as the phones are going to start ringing with these upset young ladies, their parents and the media. What the hell were you thinking?"

"I was drunk. They all looked good at that time……I think."

"Geez." Stefan was about to reprimand Ivan more, but the phone rang. "You answer that. You created this mess. You fix it." Both men ignored the ringing phone as they stared at each other.

Stefan stormed out of the room bracing himself for damage control when he would face the other members on board of directors of his company, The East European Flower Company, later in the day.

The land line phone stopped ringing but seconds later, it rang again. Ivan ignored it. Ivan read the three newspapers in detail. He racked his brain trying to recall the previous night's events. The party at the Symanski's started early. Marlena and her sister, Lavinia were leaving at five a.m. the next day for a year in France. Everyone was out of the house by ten. Ivan recalled why he wasted himself.

Marlena going to France with Lavinia. It wasn't a study venture in the French language as they announced to the guests. It wasn't a scholarship either - it was a cover up. Marlena's ultra conservative parents were sending her there because she was pregnant. Poor Lavinia, he surmised, she is to be Marlena's companion and nurse maid.

Ivan recalled driving to Marlena's home two days before with the intention of asking her out that night. He could have phoned, but he wanted an excuse to see her in person. He also thought it would be polite, especially with her conservative parents, Dominik and Maja Symanski. Everyone played their old-fashioned game. He pushed the security code to open the large, heavy iron gates. He wondered why they even bothered with the code as everybody he knew and was certain a good number of people including many he did not know, knew the code. He drove the car up the long curved stony driveway towards what he considered a mini castle.

Five bedrooms each had a generous sized en suite, a private mini-lounge and a kitchenette. The rooms were accessed by a two-metre-wide hall. Along the passageway were works of art and family portraits. They had ensured the family had stamped itself into this part of the house. The hall led to a large commercial kitchen which divided the house into living quarters and entertainment. The entertainment section of the house was split into left and right sides. Partitions normally separating the sections would concertina back into the cavity of the walls to create a hall. The informal dining room abutted the informal lounge. Then behind a much larger formal dining room and a large formal lounge were nestled directly behind. If necessary, all four rooms could be opened to form a mini-hall capable of holding up to 100 people. Spacious his and her powder rooms for the area was located discreetly behind an alcove. From the informal dining room, a set of stairs went down to a den. Recalling what he was told, it was a playroom for Malena and Lavinia as young children. Over the years it changed with their age and evolving interests. Now it was a gym complete with a music system and a game room where electronic games competed with table tennis and darts.

Ivan parked outside "the castle" as he as he preferred to call it. He walked up the small set of stairs leading to the front door and wondered if the faulty intercom system had been repaired. The system was old and required people to push the doorbell button several times before the sound alerted any occupants inside. Ivan stopped dead in his tracks. He lowered his hand from the doorbell button before he pushed it for the first time. He listened. The intercom system was on, whether it was accidental or just another fault, it didn't matter. Their raised voices drifted through. The argument inside was heated. Although some of the words were barely audible, there was enough for him to know what was going on.

All hell had broken out with Marlena screaming defiance and denial while her parents were screaming accusations. He heard a list of male names coming from each of the parents. Malena would scream back definite no or don't know. He heard is name. He paid attention. Marlena screamed out, "No!"

He now knew Marlena had been playing a wider field than he ever did, and she got caught in the worst way possible. Knowing he was not exactly a saint; he couldn't be judgemental. He listened a bit longer to the voices fluctuating in volume through the intercom system. He closed his eyes and shook his head. He returned to his car and vowed never to say a word about this argument to anyone.

He liked Marlena since they were teenagers going to the same posh school in Poznan. They were in different classes. She was one grade behind. At times, the classes were combined for sports or if there was a guest speaker. Each class was a very small size of twelve – it was almost private tuition in every subject. It was a school only the wealthy could afford to send their children. The social upside was everybody knew each other. Small classes meant you got to know everybody. The downside was that nobody got away with anything – homework was always done, and strict rules were obeyed at all times. Everyone looked out for and respected each other. It was like an extended family.

But on weekends, everyone congregated in shopping malls or sporting grounds and they partied like no tomorrow. The training of watching out for each other carried over to all after school occasions.

Outsiders were respected but as soon as someone tried make a move on a member of the group, the newcomers were quickly made to feel uncomfortable for invading. They moved on to leave the untouchable to the group's fate.

Ivan and his friends frequently went out in mixed small groups which, through the night, grew into a much larger gang. Ivan knew and observed, people would pair off through the night, especially in the early hours of the morning. It just wasn't always bed jumping a he termed it, it also included who was going where and needed a lift to a pre-determined destination. It was ingrained at home and in their strict, poshy school, women never went home unescorted or were carefully placed in a cab with an escort before all departed in separate directions. What people did behind closed doors, was strictly never spoken about. It was none of their business. It was the unwritten rule which everybody abided by.

Now Marlena was basically ordered away from home to hide her pregnancy. He wondered if Marlena knew who the father was. He shook his head and thought at twenty-two, Marlena an adult, didn't have to put up with that ultra-conservatism in this day and age. He didn't want to walk into the family fight. It was something private which they had to sort out. He knew he wasn't the child's father as they never had any intimate moments. They had never been more than good close friends hanging out not hooked up.

When he was driving back to his home on that fateful day, his father called him on the mobile phone. He wanted him to go to Gdansk, a northern coastal town, to pick up a delivery that had been late for three days. This delivery was not only three days late but for some unknown reason it was shipped to Gdansk instead of arriving by truck at the distribution centre on the edges of Poznan. It was an urgent job and the drive from Poznan to Gdansk would take two hours one way. At the start of his drive to Gdansk, he phoned the depot and ordered a semi-trailer to meet him at the Gdansk port.

The company traded in flowers. Flowers from the east were sold to customers in the west and vice versa. Due to their short shelf life, flowers arriving late were always disastrous. Old flowers for the family company would be useless or would bring prices less than what the cargo value was. At Gdansk, he would attend to the custom's paperwork and then ensure the shipment was loaded on the semi-trailer. He had already downgraded the shipment to seconds. Seconds were sold at local markets at a much lower price.

Ivan sipped on a now cold cup of coffee and thought more about that day. He had mixed feelings when he found out about Marlena and how her parents reacted. He was just as angry now as he was two days ago. It was such an archaic idea to send their daughter away when she needed the most support. He felt sorry for both Marlena and Lavinia. Marlena for being pregnant at the wrong time and the push for the younger sister, Lavinia, made to look after her older sister. No matter how he looked at it, he was both annoyed and disgusted. But at the same time, he felt a bit cheated. That was bothering him more than anything else. He couldn't wrap his mind around it.

He had been out of sorts since overhearing what was going on. Two of this three friends with whom he associated with in that short period of time, picked up on his moodiness. Antoni Grabowski had a big crush on Lavinia. Ivan hesitated to tell Antoni that Lavinia was being forced to move out with Marlena. Szymon Sawicki also knew something was up. But because they made a pact years ago, they swore they wouldn't pry into each other's problems until the person was ready to speak. Ivan kept this information about the girls to himself and intended to keep it that way.

At the party, Antoni was spitting seeds when he heard Lavinia and Marlena were going to be away for a year. Their parents made the formal announcement to the crowd while both Marlena and Lavinia forced a smile to the surprised crowd. Antoni and Ivan now had their separate unsaid excuses to get trashed at the farewell party.

Szymon, stayed quite sober by comparison. His girlfriend, Julia Tomasczewski, was by his side all nearly night, teasing Szymon with flirtatious moves. Ivan recalled telling them to find a bedroom or find a secluded place in the spacious gardens outside. They grinned back while giving the one finger salute before returning to their insular focus.

Ivan recalled chatting up a blonde-haired girl, Beth, who was now staring back at him in the top newspaper. He recalled some parts of the conversation he had. He recalled trying several times but was unsuccessful in planting kisses on her lips. But he couldn't recall asking her to marry him. *Hell,* he thought, *I only just met her. If I did ask, she couldn't have taken me seriously. What person in their right mind would take that proposal seriously after just meeting them and from someone who was obviously very drunk?* Ivan looked at the picture in greater detail before reading beyond the bold print in the first paragraph.

The ring was hers. He recalled clowning around kissing her jewelled hand and slowly bringing it up to kiss it again at eye level. That is what the photo was showing that drunken eye-level kiss on the hand exposing the semi-precious stoned knuckle buster to the photographer. Ivan frowned and asked himself, *who was the photographer?* He entered the question on his mobile's to do list. He read the article:

Exclusive to the Mail.
Ivan Nowak, the only son of Stefan Nowak, proposed to Beth Konradin, the only daughter of Charlee and Martin Konradin. The proposal took place at a farewell party for Marlena and Lavinia Symanski who won scholarships to study in France. The Nowak family own the flower distribution company, The East Europe Flower Company. The Konradin family own the large Trans-Europe Transport Company based in Germany. Beth and Ivan intend to marry early next year.

Ivan groaned, "Bullshit!" as he pushed that newspaper away and sipped his cold cup of coffee. He wondered how much of the text was relating to Beth was true. They had him right. *I didn't even know she existed before that night and promptly forgot her name seconds after she said it. It is bad when the newspaper had to remind me.* Then Ivan shook his head and cursed, "Anything to make quick money. Don't bother whose reputation you stuff up. It's all just about the money." The phone rang again. He ignored it. His mobile rang. He ignored that. Then both phones rang at the same time. He looked at the mobile; it wasn't a familiar number. He stopped the call and then switched the phone off completely. He stared at the photo in the Times.

Exclusive to the Times.
Ivan Nowak, son of Stefan Nowak of The East European Flower Company proposed to Helena Begen, a secretary who works for the German import company called Burch. The proposal took place at a party held at Mikal and Thea Mazur. Ivan gave Helena a large diamond ring which

belonged to his long-deceased mother. The couple plan
to marry early next year.

Ivan's eyes flashed back to the picture. He frowned at it as he reached for his phone, restarted it and dialled his father. Stefan answered, "What is it now?"

"Dad did you look at the picture in the Times? Look at it closely. And what do you see?"

"Just a minute." Stefan called his secretary to bring in the newspaper and pointed to the newspaper. He signed for the secretary to leave. "I have a copy. What am I supposed to see?" asked Stefan.

"Mum's ring. When was the last time you saw the ring and is it still in the house?"

Stefan pushed his hair back as he contemplated, "Are you still at home?"

"Yep," Ivan replied.

"Go to the safe and see if it is still there. I'll wait."

Minutes later Ivan returned, "It's there."

Stefan gave a sigh of relief, but he was clearly puzzled. "The paper must have dug up some archive pictures to publish that. Do me a favour. Pull out the photo albums of your mother and me and find a picture of me and your mum in the same or nearly the same position. The album should be close to the bottom of the pile. I'll wait." Ivan switched the music on the phone as he dug around in the lower draw of a wall unit.

He found two albums at the bottom. He flipped through both books. It was near the end of the second book when he came across the same picture. The one in the newspaper had been photo shopped: his father's head and his mother's head had been replaced with his own and Helena's.

"Dad, I found the photo towards the back. The newspaper photo was definitely photo-shopped." Ivan could hear Stefan sigh. "Dad. Who was the photographer back then?"

Stefan fought to recall, "I am not sure. Nyro something or other. He would be dead now or in some nursing home. He was in his fifties then."

"I have a bad vibe. Now you know I didn't propose to at least one. The papers are making things up. Scandal sells and I guess I am the flavour of the month. What time are you coming home tonight?"

"Hopefully no later than eight." Both men hung up. Ivan returned to the dining room where the three newspapers stared back at him. Reluctantly, he picked up the last newspaper, The Tribune, the one which had a reputation of mixing up facts. It had an unwritten motto: scandal, true or fake, sells.

He looked at the red head lady who may have been slightly older than himself. He recalled Mikal Mazur senior went ballistic at him. Ivan grinned as a hazy image formed. *I peed over the Mrs's orchids in the newly constructed greenhouse designed for tropical plants. Poor Mikal having to put up with that stepmother.* The woman had come into the green house to show her friends her new acquisition, an orchid. Ivan smirked to himself when he remembered being caught zipping up his trouser front. All hell broke out. He recalled Mikal senior throwing him in a cab and Mikal's senior voice giving the cab his home address. As the cab drove off, Ivan recalled, redirecting the cab to a night club where he knew some people who regularly visited the place would be there.

He found himself a booth and ordered one more drink and then drank water for the rest of the night while he sweated out the alcohol. The waitresses and a myriad of others walked by all ignoring him. The only person to notice him was this red head with long flowing locks. She sat down beside him for a few minutes, but only for a few minutes. He couldn't recall anyone taking photos at the club. Sometimes the newspaper social the columnist would venture into such haunts taking pictures of customers. It gave the venue free advertising. Again, the newspaper had to remind him but this time the paper was so wrong.

Exclusive to the Tribune.
Ivan Nowak, the only son of Stefan Nowak who owns of The East European Flower Company, proposed to Ravennah Hartoviski at the exclusive Fireball Night Club last night. Ravennah Hartoviski is the daughter of Kostya and Lothar Hartoviski who own the Fireball Night Club and several others around town. Ivan and Ravennah intend to marry early next year.

Ivan mumbled, "That's not Ravennah. Bastards. The real Ravennah is about fifteen and not permitted in the place. Liars. The poor kid is going to cop it at school." He pushed the newspaper away and downed the rest of the cold coffee.

The phone kept ringing in the background. He eventually stood up and removed it off the hook and double checked his own phone to ensure it was switched off. He showered before going to bed at ten in the morning. It was fitful sleep. The previous night's events and newspapers reports kept looping through his mind. He woke up with a start but couldn't explain why. He rolled over towards the window where unfamiliar noises outside floated through his window. Lazily, he lifted himself just high enough to see over the window ledge and groaned. Hordes of media vans and cars waited outside. He rolled on to his back and placed a pillow on his face wishing he could die there and then.

There was a knock on the bedroom door before it was opened. Pawel, his family's bodyguard come limo driver, looked in. "Sir. I know you are awake and know of the media outside. What are your intentions?" Ivan groaned as he pulled the pillow off his face. "Sleep." He rolled over on to his stomach and placed the pillow on the back of his head in a feeble attempt to block out the noise. Pawel politely coughed. "Sir, you have an appointment at three and another at five. Your father is on my phone wanting to talk to you. Since you had the house phone off the hook and yours switched off, he is calling you on mine. I think you should take the call." Ivan slowly sat up and extended his hand. Pawel waited outside the bedroom until the call was over. Ivan handed the phone back and mumbled, "Thanks. Check to see if there is media at the back entrance. I'll get myself ready for the three o'clock."

Seeing no cars or vans were at the back entrance, Pawel drove the family's limousine as Ivan sat in the back going over the work papers his father had left him. If it wasn't such an important meeting, he could have cancelled but that would have reinforced a playboy image which was clearly displayed in the newspapers. He braced himself for smirks, frowns and anything else anyone at the meeting would show. Damage control was important.

The meeting with the new marketing company went well. No one mentioned the notoriety, or they were too polite to mention it. It was a relief. Then it was to the next meeting on the other side of town to meet with a familiar client wanting to increase their business. This was the second meeting with Burch and Burch was named in the Times.

Ivan cringed but quickly recomposed himself when one of the younger of the senior men at the meeting mentioned the newspaper events while his secretary was out of the room. She had been assigned to another task before the meeting began. She was to join them later. The man probed for more details. Ivan ignored the unnecessary distraction and kept steering the meeting to the pre-set agenda. When the meeting was half-way through, the secretary arrived. Ivan gulped when he recognised her from the newspaper, He looked across the table and then quickly looked down. She had recognised him as the drunken slob making passes. She watched him in silence while diligently taking notes and sliding her laptop to the bosses on either side of her. They quickly glanced at the prepared information before continuing with the discussion.

Helena looked at her watch, stood up and exited the room. She returned shortly carrying a tray of sandwiches. She placed the tray slightly off centre on the table and left the room again. Ivan excused himself from the others to follow her. He sensed the others in the room making comments and felt all their eyes burning into the back of his head.

He called after her. She ignored him and continued walking down to the staff kitchenette where other trays of food were to be carried to the meeting room. She slammed the door in his face and held back from turning around to face him. Ivan opened the door slowly and gave a soft cough.

"Sorry. I was drunk. I can't recall you or the others. And sure, as hell, I don't recall proposing to anyone. I am sorry."

The secretary spun around, "You didn't propose. We only spoke briefly. You were trashed so I went away. Not a great first impression. I didn't put this," she held up the newspaper, "in the paper. Look carefully. It is photo shopped."

Ivan sighed in relief. "I know. The original photo was my father and my mother on their formal announcement of their engagement. I don't know how they got the picture unless the person spent hours going through archives at the newspaper office."

"I had some explaining to do. No proposal took place."

"Obviously someone doesn't like me or my family. More dirt, the worse the reputation and less business. I knew this would have been equally as hard on you as it was for me. Can I formally introduce myself? Ivan Nowak." He held his hand out.

"Helena Begen" She shook his hand.

"Let me help you carry one of those trays," offered Ivan.

She smiled. "Thanks. Take the largest one with the fruit and cheese."

Upon returning to the meeting room, the clients looked up with surprise to see Ivan assisting Helena with the trays. They said nothing but one of the older men raised an eyebrow as if they were confirming something in the newspaper may have hinted on something that was true - they at least knew each other.

When he arrived home, Stefan was waiting. He was more relaxed than he was in the morning. "How did the two meetings go?"

"Good," replied Ivan. "I'll do one of the reports tonight. I found out something which is like a double edged sword." Stephan looked puzzled but allowed Ivan to continue. "I met Helena the secretary from Burch. She also had to face similar rubbishing. She knew the photo was faked and confirmed I didn't propose. One photo was photo shopped and the other was just an opportunistic shot. And I have met Ravennah, the real Ravennah Hartoviski. She about fifteen and is not permitted into the night club. I have no idea who this red head lady is."

Stefan looked up in relief, "That confirms what I was thinking. Others on the board will be relieved. The chairman, Jakub Kamirisky knows Ravennah and her family. He instantly knew the paper was printing rubbish. However, he wasn't so sure about the other two."

Ivan nodded. "I know I got wasted and that was as far as I went. Sorry. I have no idea who or why these were created other than to discredit us."

Stefan asked, "What triggered the drinking binge? You've never binged before."

"Dad, I can't say. I accidentally overheard something which I wish I never heard. I can't tell you just yet. I was very upset. You can breathe. It wasn't related to the business. When I am ready, I will tell you. Promise." Stefan nodded. In the past, Ivan did tell him what bothered him, but always did so in his own good time. He smiled as he recalled, his mother was like that. Issues were brought up, but the timing had to be right. For a child who lost his mother at very young age, it was uncanny how a few traces of her personality were displayed by Ivan.

Just then the doorbell went. Stefan went to the video screen near the door. He frowned as two strangers who were at the door. Stefan spoke through the intercom system, "We are not doing any interviews especially at this time of night." One man rummaged in his pocket and held up a badge.

"We are the police. Detectives Radoslaw Lanski and Eryk Wojcik. Can we come in?"

"What is it about?" enquired Stefan.

"This is not a matter to discuss through your intercom. If we can't come in, then come to the central police quarters tomorrow as soon as possible."

"Wait." Stefan pushed the entry button. A loud click was heard. The detectives pushed the door open. Stefan greeted them at the door, ushered them into the lounge room and introduced Ivan.

CHAPTER 2

The men smiled as they introduced themselves again and re-showed their badges.

"What is this all about?"

"Not good news. Mr. Nowak, we believe your life and that of your son's is in danger," said Radoslaw.

"How?" asked Stefan who was now feeling vulnerable.

"Do you recall witnessing a crime about twenty-five years ago?"

"Yes. I do recall and I have put that part of my life well behind me. The accusation I was a part of the crime and the tortuous subsequent court case, broke me. That episode is left best buried."

"I am sorry to give you bad news. The criminals have been released after completing their long stint in jail. We tried but couldn't stop the release. That happened just three days ago. We tried to contact you, but you were out of the country. And today no one was answering any phone," said Eryk in an almost frustrated manner.

"Yes. I was in Switzerland helping a new franchisee. The first one for Switzerland," Stefan replied reliving the pride of the new expansion. "And today, we ignored the phone thinking it was all media."

"Mr. Nowak, we believe the criminals are out to destroy you, kill you, and maybe kill your son.

Rumours before they were released indicated that, and we tried hard to stop their release by citing the rumours. We also cited other possible criminal activity. The prison administrators wanted proof not rumours. We didn't have enough proof to satisfy their requirements."

"We believe the newspaper articles are the start of their attack. The red head-lady falsely called Ravennah is the daughter of one of the men, Norbert Zielinski. Her name is Roza Zielinski. The other is Wikto Duba. Do you recall those names?" Stefan nodded."

Radoslaw continued, "The real Ravennah is about fifteen years old. We checked that out and she doesn't even look like Roza. We visited the Hartoviski family today. They were fully aware of the newspaper and the false use of their daughter's name. They were very upset. They want to press charges when these people are found."

"What was their crime?" asked Ivan.

"It is best for me to answer that," said Stefan as he started to relive the incident.

"It was in summertime. I had met your mother some six months before. I was nineteen at the time. I couldn't sleep so I took myself for a walk hoping that would settle me. At that time, there were few phones in houses, certainly no mobiles and no all-night venues. Just a few streetlights generally placed at each corner and half the time they were out. So, any light from any building stood out and helped anyone walking around. I was just three blocks away from home when I noticed the corner store had a light on. I was curious and walked over. That shop always had the lights off at seven at night. The owners lived upstairs. It was usual then that most shop owners lived ups stairs and just about everyone in the town had lights off between ten and twelve. I was out walking at two in the morning. It was construed as suspicious behaviour by the police of that time."

Radoslaw added. "We were under the influence of communist rule. Non-conformity was almost a crime in itself." Stefan grimaced recalling the restrictions on life. "As I was saying. I looked into the window and saw the shop owner and his wife in their pyjamas looking terrified at two men pointing guns at them. I ran to the nearest phone booth a block away from the shop and called the police.

I was told to stay where I was but to keep watch from that distance to see which way the robbers would go. While I was waiting in the booth, I heard two gun shots. I told the police over the phone two shots were fired.

"I ran from the booth scared I would also be shot. The phone booth was lit up, and in the darkness, it was like an advertising sign which said 'shoot the caller.'

"The police arrived to see two bodies and a safe opened. Since food was also expensive at the time, the criminals also helped themselves to some of the food. I approached the police with the intentions of giving details of what I had witnessed. Because I was out at this odd time of night, they listened to the details and then arrested me. In their eyes, I was a part of the gang who just got cold feet and snitched on the others. I had a hard time convincing them I was the witness and the one who called for them. I was cuffed and taken to the police station and endlessly quizzed." Stefan rubbed his face recalling the violent slaps and the week spent in the watch house.

"Seven days later the men were caught and told the police I was a part of the robbery but got cold feet and left the get-away car to call them. The police found their fingerprints in the car and at the crime scene. They turned over their apartments and my apartment looking for evidence of my connection. Of course, they found nothing, but the men insisted I was a part of the crime. I was freed but was carefully watched. No evidence was ever found.

"In the courts, the police were softer in their approach but the defence for the criminals grilled me much worse than what I experienced in the police station. Anything I said was twisted to make it look like I was a part the violent crime. They did their best to discredit me by digging up anything and everything and twisted things around. I was treated badly like a criminal. The event changed my life. Your mother didn't want to know me. I was disowned by everyone. Mud sticks even when you are clean." Stefan pointed to the three newspapers still on the coffee table.

"They got twenty-five years. The aftermath for me was, I lost your mother and had a hell of a time convincing her and her parents of my innocence. I lost my job and eventually kicked out of the apartment I was living in. I was on the streets."

"Both of my parents had died. My grandmother was on her death bed in some horrible rundown hospital. The house we shared was rented out a day after your grandmother moved to into the hospital. Our personal belongings were left on the kerb. People who were equally as poor as we were, stole the items. I was left with a few clothes and a couple of photos. It took me a while to get an apartment, more like a one room hovel and that was after getting a new job. In the communist period, 1945 to 1989 living on the streets was a crime. The police still had this view until 1993 when the Russian military left the country - a hangover from communist rule. I was hiding at night and nearly freezing to death in winter. A very bad time for me. It took me two years to re-build my life and all the time dodging the police for vagrancy."

Stefan smiled at his plan which started him on his path to riches. "I was becoming depressed and fearful of the chances of being caught were getting higher. Police were under orders to round up vagrants and move them to wherever. No one knew where they went, and no one ever came back. To disguise myself, I would weed the council gardens, talk to anyone and everyone who happened by. When the real council workers came, I joined in with them weeding the gardens and this time with tools instead of my hands. Eventually, a supervisor came by when the others were designated to another part of the gardens. Naturally, they took the tools. He saw me at work using my hands and questioned where my tools were. I told him I was on the streets and was trying do some useful community work for my self-esteem and in the hope, I may develop some skills to become employable again. The next day the supervisor offered me a job. A vacancy had occurred two days before, but the council hadn't advertised the position vacant. In those days wheels of bureaucracy turned much slower than they do today. I was employed again. Eventually, I worked my way up two levels in the council before deciding to leave and make my own fortunes. Still very hard under communist rule. But times were changing."

"Why didn't you tell me any of this?" asked Ivan somewhat stunned by the revelations.

"It was too painful. I didn't want to relive that part of my life."

Eryk leaned forward. "Mr. Nowak, we feel the past is going to catch up again. The men have had years to plan their revenge. The newspaper articles about you and your son is just the start. We suspect they will cause you disrepute or even kill you. They want revenge. For the next few days we are going to have police escort you and Ivan to and from work while we make plans to shift you to a secure location."

Stefan's and Ivan's faces paled at the foreboding changes. Stefan's hands trembled as pulled out a handkerchief to wipe his fogging glasses.

"Yes, of course. But give me time to plan out and implement some actions of my own."

"Make sure you run them past us first as we don't want your ideas to jeopardise protection for you and Ivan," said Radoslaw. Stefan nodded as he felt his stomach churn. Ivan reached over putting a comforting hand on his father's knee. Ivan could see and feel the distress surfacing in his father.

Eryk and Radoslaw stood up ready to leave. Stefan remained seated trying to come to terms with the new life events which now lay in front of him. Ivan led the detectives to the door. Eryk whispered, "Look after your father. He went through hell in those years. Now he is close to retirement, the last thing he needs is this disruption." Ivan glanced back at his father sitting in the armchair. He was dazed and white with fear.

Ivan whispered, "I was told mum died in a car accident when I was three. Did the car accident have anything to do with this?"

Radoslaw frowned. "As far as we know, no. It was very common in those days for cars to slide and crash on icy roads. Wheel tracks for cars where almost impossible to get back then. They were common in the west but not here." Radoslaw shook his head. Eryk nodded his head in agreement. "If you want and have the time, come down to the station. I can arrange for the archived file to be viewed."

"I will take you up on that. Will tomorrow afternoon at four be suitable?"

Radoslaw thought for a second running his brain over the shift time. "Can you make it two?"

"I will change a bit of my work schedule. No problem," replied Ivan.

Ivan went to the police station and met both detectives. They escorted him down a corridor then down some steps to a files room. He was told to sit at the small desk near the window. Eryk had pre-prepared the clerk for the file request. When Eryk requested the file and signed for it, it was handed over to him. Radoslaw reminded Ivan of the rules and said it loud enough for the clerk to hear. The clerk looked up to see the file being handed over to Ivan. Ivan sat quietly reading the faded pages and looking at the grainy photos. His dead pregnant mother looked back. A tear ran down his face. He racked his memory. He couldn't recall he was supposed to have a brother or sister. He read the accident report but focused on the car report.

On an A4 piece of paper, Ivan wrote some details. He would check the information out on his computer when he went home. The first place of call would be going to the south-western corner of the back yard where an old shed was concealed by significant overgrowth. He knew the old shed housed his mother's car. His father had purposefully let that corner be unchecked - the overgrowth was just enough to conceal the shed. Ivan now thought it was somewhat symbolic. The car in the shed hidden by shrubs, hiding painful memories that can be exposed at any time. Here was the exposure time. He didn't know what he would find in that shed, but he would be prepared for anything.

He had been in the shed only once in his life. The wreckage to him at that time was just wreckage. Now he had a reason to look at the morbid keepsake. In his way of thinking now, something could have been missed. The icy surface was definitely a problem. But was there more?

Ivan returned the report and thanked the officer. "Please wait. Visitors have to be escorted out." The officer behind the desk spoke into an intercom system. A junior officer appeared at the door minutes later.

When Ivan was at home, he asked Pawel to accompany him to the old shed. Ivan was armed with hedge cutters and a couple of garden tools. Pawel armed himself with a few car tools, a torch and two sets of disposable gloves. Together, they examined the wreck. Both looked at the wreck and then slowly examined each section.

The baby's pram was still in the back. It was now covered in mould and dirt. Ivan pulled it out completely and placed it outside. He examined the rest of the compartment. It was smelly and the mix of dirt and mould flying into the air caused Ivan to cough. "Stop," ordered Pawel. "I'll get some masks. That mould can kill or make you seriously ill." Pawel left the shed, but Ivan continued searching in a different section of the car.

When Pawel returned, he saw Ivan was now covered in a mix of dust and mould. Ivan said, "There is nothing unusual that I can see in the back seats, or what is left of them." He held up a ball. "One childhood toy recovered. I can't even remember losing this." He put the ball aside.

Pawel looked at the ball. "Your father replaced it with an identical ball. You didn't even know it was missing." Ivan nodded. "I suppose it was one way to shut me up or bluff me. It was so nice of him to do that. Let's have a look at the back again."

They pulled up the rotting carpet cover. A cloud of dust plumed out. They tried fanning the cloud away with their hands. They knew it was hopeless, but it was a reflex response. About a minute later the filth settled again. Ivan's and Pawel's eyes searched for any anomalies. Pawel pointed to a cable.

"Follow that cable and see where it leads."

The men did their best to follow the cable. Ivan returned to the back seat and ripped up the carpet to expose the near rusted out floor. He continued to follow the cable towards the front. Pawel left the rear and entered the front seating area or what was left of the front seat. Pawel followed the cable further. It led to the mangled engine. Both men picked their way around the crumpled engine shaking all types of cables and wires to see which led back to the one of interest. Pawel pointed to cable which he was sure was the one they were investigating. He brought Ivan's attention to it before giving it a tug. The cable came loose. Pawel said, "I think this was the brake cable. Look. It was cut, not all the way through but enough to weaken its functioning if the brakes were heavily applied."

Ivan pulled back. "Are you sure? This thing has so many rotted bits, it could be another rotting piece." Pawel looked at the cable again and pointed, "Here is a partial cut. Nice and clean and the rest is wear and tear. Your mother would have difficulty bringing the car to a safe stop and icy conditions would have stressed the brakes by frequently applying them. If she slammed them on for any reason, it would have been enough for them to snap. The cable would snap at any time at any location, but cold weather would have shortened the life span of the cable. The cable would have been more brittle and would snap quickly."

Pawel moved to the battered glovebox. He pulled out a maintenance book and flipped through the pages. The last service was done twenty days before the accident. The service station was long gone, swallowed up by a small group of neighbourhood shops. The owners were long gone. They replaced the cable and the book. Ivan became anxious.

"Dad is already very upset over the recent events. I am not sure if he could handle that mum's car had been tampered with. This information might be too much for now. He never re-married as he loved mum so much. He would always say, there was no one who could fill her shoes."

Pawel nodded. He had often seen Stefan quietly weep or his eyes well up on the days of her death anniversary. Pawel saw the emotions in the rear-view mirror of the car. Those days, he always noted, Stefan was always moody. He just couldn't let go. "I think we should just let the police know. Get them and their team to take another look at this wreck." Ivan nodded.

"These crims would have organised someone to do this while they stayed behind bars. Someone who visited them would have been given the task. Are the prison visitor books kept this long?"

Pawel shrugged. "Who knows? The faster you and your father leave for safety, the better it will be."

Ivan looked serious. "What about you and your wife? You both have been working for us since 2000, almost the year dot. What about your safety?"

"They are more interested in you and your father not me and Nikola," said Pawel and he thought, *I hope I am not included.* "Both of us better clean up. The police have already stationed unmarked cars outside the place. We can get one car to notify Lanski and Wojcik about the tampered car brake. Now go. Clean yourself up and start packing. I will handle this."

CHAPTER 3

Stefan went through his check list. The board of directors knew of his circumstances for leaving.

He was now just a majority shareholder. The company, he felt was in capable hands. He could check in at any time when it was safe to do so. He and the others had made a code for identification if he or Ivan did call. No name, but numbers were used. With the advice of the police, the company was under-going major security upgrades – on premises at every venue and in the headquarters. Nothing was left to chance.

Stefan looked at the new bank account. The previous accounts were closed, and all shifted into new accounts under a new name in a different bank. The police had supplied him with the new identity papers. They were able to keep their first names, but the surnames were changed. Stefan Nowak was now Stefan Wozniak and Ivan was now Ivan Kowalski. Stefan said just loud enough for Ivan to hear, "The lying now begins." Both groaned at the new names supplied. Detective Eryk Wojcik had commented, there are over ten thousand people in Poland alone with those surnames. Eryk had told them it was better to hide in the flock. It made the criminal's work much harder to find them.

Ivan walked out to his waiting father. "All the social media is closed off. All the goodbyes are done. The bags are packed. He looked at the three bags he had around him. "What reason did you say to your friends for leaving so abruptly?" asked Stefan.

Ivan smirked. "I realised I needed to go into rehabilitation for alcohol addiction. And that is in Switzerland. There is a place there. Some were a bit surprised and others thought it was expected. I said I will be only released when the therapists saw it fit. I did inform them my social media was down and that was the start of the therapy. I made sure I said they would not be permitted to contact me, and I would not receive any of their messages. They swallowed it."

Stefan nodded. "The lying has already started."

"Dad, I am concerned for Pawel. I am sure he and Nikola will be targeted. They have been with us for so long." Stefan placed his arm around Ivan's shoulder and said softly, "Pawel and Nikola have been taken care of. They have a rent-free home where he and his wife can live out their days. I placed a sizeable amount in his bank account. Then at the end of each six-month period, a small amount of money goes into Pawel's account to cover general expenses. The only thing he needs to do is make sure this place looks like it is lived in. The gardener will continue to come but only once a week. Pawel will pay the gardener from the special allowance."

Eryk Wojcik knocked on the door. Stefan let him in. "All packed?" Eryk asked.

Both men nodded. Eryk handed them their new passports, new driver's licences and new birth certificates. They opened the passports. Ivan and Stefan frowned at their faces and at their new identifications. Stefan and Ivan placed the identifications in their pockets before glancing at their new birth certificates. Both men slipped the certificates into an outer compartment of a suitcase. "Shall we go to the airport?"

"Airport?" echoed Ivan.

"Yes. You're not staying in Poland. You're going to the U.K. Private jet. The British know of your arrival and will meet you. They will take you to one of their safe houses. Even I don't know where any of them are. The British send their people here sometimes. It's a nice arrangement. The aim is to make things more difficult."

From the departure lounge, a man wearing a business suit watched all departing planes. He spotted the private Lear jet with a limousine beside it. He looked closely at the movement of the people getting out of the vehicle and into the jet. He cross-checked the two passengers with the text message and supplied photos. He nodded to himself when it was confirmed. He called the office on his encrypted phone. "They are flying out, most likely leaving the country. Lear jet registration P25-K492." Then he phoned the other men also observing all departing planes.

CHAPTER 4

Eight hours later, Stefan and Ivan were met on the tarmac at the far end of Heathrow airport. A limousine with blackened windows had pulled up beside the plane. Detective Thomas Poole extended his hand and introduced himself. "Detective Thomas Poole." Poole was in his late forties with a receding hairline. He wore a dark navy suit with a pale blue shirt and a black tie with a small police motive worked into the fabric. Ivan and Stefan reciprocated. Poole opened the door of the limousine and ushered them in. Poole quickly introduced the driver, Ian and the extra security officer as David.

After thirty minutes of silence, Ivan spoke when he noticed the car was turning away from the city and going onto a motorway. "Aren't we staying in the city?"

"No. A smaller town just one hour away. Smaller towns are easier to keep you safe. The people who are out to get you are in the bad news category. Sure, they did their stint in prison, but they were very busy."

"Besides wanting to kill you both, they are also wanted for orchestrating a number of murders while behind bars. The Polish police did their best to keep them inside, but the prison administrators wanted iron clad proof. Those two men also joined the Russian mafia while inside the prison."

Stefan coughed. "How is that possible?"

"Bad attracts bad. Evil has a way of consolidating. Where there is a will, there is a way. If they hadn't joined the Russian mafia and plotted so much, you would still be in Poland. Welcome to Britain."

The car pulled up outside a country pub. "Your safe house," said Thomas Poole. I'll introduce you to the publican, Sargent Graham

Smith and his wife Linda." Ivan just stared at the pub. He didn't move. "You're kidding me!"

"No. Graham Smith is in semi-retirement thanks to a bullet wound to the leg. He bought the place five years ago. He will assign jobs to you to make it look like legitimate working-holiday makers.

You're here for two weeks and then you move on. Which of you can pull a beer?"

"I'm not that good. I drink it better," replied Ivan with a smirk which earned him an elbow nudge from his father.

"Cook?" asked Poole.

"I can boil water. Maybe one or two other basic stuff," said Ivan.

Poole looked to Stefan and before Poole asked, Stefan offered, "Gardening. I do gardening, and bits of other administration work. Ivan is also good at running messages, customs paperwork and alike."

Poole nodded. "Okay. Smith will find your skills. He expects people to give assistance."

Graham Smith looked at the men as they entered the empty pub. He stopped cleaning the tables and went to greet them. Smith was younger than what both Ivan and Stefan had thought. The man was in his late thirties with greying hair starting at his temples. In spite of the limp, he was still athletic. Well-formed muscles on his arms and legs said he kept in good shape. Linda looked about ten years younger than Graham. Her long jet-black hair framed her freckled face. Ivan kept staring at her piercing crystal blue eyes. To him they looked bewitching. After a short introduction, Graham guided the men through the 'staff only' door to the second of the three rooms at the back. "Settle in. Rest. The bath is over here." He pointed to a green door. There were no signs indicating it was a bathroom. To Stefan, the door looked brand new.

The next morning, Stefan and Ivan entered the pub via the staff only door. They went to the kitchen where Graham and his wife, Linda, greeted them. Linda had just about completed her breakfast. Linda gave a warm smile and invited them to sit down at the table. Graham set the table for them – cups, saucers, cutlery and a plate. Linda offered, "What will it be? Eggs, bacon or cereal."

"Just eggs and toast. Thanks," said Ivan.

"The same. Thank you," said Stefan not wanting to make Linda fuss.

Graham munched on his toast laden with jam. "Today, I just want you two to walk around the village and get to know the place. I mean know the place. Places to hide, what links up to where, and who lives in what house." Linda gave Graham a kick under the table. She added, "That will take half the morning. Then come back and tell us what you observed. We get all short-term stayers to do this exercise. It is just in case the bogeyman comes, and you have confidence in knowing where to go."

Graham kicked Linda under the table.

At eleven o'clock Stefan and Ivan returned to the pub. The pub had several people inside. Ivan ordered and paid for two drinks of beer. He took the drinks to one of three empty tables. As soon as Graham had a moment, he gave a nod, *well played* was written across his face. After the drinks were finished, Stefan and Ivan walked over to the door which led them to the back rooms. Stefan fell asleep on the bed while Ivan paced the room.

There was a knock on the door, Linda whispered,

"I need help in the kitchen. We just got notice of a crowd coming in at three o'clock."

"I can't cook," said Ivan.

"You'll learn. You'll get the hang of it. Simple kitchen hand stuff."

Ivan shut the door and followed Linda to the kitchen where he had earlier had breakfast.

She handed him a potato peeler and a sack of potatoes and showed him the basic action. "When you finish each potato, put them in this bowl of water."

Ivan did as he was told. Linda engaged in conversation, "We don't normally get a big crowd coming in, well not this big. There are thirty people coming. It is usually ten to fifteen. It is always a day's notice and never at three p.m. An odd time but who cares if it brings in a few pounds. The machine which peels the potatoes broke down late yesterday. We haven't got around to replacing it. Where you lived in Poland, didn't you or your father cook? Where's your mother?"

Ivan replied, "Mum died in a car accident when I was three or four. Dad never re-married. We had ladies who would come in and cook food for us. They would come in the afternoon and have the meals ready. We just warmed them up in the oven or in the microwave. That was it."

"Then this is catch up time. More independence. When you finish those potatoes, start on the beans, head and tail them."

"What? I've never seen heads or tails on any beans."

"Well of course you hadn't. They were chopped off before you saw them on a plate." She bought over a bag of beans. Ivan looked at the bag. "Are you teasing me? I don't see any heads or tails."

Linda chuckled as she pointed. "The tips are called heads and tails."

"How can you tell which is the head and which is the tail," asked Ivan.

Linda rolled her eyes. "I'll show you." She grabbed a few beans, lined them up and cut the tips off. Then she swung them around and did the same. Playing on his naivety, Linda said, "The first cut is the head and the second is the tail."

" They all look like cut tips to me," said Ivan.

"Exactly," said Linda. "It is a cooking phrase, head and tails." Ivan nodded and then asked, "A British cooking term?"

"Not quite. The chefs in any restaurant use the term," replied Linda as she returned to the meat she was slicing into steaks.

The expected crowd walked in. They immediately ordered drinks. Stefan was assisting Graham at the bar by acting as a drink waiter. Ivan assisted serving the meals but only carrying two plates at a time. This slowness was noted by a well-dressed man wearing a long sleeved pale blue shirt which covered numerous tattoos. "Hurry it up," he grumbled.

"I only have two hands," retorted Ivan.

"I've seen waiters carrying three and more plates," said the impatient man.

"I am not other waiters," said Ivan trying to remain calm and polite.

"Where did management find you?" quizzed the man. Ivan ignored the question but felt something was wrong with the man. There was a vibe – an uncomfortable vibe. He would mention it to Linda and Graham later.

One week later, Stefan had converted the over-run garden in front of the pub into a picturesque display worthy of any five-star venue. He was now working on the overrun and poorly kept vegetable garden. He was happy doing the task, but his mind kept wondering if the company was running smoothly. He had focused his attention on Ivan running the show but the events of Ivan in the newspaper was the start of a revenge campaign. That worried him. The official line to the public and many clients was his health took a turn for the worst and was convalescing at home. No disturbances. Any questions about Ivan - he was in Switzerland undergoing rehabilitation and then doing company errands in other countries. But after a week, Stefan was becoming anxious. He was still not permitted to phone. He had to wait for Thomas Poole's return with a phone which was heavily encrypted and then every word would be monitored.

He kept plugging away at the garden which now seemed to be a mix of therapy and terror. Therapy because it relaxed him. As he relaxed the terror of being homeless on the streets of Poland when the communist ruled crept back. He lived through the uprisings and the political struggles which made him appreciate the peace which followed. He never took that political peace for granted. But now the criminals were out of their cage, ready to attack and kill. Twenty-five years of pent up revenge terrified him. He dreaded the thought of what horror they could unleash.

Stefan looked up from the garden when he heard footsteps approach. Thomas Poole and Graham Smith were standing together. Their faces grim. Ivan came up beside them. Ivan saw their expressions as well and wondered what the bad news could be.

Thomas breathed in a deep breath, delayed speaking for a moment to search for words that would be as gentle as possible, but there were none. Eventually, he said, "Pawel and his wife, Nikola were shot. Nikola is dead and Pawel is in hospital. They were doing their regular checks in your house when they noticed what they thought was an attempted break-in. Nikola was calling the police when gunshots fired. The operator heard the shots over the phone. Nikola was dead instantly. Pawel had a few seconds of time to conceal himself and from where he hid himself, he could see Nikola on the floor and motionless. At that time, he wasn't 100 percent sure if she was dead. The intruder found Pawel and shot him in the thigh and then in the shoulder." Thomas stopped talking when he saw Stefan beginning to pass out. Graham and Thomas caught Stefan on the way down to the ground. Ivan went white at the news and at seeing his father collapse. Linda came in and held Ivan just in case he collapsed as well.

Half an hour later, when everyone was inside, Thomas asked, "Did either of you phone or use the internet to contact anyone back home?" Both shook their heads. Stefan spoke softly, "I was waiting for that special phone. Can I ring Pawel in the hospital?"

"No. We will send a message via the police. Pawel is under police guard at the hospital," confirmed Thomas.

Stefan cried, "Pawel didn't deserve that. I suppose it is out of the question to be permitted to go to Nikola's funeral."

"Going there will ensure your death. It was a ploy to get both of you out of hiding. I want every person both of you know to be written down on a list. If you have their phone numbers and addresses, that will be helpful. Sorry. We think other associates will be targeted."

"Good lord," said Stefan, "Business associates too? I have hundreds and all the franchise people are they in danger too?"

"Maybe. We can't tell at this stage. How many people are in the franchise?"

"A few hundred. They're scattered all around west and east Europe."

"I didn't know selling flowers was such a big business," said Graham.

Stefan looked firmly. "If it is done right, big money. Bigger when a celebrity dies. That's when we can run out of stock. Valentine's Day is another spinner. People buy flowers for all occasions to express their feeling. Here I am going back to my basics, gardening. That is how it all started, weeding and caring." A tear ran down Stefan's face. He wiped it away. His mind kept jumping around – *Nikola, lovely Nikola, gone. Pawel, honest and reliable, injured and I can't even visit him in person.* The criminals, the past court case, the escape from Poland kaleidoscoped. He now looked at the others and asked, "Are we ever going to be safe?"

Poole shrugged. "When the Russian mafia want revenge, they do their ugliest best. They are like wolves following a trail and never letting go until the prey is killed. You may make several moves over the next few years."

"What country can we go to escape these animals?" asked Stefan.

"At the risk of sounding flippant, and I do not intend to be that way, the only place is Antarctica," said Poole. "The mafia aren't too impressed by the cold and isolation."

Ivan butted in, "Give me a break. Really? You have to be a scientist to set foot on the ice."

Graham blurted out, "How about the Congo. Lots of mad terrorists there sending the place bankrupt. That is the only other place the mafia won't bother going to. It's too screwed up for them. Lots of tropical and rare highland flowers. That would be a bonus."

Linda gave Graham a dig in the ribs. "Stop being an asshole."

"Well it's true. The Congo is a no-go zone for the mafia….and for the rest of civilised people."

Thomas broke up the small domestic argument. "Next week we are going to move you. We are just waiting for the place to be cleared and checked out. I will see you then."

Four days later, Graham knocked on Stefan's and Ivan's door. "Come to the kitchen. We need a chat." Ivan put down the magazine he was reading. Stefan wiped away tears. He tried hiding his grief over Nikola's death and Pawel's near death.

They walked into the kitchen to see Linda at the table guarded by two men holding knives to her throat. Ivan recognised one man. It was the same man who complained about the slowness of receiving his meal. Graham looked calm but underneath he was very nervous. He hoped the silent alarm button hidden in the bar had done its work alerting police thirty minutes away.

Poole would also receive the alert and would be here as fast as he could. "Is this all the people here," demanded the man which Ivan recognised.

"Yes," said Graham trying to control his emotions. "Go and check yourself, if you don't believe me."

A gun was pulled out of the back of one intruder's torn dirty jeans. "Everyone sit down," ordered the man with the gun. The other man pushed his way past the small group and searched the building. He walked back in, "No one else around. Where's the cash?"

Linda pointed to the small safe. The man walked over to Linda and stared her in the face. "Open it darling if you know what's good for you." He gave her a wink and a grin to reveal some front teeth were missing and others were chipped. Linda opened the safe. The man placed his hands inside and pulled out less than two hundred pounds. Then he felt something else which took his interest – a handgun.

He looked at the gun and smiled at the acquisition. The firing pin was missing. "Where's the pin?" he looked directly at Graham. Graham tried to stall but was given a firm swipe across the face with the butt. He put his hands up to shield his face and offered submission. "I'll get it." He walked over to a draw in a cupboard which lined one wall in the kitchen. By pulling the draw open and pressing an internal mini button, triggered another silent alarm. He hoped the second would make the backup come faster. He pulled out a small pin and handed it the intruders.

Now both intruders were holding guns. The knives were put away. "Sit," ordered one intruder holding his own gun. "Hands flat down on top." One of the intruder's phone rang. He nodded and confirmed the place was under control. He moved his eyes to Stefan and Ivan. "We had a lot of trouble finding you. Which of you two is Stefan Nowak?"

No answer. He yelled again, "Stefan Nowak?" No one moved. Then Ivan said, "Me."

"Bullshit you are. You're too young." The man took out his phone, re-checked the photo and turned the gun to Stefan.

Ivan sighed. "You people shot Stefan. He and his limo-driver swapped places."

"Bullshit," yelled the man holding the phone.

"That was the driver. You, old man. You're Stefan Nowak."

Stefan reiterated what Ivan just said, "You people shot Stefan Nowak in Poland. The swap was withheld by the police." The man hit Stefan on the face with a gun. Then he pointed the gun back at Ivan. "You. Stand up and come with me."

Ivan stood up and walked out of the room with the gun now firmly pressed against his head. When they cleared the doorway, Ivan pretended to trip over the half size step, the one he tripped over several times in the first week. As he fell, he kicked his leg up into the man's stomach. The gun accidently fired into the ceiling. Ivan then picked up a stone statue on a pedestal in the corner of the dining room they were now entering and slammed it over the man's head. The man fell in a heap. Ivan took the gun and ran outside to go to the window for the kitchen.

He crept slowly and quietly. It was clear the other intruder was agitated. Everything was too quiet after the shot and a loud crash. The man suddenly didn't like the odds. Ivan tapped the window to distract the man. Graham seized the moment and punched the man with all his strength on the back of the head. The man stumbled. Ivan took aim and shot the man in the stomach. He fell. Ivan ran inside to see the others staring at him. "Not much of a choice, you or him. It was him." He looked over to his father who was now absolutely stunned, "Just who taught you those moves? And to shoot."

Ivan sighed. "You obviously didn't read any of the sports section on the school report card. Let's just say, I am trying to payback that expensive investment of my education. Self-defence classes, shooting, archery and a pile of other sport were on the curriculum. It was compulsory to do a new sport every semester so we could talk with confidence and do that activity when social situations required. I liked the sports stuff most and often stayed back for extra tuition." Ivan patted his father's shoulder. "You did good dad. Just very, very good."

The cavalry of police cars and two ambulances arrived first. They were joined by Thomas Poole seconds later. He stepped over the body in the hallway and peered through the door. He soon saw the bleeding man on the floor. He yelled, "Medic! Medic!" And to the small group, he asked, "What exactly happened?"

Graham stood up still nursing a sore hand, "Just a bit of inconvenience which Ivan largely sorted out. These guys have to move now. I did a body search." He put two driver's licences on the table. "I suspect these two intruders belong to the mafia." The man on the floor groaned. His breathing was shallow. Graham pointed to the man bleeding out. "This one is nearly dead." He pointed to the motionless body in the dining room. "I am not sure about him. He took a major blow to the head."

Stefan stood up and stepped on the bleeding man's leg as he approached Poole. The man screamed. Casually, Stefan looked down. "Now you know how I feel. You and your friends killed a very nice innocent lady and tried to kill her husband. Pain. You don't know what pain is." He deliberately kicked the man again just as the medic brought a stretcher in. Stefan looked at the medics. "Treat Graham first. Leave this piece of crap for later." He gave the man another nudge with his foot. "Tough bastard. He's still alive. Tsk…tsk…"

On a knoll just over a kilometre away from the pub, a bikie overlooked the scene. He took out a powerful pair of binoculars. One stretcher had a person connected to a drip. The person was carefully loaded into the back of one ambulance. A second stretcher came out. This time the person was in a body bag. From the distance the observer wasn't sure who was who in the body bag until he saw the Nowaks were still standing. The man took out his phone, sent a text message, put the phone away and rode off.

On the way out of the town, he passed another rider. They nodded at each other and each continued. Two more bikies were passed. They saluted as they passed each other.

The duo went halfway up the knoll. They each would follow an ambulance. The man who observed everything checked himself into an inn in the next village some ten minutes away.

Back at the small dingy office in a backroom of a legitimately set up tattoo parlour in the heart of London, an encrypted message was sent by text to all members in the British sector – the hard core mafia and to bike gangs who were remotely controlled by the mafia. Included were independent gangs who regularly traded with the mafia. The message came via head office in Saint Petersburg. Two photos appeared with the words underneath:

Wanted Stefan and Ivan Nowak. Polish informers. Captured alive and taken to headquarters in London 500,000 Euros. Captured injured – 400,000 Euros. Captured dead – 300,000 Euros. Open season.

CHAPTER 5

Stefan and Ivan with their belongings got into a large four-wheel drive. "Where are we going?" asked Ivan.

"We've secured a two-bedroom apartment in Edinburgh, Scotland."

You'll stay there for two months until we I.D. the two characters who invaded the pub. That will determine if you stay permanently in Edinburgh or need to move on," said Poole.

They were close to ten minutes away from the outskirts of Edinburgh when Ivan said, "Maybe I am getting paranoid, that bike has been following us since we left the pub." Poole glanced into the rear-view mirror. "I know. I placed an alert to the station a few minutes ago. Silent alarm system with GPS. We are going to get company." The words barely left his mouth when a siren screamed behind the bikie. The rider not wanting to draw attention, pulled up at the side of the road. "All fixed. The driver and passenger in that very ordinary police car is really one of us. The rider will be questioned, breath tested and searched for anything that could make him take a trip the nearest police station." Poole glanced again in the rear-view mirror to see the rider was now being cuffed. "They found something on him." The others swivelled their necks back to see the officers place the bikie in the back of the police car.

Twenty minutes later Poole pulled up outside a small apartment block. "We're here. The unit is to the back. I'll introduce you to your minder. He lives next door. There are cameras going from your apartment to his. Kitchen, lounge, and dining areas only. Twenty-four-hour surveillance and alarm systems throughout."

They walked down a narrow path. Poole knocked on the minder's door and introduced the new tenants. John King who was in his mid-forties and looking much fitter than most twenty-year olds, greeted Stefan and Ivan and quickly showed them the apartment next door.

"Make yourself comfortable. Tomorrow will be orientation day – rules for your safety, neighbourhood, shops, entertainment and the rest. You two have some big heavies chasing you, so we have to be tighter than most times."

Poole mentioned the incident at the pub. "We have to find the leak." Poole's phone rang. His face went white. He slowly looked towards the other three as tears formed in his eyes. "There's been another shooting. Linda and Graham have been shot. They are still alive, but both are in a bad way."

Ivan looked at his father who was visibly shaken. "No. No. When will this nightmare end?"

Ivan slipped an arm around his father's shoulders. "For now, we are safe." He looked back at Poole. "Are we safe?"

Poole nodded. "For now. I will keep in touch." As he walked away, he swore under his breath. "A traitor in the force. No doubt getting big tips. Someone better find him or her before me. I'll rip them up if I get to whoever it is first." Thomas Poole kept muttering to himself. He solved all his problems that way. His juniors called him the Mutterer.

Stefan and Ivan had been in the safe home for just over a month. Both worked hard to resist calling others they knew. Finally, Ivan said, "I am going to open a new Facebook account and under a third name. I won't post any pictures. I just want to see what my friends are doing. I won't write any posts."

Stefan nodded. "Run it past John. "Just don't give us away. The bastards will be watching."

John felt uncomfortable. "I will set you up with a third name." Fifteen minutes Ivan was now Albert Brown of London. John supervised his actions on an encrypted computer.

Ivan clicked down the posts for Marlena. It said south France, Bayonne. He smiled to himself at his success in locating her. Her pregnancy was now showing. Then he moved to his friends Mikal, Szymon and Antoni. Then he clicked off. Ivan gave a sigh of relief. There was some chatter about him, but nothing nasty. He smiled at the speculation and wished it was true. Stefan asked John, "I would like to do some checking at the office. I will use the same Facebook account to see what is happening. I'm looking at customer comments. I feel very left out of the loop. A bit lost." Again, John supervised the action on Facebook. Stefan sighed. "The new franchise person in Switzerland is having issues and no one is really fixing them up. Grr." He clicked off.

It was near the second month of the stay in the safe house when Poole arrived. Before Poole could say more than the initial hello, Stefan jumped in. "Please no more bad news."

"No just an update. Ivan, the man you slammed the statue over his head and subsequently died was Gregori Zielinski. He was the brother to Norbert. Whispers on the grape vine - Norbert is now criminally insane and is offering a reward for your deaths. The man who was shot at the pub, also died. He was a member of the Russian mafia. His name was Andrik Chaban. What we know he was low on the mafia ladder but still a thug. You two really know how to piss people off." Poole looked at John. "They stay one more month and we have to move them."

Every day, John took both Stefan and Ivan to a shooting range. Here they took lessons in both rifle and pistol. Then it was to self-defence classes. Stefan complained at night about the discovery of new muscles. Ivan felt more relaxed and more confident. Getting out of the area was fresh air in itself. John then gave them a booklet for them learn the British road rules. He followed with defence driving lessons.

It was four days before the end of the extended stay when the group returned from their lessons in advanced driving skills. Ivan lapped up the lessons, but Stefan felt apprehensive at each new manoeuvre. They parked the car in its designated bay when they returned to the apartment.

Stefan was leading the way when he suddenly stopped and held up his hand. He pointed to the ajar door. John pulled out his gun, called for backup, and signalled them to stay back.

John waited until Stefan and Ivan were crouched behind the car. He hesitated. Scenarios were running through his mind. He decided to wait for backup which arrived in less than five minutes. Only flashing lights signalled the police approaching. John flashed his I.D. and had the new arrivals circle the building. When he was assured Ivan and Stefan were protected, two of the policemen and John approached the door to the secluded apartment.

They were expecting an attack. There was silence. Cautiously, each officer entered a room each with their guns at the ready. One of the policemen called out, "Here." The men rushed over to him. Two dead cats were on one bed. A note written in Polish said:

Finding you is easy. Just a reminder how you will look like in the very near future.

John immediately contacted Poole.

Poole who was heading across the city to check in on another couple sheltering in custody, turned around. He went directly to the apartment complex where Ivan and Stefan were being held.

Gunshots were heard outside. John and the accompanying officers cautiously approached every window in the apartment. They looked outside and noted the car which they had used was riddled with bullets. John cursed and wondered if Stefan and Ivan were safe enough. He knew they were crouched behind the car, but he wondered about where their location was now. His thoughts were smashed when a bullet flew through the window and narrowly missed him. He pulled back and noted the other police with him had taken cover. They all felt trapped as more bullets flew into windows.

Then there was an explosion. Then everything went deafening quiet. Then voices were heard again outside – screams, orders yelled, running, more and more shots. Silence again. Another explosion somewhere much closer. To John, it sounded like the entire neighbourhood was going up.

John felt the vibration of his phone. He answered in a whisper. He recoiled at the message and the voice. Someone had his number and were threatening to kill him for helping the Nowaks.

John contacted Poole. When Poole received the call, he was furious. Only certain people knew that number and now the mafia had it. The leak was bigger than he thought. Poole knew he was about five minutes away. He stepped on the accelerator.

The cat and mouse game continued for another hour. It was like a war zone with spasmodic shooting breaking an intolerable silence. Poole arrived, flashed his identification before venturing into the main war zone. He looked around for Ivan and Stefan but couldn't see them. He asked around and for an update as to what was happening. More police cars came with their sirens announcing their arrival.

Ambulances followed and stopped at a zone behind the hastily set up perimeter. Silence again. A lone shot slammed into an ambulance window killing the driver. Then there were three smaller explosions. The final explosion was so close that it sent rubble flying into the apartment. Some pieces narrowly missed John and another officer. Then a few more gunshots followed by shouts. The suburban war was over.

John and the other officers in the house emerged. They looked at the mess around them. To John, it reminded him of his military days in Afghanistan where he and others of his troop were assigned to flush out a terrorist group hiding in partially demolished buildings. In one block, damage buildings and rubble scattered into the surrounding streets. Bullets shells had lodged in the walls of brick fences and surrounding buildings.

The peaceful suburb would never be quite the same. There would be scars, both mental and physical. It wouldn't be just people who suffered but the buildings themselves. Whispers of the events would be retold for a decade or two. Trust in the area as a place of residence had been smashed. Only time will restore safety and comfort.

John looked around for Ivan and Stefan. He found them under separate police vehicles behind the secured area. Both were shaking and uninjured. John bent down. "Found you. You can come out. That wasn't the safest place to hide but under the circumstance, it was better than carrying a few bullets." Slowly Stefan crawled out. Ivan was faster to move. They were still shaking. They huddled together. Their attention was drawn to Poole who had just arrived from somewhere else on the scene. "Gee, you two are problem kids. Get you bags. You're moving again."

As they packed their bags, they heard ambulances scream away taking with them the injured and the dead. How many dead from either side? Stefan and Ivan didn't know and most likely never. How many were injured was another unanswered question. They had no time to deliberate.

Poole watched them pack their belongings and engaged in small talk. He noticed a stud fell off Stefan's bag. He picked up the stud to examine it closely. "Shit," he whispered. "This must have been planted when the dead cats were put on the bed."

He stopped Stefan and Ivan from packing and yelled into his phone. "I need the place to be debugged! Now!"

Sixty minutes later, a specialised unit entered the bedroom. When one of the testers went over Stefan's bag, it blipped again. Stefan looked stunned and stuttered, "I didn't know. Sorry. I didn't know." He sat on the edge of the bed angry, ashamed and disgusted. He began to weep.

"I feel sick. Really sick. Those good people out there were killed because I didn't know I had a tracker on me." He repeated the guilt he felt. Thomas interrupted the self-deflation. "I don't think the devices were there when you came. They were planted in the break-in. Stop beating yourself up. We were lucky we found them when we did."

Ivan tried to hug him. "Dad, we are not guilty of the carnage outside. They did it."

Stefan didn't look at Ivan, "That wouldn't have happened if we were not here. Those poor innocent people."

Poole leaned over and patted Stefan on the shoulder. "When you get to the next destination, we will ensure you get some help. For now, I want you to try very, very hard and compartmentalise this event. Shut it away." Both Stefan and Ivan looked perplexed at the request. Compartmentalised as if it didn't happen? That was somewhat beyond their current abilities. The sounds of the bombs and gunfire resounded in their minds. It was easier said than done.

The beeper was now in another room. It blipped again. Poole came running in. The officer pointed to a pair of shoes Ivan had been wearing a couple of days ago. When Ivan was notified, he felt sick. "Put them in a bin. I don't want to see or wear them again." He walked back to his sobbing father. The officer in charge of the sweep said, "This placed needs to be ripped apart. John's apartment too."

"Great," whispered Poole. "This operation is a total train wreck."

From a distance an encrypted text message was sent to the tattoo shop in London.

Five members dead. Two going to hospital. The Nowaks are on the move.

The observer received a reply.

Stay with them. Observe only. Report back with details.

At the headquarters in Saint Petersburg, an encrypted text went out and pictures of showing the Nowaks and John King.

Underneath the photos of Stefan and Ivan, the bounty increased.

700,000 Euros captured alive and brought to London headquarters.

600,000 Euros captured injured.

500,000 Euros dead.

Under John King's name:

200,000 Euros dead or alive.

Open Season now extended to all affiliates, friends and family in Britain and Poland.

Orders were given to cover all airports, shipping ports, stations and at the entrance of the tunnel to France.

Hours later a text message was sent back to headquarters in Britain and relayed to Saint Petersburg:

Stefan and Ivan Nowak are going on a Lear Jet. Registration P25-K492. Heavy protection.

CHAPTER 6

They were on the plane again. This time they touched down in, Paris, France. They were met by one police officer who whisked them away. The officer introduced himself as they drove off the tarmac. "I'm Detective Louis Bellin. And your driver is Jules." Jules gave a look in the rear-view mirror, gave a grin and a nod. Both men were in their mid-fifties, average in height and very thin. "I have received copies of your files from Poland and Britain. Also, our sources know there is a bounty on your head. A very big bounty. 700,000 Euros if captured alive, 600,000 captured and injured and 500,000 if killed. All this because you witnessed a crime twenty-five years ago." Louis shook his head. "The bounty that is out took a big jump when more of the Russians were taken out. Holes are being created in their organisation. They are not happy."

Stefan commented, "We are not exactly jumping with joy. Everywhere we go, death follows. What about the holes in the police force? Did the bastards consider that? Lost partners, lost parents."

The vehicle drove west towards the coast and then south. Ivan smiled at the change of fortune. *Malena's territory*, thought Ivan.

They stopped at La Rochelle. It was a usually busy tourist town. It was quieter now that the weather was turning cooler. Assorted boats lined the shores. The beach cafes, coffee shops mixed with tourist traps fronted the road running along the beach. Ivan smiled as he tried to lighten his father's brooding. He whispered, "See the continent at the expense of the government." Stefan turned his head. "Not funny." Ivan sunk back into his seat.

The car went up a narrow steep road, gave a few twists before turning into a driveway. This house was very similar in size, colour and vintage as the surrounding houses. From this position, they could see the ocean and any traffic along the beach front road. "This is more like it," said Ivan. It earned him a dig in the ribs from Stefan and a blank look from the driver. In broken and heavily accented English Jules said, "This is not a holiday. I believe you two have some …" he paused to search for the words in English, "devils wanting you." He pointed to a church almost directly above them on the next street. "That is where you need to go. Pray the devils do not come again." He sniffed the air, "The ocean air is tainted in summer. Too many dealers selling rubbish. This time of year, less dealers as the holiday customers have moved on."

Louis introduced them to their caretaker. "This is Michel. Mr. Michel to you." Stefan and Ivan introduced themselves and shook hands. "Welcome to France. I believe you two have a target on your back. That is what the Brits say."

Stefan nodded and muttered, "Not just on the back but everywhere else."

"Now be positive. The British did the hard work finding the trackers and downsizing the Russian mafia. I have to say, they are very good in downsizing gangs. But we French are very good in babysitting." Stefan looked blank at Michel. Ivan chuckled.

"Did I use the wrong word? asked Michel.

"No. No. Very appropriate," said Ivan as the smirk grew wider. Michel was sceptical.

Michel introduced Stefan and Ivan to his wife, Maria. "We are both trained police," said Michel. "I will show you to your rooms."

The rooms were smaller than what they had before. The bed was jammed up against a wall to allow for a free-standing cupboard. "Have you eaten? It was a long journey. Hungry?" asked Maria.

Stefan was more tired than hungry. "Is it possible to have a biscuit and a cup of tea?" Ivan asked for the same. When Maria took the food and drinks to their room, both men were asleep while fully dressed. Their bags were still packed. She left the sleeping men. She said to Michel, "They are sleeping like babies. Give me another look at the Polish and British reports."

"More mafia will be coming. More information will be coming by email. They were the main targets for that shoot out. The one that was on the news and every newspaper. We may have our work cut out with these two," said Michel as he looked over Maria's shoulder towards the closed doors.

Two days had passed before either Stefan or Ivan felt they wanted to move beyond the doors of their new safe house. Both were now feeling more relaxed. Ivan ventured to Michel, "Is it possible to go to Bayonne?"

"What's down there? A girl?" asked Maria.

Ivan half nodded and pulled himself up. "No. I believe it is beautiful down there."

"True," said Maria. "It is a bit cold for a swim."

"I am not a swimmer. Neither is my father. Just a day away from walls," said Ivan.

"I will have to get clearance," said Maria. Ivan nodded and when he left the room, he gave the air a punch.

The drive to Bayonne was two hours. Stefan looked at the countryside as they drove.

Ivan had a hundred conversations running around his head if he should run into Marlena or Lavinia.

They were on the outskirts of Bayonne. Suddenly, Stefan said, "Stop. I want to visit that store over there." Stefan recognised it as one of his franchise shops. It was one he had never visited. "I need to smell the flowers. It would make me feel so much better."

Michel stopped at the flower shop. They all went inside.

The owner looked up when the bell at the top of the door rang. He smiled at the possible customers. He watched the group walk around the shop. He noticed Stefan bending over to smell flowers, he bobbed so many times that he began to look like a bird pecking at the ground. One man looked bored. To the flower seller, it looked like he was the driver who had to stop to fill the desires of the others. The lady walked around the shop and selected a flower. The older man stopped her. He put the flower back and directed her to another. The flower seller listened to what the older man was saying. He thought, *this man knows his flowers.* He continued watching. For some reason he felt he recognised the man, but then he wasn't that positive. The older man bought an arrangement of the most expensive flowers and presented it with pride to the lady. The group went back to the car and drove off.

The shop owner went back to his work area. Then it dawned on him. It was Mr. Nowak. He had seen his picture on some correspondence from the company. They mentioned Mr. Nowak was resting after an illness. He picked up the phone and dialled the Polish head office.

Stefan's secretary, Paulina, took the call which was redirected to her via customer service. She confirmed that Mr. Nowak was convalescing. No longer at his home but at a friend's home. She couldn't give the caller a date of his return. The franchisee wasn't convinced and gave his details before hanging up with his last words stating he was going to send photos taken from his closed-circuit television in his shop. He wanted verification that the owner of the company had come to his shop. He was surprised and proud that the unsuspecting event had taken place.

Two blocks away was a small, rented office. Two small teams belonging to the Russian mafia were monitoring twenty-four hours the phones and all electronic equipment of The East European Flower Company. The teams worked in shifts recording everything. One team had tapped the phones of the East European Flower Company and the other had tapped into the computer system. For weeks nothing of any significance piqued their interest. All was not a complete waste as they were now very clued into the workings of the company. That, in itself was a bonus. Now for the first time in many months, there was something about the Nowaks. The caller was traced to France on the outskirts of Bayonne. It was the first lead after the Lear jet left Edinburgh. The hackers had now hit pay dirt - the location of the Nowaks. A message was sent to Saint Petersburg. Picture confirmation would be coming soon. The men were instructed to continue monitoring while the bosses redirected the other mafia members to focus on the west coast of France.

An email sent to customer service was redirected to the secretary. Paulina knocked on the door and gave the photos to the new chairman, Jakub Kamirisky. Jakub studied the photos and looked again.

Stefan has aged so much in the last seven months. Ivan looks older too. He drummed his fingers on the desk and recalling the strict instructions what both Stefan and the police said, "Send an email back. State this in not Stefan Nowak. He is here in Poland. I saw him earlier today. It is someone who just happens to very similar to him. Also, add thank you for his interest and we all hope Mr. Nowak will recover from his illness." Paulina nodded and left the room.

The hacker watched the emails go through the system. It stopped in Bayonne, France. More checks pinpointed the email's location to a flower shop on the outskirts. The man grinned. "Got you."

He forwarded the intercepted email to the head office in Petersburg.

The head office was disguised as a patisserie, a small store in the heart of Saint Petersburg. The hacker wondered just how many innocent Russian citizens would be horrified if they knew they were assisting the finance of the mafia.

The hacker began expanding his invasion to include other franchise stores. At the same time, the Russian mafia, head office sent text messages to all in Britain, France and Germany.

Converge on Bayonne and other coastal towns of France. The Nowaks are in France. Still open season.

Stefan was feeling so much better after the unofficial imposture inspection. For those few minutes, he felt he was back in the loop. The shop was how he expected all his franchises to be – clean, good service and fresh stock. He smiled for the first time in two weeks. He glanced towards Maria. She was smelling each flower after examining each in detail while Michel continued to drive.

The car pulled up into a parking lot, the only parking lot to service the northern end of the narrow two-way road running along the ocean front. Michel pointed in the direction they were going to walk. Ivan had a skip in his step, the fresh air and scenery change was invigorating. He looked towards the water at the numerous anchored boats of assorted sizes and types. Stefan occasionally looked over towards the sea, but he was more focused on the assorted small shops which were largely tourist traps. Both Michel and Maria flicked their eyes between Stefan and Ivan and at the surrounds. They were on guard.

Michel directed the group up a small set of steps to an outdoor restaurant. The view to the ocean captured their attention. In the distance was a large long-range motor cruiser. Ivan stared at the vessel before commenting, "That is something I would like in the future." Stefan turned his gaze towards the cruiser. "A couple of my business deals have been on such boats. They're very expensive to run, not just in fuel but also to staff. Not really my idea of splashing out in luxury."

Maria squinted her eyes at the distant cruiser which was now turning towards the bay area. She sighed. "They are out of luck with moorings. The place is full. The big boat section is full. Some crafts are already anchored offshore because there is no room. The owners will not be happy having to use their speedboats to come ashore. Another boat having to do the same will add pressure to the moorings for small boats." Their attention was interrupted when the waiter came to take their order.

Ivan continued watching the cruiser. It had stopped halfway to shore. Two small speedboats were lowered to the water. Bags followed. Two men per boat headed towards the shore. They anchored six peers away from the restaurant. Each man carried two long bags.

To Ivan they looked like Szymon's gun bags, the ones he used for rifle shooting training. He dismissed the thought as the bags could be used for clothes and other personal items. He saw the men had focus. They walked past the restaurant, up a path towards a small motel. Others on board seemed to busy themselves with a mix of chores and fishing.

Maria noticed the lines being tossed into the ocean. She shook her head. "Dummies. They won't catch a thing. Too much boat traffic scaring the fish away. It is all for show." Michel glanced over the crafts. "Typical snob class. Lots of spare money and spare time and low on grey matter."

Ivan and Stefan chuckled. "You don't need too much brains when you're rich. You employ them," said Stefan.

Ivan pulled his hat down as far as he could. He nudged Stefan to do likewise. Stefan resisted for a few seconds, then hurried to lower his hat. Ivan and Stefan were now hiding their faces from view. Their hands covered their faces when the elbows touched the tables. Michel asked, "Who do you see?"

Ivan said softly hoping his voice wouldn't carry beyond the constraints of the table, "Two friends from Poland. The pregnant one is Malena and the younger one is her sister, Lavinia."

Stefan said, "I didn't know Malena was pregnant. Do you know who the father is?"

Ivan sighed. "Definitely not me. Do you remember that night when I got so drunk, the night my face appeared in the newspapers? The night which started all this hide and seek stuff?" Stefan nodded. Maria and Michel leaned closer. Gossip was always good entertainment. Ivan continued. "Two days before I went to their house with the intentions of asking Malena out. The door buzzer was faulty. It had been faulty for weeks. But this day their voices went through the intercom system. There was a big argument going on between Malena and her parents. I turned around and left their house. I was very upset to learn she was pregnant but more with her parent's ultra-conservative behaviour. They had a farewell party to say Malena and Lavinia received a scholarship to France to study the French language. It was a ploy to deflect that Malena was pregnant. And here she is almost waddling. She looks like she is about to drop the baby any day."

Maria looked at Malena and Lavinia. Both women had now set themselves down at a table just inside the front doors. Maria did a quick calculation, "Looks about eight months. You try carrying that load around. Yep, you men really need to experience the inconvenience. If you don't waddle when you walk, you feel like a beached whale lying down or getting up from a too soft lounge chair. Don't even mention trying to get up from the floor. Umpf! Men!"

They hurried their meal. Michel paid the account. They stood up ready to go. Malena called out, "Ivan! Ivan!"

She pushed her chair back in a hurry. It tipped over. Lavinia stood up, pulled the chair upright before joining Malena to approach the table. Ivan had already joined other patrons in looking around the area. He continued leaving with the others in his group, but Malena grabbed his arm to hold him back. He turned and did his best to conceal his recognition. "Excuse me. I think you have mistaken me for someone else," said Ivan in perfect French. This was a phrase he was made to learn. Malena looked carefully and pulled back, "So sorry. You look identical to a friend back in Poland or he could be in Switzerland now." She studied Ivan's face. She was certain she was right. His eyes contradicted the expression on his face. Her eyes questioned him before pulling away to apologise again, "I am so sorry to have disturbed you." She walked back to her table. Lavinia followed.

When Ivan and his group left the restaurant, Malena wiped away tears. She sniffed hard. The food they ordered arrived. She looked at the food. Her appetite was gone. "That was definitely Ivan. He did recognise me but pretended not to know me. He didn't want to know me anymore." As she cried, Lavinia slipped an arm around Malena's shoulders. Lavinia glanced up to see the group of four at the bottom of the stairs. Ivan turned to look back. Their eyes met. Ivan mouthed, "Sorry. I had to."

He held a finger to his lips, "Shh." Lavinia nodded but was puzzled.

Back at the safehouse, Michel and Maria continued teaching Ivan and Stefan some basic French.

"Ivan, today you were recognised by a friend. You did well to conceal your identity. But that was not enough. Tomorrow morning, we go shopping in the local area. Wigs and other disguise items. You two must learn to disguise yourselves whenever you go outside. There will not be a repeat of today: past girlfriends, friends and relatives are off limits."

"Are we going to have more self-defence classes?' asked Ivan.

"Yes. I will be teaching you. Beside the church, I pointed out before, is a gym. We practice there."

For a week, Michel revised, and fine-tuned self-defence lessons Stefan and Ivan were taught in Britain. Then he added a few more techniques. Michel finished each session with a treadmill and a rower. Stefan complained his legs were like jelly, but only after the treadmill. Michel just repeated, "Curse me now. Love me later. Running could save your life. Those bastards are fit, very fit."

It was a few weeks later, a Wednesday when it happened. Ivan opened the door to lead the group out of the gym. He shut the door and held it firmly. He said between gritting teeth, "Malena and Lavinia are outside coming up the steps." Michel took hold of the door and ordered the other two, "Go to the back door. It leads to the church. Go around the back of the church. A path will lead you back to the road. Ivan and Stefan ran to escape.

Michel opened the door. "Sorry ladies. This door has a habit of sticking." He stood aside to allow the women through. Malena asked, "Didn't I see you at the restaurant a few weeks ago? The restaurant where I made a fool of myself by mistaking a person for a friend?" Michel slowly shook his head and switched on the charm. "I think you made a mistake again. I would remember such pretty women." He held out his hand. "I'm Philip. And you two are?"

"Malena and Lavinia. Sisters," said Lavinia.

Michel ushered the women in before leaving. "The gym is all yours. Are you coming back tomorrow?"

"We come every day for gentle work outs," said Malena. "We moved from Bayonne just two weeks ago. Too expensive to live there long term. Normally, we come here much earlier. But today the baby was giving a protest. One or two weeks to go." She rubbed her stomach. The baby gave a few kicks back. Malena sat down on a chair. The baby kicked away before settling down again. She looked at her stomach. "Now it is my turn to exercise." She stood up and walked over to the treadmill. Michel watched. "Are you sure you will be okay on that?"

Malena adjusted the controls. "Walk only." She smiled back. Michel left the gym.

Thirty minutes later, everyone in the safe house heard an ambulance screech to a stop. Michel and Maria ran to the back of the safe house and up the stairs. Michel whispered to Maria, "Malena has gone into labour."

They barely turned around when they saw Ivan running towards them. "What happened?"

"Your friend, Malena who is at the gym has gone into labour. You can't go. It is not your place and you could risk attracting the mafia. You could put her and the child at risk. Sorry." He blocked Ivan's attempt to pass them.

Ivan quickly asked, "Can I at least send some flowers.…anonymously?

Michel shook his head. "Still too risky. Besides, you said it wasn't yours."

"I know. But she is still a friend," protested Ivan.

Maria grinned. "You're in love with her? Am I right? Even when she is pregnant to someone else? You have it bad." Ivan stared at Maria. It never occurred to him he was into her in such a big way. He walked back to the lounge where his father was just picking up a French book to practise his French reading. Ivan sat in an armchair thinking what he wanted and could do.

He took out his new phone and looked up hospitals in the area. There was only one very large hospital. He switched off the phone, took the phone and handed it to Michel. "Take this. I am tempted to call the hospital." Michel raised an eyebrow and took the phone. "Smart move." He stuffed the phone in his shirt pocket.

Later that night, Ivan crept out of the house. He walked down the street to a cab rank.

He jumped in the cab and directed it to the hospital.

The administration office was manned by two staff. He could see the office would have many more through the day. The night shift was a mere skeleton. The staff questioned his late arrival and relationship to Malena. He lied, "I'm the child's father. I came as soon as I could from Germany." The nurse gave him directions to Malena's room.

Through the glass panel on the door, he could see Malena was sleeping. He crept in and kissed her on the forehead. She stirred but did not wake up. He pulled out an A4 piece of paper he had folded into his pocket before leaving the safe house. He pulled out a pen and scribbled a note on the paper:

I had trouble finding you. Sorry, I had to deny knowing you. Things are complicated. If you see me, pretend not to know me. It is for your safety. Facebook name Albert Brown. Love. I.N.

He saw a bouquet of flowers on a side table, a mix of roses. He grinned when he saw the back of the card, 'All Occasion Flowers.' *Appropriate*, he thought. He flipped the card to see who the sender was. The card was from her parents. *Hypocrites*. He slipped his note into the fastening ribbon securing the flowers together. He turned to Malena again and watched her sleeping for a minute or two before leaving.

Ivan crept out of the room and caught the cab back to the safe house. He thought he got away with it, but Michel turned on the kitchen light. He growled, "Where in the fuck did you go?"

Sheepishly Ivan bowed his head. "To the hospital. Malena was asleep. I didn't wake her. It's out of my system now. I can settle."

"Out of your system? Idiot. Love-sick puppy." Michel shook an angry finger at Ivan. Words failed him.

"Get to bed. Stay there. You better pray that no one saw you."

Two weeks later, Stefan, Maria and Ivan were winding up their gym session when Lavinia and Malena entered. They pretended not to know each other but Ivan noticed they placed their gym bags not far from theirs. There was only one bench at the door near the gym. Everyone placed their belongings on it rather than use it for a rest spot. Keeping to instructions, Malena and Lavinia ignored Ivan, Stefan and Maria. They started their warm-ups.

Ivan glanced to see the baby was wrapped in blue. *A boy*, he thought. *I wonder what name she gave him.* When it was time to leave the gym, he bent over to pick up his towel. He spied a note and tucked it into his pocket. He would read it when he was out of everyone's view.

Back at the safe house, Ivan went to the toilet to read the note:

I had trouble finding you too. You disappeared. When things are 'uncomplicated' as you put it, let's get together. The boy's name is Leon Ivan. M.S.

Ivan smiled and thought about the name. *Leon was her favourite uncle. She didn't have to add mine in the mix. That will piss her parents off. They will think I am the father. I don't need angry parents coming after me as well. I hope it was just wishful thinking on her behalf.* He flushed the note down the toilet to save another argument.

Three days later, Maria and Michel ordered Stefan and Ivan to pack their bags. "You two are on the move again. Reliable sources have indicated the Russians are on their way. You leave now. Pack up."

A blue four-wheel drive stopped outside the safe house. Stefan and Ivan said their farewells to Maria and Michel who were also packed and ready to leave the safe house. Jules was driving them again. He was silent as he drove them north-east towards the German border. At the outer edges of Nancy, they alighted the vehicle. They were at a farmhouse.

A middle-aged couple met them outside and introduced themselves. "James and Tina Smith." Tina quickly added, "You look puzzled. We are British. The French team who run this safe house are on vacation. Sometimes we do swaps." Jules sped away leaving his charges in new hands.

Stefan and Ivan were led to two bedrooms at the rear of the house. The rooms were large and each had a very small en suite. Tina directed them to unpack and then join them in the lounge.

James showed them a map of the small farm. "Tomorrow we will start learning each escape route. Two over here and one longer one here." James pointed to the unmarked map. You will need to know these escape routes for obvious reasons. The word out is the mafia have converged on France. They were spotted in La Rochelle and were in the area where you two were living. They systematically comb the streets door knocking residents with sob stories or impersonating police. Anyone could have directed them, without understanding they were duped into providing information, to the safe house. We are unsure of their numbers. But now you are going to dye your hair. Ivan you have dark brown. Stefan, you have black. Tina will assist you." James handed them their colours and a towel each. Tina directed them to the laundry area where a chair leaned against the laundry tub. A tap on a flex hose made the set-up look very much like a hairdressing salon.

Stefan looked at his new hair. "My, I look so much younger." He looked at himself in the mirror and frequently switched angles. Ivan frowned at his new colour as he turned his head from side to side.

Tina said, "Ivan you are not finished yet."

"This is enough. What else?"

"A pierced ear," replied Tina.

"No way. I don't like them," protested Ivan.

"Then a tattoo?"

"Okay one ear pierced and no more changes."

Two minutes later Ivan's left ear was pierced and studded. He wasn't impressed. Tina said calmly, "Three weeks of care and you should be right. At a later date, you can remove the piercing for a day or two but not longer. It will close up again and will need to be redone. If it closes up, it may leave a tiny scar but that is about all." Stefan frowned at the stud. "Ugh!" He shook his head. "I better get used to that girly thing."

Two days later, James gave Stefan and Ivan small backpacks. "Lunch and drinks. Ready to start?" He led the men back to their rooms. He directed Ivan. "Look at the timber panelling at the side of your bed. Look at semi-circle carvings running down the side. The one at the bedhead height, give it a bit of a twist. You will need a bit of force. The narrow panelling swung on well-oiled hinges. "Go in. Take the torch on the left inner ledge and go inside. Follow the path to a seat. Stay there. I will show your father where his opening is. We will all meet in a minute or two."

Stefan followed James to his room. "The panel over here behind the hatstand. That hatstand is nailed to the floor as you may have already discovered. Go to the narrow space behind the hatstand. At your shoulder height you will see what could be construed as bad workmanship in the decorative carving. It is a lever. Pull down on the lever. The door should open." Stefan did as instructed.

A panel slipped sideways into a wall cavity to reveal an opening. "In we both go. Take the torch just inside the doorway." James pointed to the narrow shelf beside the door. They took a few steps inside and met up with Ivan.

"Follow me down this tunnel. It was left over from the last war. The French resistance used this tunnel very effectively." He switched on a light. We put in lights a few years ago. You can turn off the torches but keep them handy as they will be needed further down the tunnel. The tunnel is partially powered." They walked for ten minutes before there was a slope. "Torches on again," directed James. He switched off the light. They went up the slope and made a few turns. It came to what appeared to be a dead end. James pointed to a rusting lever at the side of the door. "Push that down." Stefan did as instructed. The door creaked open.

They were in a large drainpipe. A camouflage netting draped the entrance. James pointed to a thumb map. "This just gives you some baring. Nothing more. Ignore the positioning of the town. That is there to misdirect others who come after you or come from what would be our exit." They were now two kilometres away from the farmhouse.

James lifted another net. Two bicycles were hidden in a crate. "You push these bikes through this small cluster of trees and bushes. You go that way." He pointed south east. "There you will meet up with a road which will take you directly to Strasbourg on the border. A sign will tell you Strasbourg or Metz. When push comes to shove, from there you have a choice to continue towards Germany or back east to inland France. Now, try finding that road. When you come out of the bushes, you will be just meters away from a signpost. It is only a short walk through the bushes. Use the traffic noise to direct you. For now, take the road to Strasbourg. I will meet you at the edge of Strasbourg. There is a sign which says Strasbourg, six kilometres. That is where I will meet you in two hours." James handed them a bike each and turned to go back through the tunnel which lead to the farmhouse.

Ivan and Stefan looked at each other and nodded. When they reached the road, Stefan sat down. "I'm too old for this. Run here, run there."

Ivan was somewhat sympathetic. "We rest and then we start this cross-country race."

Stefan stood up after ten minutes. "Let's get this over and done with but we go at my pace."

An hour later Stefan groaned, "He didn't tell us about the steep hills. My legs are like jelly now."

"Dad we walk the bikes up, if that is any help," said Ivan. Stefan nodded.

Another hour passed when they reached the top. "It's all downhill now," encouraged Ivan.

Stefan got on his bike and followed Ivan. Stefan held his breath as each car whizzed past. He cursed under his breath. When the road flattened out, he smiled. "Much better." Another ten minutes they came across the sign which said 'Strasbourg Six Kilometres'. John was already there at the side of the road. "Nearly two and a half hours," he said as he moved towards them. "I'll help you put the bikes in the back. Anyone for a beer?"

Ivan grinned. "Sounds great."

Stefan licked his lips. "A beer and a bed."

The next day Stefan and Ivan discovered a few new muscles. They were happy to sit around the farmhouse. But James had other ideas.

"That was one escape route. Now the next one. It won't be so bad." He handed them the same backpacks filled with fresh food and water. "We start the same way as yesterday, but we detour. It is torches all the way."

This time they all met in the same dark place in the tunnel. They only walked a short distance.

James stopped and pointed to a hatch above their heads. "To open this up, twist right." Ivan was given the chore. He puffed and strained. "Is there something on top closing this off?"

"No. Just more muscle power." Ivan tried again. There was a distinct click. He moved the hatch sideways. He was surprised to see he was in the neighbouring house. "It's the next farmhouse!"

"Yes. Also, a part of this complex. They all went through the hatch. The house looked identical to the one they were living in. James led them through the house. He took them to one bedroom. He pointed. "This is the only access in the house. There is another in the shed." He led them to the shed at the back.

"Here is another escape route. He rolled two motorbikes out of the way. "Can either of you ride these?" Both shook their heads. "Looks like riding lesson coming up." James pulled up a lever on the floor. It was a large spanner hinged at one end. A ladder went down the hole. James led the way. He pointed to another torch just under the floorboard. "Just follow me."

The dark tunnel was slightly narrower than the one they took yesterday. The tunnel came to a sudden halt. A bad odour wafted through the air. "We are beside the sewer line. We go through the sewer. Always follow the yellow dots. It will take you to the inner heart of Nancy. Come on." James waved the torch to get them started. One and a half hours later, Tina met them in Nancy. She had the car interior covered in plastic and towels. She handed them a plastic bag and some fresh clothes. James tossed the bag of soiled clothes in the back of the dual cab ute. The men climbed into their seats. "Phew! Lemon baths for you three," Tina said as she wound down the windows.

The next day was a rest day. Stefan lapped that up and stayed in bed nursing his aching body and twitching his nose. He was sure the sewer smell was still hanging around.

Stefan took two more baths through the day. At night, both watched television news. Ivan and Stefan concentrated on the French, but Tina would interpret to ensure they comprehended what was going on. In La Rochelle and in Bayonne in two different towns incidents occurred. The shop owners of 'All Occasion Flowers' just outside Bayonne was attacked. The CCT showed men carrying rifles storming the shop near Bayonne. They displayed the face of one attacker. Ivan felt sick when he thought he recognised one man. He had seen him while at the café in Bayonne. He and others had come off the large cruiser. They were holding long shaped bags. Now he understood what the bags were for – concealing rifles and maybe other weapons. He gulped and then blurted out, "I recognise that shooter. He was off the cruiser. Christ, the mafia own cruisers. Stefan went pale as he realised his innocent people were now the brunt of the mafia attacks.

"The franchisees are being attacked. The mafia are going to try to destroy the business. It's not right. No! No! Leave the innocent people out!" Stefan could feel his blood pressure rise and he felt sick. "This is not worth it!"

Tina reached over and cupped his chin in her hands and snarled between her teeth in a bid to disguise her own anger and disgust. "Look at me carefully. The mafia are responsible, not you. Compose yourself."

There was news of a house fire in La Rochelle. All recognised the street and one of the neighbours. The neighbour being interviewed said the occupants left just over two weeks ago for a holiday. Stefan turned white. "Bastards."

Then the news switched to another topic.

"The new chairman of The East European Flower Company, Jakub Kamirisky who replaced Stefan Nowak, died suddenly at his home. This follows the sudden departure of Stefan Nowak who was taken ill and is convalescing at his home. Jakub, like Stefan Nowak, was a well-liked director who cared well for his employees. Staff say he will be sadly missed.

Stefan gasped again. "Died suddenly? More like assisted to die." Stefan looked at Tina and then at James who was now entering the room.

"Your company is being attacked because they can't find you," said James who had more than a touch of anger in his voice. "Tomorrow we learn the final escape route."

A car pulled up outside. The lights shining in didn't turn off. James cautiously went to the window and peered outside. Armed men were starting to surround the building. "We get out now. We take the new route. Tina you're coming too."

They rushed to the known escape exits. They took the one which led to the next-door farmhouse. James led them to another tunnel. This tunnel went under a small hill and came out the other side. As they walked James explained, "This is an old German war tunnel. It is closed off to the public with the excuse it is collapsing. Some parts are but other parts are safe as the day it was constructed."

On the other side of the hill was a used car yard. They entered the caryard via a narrow wire steel-framed gate. James weaved them through the yard towards the office. "Stay here," he said before he disappeared to the rear of the building. He returned holding keys to the door. James opened the doors, removed a set of keys and led the group to a sedan. He ripped off the sold sign. He looked at Ivan. "The sign is a decoy. It is my car. We have to stop interested parties from trying to buy it." James said calmly, "I sometimes work here when I am on duty in France. Sometimes, I train people like you in this job. That is if they stay around long enough. New identities and new occupation."

They drove off towards Strasbourg. On the way Tina called in to headquarters. In the distance Ivan saw a reddish glow. The farmhouse was on fire and all their possessions inside were up in smoke. Stefan looked back and shook his head. Tears threatened to roll down his face. He wiped them away and sniffed, "Bastards. Unbelievable. Just how did they know we were here?"

James who was driving as fast as he could said between gritted teeth, "That is the million-dollar question."

In Strasbourg, they pulled into the headquarters of the witness program. James and Tina were furious. Their raised voices could be heard through the walls. Neither Stefan nor Ivan could make out what all was being said. It was a mix of French and English. James and Tina stormed out of the room. "We stay across the road in the motel. We have rooms on permanent standby."

Two days later they were handed new passports. Ivan was now Peter Schmidt. Stefan was now Thomas Brennen. Stefan looked worried, "I can't use this name. It is a name of one of my franchisees."

James shrugged. "You don't get a choice. I didn't select that name. It is done randomly on the computers." Stefan was very uncomfortable and tried to protest. "I can't put my people in danger."

James coolly replied and ignored Stefan's protest. "In Germany, there are over 100 Thomas Brennens. You are hiding in a flock. Remember that. The mafia could start killing all people with the name Thomas Brennen. But they are not that stupid."

Ivan placed his hand on his father's back. "We just have to live with these frequent changes until we find a nowhere place that can hide us."

James's phone rang. It was Tina calling. Tina spoke with haste in her voice, "We have to move now. I just got word about an intercepted message from the Russians. They are asking the Italians to join the hunt."

James was sceptical, "Are you sure?"

"Yes. In the message, the bounty has been upped, and our charges have just had a series of mafia offences added to their list. All fabricated to make them look bad and create motivation."

James placed the call on speaker. "Here is what is circulating in the criminal world about you. The Russians now have the Italians siding with them."

Tina relayed the offences circulating to make the Nowaks an urgent and desirable target. "Informing police of drug trafficking, informing on hit men and women, organising a new and separate drug cartel in known territories belonging to both Russians and Italians, raping some of their women and leaving a couple severely injured and a few pregnant, hacking into telecommunications and stealing guns from them."

Stefan blew a puff of air. "The bosses have a good imagination. Unfortunately, one that could leak out and become news. We're fucked."

Ivan rarely heard his father swear, "Where do we go from here?"

"Berlin," said James. "There are two safe houses in Germany. Berlin and Munich."

A cryptic protected text was sent to Saint Petersburg.

They were at the farmhouse. They escaped. We have their old and new passports. Sending photos of each now.

The person receiving the text sighed. He looked to the others in the room. "Start the character assassination now. Get the invented rumours moving and hopefully to the press. What are the plans so far for the demise of the company?"

"Stage one is underway," said a voice on the other end of the room.

CHAPTER 7

One semi-trailer owned by The East European Flower Company left the Poznan depot. The air-conditioned shipping container was painted maroon on the sides and on the end which attached to the wheel coupling. Along the two sides were plain white lettering The East European Flower Company. Directly under was the website and phone number. Below that, were pictures of assorted flowers. The backdoor of the container had all the legal requirements of registration, ownership and carrying capacity. The name of the company, its phone number and web address were spread over the two rear doors.

The driver had been with the company for close to six years. He did the same run twice a week – from Poland to three stops in East Germany and then down to Czechoslovakia before returning to Poznan. At its various stops at the local depots, flowers were dropped off and others picked up. The driver turned on his radio as he pulled out of the Poznan depot. It was just going to be another routine drive which would see him home late-afternoon the next day.

He liked the overnight stay in the Prague as it gave him time to unwind or he could enjoy the evening with other drivers who stayed at the same motel or with his daughter who lived in the city. The motel had permanent rooms for the company. The company always picked up the bill for accommodation, but food and other refreshments were always the individual's expense. There was no mini bar in these rooms. It was to ensure the drivers were alcohol free the next day. Should they be picked up and tested with alcohol, it could cost them their job. Most drivers didn't really care. The small bar next door to the motel always provided refreshments.

The driver neared his first stop, Frankfurt an der Oder, in East Germany. He radioed in his expected arrival time, just fifteen minutes.

The depot in Frankfurt an der Oder would make sure a loading bay was free. Some of the shipment would be unloaded while new stock was added to the consignment.

The entrance gate guard wrote on his form the truck number, driver's name, registration and the time of arrival. The guard would tell him which bay was clear before waving the driver through.

The first exchange was very routine. The driver waved to the depot crew as he left the bay. When he approached the exit gate the guard noted the time the truck departed before the bar at the exit gate was lifted. The men exchanged waves.

The driver fiddled with the radio stations before settling on one which played mostly the latest pop music. The traffic was light, much lighter than usual. He liked that as it gave him a clear run to the next depot in Lubben. In Lubben, the routine was the same, unload and reload and more paperwork. Then, it was to Dresden.

Dresden was going to be his last East German stop before heading into Czechoslovakia. The driver had one more turn before he got onto the highway. He slowed the truck to a near stop to go around the sharpest and tightest bend for the entire journey. This particular bend was his pet hate. The road was narrow and the bend very sharp for a semi-trailer. Not long after starting with this company, he had jack-knifed the truck at this point and he vowed never to do that again. Precious time was lost, and traffic built up kilometres behind him. When he was rescued and the traffic began to flow, he had received the wrath of abuse from frustrated motorists.

This time it was different. He came to a stop. A motor cyclist was on the road half pinned under his bike. A ute at the side of the road showed it had struck the rider. The semi-trailer driver called an ambulance just before getting out of his cabin. He approached the downed rider. He stopped suddenly when he felt a metal object at the back of his head. There was a click. The driver froze when he realised a gun was now pointed at his head. The downed rider moved the bike away with his foot, stood up and wheeled the bike to the side of the road. A man speaking in Russian nudged his head with the barrel of the gun. The driver complied as he began to sweat. The rider who was once on the ground approached the driver and spoke in Polish, "Hands to the front." The driver placed his hands forward. The rider tied his hands with grey duct tape. "Walk this way."

The rider shoved him towards the nearby bushes. "Kneel." A large plastic bag was placed over his head. The truck driver felt a thud across the back of his head. He was out. The man holding the gun, tucked it away in the back of his jeans. Both men dragged the driver further into the bushes and secured the bag around the man's head by taping the opening around the man's neck.

The bike was loaded onto a ute. The rider got into the semi-trailer and drove away down the highway until he reached the first right hand turn. The semi-trailer was heading back to Lubben. The man in the ute followed the hi-jacked semi-trailer.

Hours later when the driver failed to reach Dresden at his designated time, the Dresden depot began making calls – first to the Lubben depot and then back to Frankfurt an der Ober and finally back to Poznan. The two late night duty people at the Poznan depot knew there would be no one at the main office. The night duty clerk at the Poznan depot called the late-night manager in Poznan. The contacted manager then called a board member, Joanna Lewandowski.

Joanna Lewandowski was the only female member of the board. She had worked her way up through the system. She was well respected for her firm and just handling of staff. To receive the call at seven p.m. when she just got home annoyed her. The news rattled her. Never before had a truck not turn up at any depot at any time. She hesitated at first thinking the truck may have broken down somewhere on route.

She made more calls, and all drew a blank. Now she was worried. With Stefan and his son, Ivan, in protective custody, fatal attacks on Pawel and his wife, and on the franchisee in France, she didn't leave anything to chance. She called the police who initially dismissed the concern. She threw a tantrum over the phone and demanded to speak to someone in higher position. Eventually, she was in contact with Lanski and Wojcik. Knowing there were a series of attacks on the company, they took her call seriously. Another attack. Another innocent victim. The pressure was mounting.

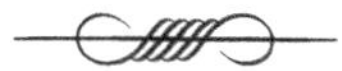

On the afternoon of the hi-jacking, the hi-jacked semi-trailer pulled into an unnamed warehouse in Lubben. The boss examined the acquisition. "Excellent work. Move a quarter of the flowers out. Put the drugs at the back. This shipment is going to Italy. The truck leaves in three hours." The men busied themselves making a path to the back and then restacked the flowers to conceal the drugs. Excess flowers were discarded in the industrial bins in the next warehouse complex. Two men waved as they left.

As they neared the Italian border, the customs looked at the semi-trailer and then at the passports. Sniffer dogs walked around the semi-trailer and paused now and then but they never sat down to indicate drugs even when the doors were open for inspection. The flowers had done their job to disguise the smell of the drugs hidden at the back of the shipping container. The passports were stamped. The men waved through. When the two men were at a safe distance from the border, they grinned broadly before breaking out into a laugh. The passenger sent a text message to Lubben:

Just past the Italian border. It worked. The flowers disguised the drugs. Heading to Rome as scheduled.

The drivers received another message telling them where they were to make the delivery. The drugs were transferred into a plain cream and brown van. The semi-trailer drove away. They were to return to Lubben.

The van driver drove a short distance to a deserted run-down warehouse zone. The area had signs indicating private land. There was another sign showing plans for redevelopment. The men in the van opened the unchained and unlocked gates and drove through. The gates were to remain open for the in-coming traffic. In less than a minute after arriving at their destination, their boss appeared in a hired black Audi.

Another car pulled up shortly after the black Audi. The men in the second vehicle, a navy four-wheel drive got out and opened up the back. Both men slid out one crate and opened it. Eight machine guns and a number of assorted pistols were on display. They slid out the second but smaller box. It was full of ammunition. The new arrivals were led to the side of the cream and brown van which now had the side doors wide open. The men inspected each other's merchandise, made the swap, and shook hands. Hardly a word was spoken.

This cream and brown van would meet up with a mini convoy before traveling along long isolated and badly maintained back roads heading north-east before going onto the main highway. The convoy with the merchandise, camping equipment and assorted other products, generally food and medicine, would now travel north east to Romania and stop over at the coastal town of Constanta - a three-day journey.

A few days later, the cargo would be exchanged for drugs. The exchange was always rotated between three ports on the Caspian Sea. The delivery site depended on what was happening in the port towns and when the paid customs officers were on duty. All the cargo would end up in the tribal controlled foothills in Iran and exchange for drugs, mostly opium. Occasionally, a stolen artefact would surface – that was more lucrative than the drugs. The drugs and the rare artefact greatly outweighed the value of the guns and ammunition, but the marauding tribesmen didn't mind. Guns and bullets were precious and a product of trade within their own country. They did accept other items such as fabrics, clothing, food and electronic equipment. The tribal people also saw these as valuable exchanges with their people and other local tribes.

The trade always got through. The bribed border guards saw this as regular income outweighing their pathetic wages paid by their equally corrupt governments. No one was going to stop the trade. The three wise monkeys came into play and danced their way back and forth across two continents. Interference meant certain and instant death.

When the Russian boss, Artem Orlov, returned to his stylish home in Moscow, Roza Zielinski was there to greet him. Immediately, she poured him a vodka topped with ice. She knew never to talk business for the next twenty minutes. As if reading her mind, he said, "At least one part of the business runs smoothly." He sat in his favourite armchair, flicked his shoes off and placed them on the expensive coffee table. He lit up a cigar and blew a few puffs into the air. He patted his thigh. Roza sat on his lap, slipped an arm around his neck before planting a kiss on his lips.

He turned on the television. The news indicated that three children riding their bikes in bushland in East Germany found the body of the dead driver reported missing three days ago. They indicated the driver's semi-trailer was still missing. They did not say the semi belonged to The East European Flower Company. Artem smirked. The police will only release what they want the public to hear. They displayed the numberplate of the missing semi-trailer. The omission to say which company was missing a semi spoke volumes to Artem.

Artem's mobile rang. Roza reached for the phone on the coffee table and handed it to Artem. He signalled for her to get off his lap and move away for a while.

"What? They escaped again! How?" his voice was raising with every question.

"We have their passports and other identification papers, not just for the Nowaks but also of the minders, James and Tina Smith. Both are British police," said the deep voice on the other end of the phone.

"Does the mole know where they are?"

"Maybe Berlin. At this stage the mole has not confirmed exactly where."

"How long will it take?" said Artem with firmness in his voice.

"The information will be coming within two days."

Artem grunted and hung up. "Don't tell me the bastards escaped again," said Roza.

Artem didn't say a word. The expression on his face said it all.

"The only good thing is that the mole has been very accurate so far. Now, how about a top up?" Artem tilted the glass. Roza obliged.

Roza's phone rang. "It's dad. Do you want to talk with him?"

"After you," said Artem and gestured with his hand for her to go ahead.

"Hi baby. Put me on speaker, I want Artem to hear this." Roza turned on the speaker.

"Pawel who was the driver of the limo for the Nowaks is now dead. I made sure he had a car accident. His fancy little house has reverted to the ownership of The East European Flower Company. Pawel had life tenancy – free life tenancy. We should buy the place. We know Pawel's lawyers will find the house belongs to The East European Flower Company. We get an innocent accountant or lawyer to buy the place on our behalf. When all the searches are done, they assign the property over to us. No second transfer fees. A pure switch. The place is across the road from the Poznan depot."

Artem grinned. "I like the plan. When is it going for up for sale?"

"We make an offer to the lawyer of the deceased person's estate. An interested party making an offer before the property goes to market before they make alternative plans."

"Go ahead. Make the purchase but no more than 250,000 euros."

"My homework says it was purchased for 220,000 euros. A bit extra and a cash sale in two months. We offer them the same with us paying the legals. That should clinch the deal. The legal cost will amount to 15,000 Euros."

Artem nodded. "It's your baby. You go ahead. Ask about the furnishings. See if that can be included, preferably free. They have to unload it so it saves them more by leaving the items in place.

There could be more valuable information hidden in the place like bank accounts etcetera. Being across the road from the depot, is an ideal situation for us."

CHAPTER 8

Ivan and Stefan walked around the block of their new home in Berlin. Their new home was an apartment above a shop. The shop was owned by the German police, a safeguard for the occupants above. The shop was a mishmash of second-hand items in good shape but no longer wanted, a disposal centre. Old electricals and furniture from privately owned police homes were sold to the general public. Very few items from the public were accepted with the excuse - over supplied or no call for such an item. Stolen or lost items which were unclaimed by their owners or the owners had already received an insurance payout, were disposed at this location. The police joked it was their very own disposal centre raking in more cash than the assorted vehicle fines issued for two blocks around. It worked like a dream for well over ten years. The public knew no better.

Like at other safe houses, Ivan and Stefan went for walks and noted what every structure was and where all the lane ways were, where each led and how they linked into nearby streets. In most lanes, bins overflowed allowing gusts of wind to scatter dirty wrappers and paper soft drink cups. Stefan quietly said, "I hope we never have to use these filthy, smelly places." He coughed. Ivan agreed and encouraged his father to walk faster to get past the smell.

They returned to the second-hand shop with the intentions of using the internal steps to their apartment. Customers were in the shop. They waited a while for the customers to leave. Recalling instructions if customers were in the shop, they had to use the external narrow rear steps. That would mean a walk down the smelly lane again.

Both liked the location of the apartment. On the ground level was the second-hand shop. One neighbour was a coffee shop which sold assorted German style pastries and cakes. The other side was his/her hairdresser.

"Coffee? Before we go upstairs?" asked Ivan when he noticed his father looking a bit drawn. Ivan opened the door for his father. "Latte?" asked Ivan.

"Sounds good." Stefan searched his pockets for the wallet. His card was still inside.

They placed their order, but the cashier softly said, "Sir, the card has declined. Error 02."

"What does that mean?" asked Stefan.

The cashier looked at the men before leaning forward, she whispered to avoid embarrassment for them. "Insufficient funds."

Stefan gulped while Ivan looked on shocked. "There were funds yesterday. Plenty of funds."

"Sorry Sir. Not now." The cashier handed the card back.

They went to the apartment on top of the second-hand shop. Tina was there and noted the concern on their faces. "What's up?"

"My bank account has been hacked. No funds. I need to use a computer to access my account."

Tina ushered them into the minder's room where a laptop was set up. "Go ahead."

"Stefan logged in account number. Then the password. It failed. He tried again.

"The password has been changed. There is no other explanation."

"How?" asked Ivan who was now quite anxious.

They must have searched the safehouse before they burnt it. Did you have the bank details written down?" asked Tina.

"No. Can we ring the company? Each month, money goes into this account. We need to stop those transactions. They will be routinely drained."

"Can we do the security checks over the phone?" asked Ivan.

Tina sighed. "We can try. I'm not holding my breath."

Twenty minutes later, Stefan opened his account. Only 2 euros were there. 10,000 euros had been taken out, transferred to a N. Zielinski. "The bastard stole my money." Tina pulled back Stefan shoulders, "We can use that information to trace Mr. Zielinski. He has made a mistake." She picked up her phone and started making numerous calls. She gave Stefan her phone. "Use my phone. It's encrypted. Call your office and get someone to cancel the transactions and run security checks on all bank accounts."

Stefan was immediately put through to Joanna. She dropped what she was working on and cancelled the automatic transactions. Then she moved into social mode. "Stefan, I have some bad news. Pawel died in a car crash a few days ago."

Stefan began to weep. Ivan took the phone. "Joanna did the police check the car for tampering?"

"No. I don't think so."

"Just where did he crash and when?"

"His car spun out of control on the highway."

"Can you get someone to check the wrecked car and give a detailed report? The brakes are a point of interest. Please, Joanna. This has happened before. My mother's car was tampered with."

Stefan glared at Ivan and stuttered, "Wh…what are you saying? What makes you think that?"

Ivan lowered the phone. "Pawel and I went over the car just before we left. Someone sliced halfway through the brake cable then allowed nature and time take and course."

"Why didn't you tell me this before?"

"You were busy, very busy. I just didn't know how to tell you," said Ivan who was now biting his lower lip.

Stefan nodded. "Yes I was busy. You were right. I would never have handled that news then."

Stefan took the phone. "Joanna one more thing. The house I bought in the company's name, the one Pawel lived in for such a short time. Don't sell it whatever you do. Tell the board members not to sell it. I have some valuable items in there. If the board wants to sell the house, strip it clean before placing it on the market. Put all the items in storage with my other contents. That includes all cupboards even if they have to be ripped from the walls. I mean all."

Joanna agreed. "Sir, I thought the house was in Pawel's and Nikola's name."

"No. It was life tenancy. It's in the company's name. I repeat, don't sell the place but if you are pressured, put all the stuff into storage. Promise?"

Jonna replied, "Promise. I will have to give a reason to the others."

"Tell them the truth. Important items in there. I am so tired of lies."

"Sir what are you going to do for income?"

"I will send you details of a new account and name."

While Joanna was talking she was opening a letter from a local legal office. She frowned at the note. "Stefan, I just opened a letter from a legal office. Someone is making enquiries about the house – to purchase and even offering pay the legal transfers."

"They want the property a little too much. Reply: it was discussed with the Board of Directors. The company advises it will be retaining the house as the company has other plans for redevelopment."

"Okay. What plans?"

"None yet. But it will give the police time to check out the buyer or if the buyer was a proxy. It was nice talking. I'll get back to you soon."

"Good luck," said Joanna as she put the phone down.

An email popped up on her screen.

Joanna,

You're next.

Joanna screamed, "Get me security! Get the police. NOW!"

Norbert Zielinski and Wikto Duba drove to Pawel's home. Under the cover of darkness, they used a hammer, to break the glass panel beside the door. Wikto covered his arm with layers of cloth before inserting it through the jagged edged window and twisted the lock. The door opened. Norbert entered first and turned on one light. They looked at the tidy kitchen which had one unwashed cup sitting in the sink. They inspected each cupboard and examined all contents in turn. There was nothing of interest.

They moved into the dining room. To Wikto and Norbert it was just old furniture and rickety at that. They moved on. The lounge was modest. One old lounge suite which had seen better days, a new recliner, a television of medium size, an old radio was on a side table with a couple of magazines under it. They opened the sideboard. Nothing. On top of the sideboard were few old family photos and old-style household items. Nothing to pique their interest.

They entered the first of two bedrooms. They turned on the lights. The bedrooms always held items of interest, but this one was almost bare. There wasn't anything under the bed. No cupboards to explore. One single king-size bed was neatly made. A teddy bear rested on the base of the pillow. Beside it was small bedside table with a couple of children's books. Nothing was in the drawers. One rocking chair was placed near a window. They moved on to the next bedroom.

It was the master bedroom. Two bedside tables with old lamps decorated the top. Nothing special to look at and the drawers held nothing of interest or value. They moved the bed around to examine what was under it. Nothing. They turned to the cupboard. The drawers were neatly stacked with socks and underwear and a drawer full of bow ties. The others were empty. The women's clothing had been removed.

Wikto opened the double doors to the wardrobe. After a shuffling of the clothes, still nothing of interest. Above the clothes rail was a narrow shelf. That took Wikto's interest.

Wikto pulled out an old wooden box. He opened the box while still at the wardrobe doors. Before he could say anything, gas shot out. He coughed and gasped. Norbert looked on in horror as Wickto gasped for air and held his neck. He went into an anaphylactic shock. Within three minutes, Wickto was dead. Norbert fumed at the reversal of fortune. He stepped back from Wikto. "No. No. The bastard has booby-trapped the place." Norbert began coughing. He ran out of the room.

There were flashing blue lights streaming into the window. Norbert cursed, "Cops."

He tried to make a dash for the front door but too late. One policeman was there with a gun pointed at him. Norbert put his hands up as if to surrender. He allowed the policeman to walk closer. Suddenly, he kicked the policeman as hard as he could in the groin, took the gun and fired into the policeman while he was on the ground. The second policeman with his gun pointed ran for cover behind the still opened car door. Norbert shot the policeman in the arm. Norbert ran to his car, fired again at the policeman before speeding away.

Lights in the surrounding houses were now turned on. People craned their necks to see what was happening. They called for help for the now visible injured policeman.

Norbert cursed as he drove. He slowed down when he saw police coming in his direction heading to the house. He muttered to himself, "Joanna you are definitely going to get it now. Bitch."

He drove his car to her home and fired the stolen police gun into her windows. Glass shattered waking her up. Joanna pressed the alarm button which sounded down the street. House after house turned on their lights wondering which person's house was attacked. Norbert was now out of the street and heading home, he spoke to himself pouring out his venom and frustration, "That was a warning, bitch. Next time you get it. Not at your home, somewhere else much less secure. You and the Nowaks and the rest of the Nowak club are going to pay."

CHAPTER 9

In the Berlin apartment, Ivan twiddled with the radio dials. He picked up a Polish radio station. The music was interrupted for a news flash. He called all to be quiet as he turned up the radio. James and Tina saw the distressed looks on Stefan's and Ivan's faces. They asked for a translation.

"Two police were shot when responding to a house intrusion. There was a drive-by shooting at Joanna's house. We go back to Poland," said Stefan. "No more running. Too many innocent people are dying. They are going after people we know. Bastards!"

James and Tina cringed at the statement. Stefan continued, "The Polish police need our help. They may see these as unlinked incidents."

James and Tina left the room to discuss the options. When they returned, they gave order to pack up. "We will drive you to Poznan police station, but we only speak with Detectives Lanski and Wojcik. James gave his mobile to Stefan. "Can you phone them and let them know you are on your way."

When the group of four entered the Poznan police station, they immediately asked for Lanski and Wojcik. They were ushered into an interview room. Lanski came in first followed by Wojcik.

Lanski said, "Wikto Duba was found dead in your company's house last night. We did not release that bit to the public. He was gassed. The gas is still being analysed. Duba opened a wooden box in a bedroom cupboard. Opening the box released the gas. Just what was the gas?"

Stefan frowned. "I don't know anything about a box of gas. Pawel must have obtained it just in case he needed protection. I have no idea what was in the box or what it was for other than a decoy in a break-in.

Ivan thinks Pawel's car brakes were tampered with. Poetic justice. The dead man kills his assailant."

Lanski raised an eyebrow and looked at Ivan. "How did you come to that conclusion? An accurate conclusion at that."

Ivan gave a small cough. "Just before we fled to Britain, Pawel and I checked out my mother's smashed up car that is stored in an old shed at the back of our home. We found the brake cord sliced half-way through, just enough to weaken it so it would falter over time. It would make sense the same order would have been dished out to Pawel. A murder disguised as a common accident. No questions asked."

Wojcik nodded at Ivan explanation. "You are right. We did not release that to the public. All of you follow me to the operations room." While walking to the operations room, Eryk added, "The hacking into the company's phones and internet was never released to the public. It would disturb the investigation."

Lanski pointed to the pictures of faces pinned to the wall. This group are suspects and the crime these people we know are associated with. Proof has been difficult. They clean up very well."

Lanski pointed to another board half covered in faces. The word deceased was neatly written at the base of known victims – Pawel, his wife Nikola, the shop owner in Bayonne, France and the truck driver. Lower down were pictures of board members. Pinned to the base of Jakub Kamirisky's photo was a notation – decease. Heart Attack. Joanna Lowendowski – attacked, bullet through her window.

Stefan stared at the notation before adding, "Assisted into a heart attack. The man was fit. He had a full medical before I left." Stefan took the photo out of its position and placed it near the other decease people. He looked at Joanna's photo and shook his head. "Is she under protection too?"

Erik nodded. "Actually, we are considering all the board members be under surveillance for their protection. With luck we may identify a person or two planning attacks."

James added, "In Britain, our safe houses were compromised. Add more names of police and criminals. I have the list."

Erik Wojcik gulped as he picked up a whiteboard pen. "Okay, who are they?"

"At the first safe house: Police officers deceased are Sargent Graham Smith and his civilian wife Linda Smith. The dead criminals are Gregori Zielanski, the brother to Norbert Zielanski and Andrik Chaban."

Lanski was surprised. "What? Gregori Zielanski. Oh Christ. He was high up in the Polish mafia and joined the Russians. Andrik Chaban is a new name. He must be a recent addition to the clan or until now, kept a low profile. Any photos?"

"I can organise one for you. Now in the Edinburgh shoot out we have a bigger list of injuries and a few deaths. The injured police are Constable Simon Downes and Sargent Ryan Obbs. Civilians injured by the criminals are David Palmer and Sibel Yardley. Civilians who got caught in the crossfire and subsequently died - the bullets were confirmed to be from the criminals' guns are Toni Marshall, Andrew Whitehouse and Callum Ashby. The criminals who died were Helge and Gerasim Elin who are on our books for making explosives for any person for any reason. This time they got a little too close to their own bombs. And another was a female from a bike gang, Blanka Pawlak. The criminals who were injured were Peter Landon, Marcus Townend, Julia Ambros, Saul Brown and Levi Lacey. These crims were checked out and found to be from a motorcycle gang. Word on the grapevine is they were after the bounty placed on Stefan and Ivan. Only Saul had mafia connections. That is how they got wind of the bounty."

Stefan jumped in, "A bounty on us? Good Lord. Bastards."

James continued. "You can add a break-in and theft of identity documents, followed by arson of the safehouse in Nancy, France. They set fire to the safe house in La Rochelle. I think that is it for us and your recent additions, the police officers who attended the break in at the house opposite the depot," said James as he looked across to Tina, Stefan and Ivan for confirmation. "Who would target that house unless they knew it was associated with Stefan and Ivan?"

Eryk softly said, "The last bit sounds like the work of the Russians and Poles."

Eryk and Radoslaw both blew out a puff of air. Radoslaw muttered, "Hell. Destruction everywhere. And now some confirmed proof. This is just the tip of the iceberg. It's not enough to get the crims higher up. They are still at an arm's length. Too clean. We need dirt, mud, glue."

Eryk asked, "Where are you staying?"

Stefan replied, "Nowhere yet. I need my identification papers to access my accounts in person. Is it possible to go to the house outside the depot? I have stuff stored there."

"No. It is still being processed. Tomorrow at the earliest. I will arrange accommodation for the four of you."

The next morning Stefan and Ivan and the police went to the house where Pawel and Nikola previously lived. Stefan immediately went to the rundown shed in the back yard, tilted a large flowerpot just inside and to the left of the door and pulled out a key. He walked back to the small group and showed them the key. "It's for the backdoor. Come." The group followed Stefan to the rear of the house. The broken panel had been boarded up.

The rear door opened directly into the kitchen. Stefan told Ivan, "Get the largest containers out of the kitchen. We are going to need them." Stefan took a knife from a draw, opened the door directly under the sink. At first the interior panel resisted the attempt to prise it open. Then it made a crunch noise. From then on Stefan was able with ease to lever the panel off. Inside the panel assorted euros and Polish money tumbled out. Seeing the others with surprised looks, he said, "A trick I learned when the Russians ruled this country. The KGB would ransack all containers and rip open soft furnishing, tear up beds and any possible wall panelling looking for anything that they considered illegal. Extra money was one of those. It was pointless hiding stuff in the ceiling. They would tear down that as well and leave you with the repair bill. We had to be inventive and learn to hide things in plain sight." Stefan placed the money in one of the containers and secured the lid.

He looked at Eryk. "Help me flip the table over." When the table was upside down in the centre of the room, he started to unscrew the legs. He gave each a shake. Assorted coins and more notes floated out. He slipped his hand into each leg to check if anything was stuck inside. His hand went a quarter of the way down the leg. There was no point making cavities go deeper. He pulled out a few documents and a few more notes. Ivan collected everything that slipped out of the table legs. Eryk helped Stefan reassemble the table and put it upright.

The group followed Stefan into the lounge. "Ivan, please get me that very sharp knife from the kitchen." When Ivan returned, he saw his father had removed the couch cushions. They were scattered on the floor. Stefan held out a hand for a knife. He carefully cut around the edges and tore back the fabric concealing the rough base construction. "Another trick from the past. The KGB would attack the cushions but not the base upon which they were placed on. Container please."

Ivan handed over the next container. Stefan scooped up collectable coins and his wife's jewellery.

In stunned silence, the others just watched. Stefan returned the cushions. He moved to the dining room chairs.

He prised open the bumpy looking padded cover and removed assorted documents – company papers dating back to when the company started, all the legal set ups, changes to the company to make it compliant to the changing laws over a thirty year period. He cut open another seat cover to pull out a number of SIM cards and USB sticks. As he dumped them into a fresh container, he said to the others watching, "I was transferring all the stuff to USB sticks and SIM cards. Easier to move around. Most of these are bank items – accounts, identification papers all scanned and passwords to the different company computers. The setup security stuff as well. I believe it needs changing. Everything has been compromised." Stefan held up a large flash drive. "Let's give the hackers something to think about - like a rival gang."

At the police station, Radoslaw set up a computer with the links to the computer network for the flower company. Stefan inserted the flash drive holding the setup of the computer network. He typed in a password. The screen opened up to the vital drives. "Here it is. Are you ready?"

"Ready to go," said Radoslaw.

Stefan found the hacked linked. The system was designed to trace the invading link even after it was trashed. "Type in your rival gang's message," said Stephan.

Radoslaw typed in:

Morning boys. This is Antonio Verdi. The East European Flower Company is mine. I was the first to hack into the system. It took a while to get it back to us. Find another company.

The hacker stared at the message on the screen. He was already frustrated as the company had just reclaimed the internet and he had to re-hack. Now this appeared on the screen. He immediately called the office in Saint Petersburg. The person answering the call immediately contacted Artem Orlov. Artem cursed, "Bullshit. I will check this out with the Italians. Call in…" He gave a list of names of staff in each of the European countries. "The meeting takes place at the Warsaw office at ten a.m. tomorrow. Vacate the building now and set up at the Warsaw office to track the source. Fuck the Italians."

Radoslaw and Erik grinned. "Okay we have a war to take the focus off your company. Alert all police stations here and place a watch in all countries, just capital cities. Put watches on all airports, check points and train stations. I want a list of all people who make late booking to all capital cities. Somewhere a meeting will be organised." The office was awash with activity. He turned to Stefan and Ivan. "You can go home, to the safe house I mean. Stefan, if you want to go into your office you will need to contact us first. We will always have a plain clothes officer escort you. His name is Natan. James and Tina it is up to you as to what you want to do."

Tina said in a firm voice, "We go where Stefan and Ivan go. That is final."

Eryk nodded.

CHAPTER 10

Stefan and Ivan followed by the small group of police officers walked into the ground floor of The East European Flower Company. Ivan noticed the new girl at the reception. He nudged his father. "She is new. I am going to get some information out of her. A bit of flirting loosens lips." The others moved away to sit in the foyer's lounge. They helped themselves to the coffee machine. They glanced over now and then to see Ivan chatting with the new girl. Minutes later he returned. He read out the details for the police.

"Sonya, wait for it, Duba. Sounds familiar?"

Natan ran a check. He whistled. "A relative of the deceased Duba."

"I have her phone number and address."

Stefan gasped. "That was quick."

Ivan grinned. "I want to wear a wire. She gets off work at five. We are going to the coffee shop across the road. I tried for tomorrow, but she says she has the day off tomorrow to attend a relative's funeral. Do I get to go?"

James said as he glanced across to the police officer. "No. Too much too quick."

Stefan stood up to lead the way to the lifts. "The main office is on the top floor. The fifth floor."

When Stefan and Ivan entered the main office, people dropped their work and stared. A crowd coming in was a rare event. Two men were distinct strangers but the other two men, Ivan and Stephan made people look – familiar, maybe not. Joanna rushed out to greet them and quickly ushered the group into the conference room. They were quickly followed by other board members. After the introductions, the groups swapped some notes.

Stefan was now very concerned at what he heard. Sales had dropped. Customers were keeping away. The odour was spreading. Damage control was urgent. Personal safety needed upgrading.

Two hours had passed before the two groups parted. Ivan found himself at the police station getting wired up for the meeting with Sonya Duba. To her, he was Peter Schmidt. "Be careful. And try to act normal," said Eryk.

Ivan stated, "Act normal? I haven't done that since leaving - just coming up to a year."

"Do up your shirt. Let's do a test."

Ivan met Sonya at the front of the coffee shop. He guided her in as he switched on the wire. He glanced to see the driver in unmarked police car across the road blow a puff of smoke out of the window – the sign all was working. If Ivan saw the smoke again, it was time to cut the meeting.

Ivan directed Sonya to a window table where he could see the driver in the car. While they were waiting for their order, Ivan began the flirtatious questioning. Two hours later, the meeting was over. At the front of the shop, Ivan gave her a peck on the cheek before he observed her walking away towards a group of motor scooters parked on the street at the next block. He waved as she sped off. Ivan walked across the road to the waiting car. He flopped into the seat, buckled up and asked, "Was there anything useful?" Natan replied, "Useful? Bloody hell. You're a natural. When all this is over, I recommend you sign up. In two hours you get the life history, a bucket full of names and a few useful dates and events. And you ask, was anything useful. Man. You really don't know how good you are." Ivan sighed. "What do we do from here?" "You can go to the safe house and I will go back to the station. You've done your share." They sat in silence.

Natan played back the recording to Radoslaw and Eryk. The men drew up a time-line. A major meeting in Warsaw in the morning. Eryk would organise eyes at the airport as most will fly into Poznan in the afternoon. Radoslaw read in the death section of the newspaper the funeral time for Wikto Duba. The mafia and the police in disguise will attend Duba's funeral at four p.m. A reception for Wikto Duba was going to be in the small hall attached to the church. Eryk muttered, "I don't know why they bothered with a church service. That mob have broken every law multiple times. I don't think the man upstairs will open his pearly gates. Hypocrites."

Positioned high up in surrounding buildings, police snipers were watching over the funeral. Eryk and Radoslaw took photos with high powered cameras. They identified several people on the wanted for questioning for a list of crimes. Sonya was there at the entrance greeting people with pecks to the cheeks or handshakes and on occasions, a hug. When all were inside, Sonya shut the door.

The doors reopened thirty minutes later. The crowd slowly filed their way into the neighbouring hall.

Radoslaw cursed, "What a lost opportunity. All those bastards here and all we can do is just look, count and identify."

Natan said, "The cameras are working overtime. Tina and James hid themselves in the church one hour before the service. They recorded the entire service and I hope they have good pictures of the people inside."

He pointed to movement at the back of the church. James and Tina under the dimming sky moved carefully down the side of the church on the opposite side of the hall. They hid behind a pillar when they saw two people go outside and engaged in a private conversation. One went inside and the other drove off in an expensive Mercedes. Tina took a picture of the car and hoped the angle was sufficient for the numberplate be identified but then she thought all the cars would have been identified. James and Tina raced towards a waiting van which was disguised with painter's signage. The fake painter climbed down from his scaffolding, went to the van and drove away.

At the station they watched the service, but the focus was on the congregation. One by one people were identified. Only ten were a mystery. Photos were added into the operations room. Radoslaw asked, "Is Ivan willing to go on a date with Sonya?"

"I think so. He said he has to wait a few days for all the funeral stuff to die down," said Natan. Radoslaw nodded. "Good. But I do feel uncomfortable for him to do the task. He goes one more time and then we send in someone who will intently nudge Ivan out. We make it look like two guys vying for the same girl and Ivan is muscled out."

Four days later, Ivan met Sonya at a market. They moved slowly along the stalls. Ivan pushed a hire trolley. Sonya slowly filled it with assorted items. As planned, a police officer in plain clothes met them half-way down one isle. Ivan was going to introduce his close friend, Oskar, to Sonya. From there Oskar would slowly manoeuvre himself to be Sonya's new friend. Ivan deliberately asked Sonya for dates which he knew would clash with Oskar's dates. He heard her give excuses for each decline but was surprised she accepted one date two weeks later.

Wired up again, Ivan reverted to be Peter Schmidt. Now he was armed with a bit of invented history should he be questioned. They met at the local fairground, near a beer garden. Everything was staged.

He would be with Sonya for about twenty minutes. Then Oskar would suddenly appear. A fight. Both would be tossed out of the area. Peter is arrested for the barrage of foul language and an assault on Oskar. He is unceremoniously dragged away by the police. Sonya is left with Oskar.

Back at the police station, Peter Schmidt was arrested for disorderly conduct by police who didn't know of the plan. Minutes later, Eryk tore up the charges sheet. "He's one of ours. He was doing as instructed." The charging officer looked sceptical and decided to observe what was going on. He would reprocess the charge if necessary.

The police officer who was suspicious of Peter looked up from his work to see Oskar giving a high five with Peter. Peter/Ivan apologised for the inflicted bruises. "What is Sonya doing?" asked Ivan.

Oskar shrugged. "Not sure. She was a bit confused and pushed me away, saying I was an overbearing creep and deserved to be beaten up." They started walking down the passageway to the situation room when Ivan's phone rang. "It's Sonya." He looked at Oskar. Eryk opened the door to hear the name of the caller.

"Put it on speaker," said Eryk.

Sonya cried, "Are you okay? I mean, have you been arrested?"

Eryk shook his head. "No," said Ivan. They put me in a cell to cool off."

Sonya sighed. "That's a relief. If they had, I was going to get an uncle who has contact in the police station and see if the charges could be dropped and have Oskar arrested. He was the one out of line."

Without prompting Ivan asked, "Just who in the police force has enough power to get a charge dropped?"

Sonya hesitated before answering, "I am not sure of his name. Inspector….It's an Inspector. I really don't know his name. Just inspector."

Ivan, like the others silently watching, stared in shock. "It doesn't matter. I haven't been arrested. Actually, Oskar has just arrived. Do you want to speak with him?"

"What? You two are talking to each other so soon? The f…" She paused for a few seconds gathering her thoughts. "Are you two being pigs competing with each other?"

"Sometimes we do," said Ivan. "More so when it comes to ladies. We have a similar taste. That brings out the competition but on everything else, we are cool. Do you want to talk to him?"

"Yeah. I need to have words with him," said Sonya as her voice tightened.

"Oskar here."

"What got into you?"

"I don't like my girls going out with other guys," said Oskar and shot a wink to the others.

"Ease up and stop being a total jerk. I was going to say to Peter I preferred you and it was going to be good-bye. Now it is good-bye to both of you. You two have no room for me. Triangles don't work."

Oskar swore softly but not soft enough, "Fuck."

Sonya heard the word. "That's right you two can go and fuck yourselves." She hung up.

Radoslaw smirked. "That was a bit over played. But we got valuable information. We don't need her anymore. Having an inspector as a mole….. Which inspector? There are about twenty."

Eryk sighed. "Twenty is smaller than a few thousand internal suspects. We can go over the records and see who contacted the British mole. All calls are recorded unless there is a private phone used elsewhere."

"We need to get clearance. Who?" asked Eryk.

CHAPTER 11

Thomas Poole was in his British office. He was about to leave when his phone rang. He didn't recognise the number. James Smith introduced himself. Immediately Thomas Poole switched on the scrambler and did an identification check on his computer. James and Tina Smith were sent to Nancy in France to look after the Nowaks. The place was burned to the ground. All were reported missing. Now they have popped up in Poland, the start of the problem. Now it was the creation of new and more significant problems.

James gave a quick update on the Nowaks. Then he preceded to say, "The mole in Poland speaks to a mole in Britain. The Polish rank identified is an inspector. Just who is still unclear. The phone dates of the upper ranks need to be looked at."

Poole sat stunned. "Thanks. I guessed someone was on the take but wasn't sure just how far up to start looking. Ranks attract ranks. I will start my checks. Keep safe. The Polish police have sent us their updates. Thanks for arranging that."

Two days later, Thomas Poole was assigned to another office to take one mother and child into protective custody. While he was waiting directions, he looked at the photos lining the hallway of the police station. The honour board had ten fallen police: photos, name and rank. Lower down was a small mention on how and when they died. Further down the hall was, what he called the skite board. Every police station had one of those. Here were pictures of international efforts and joint training. Pictures of international police cooperating in training sessions for terrorist attacks and major emergencies.

The group of pictures which drew his interest were ones showing East European police at a convention about drug trafficking. He pulled out his mobile phone and took pictures of those photos.

He put the phone away and wandered back to his seat. Minutes later, Inspector Gerry Randale invited him into his office. "Sorry to keep you waiting. I was just finishing off some details concerning the case. Please sit down."

"I called you in on this one. The mother, Lisa White and her daughter, Jennifer, are ready to leave their home in London and go to Swansea, South England. They are waiting for you in the interview room. They will be handed over to the police at Swansea. Drive them to the police station down there and hand them over to Detective Henry Gables. He will do the rest." Thomas nodded. "Being a taxi again, aren't I?"

"After what happened before with the Nowaks, yes. Any word about the whereabouts of James and Tina Smith?" Thomas shook his head. "Any word about the Nowaks?" Again, Thomas shook his head.

"People just don't vanish. There were no body remains after the fire. Find out where they are," ordered Gerry.

Thomas took the file from Gerry's hand. "I am sure the mafia kidnapped all four people and disposed them elsewhere." Sarcastically, he added, "Chopped up, and dumped overboard to feed the fish. Chopped up and shoved into a crematorium. That was done before - people's parts in the coffins for burning."

Gerry leaned over Thomas and snarled, "No more wise cracks. Four people are missing. Find them."

Thomas left the office carrying the folder. He walked into an interview room where he found his new charges. He introduced himself. They gathered their bags and followed him to the waiting four-wheel drive. He helped them load their few possessions inside. "We're going to Swansea police station where you will be handed over to the local police. Detective Henry Gables will look after you."

The four-wheel drive went along the M4 heading west. When they reached Bristol, they stayed the night in a cheap motel. The next day they were supposed to continue along the M4 and then change to M32 which would take them directly to Swansea. But Thomas decided to change plans. Something was niggling at him. The following day he drove the ladies to a small airport, paid for a small plane and its pilot to fly them to Birmingham where he knew another detective would quickly place them in safe custody. He flew back to Bristol and drove back to London. He signed in at his regular station then went home.

At Caldicot, just on the other side of the inlet near Bristol, two men in a blue van waited patiently for the four-wheel drive to materialise. It never happened. The men phoned Gerry Randale on a private phone at his home. Randale cursed and then contacted the Swansea police station. No one had arrived. Randale phoned the station two more times over the next few days, nothing. Frustrated he ordered Thomas Poole back to his station.

"Just where did you take the Whites?"

"They are in safe custody as directed," said Thomas as he looked around the room for more clues to the links with the mafia or to a Polish mole.

"They were supposed to be in Swansea," hissed Randale.

"Yes. I know. But after reading their report and who they were running from, it was much better for both of us not to know where they are." Thomas stood up ready to go out of the room.

"Sit! I am not finished," hissed Randale. "You are supposed to follow orders, not make up new ones to suit yourself."

"My job is to make sure people are safe. It says in my charter I can make sudden decisions if I see danger. I sensed danger and made a decision." Thomas stood up and went out of the room. Through the walls, Randale's voice was heard yelling his name. Other officers stared and shook their heads at him as he left the station.

Poole spent the day in a park with a new mobile phone. He contacted James Smith and Internal affairs. "It's Randale. The mole is Randale. Today I put a bug in his office. I have sent the link to internal affairs. The bastard tried to kill Lisa White and her daughter, Jennifer. Lisa's ex-husband was released from prison. He has vowed to kill them both. He has links to the far-right communist group. Stay where you are. I will check in every two days with any progress."

"I'll let Tina know that you found the mole. I won't say who it is just yet. She will find it hard to believe."

CHAPTER 12

Roza Zielinski returned to her parent's home. She tried to comfort her father. One brother and one friend down hurt him. He was bitter. The deaths of the others in Britain didn't bother him. They were pawns unknown to him. The gap was easy to fill, trust wasn't.

Roza said as she tried to comfort her father. "Nowak's can't run forever. They will tire. If we could separate them, it would be easier."

Norbert looked at his daughter and waved a finger. "I like that idea of weakening the team. The problem is, we don't know where they are."

Roza went to the computer and pulled up a photo of some of Ivan's friends.

"I have been busy searching for Ivan's friends. All well connected families – rich and cosy in their bubble. I think we need to burst a few bubbles."

Nobert looked at the photos of four young men. He pointed to Szymon. "We start with him. What does he like doing?"

"His parents own Sawicki Engineering. They build pipelines for new commercial and residential areas. They are doing a large contract for the new estate between Poznan and Warsaw. His interests are skiing, ice-skating. He is training in the Olympic team. Shooting. This is his last semester in university. He's a bit of a hard worker. He has done some units in commercial law. He has a girlfriend Julia Tomasczewski. She is also a student. Her parents own that big shopping centre on the southside. She is doing law part-time because her father had a heart attack and never quite recovered. Her mother is wheelchair bound after a car accident. She is training to run the family business. She has two years to go."

Norbert grinned. "Devise a scheme to give Szymon a criminal record and a one-way trip to jail." He added, "If push comes to shove where Szymon is concerned, add her to the list. If the parents are in the way, dispose of them too. All guilty by association."

Roza nodded. "It will take a bit of time to create a sting. I will need to do more homework on all of them. Consider it done." Norbert smirked.

He pointed to Antoni Grabowski. Roza gave a smirk. "Now his family could be useful. They are in the health industry." Norbert looked puzzled. "I'll explain," said Roza. "They have trucks of all sizes shifting supplements around and they are also into dehydrated food. I believe they are going to add snap frozen dehydrated food." She looked at Norbert who was a bit confused. She added, "The first steps in making space food." Norbert grinned wider as his mind went on a tangent. "If we get our paws on this company, we may be the first dealers in space." Roza and Norbert chuckled at the thought. Roza tried continuing without laughing. "That maybe a few years away. We can add it to the long-term plan. Now, back to this. They pick up and deliver items from France to Turkey. If we can take over their business, the smell of the food will help disguise the smell of drugs. Bigger shipments of anything going east to west and back again. Antoni likes skiing, ice-skating and tennis. I am not sure if he has a girlfriend, but he does have a younger brother and sister." Norbert's brain was ticking over with possible scenarios. "Put the family on the list. Discredit the company by planting illegal operations. Hack into their system, insert a few cameras and some of our people in the place, preferably in the food processing area, but anywhere is better than nowhere. Is Antoni studying anything?"

"Engineering, namely robotics and automation."

"There goes a few more jobs. He definitely needs to go. No consideration for the working class - machines, machines and more machines. He just might disappear into the industrial food processor. That would discredit the company by having contaminated food. The law cases of people suing would bankrupt them. The factory will be sold for dirt. Yes. Continue."

"All this may flush Ivan Nowak out of hiding but not the father. We still attack the flower company. And the last one?"

Roza laughed. "That is well under way to destruction. Thea Sorokin has wormed her way in by marrying Mikal senior. You speak to her all the time. You know the set up; her driving a wedge between father and son. Mazur Constructions Pty. Ltd. does a lot of civil engineering projects and new housing estates. They are also working on the big development between Poznan and Warsaw."

Norbert nodded. "They will be harder to tear down. Going for Mikal junior won't be enough. We need a major scandal and a split which will destroy their father-son trust and respect. What is Mikal doing?"

"He is at university. In his final year of civil engineering. Rumour has it, he is considering electrical engineering as well. Most likely he will use the credits in civil engineering to short-cut the time to complete electrical engineering. Many students do that these days. Parents put a 6 to 9-year investment into their children's education."

Norbert slammed his hand down on the armchair, "I was denied that opportunity to do that for you; invest in your education. Roza rubbed his hand and reassured him, "I had an education. Not the one you wanted. Don't discount that." Norbert looked up with apologising eyes. In a flash bitterness returned.

He pulled out his phone and dialled a number. He called this number only once a week to check in to see how his cousin, Thea Mazur was doing. Thea always answered her phone quickly when she heard Norbert's ring tone. When the finely tuned pleasantries were over and Thea had time to move away from others near her, they got down to business. "Mikal is away at the moment. Mikal junior is being his typical self and keeping out of my way. We had another argument. The wedge is slowly widening. Mikal senior still keeps his business close to his chest. I just play happy hostess when there are associates around. There is a project in the early planning stages in Krakow, some government job. Worth millions. The conversations seem to stop, slow down or alter when I am around. The only other thing I can understand is that the contract has to do with major public housing development. It is still in early stages. Some government people and Mikal are going to have a major meeting in Krakow in three days-time. I won't be able to attend until the evening when all the wives come to dinner. I have been to one of these functions before. No one speaks any business. It is all family rubbish and where to buy the most expensive clothes."

Norbert chuckled. "Keep up the good work. Mikal Mazur and his precious son are going to pay." He clicked off. He thought about the new information he had received. A plan was formulating.

He asked Roza, "Find some mud on both Mikal Mazurs. Does Ivan have any more friends?"

"There could be. But they will be more like acquaintances."

I think we have enough forward planning. Artem needs to know of these people."

"Artem is drawing up multi plans with multiple groups. He is even looking at the army. He is thinking of using disgruntled ex-army people to train our people. It takes time to amass a private army."

"Just a minute," said Roza as she thought of something else. She turned her mobile phone on and went to Facebook. "I think there is a connection between Ivan Nowak and the Symanski girls. Ivan's social media has been taken down. I am going to switch over to Marlena's Facebook page. …Nothing. No mention of Ivan and any of the known names he is using. In fact, she doesn't friend any men. She has pictures of herself with a baby boy."

"Who's the father?" asked Norbert.

"She says she doesn't know. She doesn't seem to care. She says she is in La Rochelle, France.

Now Lavinia is different. I am going to her social page. Oh yes, she is very keen on Antoni Grabowski.

Hmm, looks like they are engaged. There is a fat rock on her hand. She is showing it off."

Norbert sighed as he pulled out a mobile phone. He spoke briefly, before turning to Roza. "Artem says hello. We need to go to Saint Petersburg."

"Shall I continuing searching for more friends of Ivan?"

"No that will be enough for now. Antoni and the other two will be the first to go. Leave the girls alone. Let them suffer."

CHAPTER 13

After the meeting in Saint Petersburg, the men dispersed. Each had their own task. Their wave of destruction was sectioned off. Sonya Duba was contacted. She was the only person who had secured a job in The East European Flower Company. She was considered a valuable asset in the right place. At reception she could keep tabs on who comes and goes through the day and any possibility of job vacancies.

At the funeral of her father, Sonya briefly mentioned to her mother she met a Peter Schmidt, a German businessman who had asked her out. Then a couple of weeks later, a friend of his, Oskar Byko caused an incident at a fair ground. She said she told them where to go after a fight which led Peter to be arrested and Oskar to a local doctor for a quick check up. Her mother had passed the information on to Artem.

Artem spoke to Sonya's mother, "Do you think you can get Sonya to reconnect with this Peter Schmidt and Oskar Byko? Business people can be bribed."

Sonya Duba looked at her mother with disgust. "I actually like that job. I don't want to do anything to jeopardise it. It is about time this family made an effort to go straight. I am fed up of looking over my shoulder to see who is coming." Sonya's mother slapped her hard across the face. Sonya almost fell to the ground. Her mother snarled, "You ungrateful whore. It is crime money that got you an education and pays the rent in your fancy apartment. You do as you are told. You were born into this and you pay your debts. Phone those suckers. See which one will nibble at the bait."

Sonya nervously picked up the phone. She dialled Peter's number first. The call was rejected. Then she tried Oskar's number.

Before answering Oskar signalled to Radoslaw and Eryk to listen in. He pushed answer. "Hello Oskar speaking. Sonya it is so nice to hear from you. Finally, after what......nearly two weeks?"

"Yes. I have to apologise for my behaviour. I was rude. I would like to make it up to you. Can we start again on another date?"

Before he answered the question, he looked at the two detectives. Both nodded.

"I can meet you after work this Friday. How about I pick you up and take you to a restaurant in the Sheridan Hotel, Bukow Ska."

Sonya glanced across to her mother who was now smiling and nodding. "That would be nice. I will see you then."

In the station, Oskar looked at the two detectives in front of him. "Something is brewing. I can feel it."

"We will be in the place with you. Wear a wire," said Radoslaw. "Definitely something is brewing. It will be big."

Oskar met Sonya as arranged. He found a street carparking bay two blocks away from the Sheridan Hotel. They entered the large dining room. A waiter led them to a pre-set wall table. They ordered their meals. Eryk, accompanied by a policewoman, were ushered to a table set for four after mentioning other people would be arriving soon. The waiter nodded, handed them a drink menu and quickly left. Across the room, Sonya's mother entered with a man Sonya didn't know. The waiter ushered them to a table not far from Sonya and Oskar. Oskar noted the surprise look on Sonya's face. He looked at the same direction. "Someone you know?" he asked.

"Err yes. The lady. I don't know her partner," she said softly as she raised a glass of wine to her lips.

"Do you want them to join us? It will be fine with me," said Oskar trying to gauge her.

"No. No. The man I don't know, and the lady is a phenomenal gossip. By tomorrow morning, the whole of Poznan will know about this date."

"That bad is it?"

"You have no idea. She is a person my dear bossy mother is fond of. Really, I think she is trouble," said Sonya. Oskar couldn't help noticing the anger in her voice. He suspected she was lying and about what was already eased out of her. Sonya shot a weak smile to her mother.

Her mother gave a wave and headed for them. The man she was with followed. "Shit," cursed Sonya. "Say nothing."

Her mother put on a fake voice, "Darling how nice to see you?" She bent over and gave Sonya a peck on the cheek. Sonya cringed.

Sonya put on a fake smile. "So nice to see you, too. And who may be your partner for the night be?"

"Sorry, I don't mean to be rude. This is Norbert Zielinski. And this fine young man be?"

Oskar stood up. "Oskar Byko."

Sonya's mother grinned broadly and blew Sonya a kiss. "Well, my sweet dear, I won't hold you up with your meal." She sauntered off taking Norbert's arm.

When she was at a distance, Sonya whispered under her breath, "Bitch."

Oskar frowned. "Okay, you don't like her. Some consolation is you don't live with her."

"She is over so often at my mother's home; she almost lives there. Drinks herself stupid and then sleeps over. I am sure she comes over just to get her daily fill of alcohol. That is besides all the gossip. Yuck. I've heard the name Norbert Zielinski before but never met him. He is an asshole, thug and major trouble. I didn't even know the two knew each other. Well matched – two angels of Satan."

Oskar played the part and took Sonya's hand. "Don't let her spoil this evening." He gave it a gentle kiss. He let go of her hand when the meals arrived.

By the time the night at the restaurant ended, Sonya believed she had reeled in Oskar to speak about his business dealing with The East European Flower Company. What he said, Sonya believed and hoped what she said about her mother and Norbert was enough. She allowed Oskar to take her home. He did so but refused the invitation to go inside. He observed her entering her apartment. The lights went on one after another and then slowly switched off. Oskar drove off to the station.

Sonya was shortly visited by her mother and Norbert. "It wasn't that hard was it?"

"No. But I feel like a heel."

Her mother slapped her again.

"You did good," said Norbert. "Just good. Two more meetings with that jerk and he will be in."

Sonya stared in defiance and any questions had answers spat at them. Her hate towards them was palatable. She waited until they left. She wasn't going to hang around anymore.

She had enough assaults and insults. All her life her mother slapped her across the face. She thought it was normal. But since working as a receptionist and listening to what other female staff were saying, she then realised, it wasn't normal. She wanted out – no more abuse.

She opened her computer to access her bank account. She set up a new account at another bank and transferred funds into it. Then she set up a re-occurring transfer for a period of six months. She knew six months would be long enough for her mother to stop the regular deposits. She then looked at the rental market for cheap housing. She printed out what she wanted. Enquiries would start tomorrow.

At the station Radoslaw, Eryk, Ivan and Stefan listened to the recordings Oskar made. Stefan had coached Oskar what to say for the next meeting. By then they would know exactly what Sonya's intention were. She was obviously unhappy with her life. Short phrases and the stress in her voice confirmed that. She didn't want to be a part of anything.

The follow-up dates never happened. A call had come in. Gunshots were heard in a street on the outskirts of town. The emergency lines lit up giving an address and a rough description of a man leaving the apartment and getting into the passenger side of an old car. Sonya was found dead in her apartment. A gunshot wound to the chest and stomach saw to that.

Radoslaw and Eryk took charge of the investigation. They took her laptop. On it they found a new will all signed and in the process of registration. The beneficiary was Oskar. He cringed when he was told of the find. Nothing in the recorded conversations indicated her intentions with Oskar. To Oskar, it indicated to him that Sonya was an extremely tormented person. Attempting to leave her meagre assets to a near stranger was testimonial to that. She no longer trusted anyone she knew.

There was a file which was the last to be opened. It was named poetry by Sonya. Oskar decided he would read her works although poetry just wasn't him. He read the first poem. It highlighted the abuse poured onto her through her life. Frequent face slaps from her mother but what made Oskar sick was her mother selling her virginity to the highest bidder on a paedophile website. Her mother received 50,000 Euros. All of that was to pay her way out of gambling debts.

Oskar felt sick but read further.

Radoslaw and Eryk joined Oskar. The computer was now projected onto a screen. The next poem was read. It gave details of the drug-cum-slave route going east to Iran. This time a map showing only towns accompanied the poem. The men gasped. The information was invaluable.

They pushed on to the next lengthy poem. No pictures this time but that didn't matter. There was a series of ditties about each guard: name and addresses were supplied in the poems. Fifteen border guards were mocked in the ditties. Radoslaw whispered, "She must have gone with the men on these trips. They are too detailed."

Oskar thought about the poems and swore, "She was made to have sex with these men. The descriptions are a bit on the intermit side. Go back here." He pointed to a paragraph.

> 'The dirty old man hadn't bathed for days. He stunk.
> His body odour would rival a skunk.
> It didn't hide the scar on his lower bum
> He sat on the bed drinking his rum.'

The next poem came up. It was a twist away from descriptions to depression.

There was a poem about her meeting with Peter Schmidt and another Oskar Byko. Oskar blushed.

Both poems were flattering. It revealed she was forced to do a task by her mother and her bosses. Her task was to get Peter and Oskar to be informants. She hated the deceit.

The next poem was back in the doldrums again but a realisation she had been abused. She thought it was normal until she started working at the Flower Company. There she experienced respect and learned her life experiences were not normal. She made up her mind to leave the clutches of her abusers. It was then she realised both Peter and Oskar were different from the men she was forced to be with. Not all wanted her for sex. Just company.

Her final file was her plan to run away from all she knew. She didn't want to be a part of the impending destruction. She listed what she knew. No poem this time. Just hurried notes. There was a reference to a patisserie in Saint Petersburg. She called it the rat-infested pies sold to innocent people. Radoslaw sighed. "She knew too much and wanted out. She paid the ultimate price. We keep this under wraps. Transfer this information - poems, will and bank accounts. Then wipe it. Her family, if you can call them that, will want to look at her computer." Oskar sat stunned at all what Sonya had been through, he whispered as he rubbed his face. "She was actually a sweet person. God, she had it bad. Now she doesn't have to run anymore, and she won't be abused as well." Oskar left the room. When he was in the toilets he cried. "At times I hate this job." He punched the door with his fist. "What kind of parent treats their child in such a way?"

He walked to the gym in the basement and put on boxing gloves. He started punching the bag. With every strike he saw Sonya's mother, the bitch who barged in on their date. *Christ*, he thought, the *girl couldn't even go on a date without supervision.* Norbert's face flashed. The creep was playing escort to the bitch. Oskar stayed in the gym punching the bag until he was exhausted. He quickly showered and went back to the operations room. "Let's get the bastards and that bitch of a woman who calls herself a mother," he announced to the others.

CHAPTER 14

Stefan was ushered into the police station. "You saw how Ivan went a bit underground."

Stefan nodded. "Yes. Lies after lies with a good dose of acting."

"We are going to send in a mature man to reel in the bitch, known as Anna Duba, Sonya's mother. We need you to coach another undercover officer in business talk. Get the language right. Sonya's funeral will be tomorrow. Oskar is going. The other officer is pretending to be his father supporting his grief-stricken son," said Radoslaw.

"Show me who the officer is. We can get started now. Is now okay?"

"Sure," said Radoslaw.

At the funeral, eyes high above watched the proceedings. Again, James and Tina concealed themselves inside. The crowd was distinctly smaller. A few prominent people showed up. Some people from the Flower Company were there. Genuine mourners. Oskar with his pretend father stood to the back. Sonya's mother recognised Oskar. She walked over, greeted him and thanked him for coming. Oskar introduced his father, Fabian Byko. He gave her a business card and offered her to call him at any time for any reason.

Oskar and Fabian followed the small group of mourners to the reception hall. They mingled and networked their business to the seedy group. Fabian made it a point to zero in on Sonya's mother.

He made sure he was attentive to her so-called needs. He cursed in his mind the woman was faking grief. He wanted her to think she had a new friend. *Bitch.*

Fabian and Oskar left the reception about the same time as the other mourners. Fabian slammed his fist into the upholstery of the car before starting the ignition. "What a fucking bitch. Fake tears and a master at manipulation. I don't know why she bothers with facelifts. They don't improve her looks and the make up! Oh God! You could scrape it off with a shovel. She is ugly to the core."

"If you met Sonya, it would be hard to believe she came from that horrible family. Trying to run away didn't save her. It killed her," said Oskar trying to change the subject in a bid to calm Fabian down.

"Yeah. Now I wait for that nightmare to call. I am sure as hell taking a gun with me when I have to be around her. A vomit bag would also help."

"She would think that normal - men with their guns. Did you notice three of them had guns?"

"Yeah. Totally disrespectful to wear them in church," spat Fabian.

Four days later, Fabian was in his office at the police station. His phone rang. He glanced at the number and quickly signalled to the others working around him to quieten down. The room went silent. He switched to speaker. "Hello," he said as he glanced to the watching detectives.

The female voice on the other end purred, "Do I have Fabian Byko?"

"Yes," said Fabian.

"This is Anna Duba. We met at my sweet daughter's funeral."

"Ah Yes. I remember," said Fabian resisting the temptation to stick his finger down his throat.

"I was wondering if you and your handsome son, Oskar, would like to attend a cocktail party in honour of Sonya's passing?"

Fabian hesitated but got the nod from Eryk and Radoslaw. "That would be nice. I am not sure if Oskar would be up to such an event so soon after Sonya's death."

Anna wasn't going to let both men slip away. "Well, there will be other young ladies there who no doubt will be interested in Oskar and they could elevate the loss he may feel for her. Such a sweet gentle man to be so taken aback."

Fabian felt his blood crawl. "What time does it start and the address?" asked Fabian as he was slowly shaking his head.

"At my home. I will text you the address. It starts at eight p.m." Anna continued the purring.

Fabian stalled and flipped through the pages of his diary. His Saturday was free, but he added,

"That clashes a little with a previous event. What I will do is leave the first event early and get to your home a bit later. It may be as late as 9.30 p.m. That would be the best I could do."

Anna drummed her fingers on the phone. "Okay. I will see you about then. I will be looking forward to seeing you and your son again." She hung up.

"What a bitch. The grass hasn't even grown across the grave and she is having parties!"

Oskar, we get there close to ten. The less time in that place the better. Now let's collaborate our stories."

Just before ten on the Saturday night, Fabian and Oskar walked into an elaborately decorated hall.

Balloons and streamers decorated the ceiling. Masked waiters offered assorted drinks and platters of finger food. Sonya's mother spotted them quickly and came rushing over. "So nice to see you both. You are later than expected. I thought you two had changed your minds."

"I wouldn't miss it for the world," faked Fabian.

"Come let me introduce you to like-minded men." She held Fabian's hand and began to pull him through the crowd. She looked back at Oskar briefly who was standing alone. She spoke to Roza who was taking a drink off a tray a waiter was holding. "Look after that shy man." She dropped to a whisper, "Corrupt him." She pointed to Oskar. "Introduce him to people his own age and let us oldies be together."

Roza almost purred at Oskar. She took his hand and tossed it over her shoulder. Through the crowd she led him to a mixed group of twenty somethings. She introduced Oskar. Oskar wasn't sure he got all their names as a band started playing with the volume full on. Two couples left for the dance floor leaving Oskar with two women which neither appealed to him, but they were keen to get to know him. He almost gave an audible sigh of relief when two more women approached and introduced themselves. He spoke briefly to them all before excusing himself.

He looked around for Fabian. He realised Fabian was also searching for him.

Fabian and Oskar stood together only for minutes before dragon lady pulled Fabian away. Oskar was pulled by Roza. Roza whispered, "You don't want to hang around with your father. Let loose." Oskar looked over his shoulder to see Fabian with the dragon lady being introduced to another equally ugly female. To Oskar, the second lady looked like a horse – a copper coloured dress hugged her middle-age body and buck teeth dominated her face. *Poor Fabian,* thought Oskar. *These women age badly.*

Roza slipped an arm around Oskar's waist. "Stay put. I want you to meet someone." Roza hailed over Artem. "Oskar," she purred, "This is my boss, Artem Orlov. Now don't make my boss upset by refusing his offer." Roza disappeared into the crowd.

Artem quickly looked Oskar up and down before extending his hand. Oskar shook it under protest.

Artem Orlov was one of the highest-ranking men in the Russian mafia. He presented himself like any other businessman in any other large cooperation. He didn't make himself stand out in very upper high-end fashion stakes. He dressed with more restraint. He wore a tuxedo which looked the same as half the men in the room. A pink rose gold lapel pin filled the lapel buttonhole above the pocket of his tuxedo jacket. The base of the lapel pin was gold with a small diamond which reflected the light coming from any direction. *Expensive diamond made to look cheap,* thought Oskar.

Artem smiled with an assurance of any salesperson who had won top salesman's award several times over. "Oskar, I was speaking to your father earlier. I hear your company is making a bid to take over The East European Flower Company."

"Yes. Our offer went in just a few days ago. It is still a bit early to receive a reply. We are giving them a week and then we will contact them to see what the progress is."

"Your father said they were going down the chute caused by attacks on their company – attacks on their franchisees, and attacks on their delivery trucks. The company is starting to slide. Your father says with new branding in a takeover, new confidence from consumers and staff alike will bring back profits."

"It certainly will. The price of the company is dropping. The shares are sliding. A good time to buy. We have already bought forty-two percent of the shares. We're aiming for sixty per cent. That will be achieved by the end of next week. Basically, we are forcing their hand to sell."

"Yes. Fabian did mention the strategy – a two-way attack. I have a proposition for you and your father. I ran it by Fabian earlier. He says he will definitely consider it. He has asked me to present the idea to your board members on Tuesday morning," said Artem.

"Yes. That would be nice. What are some of your thoughts?" said Oskar hoping the information would start a new line of investigation.

"I need new young educated blood to head one strand of a new line of operations. I spent a long time developing trade with some of the Arab countries. We sell them what they need, that includes items being blocked by the U.S. and European embargos. In return we get processed and semi-processed crops."

Oskar's interest piqued. Artem noticed the change of interest. "We sell the proceeds to distributors who then sell it directly to consumers. Just like any other business," said Artem feeling he was reeling in Oskar. Oskar nodded and pretended to hesitate. More than anything, he wanted to shoot the man there. "Just what part do my father and I have in this and what are our shares?"

Artem placed an arm around Oskar's shoulder and slowly walked him to a quieter location in the room. "Your skills and your equipment. Our products go on your trucks, the old East European Flower Company trucks. Old trucks painted up will do. The roads in some parts to the Arab countries are in very bad shape. The smaller trucks would be ideal as some of the roads on the mountains have some of the tightest corners to navigate. The roads are also very narrow. The smaller trucks would be much better."

"Just what is our cut?"

"Forty-five per cent on every return delivery," said Artem smiling at the generous offer he was making.

"Hmm, forty-five? We will have to think about it. The cost of vehicles...who pays for that?"

"Your vehicles, you do."

"Who drives the trucks?" asked Oskar who was now smelling a deal worse that rotting seafood.

"My people. They know the roads and the contacts," said Artem.

"I will want one person from my company on each journey. That will be a condition," said Oskar.

Artem grinned. "Your father said the same. You too are so much alike in many ways. Funny, how you do not look like him in any way."

Oskar shrugged. "I have had that all my life. If you saw my mother, you would see some resemblance on that side. But I am very much like my father on the inside, especially the way I think."

Artem grinned. "We can't have it all. I will see you and the rest of your board members on Tuesday then."

Oskar nodded. "It will be a pleasure."

Oskar turned to move away. Anna Duba, dragon lady, caught his eye. She rushed over and took him by the elbow as she guided him towards Fabian. She said in a very dominating way, "Your father tells me you two are leaving. We can't have that. The night is so young." She looked at her watch. "It's only twelve-thirty a.m. Much too early to leave."

Fabian gave a sigh of relief when he saw Oskar and looked at his watch. "We better go. We have a busy day tomorrow."

Anna queried, "Working on a Sunday? You two need to unwind. No. No." She snapped her fingers.

Two young women materialised out of nowhere. Anna gave them a nod. They knew what had to be done. Each took Fabian's and Oskar's hand to begin leading the men upstairs. Fabian pulled back giving Oskar a jolt to reality. Fabian pulled his hands free, but Oskar felt a vice-like grip take hold. He struggled to break free. Fabian had by now blocked his 'partner' and purposely kicked the back of the knee of the lady holding Oskar. She stumbled down a few steps which would have led to bedrooms. Oskar worked his way free. Roza rushed over to assist the lady who was now on the floor. Fabian and Oskar quickly thanked Roza, gave a cursory assistance and walked as quickly as they could through the closest door.

Fabian and Oskar walked across the driveway and through the gates. The guard at the gate called them back, "I need your names to cross off the list. It's a head count in case anything nasty happens like a fire."

Both men called out "Byko" The guard looked down his list on a tablet and marked them leaving at twelve-fifty.

Fabian and Oskar made sure the guard didn't see them running down the street. They jumped into a waiting police van loaded with listening devises. Fabian and Oskar started stripping the wires off as fast as they could. Fabian cursed, "Don't drive us home. Go to anywhere but. I want the stench of those people off me before I go home."

The driver asked, "To the lake?"

"Yeah, anywhere where I can deodorise," said Fabian who was now removing his shirt. He threw the shirt out of the window. He looked at Oskar, "Ditch the shirt. It smells of those last two bitches and Roza." Oskar frowned at Fabian. He did what he was told.

Fabian saw a church. "Stop! I'm going inside." He grabbed Oskar's hand and dragged him to the closed church door.

Fabian tested a couple of windows. One wasn't locked. He opened it and climbed through. He signalled for Oskar to follow. Reluctantly, Oskar followed. He sat beside Fabian. Fabian was muttering a series of prayers. He told Oskar, "Start praying. Those people are evil. We need to get that evilness out or we become like them."

Oskar asked, "Do you do this in every job?"

"Generally at the end of a job. It keeps me sane and pulls me back into normal society. But these people are the embodiment of evil. Start praying for cleansing and protection or you will go under. This is how I have survived in this job for so long. I get help from above. We need his help big time in this job. Now start praying. Repeat after me…."

An hour later, both Oskar and Fabian walked out of the front door of the church. They looked for the driver of the van and tapped on the window. The driver woke with a start. "Let's get to that lake."

Tuesday morning at a hired boardroom at a Sheridan Hotel in Poznan, Oskar and Fabian were dressed in business suits. They were accompanied by two other police officers posing as board members and using false names – Alan Gorski, a forensic accountant and Milosz Sobezak, a police lawyer. Like the two accompanying officers, Ivan and Stefan were both heavily disguised.

Ivan still had the stud in his ear. He had a painted print to look like a tattoo on his neck and another across one the wrist. The positioning was designed to look as if Peter's wild past was now an inconvenience but enough to show there could be traces of a wild boy who could be resurrected. Ivan was assured the ink would fade with every bath. It would take a couple of weeks for it to disappear completely. Ivan's hair and eyebrows were redyed dark brown while Stefan's was redyed black. Both wore different shaped prosthetic noses. Stefan had a mole added to the left cheek. Ivan was to be introduced as Peter Schmidt, as the sales and marketing manager and Stefan was introduced as Thomas Brennen the head of personnel. Both were mentioned as coming from the German head office and would be responsible for the Polish setup and operations. They were fully briefed and were working on behalf of both Fabian and Oskar Byko.

The room was wired and hidden cameras were scattered around, not only in the room itself but in the passageway and in the basin area of the toilets. In another room with a false sign saying, 'Closed due to renovations' were the police with all their recording equipment. Every so often, they would run a drill or saw just loud enough to make the sound drift into the boardroom meeting. A reminder of the renovations going on. Otherwise the room was dead quiet.

Artem Orlov was accompanied by Norbert Zielinski, Roza Zielinski who was introduced as Artem's secretary and Norbert's daughter, and Matvei Vitsin who was the accountant, Gleb Ekkov as their legal representative.

Each group took one side of the table as if it were some diplomatic Mexican stand-off. Artem asked Matvei to begin the meeting. He presented false documentation about the so-called legitimate company who was interested in taking over The East European Flower Company and their fake legal tactics. Matvei handed out a summarised copy of the company's financials and spoke about each topic: staffing costs, product costs and distribution systems etcetera. The profit and loss sheet ended with a positive cash flow of three million Euros. He pointed out that would expand if the companies could either merge or work together on a shared equipment and delivery system. Alan examined the sheet before him. He knew it was a fake, just as the fake one he was going to present to them.

Alan opened the hastily formed website for the occasion - Exotic Polish Food. He stared at the contact page. There were genuine enquiries regarding food from consumers. He flipped the laptop around. "Here is an excellent example of customer enquiries we get all the time. Three order from ex-pats living in France and Belgium." He quickly turned the laptop back to himself. Ping! He looked at the laptop. Another customer request and enquiry came through. He looked at the group before him. "See how fast we get enquiries about our products?" Ping! Ping! Ping! Alan turned the webpage off and opened another file.

The meeting lasted another two hours. There were some points of agreements, but many areas were sticking points. As the police group parted, Alan said in loud voice to ensure Artem's men were listening, "Peter, make sure those emails are answered."

Ivan/Peter played along. "I will get my secretary to respond to the emails that is if she has not responded already. She did send me a text in the meeting. Negotiations for a shop in a shopping centre in Belgium are just about finalised. We should have that outlet open before the end of the month."

The men parted ways in the lobby. Peter and Thomas got into a taxi which went to the airport. Alan and Milosz went in two separate unmarked police cars which went in two different directions. One group of Artem's people followed Peter and Thomas to the airport while the other men followed the two unmarked police cars.

One police car stopped at an office which had temporary signs saying, 'Exotic Polish Food.' Milosz, walked through the buildings and took the exit door to a fire escape at the side to another waiting unmarked police car.

The second unmarked police car just drove to a high-rise office where numerous legal and accountancy firms were located. Alan walked into the building, took a lift to one floor, got out and back down again in another lift. He got into another unmarked police car which took him back to the police station. When Alan and Milosz were escaping, unmarked police cars picked up the trails of Artem's men outside the high-rise building and the fake office.

The criminal's car, a black rundown Audi which followed Ivan and Stefan to the airport waited for a few minutes before driving off. The police tailing this car were surprised that one criminal didn't get out to follow the Nowaks into the airport. Instead the occupants drove off going west over the freeway. The police car following that vehicle stayed with them for ten more minutes before allowing another car to take on the role. The car of criminals eventually turned into a driveway.

The following car continued along the road, turned a corner before giving the final address.

Ivan and Stefan remained in the terminal for thirty minutes watching for one of the known criminals. Feeling confident, they decided to catch the train back to the city centre. From there they could walk back to the police station.

One of the criminal's car was a white van. The van followed Alan to the fake office. The driver pulled into a handicapped person's space in front of the building. He followed Alan into the building but lost him seconds later. When he returned to his van, the man cursed when he saw a parking ticket slapped across his windscreen.

The following unmarked police car trailed the driver to a car wrecker's yard. He was observed going into the office and coming out again before driving away in a yellow Skoda. The unmarked police car followed the Skoda around town for the next few hours which included picking up children from a school before driving home where he stayed.

The car which had followed Milosz to the building which had numerous lawyers and accountant officers, was a cream and black van. The passenger of the van got out and followed Milosz into the building. He watched at the ground floor which level Milosz stopped at. He walked over to the directory and looked for the name. He blew air out of his mouth. This Milosz worked for one of the most prestigious law firms in the city. That was enough for him. He had dealings with this firm in the past. They were instrumental in putting him away for three years. He wasn't going near them. He left the building. The following police car watched the van drive to the wrecker's yard. The two men didn't leave for another hour. When they did, it was in an old unregistered car. The tailing police called it in when they were a few blocks away, a standard police car pulled them over to check the registration.

While the police were waiting outside the wreckers, they took photos of all the cars parked inside. They noted a number of vans painted black and cream or back and tan and two were white and tan and one was plain white. The vans were photographed, and the number plates were recorded. It was a fleet of some description. All had the same phone number, but each colour had a different business name.

Matvei, Norbert and Gleg went in one white limousine driven by a chauffeur. The car drove all the men to one house owned by Anna Duba. The trailing police car watched from a distance for a while before driving off.

The last criminal car which had Artem and Roza inside, was chauffeured black limousine. The car went along the freeway, heading south. The police swapped trailing cars at the final exit. The replacement followed Artem and Roza to a large house in a very well-to-do street. That police car continued its way past the house. They radioed in the address.

The house was the third largest house in the street. The entrance was via a controlled gate with a guard checking the occupants of each incoming vehicle. Artem and Roza's cars had their own remote control for the gate. Unlike the other houses in the street, this house had a rotating dog patrols; just one dog and its handler at any one time. The high brick fence which surrounded the house on all four sides ensured its privacy.

The house once belonged to Gregori Zeilinski, the man who was killed in Britain. Roza was now the owner of the house after a battle with Gregori's ex-wife and daughter. Roza smirked as she drove through the iron gates recalling the battle in the courts. Gregori had provided well for his daughter, Tanya and ex-wife. Tanya received another house which was not as big. It came with a one-off lump amount of 500,000 Euros. The ex-wife received a one-off lump sum of 800,000 euros. Roza's smirk widened, when the judge's words rang loudly in their ears. "The will is a legal document and was registered." He reiterated a clause down the bottom of the will, "If anyone is not happy with their allocation, it will be given to charity. I am very close to ordering the entire estate to be sold and all proceeds given to charity. One more word from any of you, the final clause will be enacted." Roza who never contested any part of the will at any time, got the large house. As in the past, she only spoke to Tanya on rare occasions when their paths crossed at functions. Most times both women ignored each other. As for the ex-wife, she took off and remarried a small time Italian wine maker. Roza never saw her again and Tanya never mentioned her mother.

Roza held Artem's hand as they walked into the mansion. Artem immediately stripped down naked and jumped into the spa. Roza followed after stripping down. "That meeting was stressful. They are much harder to deal with than expected," said Artem. Roza nodded but looked worried. "That Peter guy, for some reason I felt I met him before. Just something about him." Maybe I am imaging things."

Artem grinned. "You have a good sixth sense. If you are not sure about him, I will get Boris to check him out."

"No don't worry. It is just me attending a meeting of that calibre. I have never done that style of meeting before. Just beginner's nerves. So formal and so…"

Artem held up his hand. Roza stopped talking. "You did well. Very well."

Two days later, Fabian and Stefan/Thomas were invited to Anna's house. There they would discuss more of the plans to take over the East European Flower Company. Artem was there with Roza. Roza said nothing but recorded the meeting by tapping away at her tablet. Thomas and Fabian worked as a team with Fabian also recording notes on his laptop.

By the end of the second meeting, Fabian's and Thomas's company, the Exotic Polish Food, who was already the majority shareholder would exercise its control rights. Then they introduce Artem's company into a joint-venture and as a minor partner with thirty per cent. The wheels were in place.

Under the supervision of Fabian and Oskar, Stefan and Ivan made a meeting with his board members of The East European Flower Company. They would meet at a motel in Lodz to be well away from possible disturbances and any possible Artem's prying eyes

The board members drove to Lodz and checked in to a motel. In the hired small conference room, they warmly greeted Stefan and Ivan. They were introduced to the accompanying police. They were briefed on the fake takeover of the company. Joanna hesitated the most and voiced her concerns.

CHAPTER 15

The Board members of The East European Flower Company sent out to all franchisees and to all administration staff stating negotiations were taking place to sell the company to a third party.

Each was given assurance all agreements would be honoured and all staff would not be retrenched.

Joanna Lewandowski didn't like what was going on. To Joanna it was deception which if backfired, would be the final demise of the company. She proceeded with her work ever so cautiously. She knew the police were monitoring everything and that in itself, was unnerving.

She looked at the fake share register. Stefan, who she had to keep reminding herself to call Thomas Brennen, was also behind the deceit. She had always held him in high regard, but this showed her a new side to his character. Ivan, now she had to call him Peter, was always a bit of a rebel. This escapade, according to her thoughts, was typical of Ivan. He always came out of left field and did the unexpected. He did that well, too well. In her eyes, Ivan was enjoying the role playing and thrived on the complication of the matters.

A few days later the three parties met at the Poznan headquarter of The East European Flower Company. The conference room was set up. Cold water and glasses were spread around the table. Tea and coffee facilities were in place. Sandwiches and biscuits would arrive at 10.30 am for the morning tea break and again at 3.30 p.m. for afternoon tea. Lunch was being organised in the adjoining room – meals ordered from a nearby restaurant would be delivered at 12.30. The lunch break would be short, just forty minutes. There was much to get through. In Joanna's eyes, the faster this was done, the better it would be.

Throughout the meeting, Joanna remained very quiet. She only spoke when she truly deemed it necessary. She put forward suggestions for the transition to be a smooth as possible. She was relieved to have reconfirmed all staff would keep their jobs.

The major change would be the older and smaller trucks which would normally be sold off to help pay for the newer and more fuel-efficient ones, would be retained and used elsewhere. They would get a facelift – new paint, new signage, and new refrigeration units. It irked her that the bill was to be paid for The Flower Company and not by the people taking over. She knew this was a sting of some description, but she felt there was a lot more to it than a sting. Something much, much deeper.

To her she knew was on the need to know basis. She had to be satisfied with that. *Not fair*, she thought, not knowing what she and the others were working towards. She knew she would work more efficiently if she just knew exactly what was going on. She and the other board members were like beads clustered together waiting to be threaded into the loop. This loop circled them, and they all knew they would never be fully informed of what exactly was going on. They played along. Uncomfortable.

When the meeting was over, Thomas and Ivan spoke to her. They made sure they were out of sight and earshot of all others. Thomas spoke first, "Joanna, I noticed you were quite upset but kept a very professional stance. We are not exactly jumping with joy. Just ride this out. It may not look like I have your back or the board's back, but we do."

Joanna stared back before asking, "What exactly is going on?"

Ivan held a finger to his lips. "Shh. Top secret. We can't say. Just do your best to play along."

Joanna grunted, "I would expect that of you but not your father."

Ivan grinned but didn't say a word but looked the other way thinking, *dad you have an admirer.*

Thomas placed an assuring hand on her arm, "This will be over before the end of the year. It better be." Thomas and Ivan left Joanna wondering.

She collected all at the paperwork from the meeting and stuffed them in her bag. She would send via email, a summary to the other members of the board. Tomorrow, she would go through everything in detail. Analysis was her strong point. *The devil,* she thought, *no, the answer was in the all-day bullshit and posturing.* She had her work cut out. She walked out of the Lodz motel, got into her car to drive home. She locked the papers in the safe.

Before going to bed, she booked herself into motel on the far side of Poznan. She had used the motel before when she had to work on delicate matters. It offered the best privacy and was free of distractions of other staff. She tried doing the same thing by staying at home but the home phone or her mobile just didn't stop interrupting. Tomorrow she would drop in at the office and tell her assistant she was going on stress leave for a few days.

When Joanna reached the office, her assistant was not there. She asked around. There was no answer. She told the two other workers in the same area; she was going to be away on stress leave and would be unreachable. However, she indicated, she would phone in at the end of each day just to make sure all was going well. Only then did she offer a small amount of time for any assistance. She walked out of the office. The staff just stared. One whispered to another, "She should have gone on leave weeks ago when someone tried shooting her." The other assistant nodded. "About time she took that stress leave. A few days won't be enough. I bet all this take over stuff has just added to the stress."

Joanna checked into a motel on the far side of Poznan. She immediately put up the 'do not disturb' sign. She unpacked her bags and ordered a meal to be sent up to the room. Then she separated the papers into groups. The Flower Company across the top with paper in their different headings, then the police faked up papers, the Exotic Polish Food company, and then the other group, East-West Products. She knew the latter company was in for the sting. How big the sting was going to be would remain unknown unless she worked it out from all the bookwork which now laid out in front of her.

She poured over the three sets of papers, underlining anomalies. She drew a mud map of each organisation and then overlayed them. The group which she considered to be from a criminal gang didn't make sense. She took out her laptop and researched everything which came to mind. They didn't exist.

She had worked for nearly ten hours straight. She carefully removed the papers from the bed and went to sleep. Figures jumbled in her sleep. Words of the long meeting came screaming at her. She woke with a start. Sweat was running down her face.

After having a drink of water, she looked at the piles of paper around her. Something was there but she hadn't seen it. She turned on the television to the news channel. She stared at the screen not really absorbing what she was either seeing or hearing – blank faced and blanked brained. She had been so absorbed in her work; she had forgotten to check into her office yesterday afternoon. She looked at her watch. It was 9 am. She rang the office and left a message for her assistant. It was nothing more than a hello, I am still around.

She went to the gym in the motel. A workout may help her thoughts and mood. When she was finished, she sat on the mat doing some cool down stretch exercises. Then it hit her. Quickly she went back to her room and called the police station. Radoslaw answered. "Hello, Joanna here. Is the team there?"

Radoslaw signalled to Oskar and Fabian to listen up. "Some are. Oskar and Fabian. What's up?"

"I was going over all the papers from the meeting on Tuesday. The company you are dealing with is a fake."

Radoslaw confirmed that. "Yes, we are aware."

"Did you know their figures don't add up? Very fabricated in two sections," she said firmly.

"We did know there would be fabrication. Alan has been going over the same things as you. He hasn't called in yet."

"When he does, ask him to call me. I want verification of my findings. When is he expected in?"

Fabian looked at the clock on the wall. "About twenty minutes."

"I'll wait until then." Joanna hung up.

Alan was late coming into his office. He looked ill. He roughly placed his briefcase on the nearest desk and ran to the toilets. After another twenty minutes, Radoslaw became concerned. He went to the toilet area, opened the main door and saw Alan on the floor. Froth was around his mouth.

While he was waiting for the ambulance to arrive, Radoslaw did C.P.R. The paramedics pronounced him dead at the scene. Radoslaw smashed his fist on the wall and screamed his anger. There was silence in the station. Disbelief. Alan had been poisoned. Radoslaw impounded

Alan's car and then sent a team to Alan's apartment. It was taped off for the forensic people to go through.

Oskar contacted Joanna to break the news. "Joanna, exactly, where are you?"

Joanna hesitated before answering, "In a motel."

"Stay there. Don't go to your home until it has been checked," said Oskar.

"We will send a team over. Excuse me a second." Oskar placed his hand over the phone. He nodded to the intruding officer and swore. Then he spoke again to Joanna, "Joanna," he said solemnly, "We just got word. Someone blew up your house. Stay where you are. I will send Ivan and Stefan to you."

Joanna screamed, "NO! NO! Don't send anybody. They will also be in danger." She hung up.

She called her office. A different voice answered the phone. "Where is Jannetta?"

The replacement said, "She didn't come in." Joanna hung up. She called Oskar again.

"My assistant didn't turn up for work today. She didn't turn up yesterday as well. Send someone to her place. I want to make sure she is okay. I will text the address." She hung up again.

Hours later Joanna received a call. It was Fabian. "I am sorry to say, Jannetta was found dead in her bed. It looks like she was poisoned the same way as Alan."

Joanna dropped the phone and passed out on the bed. When the phone went silent, Oskar placed a trace on the call.

Accompanied by James and Tina Smith, he knocked on her door. He introduced the minders. "Joanna, we have to move you. We are not releasing any news of the deaths to the public. Unfortunately, we can't hide what happened to your home. We will say, that the police are searching for your charred remains." Joanna was slow to move at first and then managed to pack up everything in a matter of seconds. "Where will I be taken?"

James spoke softly, "England."

"Not far enough," Joanna replied. "Anywhere further away, by any chance?"

"Sorry," said Tina.

Joanna handed her work over to Oskar. "Give this stuff to Stefan or should I say Thomas. He is the only person I trust who can read the results."

Oskar took the bag and said good-bye.

On the way back to the station, Oskar swore. *Everything is going downhill fast. We would have to go deeper into the criminals. This was beyond the joke. No one deserves to die like that. We won't know for a couple of weeks what forensics will come up with. Shit. Shit.* Oskar slammed his hands against the wheel of his car. Tears trickled down his face. He pulled into a parking lot at a small group of shops. He stayed there for nearly an hour before moving on. On the way back to the station, he spotted the church Fabian and he had broken into just over a month ago. He went inside and sat on a back pew. *Fabian was right*, he thought, *we need help.*

While he was sitting and trying to pray, the minister walked in. He was holding a cloth. He intended to dust some of the window ledges. When he saw the unfamiliar person sitting on a pew, he stuffed the cloth away. He couldn't help but notice the stranger sitting and sobbing. He coughed gently.

Oskar looked up with fresh tears rolling down his face. "May I join you in prayer?" asked the priest. Oskar slid over to make more room. The priest rattled off a series of prayers and encouraged Oskar to repeat them. Thirty minutes had passed before the priest stopped. "Grief is a heavy burden. You did come to the right place to ease the pain. But be careful. A vengeful heart makes errors. Just remember who is on your side. You can ask for help at any time and in any place. Just believe." The priest blessed Oskar and disappeared. Oskar sat for a few more minutes before leaving. He walked out not only feeling refreshed but also calmer. He turned around to look at the church one more time. The priest who was now holding some mail, waved to him. Oskar waved back.

The next meeting concerning the takeover of the East European Flower Company was soon to begin.

Everyone from the police force was being prepared. This was going to be different. Two people down. Another forensic accountant refused to be present but was willing to be present by skype.

He wasn't over enthusiastic about attending knowing what had happened to his team member. Joanna was indisposed and only one board member would be present via video conferencing.

Through the meeting with the two take-over companies, Polish Exotic Food and East-West Products, more formalities of the joint venture were hammered out. From the start, Roza smirked now and then. To Fabian, Roza seemed delighted to hear that no one from The Flower Company would be present. Joanna who was supposed to represent them, as Fabian put it was "indisposed." Somehow, this delighted Roza.

By the end of the meeting, formalised contracts were drawn. Signatures appeared on all documents and initials appeared on minor alterations of wording. The East European Flower Company existed no more. It was now swallowed up by two other companies, partners in a dirty takeover deal.

When Stefan was at the police station and going over the contracts, he gave a quiet chuckle. Milosz smirked back. "I hope their lawyer never sees the error. Total invalidation. When is Oskar joining the first transport group to Iran?"

"In two days-time. As soon as the trucks have had make over. Horrible choice of colours." Stefan shook his head. "Depressing."

"Desert colours," replied Milosz. "Where is Ivan?"

"Getting some self-defence lessons. Radoslaw is teaching him a few new tricks. Last time he complained he ached. Some nice bruises on the arms and legs. The way he showed me, he looked quite proud to be showing them off."

Milosz asked, "Just hope they are not grooming him to join the force. What I have read, he appears to be a natural in undercover work."

Stefan went white. "He has a battered company to fix. If he gets on those trucks to Iran, I will kill him myself if he gets back."

CHAPTER 16

Oskar went to the Poznan truck depot for the East European Flower Company. The small older truck was now repainted in the new colours of tan and cream. Only half the truck was loaded with flowers. The rest was stacked with assorted grains, dried and canned food. Oskar was briefed that the round trip would be about ten days at the most. The mountain passes were the time variable.

Oskar sat in the cabin with his new driving partner, Kamil. Kamil said very firmly, "No one says their last name. To you, I am Boss. And you are Puppy." Oskar was about to protest the name but decided less said the better. *Puppy,* he thought, *an insult. But then again, these people thrived on insults.*

The truck passed into another yard. It looked like a wrecker's yard, the same one which was on the report a few days ago. Confirmation. *Appropriate,* thought Oskar. *Hide junk in junk.* He was given an order to stay put. Kamil got out but was back within minutes. When they left, a small convoy of vans followed. Some were painted the same colours of black and cream, black and white and black and tan. Two were still in their original colours. Only those which were still in their original colours had couple of battered panels. Only the truck Oskar was in had the name East West Products. *If anything went wrong, the blame would fall on that fake company,* thought Oskar. "What's in the other vans?" asked Oskar.

"Some have camping gear, some have fresh food, which is to be eaten first, some have cargo like we do. And all have guns for protection. Can you shoot?"

"Not well," lied Oskar.

"You will learn or be killed," came the harsh reply. "Put some music on."

It was now four days into the journey. Their camp was set up. The nights were cold. The sky was crystal clear. Oskar commented about the number or stars he could see now he was well away from the city lights and pollution. Kamil pointed to a constellation. "That's Libra. The lady with the scales of justice. And that is…" his words were cut off.

A bullet whistled past his head. The camp scattered for their guns and rifles and took cover. Oskar followed Kamil. "Who shot at us?" Kamil remained silent. "Take cover." Under cover, Kamil replied, "Don't know yet. It happens all the time. I've lost a few men in these parts. Most of the time the attacks are in the mountains. Crazy people there. Hungry for money and sex and anything else which takes their fancy." A bullet whistled past and buried itself in some rocks nearby. Oskar saw the size and immediately thought Russian army. Kamil swore. He moved from his position, but he signalled for Oskar to stay put.

Ten more bullets sounded in the air. There was a scream. Then a thud. A muffled sound followed by, "Agh". Silence. Then a voice said, "All clear."

From another direction. "All clear." And, one more, "All clear." One more gunshot was heard. Coming from the same direction as the second caller, "Definitely all clear now."

The bodies were dragged to the campfire. Each was inspected. A horse neighed in the distance. The men stopped and listened. They scattered for cover again. A lone horse walked into the camp. It nudged its dead owner. Neighed again. Oskar approached the horse and tugged gently on the reigns. The horse quietened and allowed Oskar to search the two bags. One bag held rations of food and water. The other was more interesting. Oskar pulled out identification papers and cursed. "Russian cops. You killed Russian cops. The cops are going to be really pissed off." He searched the bag more.

"Cops baring gifts. They may not be too badly missed." He pulled out a fist full of nuggets. He pocketed the largest for himself before displaying the rest.

He showed the group. "Either they were accepting bribes from the locals or took a fossicking holiday. Cops with gold, doesn't look that good."

Kamil examined the nuggets. "Are you sure these are for real?"

"Yeah. Real. Fool's gold is different."

Kamil noticed there were only four nuggets. He went to the saddle bag and gave a visual and hand inspection. Nothing. He placed one nugget in three of the driver's hands. "One nugget for each team."

He looked around to see Oskar walking away and taking the horse with him. "Puppy, where are you going?"

Oskar got on the horse and whispered, "Go home." The horse stood still. Oskar clicked his legs into the horse. The horse reared up. "Okay." He said in Russian, "Go home." The horse went at a trot.

Oskar ignored the others calling him back. He noted they didn't come after him.

Two hours later, the camp was packed up and the bodies buried. Oskar had returned with two other bags, and putting on a cowboy act. "Them hills are laden with gold." He dumped a small bag of gold in front of the group. Your share. He held up one looking almost empty. "My share. Their camp is empty. They were using fossicking as a cover. Just some fossicking tools back there. He handed them the other bag. "Interesting stuff in this bag. You better look."

Kamil took the second bag. He gasped. "The Russian cops are on to us. They must have been showing these pictures of us around. I wonder how many locals saw the pictures?"

Oskar said, "Wrong question. Who was bribed – cops or the tribes?" Oskar looked Kamil in the eyes as if challenging his authority. "Where did they find the gold or who gave them the gold? We better get out of here before company comes."

"We are in nowhere," said one of the other men with confidence.

Oskar stared in disbelief. "Exactly. Being in nowhere didn't stop them from finding us. Let's move."

The convoy twisted and turned over the steep narrow road going up and over the mountains. Oskar sat nervously fearing any possible mishap. One false move the truck more so than the vans would have a one-way journey down. Humans would come out second best. Kamil saw the tension. "You'll get used to it. Just five more kilometres to go."

When they reached the town of Lviv in the Ukraine, they made a detour down a dirt trail. The cars came to a stop three kilometres later. There was a clearing about the size of a football field. A well was in the middle. The boss drove to the far side of the clearing. The others followed. The Boss said, "Time to stretch the legs and have a drink." He pointed to the well. "One of the best sources of water in the area. Natural, clean and always cool, even in the summertime."

All the people in the vans got out and refilled their containers of water. The Boss looked at his watch, pulled out a cigarette and blew puffs of smoke into the crisp air. Nothing else was taken out of the vans. Oskar wondered what was going to happen next. He didn't have to wait much longer.

Two sets of car lights appeared. The fast-moving cars slowed down as they neared the convoy. Four men got out and walked directly to Boss. The conversation was short. The men departed as quickly as they came. The Boss told the group, "We stop and unload at the Balti small plane's airstrip. Then it's back home." The others nodded but Oskar asked, "Obviously a problem ahead. What's up?" Boss tossed his cigarette on the ground and stamped it out with his foot. "Cops are everywhere for a local festival at one port. At the other, some small-time shit head placed a bomb threat. Stepped up security. Not worth the risk." He paused for a few seconds contemplating the inconvenience. "No pussy this time round. I could have used some of that. A good whore house is in Constanta has lots of good young girls. But that's life. You can't always get what you want. Maybe next time will be better."

At the Balti airfield, all the cargo was loaded into a light aircraft. The pilot was paid in cash. He would receive another payment when he returned with different cargo. Oskar asked, "My geography isn't the best. Constanta is in Romania, isn't it?"

Boss looked at Oskar. "Yep. What do you know about Romania?"

"Nothing much. Poor people. The people are more religious than in Poland - lots of Catholics and Orthodox. Internet scammers and now pros." Oskar wanted to ask more questions, but he realised if any more questions were asked about Constanta in Romania, it would raise suspicion.

"Maybe in the next trip we get to Constanta. The girls sound nice."

Boss started the engine and chuckled. "That depends on lots of factors."

"Like what?" asked Oskar.

"How long we all live on the way back. Remember those Russian cops?"

"Yeah."

"They were supposed to have reported back the night we got rid of them. The Russians cops are a bit upset. The Ukrainian government has asked the Russian police to assist investigating their disappearance. It was on the radio."

"Fuck," swore Oskar as he punched the dashboard. He turned on the radio hoping to find some music. Instead, there was news of the bomb threat and missing Russians on holidays in the Ukraine.

"While we wait for the plane return with the new cargo, we play tourist in Lviv. The girls here aren't very friendly. I advise you to keep your trousers up and zipped up. The brothels are dirty and nearly always you get a life-long parting gift. It's your decision as to what you do for the next twelve hours. Then it's back home again."

The aircraft landed in the early hours of the morning. The drugs were loaded into the vans along with frozen packets of seafood. The seafood and some packets of drugs went into the vans already set up with freezers. The vans with just refrigeration, took slightly more drugs. The drugs were mixed in with josh sticks and flowers.

Now it made more sense to Oskar as to why The East European Flower Company was targeted. Stefan and Ivan were part of the revenge but the acquisition of large volumes of cheap mixed flowers was enough to confuse the sniffer dogs. The truck and vans from a Food company assisted in not only getting the fish back in superior conditions but disguised the odour of drugs. Food and strong-smelling Josh sticks would also confuse the dogs.

When all were ready to leave, Boss was handed a parcel. The pilot held out his hand. "Bonus item needs bonus pay." Boss didn't argue and gave the pilot an extra 300 euros. "Hold this for a second until I find a safe place for that." He handed the box to Oskar. Boss pulled out a few items jamming the space under his seat. He tossed them over his shoulder. They landed somewhere in the back.

He slid the box under his seat. Oskar was busting to ask what was inside, and to have a look at the mystery item that earned the pilot extra money. He would find out sooner or later.

On the way back, they did not camp in the same places as before. Taking a different route home was the norm. They stopped at what Oskar termed as nowhere villages. Small unmarked villages looked deserted and very rundown. The deception of desertion suited these people. It was their choice to be invisible and through their invisibility, they dodged authorities. In this deception they were able to see and hear all around them. To them, if you don't exist, you don't have any-one breathing down your neck. It was a hard life, but they were happy.

When the convoy arrived at one rundown village, it was close to dusk.

Boss told the men to open up the 'store'. The camp tables and chairs came out. On top was placed new sleeping bags, some new kitchen utensils, assorted canned food and dried food, and a few other household items. They worked by the light of only one torch. When all was set up, the convoy waited.

For twenty minutes nothing happened. The men from the con-voy watched in all directions. Several cars with their headlights on low appeared in the distance. The cars were moving slowly with men with rifles sitting on the top. The women and children were tucked inside. When the new arrivals reached the makeshift shop, the engines turned off. The occupants by now had lowered their guns and warmly greeted the convoy of smugglers. They noted Oskar's presence and questioned Boss. The newcomers then hit the hard questions on Oskar.

The place was a hive of activity. The children ran freely in the darkness playing their traditional games. The women assisted by both male and female teenagers set up the evening meal. Carpet was placed on the ground and cushions were scattered, not enough for the group, but that is all they could manage in the transport. The older men traded their drugs and information for goods they required. Their shopping list always included what the women wanted. If it wasn't available here and now, it would be there on the next.

Oskar sat on a rock where others had previously sat. It was slightly away from where everyone was. He wanted an overview of the event as he slowly ate the unfamiliar food. Parts of it he didn't mind, but he wished he had not placed some items in his mouth. He really wanted a beer to wash the taste away. There was no beer but a rough brew the people had made. After taking his first sip, he guessed it would be the next best thing to pure alcohol. He discreetly tipped the drink onto the grass. He was certain the few blades of grass would be dead the next day.

Boss walked over to Oskar. "What's up?"

"Nothing. I am not handling their food that well. And their drink is a bit rough. I just didn't want to disrespect anyone if I vomited."

Boss nodded. "Two more meals and you get used to this. That's how long it took me. They tell me they dug up the Russian cops and placed their bodies and their equipment one hundred meters off the road. They set the bodies alight when they saw the Russian coming through. They have the horses and the saddles. By the way, their boss has taken a liking to you."

"Really?"

"Yeah, he would like you to stay a bit longer and we pick you up in three weeks' time."

"I don't speak their language or dialect. I would die out here, go crazy with no modern cons."

Boss burst out laughing. "I think you better take the offer. You don't have too much of a choice."

"Why?"

"His oldest daughter has taken a shining to you. The father wants to see if you could fit in."

Oskar spluttered the food he was chewing. "I'm not staying. She can have the other men. Tell the father I am not interested. Tell him I already have a wife, well a girlfriend soon to be wife."

Boss laughed again. "Here, it is common for men to have more than one wife. The mortality rate is high. It's an honour. What have you got against a wife at home and one out here? They will never meet. Two of the men have this very comfortable arrangement. That is why the welcome here is very friendly."

Oskar just said, "Then the other men can have that so-called privilege. I'm not interested."

Boss slapped his hand on Oskar's thigh. "She is the prettiest of all the available women. You're missing out. "

"Tell her father in the most respectful way possible, no. I won't fit in with their people."

"How do you know that when you haven't tried?"

"I know myself well enough to know," said Oskar feeling quite worried about his mortality.

Boss laughed. "A mature person knows what they like, dislike, can and can't do. Perfect."

Boss waved the father and the daughter over. Both, like the rest of the tribe, wore a loose flowing thick robe with hoods. The hoods and the darkness hid their faces. Oskar groaned and hid his face behind his hand.

Boss pushed it away. "That is rude."

"Good. I shall continue to be rude," retorted Oskar.

"Not if you want to live," warned Boss.

"Fuck you."

Boss looked at him in disgust. "No you fuck her…and preferably tonight. Their custom. Then you two are married."

Oskar stood up with the intentions of moving away.

Boss grinned. "A good display of manners to stand up when the father and the bride to be approach."

Oskar felt trapped. He turned his back and went deeper into the sparse bushes. The slow step turned into a run. He headed directly for the truck in which he had travelled in.

The truck's engine just clicked over when a triable person's head was at the driver's side window. The man opened the door and pointed a gun at Oskar's head. "Get out now."

The man just laughed. "She likes you. You lucky man. Her father boss here. You no stay. You dead." The man cocked his pistol. "Now get out. Be good man."

Oskar went white: his mind was running triple speed. While the engine was still running, he started to climb out. The man was also moving back slowly and kept the gun pointed at Oskar as Oskar opened the truck's door. The man was now moving slowly further back when Oskar suddenly jumped back in and drove at full speed. The open door on the driver's side swung to hit the man with the gun. The man buckled over holding his stomach before falling to the ground.

Oskar managed to just reach the highway when he was stopped. A group of the men from the camp blocked the road. He slammed on the breaks.

"Shit! How did they get here so fast!" he yelled to himself.

Four rifles pointed at him. Two men walked to the truck while the other two covered them.

Both men walking forward climbed into the truck. They held the rifle at his head. "Drive back."

Knowing the truck could not do a U-turn on such a narrow road, he slowly manoeuvred it through the bushes before going back to camp. He stopped the truck almost where he started. The guns were still pointed to his head. The two gun-holding passengers signalled him to get out. Oskar complied.

Everyone in the camp watched silently as the trio moved to the centre of the camp. The guns were lowered. There was deafening silence. Oskar now believed his life was going to be cut short. There was a slow clap coming from the rear. Then the others joined in. Then laughter spread. Oskar felt embarrassed and confused. He was their entertainment for the night. *Christ, I am never going to live this down. I am the village idiot.*

Boss came forward. "Just a demo. You can't run from these people. They have eyes and ears everywhere out here. It is their territory and their rules. If the chief here says you get married to whoever, you do it. If the chief here says piss, you do it. If the chief says…"

Oskar held up his hand to stop Boss. "I get the picture. Follow orders in this shithole."

"Boss put his arm across Oskar's shoulders. "The chief says his daughter fancies you, so you make them both happy."

"Got a condom? I feel like I am the one being raped here."

Boss laughed. It made the others look. Their silence said it all: share the joke. Boss translated.

The others laughed. Boss translated a comment from a heckler, "Are you gay?"

Oskar was taken aback. "This time I wish I was." Boss laughed again.

"The chief's son is gay. So, who do you want? Him or Her?"

"Neither. I will keep my trousers on."

Boss asked, "Are you a hermaphrodite?"

"No. I am just not into this stuff. I mean having it off with strangers."

"We need to put a touch of Lucifer into you. I have noticed and everyone else too, your upbringing has been exemplary. That rates highly out here and more so with this tribe. When you ran it told them a couple of things. One, you are a man of principle. Two you are still a virgin. That rates very high in this area." Boss pushed Oskar forward. "There are condoms in the glove box."

Oskar walked to the truck and pulled out three condoms. *I just stuffed up. I don't want to do this. My hands are shaking. I can't get my act together. Christ, I am so rattled.*

When he returned to the camp, many started to depart for their homes. Just four families remained. Most of the men from the convoy were erecting their tents.

"Are you ready?" asked Boss.

"No."

"She is. The father isn't going home until he knows she is hitched."

"Fuckin' hell," said Oskar. "Don't tell me he is going to watch?"

"No. He's a bit more civilised than that. He just wants to see the blood drops."

"No way. That is disgusting. Don't I get a say in any of this? Does the girl have a say?"

"No. The girl sealed her fate when we were eating dinner. She said to a friend she thought you were handsome. The girlfriend told her mother and she told the father. Here, when a girl's eyes starts to wonder, that is when they are pushed to marry."

Oskar was shocked. "It is just girl talk. Nothing more."

"Not here. Not in this culture. When the girl's hormones kick in, it's time for them to marry. You just made hers kick in. Go. You don't upset the chief. That's their rules. Upsetting his daughter or other family members makes him very upset."

"Why can't the other men from the convoy do it?" asked Oskar who was trying delay the inevitable.

"Put it bluntly, she didn't fancy any of them. You're it. It's a privilege. She's a virgin too."

"What? The village idiot gets the prize!"

"This time he does. Stop wasting time. We can't go until it two virgins work it out. It ought to be fun," teased Boss. "Get this job done. I don't want to be here for the next two days or however long it takes to get that thing of yours working. You do know how to use it, do you?"

"Yeah. It works well on the girlfriend back home."

"Then think of fucking her instead of the chief's daughter. Then we can get out of here."

Boss pointed to a large tent. One candle lit the interior. "The bridal suite," said Boss. "Go."

Oskar went into the tent. There was a thick layer of blankets and fur. He took off his shirt and tossed it aside. He was in the process of taking off his shoes when the young lady nervously walked in.

She was nervous as much as he wasn't interested. She slipped back the hood of her coat. She was not much older than seventeen. He froze. He started to dress himself again. He opened the tent flaps to speak to the chief or Boss – whoever was available. He gulped when two men standing guard pointed their rifles at him. *This is so wrong. So wrong. She's a kid. I can't do it to a kid. No. No.*

He went back inside. They stared at each other. He pointed to himself and said his name. He encouraged her to say her name. After a few attempts she said in a soft voice not much more than a whisper, "Preshka". The girl began to sob. Her fear was evident. Oskar couldn't speak to her in her language. He tried. She just stared back. Scared. He stripped down to his underpants and turned his back. She was undressing. When she was sitting beside him, she touched his arm to indicate she was ready. He turned to her and pulled up the cover. He blew the candle out. No more silhouettes for others to see.

He whispered, "Good night." He adjusted himself to sleep on top of the covers. The girl was muttering away in her language while she lay under the covers. What she was saying, he could only guess.

The next morning, no one disturbed them. They stayed in the tent looking at each other in silence wondering what to do. Oskar sat up. He tried to tell her of his plan. He gave her all her clothes and indicated to get dressed. He dressed himself. He pulled out the tell-tales sheet her father was wanting to see. He pushed her back and indicated for her to turn around. Oskar cut himself with a knife. Not a deep cut. It didn't need to be. He let the drops spread over the sheet. He smeared a few. He told her to turn around. She looked in shock. The blood her father wanted to see was there. She was awestruck that a stranger would do such a thing. She rushed to bandage his bleeding arm. She cried with relief. Oskar held his finger to his mouth. "Shh." She nodded and smiled for the first time he had known her. She gave a sigh of relief. Oskar held her to his side. "Are you ready to go outside?" He nodded to the tent flaps. She stood close to him and he held her hand. She held the blood-stained sheet.

She presented it to her father. He nodded his approval. He gave her a hug then told Oskar he was free to go with the others and return with some wedding gifts.

Oskar got into the truck with Boss.

They waved at the few remaining triable people. Oskar blew the girl a kiss.

Boss asked, "It wasn't that bad was it?"

"I didn't do it. She was underage. We just slept. Nothing more. I cut myself for the blood the chief was expecting to see. He got what he wanted. The girl got what she wanted and so did I."

Boss smirked. "Christ, you are a monk. Next time we come this way, make sure you do screw her. You still have to sleep with her. If she doesn't get pregnant after two goes, they will become suspicious."

"How about saying, I am at fault. Shooting blanks."

"Then it is grounds for divorce. But when she does have sex with another, the truth would be revealed. You're a dead man," said Boss.

"Then I must mysteriously disappear after the second trip back home. Do a runner so to speak. Anyway, I am here for a short time only. Company agreement."

"Tell me more about this agreement," asked Boss.

Oskar only answered Boss's questions to the minimum. No elaboration. Boss seemed satisfied.

CHAPTER 17

Back in Poznan, Oskar picked up his car from the Flower Company depot carpark.

He drove home and tossed all his clothes into the washing machine. He put on the shower, the first real bath for ten days. Near the end of the shower, he heard the front door click and the rattling of keys. He got out of the shower and quickly dressed.

His girlfriend, Lydia came through the door. She looked pale. Knowing of the two poison attacks suddenly played on his mind, he rushed to her side. "Hello gorgeous." She didn't answer. She coughed and held her stomach. "Hey, what's up?" She didn't say a word but hugged him and cried.

She sobbed and cried more. "What is it?" he asked gently. She pulled back for a second.

"Just happy to see you. And I have bad news."

Oskar guided her to the sofa. "Tell me, what is the bad news?"

"I have advanced cancer. I didn't know I had it. I started to feel ill about four days ago. The doctors gave me a series of tests. They say I start chemo tomorrow, but they doubt if it will work. It's too advanced." Oskar held her tightly. He held her as long as she wanted him. His eyes watered but he fought back the tears.

She sobbed. "Very advanced ovarian cancer. It has spread to other parts of my body."

Eventually, she asked, "What happened on the trip? Then she added, "Only what is permissible for you to tell me."

Oskar sighed. "Well I was made the village idiot and had guns pointed at me more times than I could have imagined." Then he went on to explain the forced evening in a tent with a teenage girl called

Preshka. He showed the knife cut which was almost healed over the top. Lydia smiled and shook her head. Then began to laugh. He said with concern, "Next time I go there, I have to take the kid wedding gifts. What do fourteen to seventeen-year-old girls want?"

"What happens if you show up with nothing?" she asked almost amused.

"I will be shot. No questions asked. Bang. Lights out."

"Then you better get something," she stated.

Lydia was silent for a few moments. "She is poor, backwards and invisible and chained to a culture dominated by men. Some perfume, toiletries, dresses, shoes. In her situation a sleeping bag and cookware. Want to go shopping together on Saturday? We will make a day of it. It will get my mind off this cancer. What are you doing tomorrow?"

"I have to report in at the station. There is so much to report, I will be there all day. I need to know what has been happening here. In this job, ten days is a long time."

Oskar walked into the station and went directly to the map room. He sorted through the pile until he found what he was looking for: east and central Europe. He carried it back to the situation room and mounted it on a wall. He traced over the highways to Lviv in black and then added blue dotted lines of the unmarked tracks where they camped and shot the Russians. He used a highlight pen for the Black Sea cities of Constanta in Romania, Chisinau in Moldova and Odesa in the Ukraine. He used post-it papers to indicate what got to the Black Sea and what was coming back. Guns, food, household items, medicines appeared on one paper. He wrote clearly, UN sanctions being breached. On another, he wrote drugs cannabis, but opium was in bold and in various stages of maturity, occasional antiquities. Then he added in red letters: to be confirmed – people trafficking, namely girls between the ages of ten and twenty-five. Boys could be in the mix.

In the area between the Black and Caspian Seas, he added a large post- it note. Unknown routes and towns. He listed the countries – North Turkey, Armenia, Azerbaijan, Georgia and North Iran. He drew a circle around North Iran. He was looking at the map when Eryk and Radoslaw came in. They stared at the map.

"You were busy," said Eryk.

Oskar pointed to the isolated village where he was held for an extra night. I suspect people traffickers are passing through here. I need more time. Then he explained what had happened there. He rolled up his sleeve to show the knife cut. He told them of the Russian police they battled and where the bodies were initially buried, and the locals relocated them for the Russian police to find them. He added as he brought out a nugget and a small bag of gold dust. "I don't know if the Russian police were being bribed or doing the bribing. It was mentioned on the radio they were missing tourists on holiday. This nugget and others were found in saddle bags on the police horses and the gold dust at their camp."

The others stared at the gold. Evidence. "I have a few pictures taken on the side. I couldn't do it too often or get the whole convoy or people on the way. He put his phone on the counter. They scrolled through. "We will get these developed and cross checked with what we have," said Radoslaw.

"Do you have any names?"

"No one uses their real name. All nicknames. I was Puppy." Eryk and Radoslaw laughed.

"The driver I was with was called Kamil but I had to call him Boss and he was the boss. The other nick names are Trouble, Nuts, Shorty, Ogre, and Grumpy. They were the drivers of the convoy. I didn't have a chance to interact with the others. Teams generally kept to themselves. What has been happening here?"

Eryk sighed and blew his lips. "Ivan and Stephan are using their German names to work full time in The East European Flower Company. They are getting the company on track. Joanna Lewandwoski is in Britain. Tina and James Smith escorted her there. The British contact has found the mole at their end. They are in the process of gathering evidence. We are still investigating this end. Internal affairs have identified one prison official who is on the mafia pay role. More are suspected. They are still gathering evidence on possible more prison officials on the take. At this stage, there is not much in the way of evidence that would hold up in court. Time will tell. No more linked deaths that we know of."

Mikal (junior) Mazur was sitting on a park bench. He was depressed. His studies at the university were suffering. He felt a failure in all aspects of life. He had never failed subjects so badly. His step-mother was one cause and it frustrated him that he couldn't convince his father. His father put it down to jealousy, childish jealousy. It wasn't. Mikal always felt a bad vibe coming from her. He had told his friends of his dislike for her. They listened but they were powerless to do anything. They were his support. Ivan, in particular was his main crutch and he was now out of his life. Suddenly gone. Searches turned up nothing. It was like he fell-off the face of the Earth. Mikal contemplated what he should do or could do. He had been sitting on the bench for close to an hour. His reflections were interrupted by a voice, a familiar voice. He turned around.

"Hello, stranger," said Ivan. Mikal was dumbfounded. Then a broad grin spread across his face. Instantly, Ivan held his finger to his lips. "Shh."

Mikal hugged Ivan and then pulled back. They looked at each other. It was only a minute, but it seemed longer. "I am so glad to see you," said Mikal. "I really need someone to talk to. I am going down the tube so fast." He pulled out a small pistol. "I was tossing up between this and a knife. I think I was minutes away from deciding."

Ivan pushed Mikal's hand away. "Put that away. I am going to cancel the rest of the day and spend time with you." Ivan dialled the office. "Lucia, this is Peter. Cancel all my appointments for the rest of the day and tomorrow morning. Reschedule where possible for tomorrow afternoon." He hung up.

"Peter?" asked Mikal.

"Yeah. And a few other changes, including a new secretary. Paulina left for Britain. I am not supposed to be talking to you or anyone else."

He saw the questioning look on Mikal's face. "What's with the hair colour change, tats, stud and nose job?"

"It's a long story. But I want to hear your story first. Shall we go to the bar across the other side of the park? I don't think anyone we know goes there."

Mikal nodded. Ivan sounded more interesting than what he could match in his own story, a story of his own demise.

For three hours they spoke – a recap of the year and a half. Then Ivan asked about the others in their group, Antoni and Szymon.

Mikal said, "Strange you should ask. I have tried contacting them several times, but they too seem to have disappeared. There has been no contact for nearly three months." Ivan became worried. "Did they say anything to give an indication they would be away for that long?"

Mikal shook his head. "They were going on a week-end skiing trip to Saint Petersburg. That was it. They were supposed to book into a resort about twenty kilometres out. I made enquiries. They booked in on time and then out on the Sunday afternoon. Then nothing." Mikal handed Ivan one of a few resort's business cards. "I drove up there and searched the outer resorts for a week. Then came back." Ivan looked at it carefully and tucked it in his wallet. "I will get someone to look at it. I now know a few cops who just may be able to help."

Mikal gave a smile. *Yes he would know a few. After what he's been through. He would just about know the entire police force*, thought Mikal.

"How is the situation at home?" asked Ivan.

"Crappy. I moved out to a poorish apartment. Working a low paid job to make ends meet. Uni is suffering. Failed all the subjects for the first time in my life. The queen bitch at home is making sure the gap between dad and me is as wide as the Atlantic Ocean. I wish the bitch never entered our lives. Dad is so blinded by her. She can't do anything wrong."

Ivan's paranoia kicked in. "Tell me what her maiden name was before she married your father?"

Mikal paused for a few minutes. "I saw some papers before she got married. Born as Theodora Majewski. Widowed with the name Czerwinski. Divorced some Russian rich guy called Sorokin. And now, I am obviously in the way. She's after dad's money. I even bugged her phone and have a recording of her plans. I hear her frequently speaking to a creepy cousin on the phone. He rings nearly every day. One day I followed her and saw him from a distance. He was a Zielinski."

"Norbert Zielinski?"

"You know him?" asked Mikal.

"I never met him. I killed his brother Gregori. He had a gun to my head. I faked falling. I smashed a sculpture over his head. I didn't know he would die. The cops never charged me. Too many witnesses.

Self-defence. The Zielinski's are pissed off with me and dad. If Thea is Norbert's cousin, then she is wanting you and your father out of the way. She is setting up your father's company for a Russian mafia's take over. Believe me, she is mafia through and through."

Mikal wanted to vomit. Blood drained out of his head. "What can I do about it?"

"We get the cops set up a sting. Another sting like my father's company. We need to get your father on side - urgently. The bastards will launder their money through your father's company. Do you think he will co-operate?"

"He may. Getting him to the police station will be a challenge. He won't come if I am in trouble. He has made that clear. I am on my own," said Mikal.

Ivan pulled out his phone and called Radoslaw directly on his mobile.

"Radoslaw? Ivan here. Look, I know I broke all the rules that were drummed into me, but it is worth it. I have a new development. The mafia are going after another company. And two of my friends have disappeared."

"What?" exclaimed Radoslaw. "Where are you?"

"In a bar in beside the Tutti Santi Pizza Shop in Ogrodowa St. I have someone who is in the know and needs protection."

"Move from that bar and come back to the station. Peter, if this information is useful, you are forgiven for breaking your cover. If not, we are going to give you a beating."

Thirty minutes later, Ivan introduced Mikal to Eryk and Radoslaw. Mikal told of the missing friends. Then he added the step-mother's story and how she was driving a wedge and going for the both the money and the company. He played the recordings of her conversations with Norbert. Then he finished with his statement of two missing friends, Antoni Grabowski and Szymon Sawicki. Radoslaw asked, "Did you go to their homes?" Mikal nodded.

"A few times each. I went to the Grabowski home three times. I looked through the gate. The gate wouldn't open when I punched the code. Er... we have each other's gate codes. I guessed the code was changed. I noticed the grass was very tall. It looks like the gardener was away as well. I went to Sawicki home. No one was answering either. Only the front of their yard was being attended to. At all times I thought it odd. I also assumed they were away as well, and the gardener was being a bit lazy while they were away. Why?"

"Just routine questions. Are you sure there was no one home?"

Mikal nodded again. "As much as I could tell. It was like all my closest friends and their families just vanished. It is very isolating."

Radoslaw and Eryk sat in silence processing the new information. It had never occurred to them; the mafia was aiming so high. The Mazur Construction Company did many contracts at different government levels. They were aiming at the government – getting as much inside information and eventually controlling the infrastructure. Powerful and unseen control. On the surface, it would appear the government would be democratically elected but deep down, it was Russian mafia controlled. Then they were left wondering if there were links to the Russian government itself. There were questions which now could never be answered and may never be.

Radoslaw looked at Mikal. "You get out of your accommodation now. You bunk in with Ivan and his father. You go back to university and study like hell to make up for lost ground. Even if you pick out two subjects to refocus your attention, it will be better than getting permanently kicked out. When you walk in and out of the university grounds, you wear a disguise. Everywhere you go, you wear the disguise. We will organise papers for you. Peter, will assist you in getting used to the idea." Radoslaw picked up the mobile phone and called the minder to expect another person.

When Ivan and Mikal left, Radoslaw and Eryk stared at each other. Eryk said, "I will check to see if their parents lodged a missing person's report. They should have. Rich people like to keep tabs on their kids. If there is no report, we better make a visit to their houses."

Radoslaw brought Natan in. Natan tried ringing Mikal Mazur's office. The secretary answered the phone, "Mazur Constructions, Mr. Mazur secretary speaking. "How may I help you?"

"My name is Natan Byko, I would like to speak to Mikal Mazur."

"What is it about?"

"A personal matter and for his ears only."

The secretary said in a rough way. She didn't like to be left out of any possible gossip. "I will see if he is available."

She put Natan through. Ten minutes later Mikal asked her to make an appointment for Natan Byko tomorrow at 11.20 a.m."

At 11.20 a.m., Natan, Stefan, and Eryk entered the Mikal's office. Mikal junior stayed downstairs in the foyer just in case he was needed. After thirty minutes, Mikal senior was visibly upset. He heard what Stefan went though and now trying to save his company while in disguise. He heard the recording of his wife's activities. He sat silently processing the information. He eventually asked in a wavering voice, "Where is Mikal?"

"Waiting downstairs in the foyer," said Eryk. Through the intercom, he told his secretary to get Mikal from the foyer.

Mikal walked in not sure what to expect. His father profusely apologised, gave him a hug and wiped away a tear trickling down his face. "What is the plan?" asked Mikal senior.

"We will bug your home – cameras and microphone and intercept her mobile. The application will take a day or two. We will contact you. When we are ready, take Thea out for three hours. Make sure all home staff are out as well. We will need a key and the alarm number." Mikal nodded.

When the men left Mikal senior, sat numb. He sobbed in the privacy of his office. He felt betrayed and at the same time guilty of the treatment he had given to his son. When he recovered to some degree and refocused himself, he gave instructions to his secretary, "Any calls coming from either Mr. Byko or Mr. Wojcik or my son, Mikal must be put through with no delays. If I am in a meeting, I want to be interrupted. He phoned Mikal and asked not sure if Mikal would accept the olive branch. "Dinner tomorrow night?"

"After uni. About seven p.m."

Three days later, Mikal senior took Thea out to her favourite restaurant. It was rare for him to take her out through the day. She snapped at the chance. Then he drove her out to what she said was her favourite park where they walked and talked about their lives before and through their union. At six p.m. they went home. "Where are the servants?"

"I gave them the day off. We don't need them here tonight. Total privacy. I liked having the day off. We should do it more often."

Thea started to pour two red wines. "So nice." Her phone rang. It was Norbert. "Not now. I am busy."

She hung up. She smiled. "That was my annoying cousin, Norbert."

"I have noticed he phones a lot. How come I never met him in person?"

"He moves around a lot," she lied.

"Yeah, I know that feeling. One day here and one day there and then we forget who is important." He sipped on the wine as he eyed her carefully.

Down the street, the police were sitting in an unmarked van loaded with listening equipment. The call was traced to Norbert Zielinski. The officer grinned. "One phone number in the bag." He smirked.

"We should be able to collect a few others after that. Just how big is this ring?"

"Massive. If we can nab them, the courts will be busy for years," replied the other officer. They continued listening and watching the screens.

The couple went into the bedroom, no camera but only listening devices. Mikal made an excuse to go to the kitchen. Thea followed but only after she dialled another number, Artem Orlov.

"Did the last shipment come through?" she asked.

"Yes big sister. And a little bonus. An artefact about two thousand years old. It should bring about 20,000 euros from dealers. I have Krolovic making up the authenticity papers. They should add value. How's that fool of a husband of yours?"

"He took a day off and took me to a restaurant and then we walked forever in that dreadful park he likes and I pretend to like."

Artem chuckled. "The price of love."

"I have managed to get Mikal out of the house. The wedge between father and son is wide enough so they don't speak to each other. I will be working on his will, to make changes. Block the son out. That is my next step."

"Big sister, take care. There are no room for mistakes." He hung up.

The men in the van whistled. "The bitch. Proof she is in for the money. Orlov. Do you know who he is?"

"Nope. Someone will. Sounds like a big fish."

"Krolovic is a new name. We need to run our data base on these two just in case they are in the system somewhere." Minutes later, Krolovic name appeared with information. "Krolovic is a forger of documents. Fraud squad needs to be brought in. They can organise a sting on him."

The next day, the recordings were played back to Eryk and Radoslaw. Radoslaw found another white board and propped it over one on an easel. He wrote the names to date.

Thea Mazur big sister to Artem Orlov.

Thea and Artem are cousins to Norbert Zielinski. Radoslaw stood back. "A family business. Have the photos at the two funerals and what Oskar took show up any matches on the data system?" asked Radoslaw.

"The ten faces at the Gregori Zielinski funeral match. The rest, including what Oskar was able to get on the sly, are all new faces. We only have nicknames as I.D. for Oskar's group," said Eyrk.

"Soon there will be more faces than board space," commented Radoslaw. "We need to get as many as possible. And done properly if any of these are going to jail. Umpf. Holiday at taxpayers' expense."

There was a knock on the door. Mikal junior was escorted in by an officer. Mikal handed a picture of the four friends to Radoslaw. Both detectives looked at the photos. He gave another business card of the resort they were last seen. Radoslaw looked at the photo of the four smiling young men. He noted the innocent eyes of Ivan and Mikal had changed – older and strained. Innocence lost forever. Mikal left the room with his escort.

Radoslaw asked Eryk, "Are you ready to go to the homes of Antoni Grabowski and Syzmon Zwicky?" Eryk nodded. "I think we should take a couple of uniforms with us. I have a feeling we need to."

"I trust that instinct you have. Let's see who is in the canteen," said Eryk.

CHAPTER 18

The police pulled up outside the gates of the Grabowski house. They pushed the button hoping to reach the occupants inside. No answer. Radoslaw got out of the car and peered through the thick evenly spaced bars of the gate. What he saw made him uncomfortable. Something was amiss. People like this always had gardeners and the yards were always immaculate. Here the grass was both tall, unkempt and now browning. Radoslaw went to Eyrk, "Something is wrong here. We jump the fence." He told the two uniformed police in the car behind. They got out to assist him over the fence.

When Radoslaw was on the other side of the fence, he noted the letter box was overflowing. He quickly flipped through. Bills were unpaid and there was one envelope marked overdue. He collected as many as his hand could hold before pushing the override button to the sensor which would open the gates. He ushered the others through, got into the car again for the drive to the house recessed well to the back of the property.

They knocked on the door. Nothing. They tried three times. Radoslaw ordered the accompanying officers to go around the building to see if there were any windows broken or a door which could be opened.

One officer came running back. He was almost panicking. "Sir, you better come this way and see for yourself."

Radoslaw and Eryk followed the officer around the corner. When the officer stopped, he pointed to the decomposing body half buried in the tall browning grass. "Jesus," said Radoslaw, "Another one to the body count. Set up a perimeter." The officer ran back to the car and got the tape out. While he was away, Eryk commented, "I hope this is the only body. It appears to be the gardener from the clothes he is wearing. Some tools are nearby." The officer came back with tape and a couple of stakes. Both detectives helped the officer push the stakes into the hard ground. The other officer came to the group. He saw the body and quickly looked away. "There are some French doors open."

The four men went around to the open French doors. They tapped and called out. Now answer. They ventured in. The place had been burgled. Furniture was missing, paintings off the wall, some pieces of unwanted furniture was tipped and were in disarray on the floor. Eyrk said with concern, "This is not looking good at all. We split up. Expect the unexpected and it may not be pretty." He sniffed the air. "Something smells very off."

Radoslaw with one officer went towards the kitchen area. On the floor was a decomposing female body. The person had bled out when a bullet went through her spine. Crippled by the impact and her contorted face were barely visible through the advanced decay. The stench in the kitchen had attracted flies and assorted bugs. Raw meat still in its plastic seal and vegetables were looking more like a compost heap were on the kitchen bench. The men gasped for fresh air. With a hand covering his nose, Radoslaw walked around the body to enter another room. He hoped there were no other surprises. He entered the dining room and grimaced.

The dining room was set. The guest missing. It gave an eerie and macabre site. A dinner which never happened. Radoslaw mind was now playing around. He could see ghostly shadows around the table. He shook his head. The room gave him the creeps. He and the officer moved out to enter the lounge room.

As they entered the lounge room, Radoslaw pushed the following officer back. Four bodies with bags over their heads laid on the ground. The bags were taped to stop air entering. The hands were bound with cable ties. The people were obviously shot while they knelt. The safe on the wall was open. Contents gone.

Eryk came running down the stairs with the intentions of telling the others three bodies were upstairs. He stopped dead in his tracks. "Jesus. House of horrors!" Eryk turned around. His face was ash. He noted the uniformed officer he was with was now was outside vomiting. He drew in a deep breath, but the smell of the house was taking its toll. He rushed outside. Radoslaw and the officer followed to get some fresh air.

While outside Eryk said in a weak voice, "I found Antoni. Dead and decomposing. His bag was unpacked, and the contents strewn across the room. The other room contained a younger girl, possibly a sister. Her naked body is tied to the bedhead posts – spread eagle. More than likely she was raped. There were cuts of different depths, possibly tortured. The last was of a younger boy who had been tied in a similar fashion, but he was face down. Evidence of being raped and then similarly tortured. "I'm sorry for running outside. The three bodies upstairs and five down here, were a bit much." Radoslaw patted Eryk on the shoulder. "Don't be hard on yourself. I was close to throwing up." He checked on the two uniformed men.

All the men went silent and needing time to recover. "Call in forensics. Tell them to set up camp, big time," said Eryk in a quivering voice. He walked to the side of the driveway and threw up again. One officer said, "I can still smell the stench inside. Is that normal?"

Eryk nodded. The officer took in breaths of fresh air, but it still didn't help. Gingerly, Radoslaw asked, "Anyone got stomach to visit the Sawicki's house? We can leave it for tomorrow." All shook their heads. "Let's get forensics in first. Then we go," said Eryk. He looked at the uniformed officers. "You two have a choice. It will be okay not going over. I will request leave for both of you. We are all going to need counselling. Those images need to be shifted or dulled." The officers nodded.

One said, "I would like to go home now." Eryk nodded approval. The other said, "I think I will go too. This is more than what I was ever expecting." Radoslaw nodded. "I'll organise someone to drive you home. Both of you are in no state to drive." He looked at Eryk to check his condition. He knew they were both in a bad state.

It was late in the afternoon when Eryk and Radoslaw went to the Sawicki's house. The yard looked in to be in a better state. They pushed on the gate button. No answer. "Not good," said Eryk. It looks like we jump the fence again."

This time Eryk went over with some assistance from Radoslaw. Radoslaw drove the car through the gates. Eryk didn't get in the car. The house wasn't that far from the gate. The walk gave him time to observe the grounds. No tell-tale signs of disturbances. He was hoping this house was more promising than the one before.

He pushed the front door button. No answer. He pushed it two more times. No answer. Both men froze. A possible repeat, a repeat they didn't want to see. They decided to keep together.

When they were at the back of the house, a gun fired. The bullet narrowly missed both detectives. They dived for cover. A voice yelled at them, "That was a warning shot. Hands up." The detectives complied. A bedraggled and bearded young man holding a powerful rifle slowly revealed himself from bushes some one hundred meters away. He walked slowly towards them but stopped just over twenty metres away. It was evident, fear and hatred possessed his body and mind. "Who are you?" he demanded.

"We are detectives. We had information that Antoni Grabowski was missing. We found him dead along with other household members. We are doing follow ups. Are you Szymon Sawicki?" The young man considered the question. The gun was still firm in his hand. "What's it to you?"

"Mikal Mazur reported Syzmon and Antoni missing." said Radoslaw.

"Keep the hands up," said Szymon almost in a shout. He clicked the gun. Radoslaw and Eryk pushed their hands up higher. "What's been going on here?" asked Eryk. We were at the Grabowski's house.

Death everywhere. Can we put our hands down and show you some I.D.?"

Szymon pointed the gun at Eryk. "Only you show me. Toss the I.D. here. You," he indicated to Radoslaw, "Turn around."

Eryk did as instructed. Szymon picked up the I.D. without taking his hands off either men.

"You can turn around. Take your guns off. I want to see them on the ground," ordered Szymon.

When the detectives dropped their guns, Radoslaw pre-empted the next instruction and kicked his gun. It slid across the grass half a metre away. "You too," ordered Szymon.

"Can you bring Mikal here?" asked Szymon.

"Better than that. Ivan as well."

"Is Ivan back?"

"Yes. He looks a bit different. Can I use my phone to call them? I have to put my hands in my jacket. Do you want to talk to them?"

Szymon nodded. He started to lower the rifle, but he didn't walk any closer. Radoslaw managed to get only Ivan. Radoslaw relayed the message, "Ivan only is available. Mikal is at uni trying to make up for lost classes and poor grades."

Szymon nodded, as he held out his hand for the phone. They spoke a while before Szymon handed the phone back. Szymon raised the rifle again when he heard the familiar sound of his mother's car coming towards the property. "Quick. Follow me. The bastards are coming back."

He started running for the bushes. The detectives followed.

Szymon went to his hideout, a bird-hide snuggled behind some bushes. It offered a near perfect view of the house. He pulled the detectives inside. "Shh." He handed Radoslaw a small set of binoculars.

The three men saw the unmarked police car and rifled through it. They swore at what they found. They all pulled out their guns, searched the immediate outside of the large house before returning to the front. One pulled out a key and opened the front door. With guns at eye height, they carefully entered the house. Fifteen minutes later, the men came out. One called out, "Search the grounds. They must be hiding in the bushes."

The men pointed directly to the area where Szymon and the detectives were hiding. Szymon lifted his rifle and took aim. Radoslaw and Eryk took out their pistols which they had picked up when they started to run to the bushes. Szymon whispered, "I take the one on the left and you two go for the other two." Both detectives looked at Szymon with surprise.

"Are you two squeamish?" asked Szymon. "I got past squeamish, long ago. It's them or us and they have taken a lot of us." Szymon cocked his rifle in anticipation. "On the count of three. One two three." Szymon fired. The man fell dead taking a bullet to the chest. Then the detectives fired. Their victims fell. Their legs shot out beneath them. Szymon took aim again and shot them in the chest. The men died instantly. He looked at the detectives. "Next time shoot to kill and then ask questions. Let's see who we have." He walked out of the hide towards the three dead men.

He rolled over the man he shot and went through his pockets. In his search he pulled out some police equipment which was supposed to be in the car. The driver's licence read Timofei Sorokin. The next man was searched. Igor Sorokin who was much younger than the first man. Eryk asked, "Father and son? The name Sorokin sounds familiar. Where did I hear that before?"

"Mikal said his stepmother was married to a Sorokin. A possibility Thea Mazur's son or stepson and ex-husband are now history. The bitch may laugh with joy at Timofei's death. If this is her son from a previous marriage, it is hard to tell what the bitch will do," said Radoslaw.

Szymon asked in surprised concern, "Mikal's stepmother is mixed up in this? No wonder he was having it rough at home. Poor Mikal. Does Mikal's father know about her?"

"We made sure he knows and is cooperating," said Radoslaw.

They rolled over the last victim to get to all his pockets. "Dimitri Polyakov. All these men are Russians," said Szymon. "Why are Russian men chasing us?"

"Not ordinary Russians or cops, mafia," said Radoslaw. "They are everywhere in the city. Exactly why, we are not one hundred per cent sure. Just theories."

"Follow me," said Szymon. He went back to the hide. He handed the detectives six more driver's licences. You can find their bodies over there." He pointed to another cluster of bushes. They came, they wrecked the inside of the house. They stole what they fancied. They kept coming back, obviously looking for me. If I go to prison for their murders, so be it. I will know I have killed some of the bastards who killed the people at the Gradowski's house. That night is one I will never forget. Gunshots and the screaming. I still hear it now, more so when I sleep. I don't sleep well anymore. And I have very big trust issues."

The trio looked up. A police car came through the gates. When it stopped, Ivan got out. Both the driver and Ivan were shocked to see the dead bodies. Slowly Ivan walked to Radoslaw, Eryk and Szymon. To Ivan's eyes, Szymon had changed so much. Pushing the obvious body filth aside and beard, he looked more like a man ten years to his senior.

Szymon embraced Ivan. Ivan cast his eyes to the ground, "So good to see you. It looks like I missed the action. More mafia?" he asked as he looked at Eryk. Eryk nodded.

"Your friend Szymon is an important witness and did a good job in self-defence."

Szymon asked, "I would like to go inside, have a shower and get fresh clothes. I haven't had a decent clean-up for nearly three months. Please keep watch. I am expecting more company. They come at random times."

At the police station Szymon gave a detailed account of what happened at the Grabowski house three months ago.

CHAPTER 19

"Antoni and I went for a weekend skiing trip outside Saint Petersburg. The best weekend for a very long time. We did ask Mikal to come along, but he was moving out of his home. Too much bad blood was developing.

"We arrived back at the Grabowski's home about four in the afternoon. Everything was normal. Over the weekend we had our cars parked at the airport. I have the receipt in one of my pockets. Szymon continued as memories flashed of the fateful evening.

"I'll get your skis down from the roof racks," I offered Antoni.

"Thanks. I can't wait to tell the others what a great time we had."

Antoni pushed on the doorbell to warn those inside of incoming traffic. He took out his keys with the intention of opening the door but Hanna, his younger sister, opened the door from inside, and stepped aside to allow Antoni and me in. She gave him a hug. "That trip must have been good from that big smile I see plastered over your face." She bobbed her head around and gave me an equal warm welcome.

"Excuse me while I take my bag up to my bedroom," said Antoni as he pushed passed Hanna.

Filip, Antoni's youngest brother came forward. "I'll take those skis," he said to me. He placed the skis in a cupboard under the steps which held everyone else's skis and an assortment of skates. "Good trip?" he asked.

"It sure was. Perfect ski conditions. Great time," I replied.

"Zofia Grabowski was Antoni's mother. She met me with a warm greeting, no different to her own son. She regarded me like her own. Antoni and I had known each other since kindergarten.

She planted a kiss on each side of my cheeks and ushered me into the lounge. Antoni came bounding down the stairs carrying gifts. He gave Hanna a bag. I heard him say, "Sorry, short on wrapping paper. Filip's is in the same bag." Hanna pulled out two items. She tossed the blue and white beanie to Filip and kept the red one for herself. Antoni planted a kiss on his mother's cheek. She joking asked, "What? Nothing for me?"

"Nope. Just me," he teased. From behind his back he pulled out a bottle of Vodka, the most matured one he could find. "Dad and you can share that." She smiled and called in her husband, Maxim.

"Maxim had been out the back of the house with their gardener, Igor. They had a go trying to repair the tap, but it appeared to have seized in the cold weather. The continuous drips of water were collected in a bowl. The water would ice up and form a dome. Maxim greeted both Antoni and me and then said, "Excuse me. I have to call a plumber." He dialled his regular plumber. Zofia said to Maxim, "Get him to fix the toilet in the powder room too. The valve can go any time. It is starting to play up." Maxim nodded as he completed the dialling.

"I called my parents to say I was at the Grabowski's home. I would be leaving shortly.

Zofia took my phone off me and invited my parents over. "Come over for dinner tonight. It is short notice. A spur of the moment thing." My parents agreed and would be there about six p.m. "Mum said dad would have to leave early in the evening for an early morning flight to Warsaw. They would leave early.

"I then phoned my girlfriend, Julia. I made arrangements to see her on Monday evening. I was intending to make it special. "Szymon fumbled with a small box hidden in a pocket in his jacket. He had picked out an engagement ring when we passed through Saint Petersburg. I had been thinking about marrying her for a month." He showed the box and the ring inside. "The ski trip would be the last I would make with my friends. From Monday, any ski trip would be with Julia. I told Antoni of my plans and made Antoni promise not to say a word to anyone."

"About five, the plumber came. I was near an open window and could see and hear what was going on outside. The gardener, Igor, opened the roller iron gate to allow the vehicle through. City Plumbing Service had been at our homes before and we always got Jakob. He was not only what we considered the best plumber, but also, he was a genuinely nice person. The driver leaned out of the widow. "Jakob is on another call. I'm Peter," said the driver giving what I now know is a false name. Igor nodded and directed the van to the side of the house with the problem tap. Igor said, "Before you fix this outside tap, Maxim said there was a toilet playing up. The flush valve is on its way out."

Peter went to the side of his van and pulled his set of tools and a couple of models of flush valves.

"I'll do the inside first. Show me the way."

"Minutes later Peter returned to his van. He tossed the faulty flush valve into a container of faulty parts and placed the unused models in a box with other valves. He grabbed a couple of different size tap washers. Igor guided him back to the exterior tap. Igor watched Peter strain to turn on the tap. He examined the semi-frozen water slowly bubbling out. "I'll put a new washer on but don't try forcing it with semi-frozen water. I would say if the cold keeps up, the water will be frozen up in the pipes. Let the snow do the watering." Igor nodded as he watched Peter pack up and return to his van.

"My parent's car was at the gate. I saw them push the code to let themselves through. Dad, Levi, parked his car just a few meters away from the plumber's van. Dad greeted Igor.

Igor smiled at them. He knew them well. "Hello to both of you. The weather hasn't been that good. I feel it in the bones these days."

Mum, Laura, spoke to Igor, "I have never been a fan of the cold. Keep warm out here."

Igor nodded. "I do my best. The rest are already in the house." He ushered them through the front door.

"Peter knocked on the door. Maxim came out. "All done?"

"Yes. I will write up the invoice in the car. It will take a minute of two."

"No. Just send the invoice by email. That is how we always do it. Your boss knows of our arrangement." Peter nodded. He sat in the van writing up his notes. Peter noted the front door was now closed but doubted it was locked. Igor was still outside struggling to roll up a stiffened semi-ice filled hose. Then I turned my attention to all the people inside the house.

"Two of the four armed men wearing black clothes, black gloves and each wearing a balaclava ran into the house. The other two ran around outside. Igor was still outside near the repaired tap, well, that's what I assumed where he was. He must have been shocked as much as we all were. Within seconds, two men must have been at his side with their guns pointed at him. They must have ordered him around first and knowing Igor, he would have complied. We heard a gunshot. I leaned later it was near point blank. The men outside then ran to join the other two who were inside the house.

"The men yelled at all inside to stop screaming. The cook, Igor's wife, Nina made a run for the kitchen. She was going for the nearest exit door. She intuitively knew the gunshot had killed or injured Igor. One man shot her in the back, snapping her spine. Helplessly she laid slowly bleeding out knowing no one could assist her. She would have heard more screams, more gunshots and whimpering before she died.

"Peter came back into the house wearing gloves and holding a pistol and joined the others. The first four intruders had every one of us, the Grabowski family, my parents and me corralled into the lounge room when he joined the group.

"Everyone was forced to kneel. One man walked behind each kneeling scared person and placed a blindfold across our eyes. When he finished, he ordered, "Arms in front where we can see them." All complied. All shaking as fear transmitted itself through the room. I assumed the same man bound each person's hands with cable cords. When he completed that task, he stood back to join the others.

Another from the group ordered, "We know there is a safe in this room." He removed a side table blocking the access. He barked, "What is the number?" Maxim remained silent until we heard the click of a gun which I guessed was resting behind his head. "There is nothing of value in the safe," he protested. The man behind Maxim snarled, "One more try. What is the number?" He must have pushed the gun harder against Maxim. Nervously he said, "Twenty, ten, sixteen, one, five." Another man must have been standing by the safe dialled each in turn. The safe opened. The man gasped. Nothing. "This safe is a decoy. Where is the other safe?"

"There is no other safe. Three weeks ago, everything was transferred to a safety deposit box in Warsaw." They were the last words he spoke. Bang. Maxim laid dead on the floor. The sound of plastic ruffled for a while. I guessed they put a bag over his head or someone else's head. I heard the sound of duct tape being pulled and the crackling noise. I guessed it was going over the plastic.

"Zofia was next. I heard the click of the gun which must have then been placed to her head. The same man who demanded the safe number, spoke again, "Which bank and what is the number?"

"The Polish National in the city heart" she said in a mix of fear and tears. We were all terrified by then.

"What is the account number?" snarled the man behind her. Someone must have written the numbers down on some pad or paper. "It's one, one, six, six, four zero," she whimpered. "What it is all about?" she asked. I still hear these words ringing in my ears.

"None of your business," snarled another man from somewhere else in the room. One of the men turned on the computer. It was password protected. "What is the password for the computer?" the voice demanded. Zofia was silent. The gun pushed harder on her head. She cried, "Poznanpoland%20"

The man typed it in. The computer opened. He noticed the shortcut on the desktop. He opened the icon. "Fuck," he swore. "There is information about the account. It is a high security account and not available on the net. It uses biometrics and voice recognition. Guards attend at every stage. If after two attempts, it fails to open, you cannot access it for twenty-four hours." He printed out the details and pocketed the printout.

He walked over to another person in his group and whispered but not soft enough. I could hear what he was saying, "The biometrics are eyes, handprint and voice. The cameras in this place were put in too late."

I think it was the fake Peter, who said in a loud voice for all to hear, "We finish these off, ransack the house but only take what is valuable. Don't smash things up, but we can have a bit of fun."

"I didn't know what that meant, not immediately. Then he asked, "Who are the guests here?"

"I think they are the Sawickis," I heard a different voice say.

That must have delighted the ears of the others. "We were supposed to go their house next. How considerate of them to save us the trouble. We still go, but tomorrow. Time is on our side. Pull out all internal and external security here, our cameras and we do the same with the Sawicki's home. Do it carefully to make it look like they never had proper security. Start now."

"All of us with our blind folds on could hear movement around the house. We all must have wondered what each person was doing, but none dared to speak. The busy activity in the house confirmed to us remaining hostages, a lot of things were happening. Just busy footsteps kept us worried as to when it would stop and when the shooting will begin again.

The footsteps stopped. All of us still kneeling, bound and blindfolded sensed things were going to change for the worse. Filip felt himself being dragged up. I guessed he tried fighting back and screamed and swore at the men restraining him. A third man punched him, and I guess it was to the head. If he wasn't dazed, he could have been unconscious. Whatever it was, it was just enough time for the men to tie him to his bed upstairs. He screamed that out to us all. He must have done his best to shake one man off his back. He screamed more trying to block out the sound of one voice of the man who was on top of him. That man was yelling for him to be still and it wouldn't hurt as much. Then everything went quiet. I wasn't sure if they killed him there and then or if Filip submitted to their demands. I doubted if he would give in. I guessed they killed him as well.

"All of us in the lounge room heard the returning footsteps. All cringed with fear. I certainly did. We had an inkling of what happened to Filip. Zofia screamed out, "What have you bastards done to my son?"

She never got a reply. She was shot at the back of her head. Then two more shots were fired. I wasn't sure who else were murdered, until I felt my father's body brush against mine as he slumped to the floor.

"Hanna screamed at the sounds and screamed more when she felt two men pull her up. I could hear her kick. She did her best to fight back and creating mayhem. Antoni did his best to run to his sister's aide. Being blindfolded and not knowing where the intruders were except when they grabbed him. He screamed when he felt something sharp like a needle entering his back. Then punches around the head and stomach. He yelled about the sharp administered pain. He yelled again when he felt the same sharp jab again. Then he was silent. I guessed he was overpowered and never knew exactly what happened after that other than guessed he was going to die.

In the fighting and the men's distraction, I took an opportunity and with a run of faith with my blind fold on, ran through the kitchen and out of the back door. While running, I removed the blindfold. I headed for the shrubs at the back zigzagging my way to safety. I heard the sound of voices coming after me. Gunshots fired around my feet. I felt the bushes in my face. They scratched me but there was no more gunfire. I knew I was going to be next.

"I knew these bushes well. Antoni, Mikal, and Ivan played in this area. We would play for hours. Always coming back home with torn and filthy clothes. The stormwater drainpipe which was always the escape route out of the property, was now going to be a real escape route to my safety and freedom. I headed for the pipe and hoped there wasn't too much cold dirty water. I was feeling a little safer and stopped. I rubbed the cable cords on the metal grill. Eventually the cable snapped. I opened the grill. As kids it took three of us to move the weight, now just me. I crawled inside. The water had iced. I pulled down the grill before crawling through the pipe. My hands began to turn blue. My trousers were now so wet and cold; my knees were beginning to ache.

I pushed myself. Fear kept me moving. I knew I didn't have far to go. My memory served me right, I knew I would come up two blocks away at a park.

"I managed to crawl out of the pipe. This end was open, no safety grill. I looked around from this safety point to check out the park. No one was around. I looked at each road circling the small park. I cursed. Someone in dad's car was driving slowly like a shark circling. I was its prey. I bobbed down into the pipe again to wait for the car to go and hopefully never to return. The car eventually disappeared.

"I jogged across the road where a twenty-four-hour store was serving customers. I changed my mind about entering. Instead, I ran to the back of the store and hid in the toilet block. I stayed there until daylight. I did my best to clean myself up, but I knew people would give me a wide berth.

I walked into the store and bought some food before walking home. On the entire trip, I was looking over my shoulder and at everyone walking towards me. I pulled out my phone with the intention of phoning Julia to warn her and explain what had happened. The phone was almost flat. I tried but the phone simply didn't connect. I needed to call her and urgently. I jogged the rest of the way home.

"When I got home, I did a check on his house. I went to the garage which was separated from the rest of the house but joined by a small enclosed breezeway. I smashed one of the glass panes of the breezeway. It was a pane which was designed to be smashed for emergency purposes. I felt around for a secondary switch to open up the garage door. I swore when I saw my mother's car was missing. I knew instantly, some of the murders had been to the house and had helped themselves while others were searching for me. I was a loose end.

"In the garage I found a cardboard box full of pieces of assorted metal things. I searched through the box for one of two emergency keys to the house. But my first moment of success was interrupted. A car pulled up in the driveway. An unfamiliar and angry voice floated towards me. I had to hide. I crawled into a cupboard housing assorted tools. I couldn't quite get the door shut and hoped the men wouldn't come his way. I had one hand holding the door as close to my body.

"One man was in the breezeway when he called the others to the broken pane of glass. "He's been here. Search the place." I looked around in the confined space. I placed my free hand on a hammer just in case the door was opened. The man looked around the garage but took no notice of the cupboard door being slightly ajar. He called out as he walked out of the garage, "All clear."

"I heard more noise. Furniture was being stolen. Just small items which would fit into the back of dad's car. The car eventually drove away.

"I left my hiding place, opened the door linking the breezeway to the main house with the master key. I carefully looked in each room before entering. The task was made easier as each room now had several of its contents removed. I pushed on a panel in the hallway and removed all the family's hunting rifles and all the ammunition. I closed the panel to ensure it didn't give the men any ideas to smash all the walls in a bid to find other hidden treasures. I took them to the bird hide which was to become my temporary home.

"I was about to return when mum's car came up the driveway. Two men got out and helped themselves to more household items. They didn't see me hiding in the bushes. They were too focused robbing the place. When the men were finished, they did a check around the house to ensure it was locked securely. I took aim. I shot the first man in the stomach. The second came running with his gun drawn. I shot him in the chest. I watched them die slowly by using my father's binoculars that were always in the hide.

"I dragged their bodies to the bushes some forty meters away on the other side of the house. I searched their bodies for identification and pocketed them. The shallow graves were marked with branch off-cuts and stones. You saw the stone. One, then two on the next victim and so on until six.

"I cleaned myself up. I didn't know this was going to be one of the last baths I would have. I bundled up my filthy clothes and placed them in the washing machine. While that was going, I returned the stolen furniture to the house. Now, I had most the keys to the house and the keys to my mother's car. While I was driving, I charged my phone. I had to call Julia. I was supposed to meet her that night. I had to call it off, warn her, and make sure she was safe. She didn't answer her phone. I left a message and another a couple of hours later. It wasn't like her to not return my calls.

"I purchased food. A mixture of fresh and dried with lots of bottled water and some toiletries.

I placed everything in labelled boxes before placing them in the hide. The next stop was at a gun shop. I showed my license before purchasing more ammunition. I went to a camping store and bought a new sleeping bag, one which would handle the zero temperatures and other assorted equipment I considered handy. I used the dead men's cards for some transactions. My way of compensation for the murders and inconvenience they put me in.

"I drove the car as far as I considered safe to the hide and unloaded the equipment. I drove the car out of the property, around the block to a nature reserve. I hid the car in the mixture of trees and bushes. I took a short cut back home. When I was about to settle in for the night, I heard a sound of a car. A new group of men appeared. "I watched as the men entered the house using the keys in dad's car. This time they took nothing. They were searching for the first lot of men who didn't return. I was angry when I noticed the men had decided to stay overnight.

"The next morning, the two new intruders searched the grounds and stole a couple of items from the house. They left. I waited for a few minutes before venturing out. I had made my mind up and would not go near the house without a rifle and extra ammunition. I removed my clothes from the washing machine, the clothes which were there from yesterday and stuffed them in a plastic bag. I took a few other changes of clothes and dad's phone charger. Then I raided the fridge for the milk. I was making a point not to consume all the contents just in case they did a fridge check. I picked up the land line. I heard an odd noise. I put the phone down immediately and bolted out of the house with the items I collected.

"From the hide I could see the same men returning in a different car. This time they didn't go inside but positioned themselves – one in the front of the house and one to the back. I took aim at the man at the front of the house. I fired. The man hit the ground clutching his knee. The other man came running. I shot again but missed. The man took cover. I moved from the hide to another location which gave a clearer side view of the man. This time I didn't miss. The first man swivelled around trying to locate me. Not knowing where in a general direction to aim, he fired. I shot back. This time I hit the man in the head. I took their identifications and any cards and money they had in their possession. I returned the few bits of furniture.

"I buried these men beside their friends and drove their car to a shopping centre which had an underground carpark. I placed the car on the second level to one corner, cleaned my prints off before locking it and walking off with the keys. I could use that car in emergencies. I tried calling Julia again. Still no answer. I tried her parent's home on their land line. Still no answer. I took a bus to Julia's home. I found a note on the door:

Gone on holidays with my parents. Going to see Marlena and Lavinia in France. Will call when I get back.

I took the note off the door. I thought nothing too much of the note and it offered some comfort that she was away. I could now focus on the criminals who destroyed my life."

"I went back to the Grabowski's home to use one of their cars. Through the gate I saw Antoni's car was gone. I pushed the gate code. The gate opened. I ran up the driveway to the large garage which recently was expanded to house the cars belonging to Antoni and Hanna. I opened the garage by pushing the emergency button. All the cars were gone. I swore. Then I heard a noise, looked outside and saw Antoni's car coming up the driveway. I went outside to hide leaving the garage doors open.

"As the driver came closer, he saw the garage doors open. He stopped short of the garage and got out of his car with a pistol in his hand. He went inside the opened garage, checked it out and closed the door. He circled the garage and building, spoke on his phone and put his gun away. The man entered the house, looked around and then left. I knew from the man's actions; I was still being hunted.

"I waited for fifteen minutes until I was sure the man was well away. I ran deeper into the bushes at the back of the house. I found the makeshift steps the others and I made when we were children. We made the crude steps out of stones held together with mud and out of date flour and crushed dried leaves. As boys we would go over the fence into the once raw forest. We would play at the edge of the forest and then climb the tree which overhung onto Grabowski's property to return home. I noted the tree was now gone. Going back to the hide this way was doable but difficult. I went up the now crumbling steps and hoped it was strong enough to hold my adult weight. I went over the wall. The virgin forest was now part of a government complex which I once visited in an official capacity. Dad's company had installed all the pipework. I ran through the grounds, people stared at my unkempt state. I ignored them and kept running down the street towards my home. I crossed into the park where the storm water drain would lead me back to the safety of the bird hide.

"The next day, men came to my house. The bastards were in my car. I cursed and was determined to get my car back. I waited until the two men got out and were halfway to the front door. I shot two more – one in the chest and one in the arm. I reloaded my rifle and shot the injured man before he got back to the safety of the car. I searched my car looking for any tracking devises. I didn't want to chance it. I didn't find anything but as a precaution I disabled the GPS.

I jumped when a mobile phone belonging to one of the dead men rang. I picked up the phone and answered. The caller spoke Russian. I clicked off and knew others would be coming and in greater numbers. I had to evacuate. I took the driver's licences off the dead men and raided their wallets for cash and cards. I shoved the men into the car and drove them to the growing cemetery. I again made a rough grave, much cruder than before and shoved a stick in the ground. No other markers. I drove towards the hide and loaded up with personal effects before driving away. I tossed the mobiles in the council garbage truck coming down the street and drove off to where I had hidden my mother's car. I slept in the car. Two cars retrieved.

"I attempted to go home the next day but felt something wasn't right. I drove my car away and doubled back on foot. There were about ten men crawling over the place. Some were installing cameras and burglar alarms. What got my attention, were a series of landmines. Landmines on my property? Fucking hell!"

"It's a bit over the top," said Radoslaw. He shook his head. "Bastards."

"I kept watching and noting the positioning of the landmines. I would move them to a new location. When the men left, I drove to the library. I googled landmines and printed out the different models and how to move them with safety. I didn't go back to the hide. I drove to Warsaw where I booked into a cheap motel, bathed and slept for an extended period.

"I bought some tools and then splashed out on some night-vision binoculars and a metal detector.

I drove back home but stopped at the gates. I checked every step with the detector – just in case someone returned with more mines. The detector beeped near the control panel of the gate. I stood back. With shovel in hand and at a safe distance, I started digging. The mine was scooped up with the shovel and carried to the side of the road. I opened the gate, brought the mine inside to the side of the driveway. I scanned the rest of the driveway. It was clear. I placed the mine at the front door of my house. I would decide what to do with it later. I drove the car in and parked it halfway to the house.

"Two hours later, I had dug up ten mines. I didn't disarm them but relocated them around the house. I knew the camera were watching me, but I soon sorted out the blind spots. I put a few in these locations. Then left. I knew the men were coming.

"I left the property in my car and drove into the shopping centre where I had left the other car days earlier. Here I swapped cars and used that for a couple of days and reparked it in a different location in the same carpark.

"I returned home a week later and repeated the same process – mine checking and relocating them. I only found five. I squinted at the disturbed ground to the western side of the house. The house was untouched, but a tell-tale mini crater was evident. I looked closer. The body was gone but there was evidence of flesh and clothes. Ants happily feasting – tearing the remains apart.

"This time I focused my attention on the cameras. I found the ladder in the garage. Each camera was removed, and the cables pushed back inside. I sealed the holes with duct tape and left the house again. I knew they would be back. This time I left the mines on the doorstep with a tongue-in-cheek note.

Score 7-all. Do you want to continue? If so, stack the mines on top of each other in the middle of the yard. I will know our war continues.

"I didn't return for a week. I saw the mines were gone and the cameras re-installed, but I wasn't going to be complacent. They had taken the ladder and the mines could be in the yard again.

I left the property again. Swapped cars and stayed low. I returned to the hide only via the stormwater pipe. I would scan the property later in sections in an organised grid. The metal detector was working overtime. Beeping in different locations. A couple of nights I stayed in the hide. I was disturbed only once. The night vision glasses assisted my surveillance. Two men had arrived. They were carrying suitcases. They were going to stay over. "Not in my house," I said to myself.

"When the men returned to their car, I shot them. Like before I checked out their bodies for identification. This time I checked the suitcases. There were the usual clothes, ammunition, enough for a war.

One case had a mix of drugs, guns and photos. I looked at the photo and swore.

It was a photo my parents, me and all the Grabowski family. All but my photo had a red cross drawn across. I closed the bag but took the photos. I had no idea why we were on a hit list at the start of all this, but I understood I was a loose end."

Szymon reached into his jacket and pulled out the crumpled picture to show the police. Eryk took the photo and placed it on the wall with the growing number of deceased people.

"I dragged them to another location as the area I was using was getting very crowded. It was just ten more metres away from the first group. The ground was harder, and time was short. I made the graves shallower and marked them the same way with sticks and stones. I knew more men would be on the way. I had to leave. I decided I would come back at random times to mow the grass and remove the cameras as necessary. I rarely went inside the house and when I did, I just took canned or dried food. Everything else of value was now gone, including family photos." Szymon ended his recount. "I lived from day to day. I kept low. I knew I killed and that means prison. I was too scared to go to you guys. I trusted no one."

Eryk sighed. "That is one hell of a story of survival against the mafia."

"Mafia?" Szymon said in shock.

"I killed mafia? No wonder the bastards were so persistent and technical. Which prison would I be going to? I am prepared for that."

Radoslaw looked at Eryk and tossed his head aside. The men walked out of the room. There was short discussion. Both men returned. "Here is a deal. You are still in danger, more so than ever before. Keep out of trouble. Stay with Ivan and Stefan for a while but we put you in witness protection in another country. You leave in three days. As for the murders? Killer unknown but your family's property was the unfortunate dumping ground. And if the shit hits the fan, it is all self-defence. I looked at the identifications of your handiwork. Two of the men were at recent mafia funerals. They won't be missed by anyone. We will collect all their DNA and match it to a number of unsolved crimes in the city and just maybe in other parts of Poland.

I am sure some of the surviving victims will be rejoicing at the news. Now, you keep low. Keep your mouth shut. Got it?"

Szymon nodded. Then he said, "Julia is still missing. Her family is still missing. The last text message was months ago. If they went to France, I hope they are still there."

"We can send a notice out. No guarantees on anything."

Szymon stood up to leave. He said with a tear running down his face. "Sorry for pointing the gun at you. I have trust issues. I have nightmares all the time."

"We are not surprised. You did scare us. Just who taught you those shooting skills and general survival techniques?"

Szymon thought for a second contemplating what he could say. "Climbing and camping is a mix of the sport skills taught at the school we all went to. On summer holidays, my parents insisted I went out bush to connect and survive on rations. Dad had the idea I wasn't going to be soft and city bound. He saw it as a kind of training to think your way out of trouble. I protested when I was a kid. But now I am ever so grateful he won each battle. He had foresight which I never really appreciated until all this happened. The other bits were common sense for survival."

"Ivan has been waiting outside for you. Mikal maybe here by now. He has gone back to uni. But your situation is different. The mafia will have a price on your head. Don't look surprised. Ivan and his father have a big bounty on their heads too. It seems a common practice of the Russian mafia."

"That is all I needed. A bounty. Can I go now?" Szymon pointed to the door.

"Yes. Remember the rules. We will be in touch. Practice calling Ivan, Peter and his father, Thomas. Mikal is still Mikal but his surname is now Chzov." said Radoslaw.

As soon as Szymon saw Mikal, the men embraced. Ivan was pulled into the duo. Eryk nodded and closed the door. He said softly, "When I look at that group, I see old men, not the youthful smiling guys in the photo on the wall. So sad that their innocence has been taken away from them."

Radoslaw opened the door to see the trio were still there. "Go. Go home all of you. Celebrate at home and I mean at home. Swap your stories there. I want you all here tomorrow at ten. We need you all to help us form a picture, the big picture. We have bits of a puzzle and just maybe you can add more bits."

When the detectives were on their own, Eryk asked, "Just who are running their companies?"

Stefan is trying to restore his company and is slowly fixing its reputation. Mikal senior Sawicki is altering his will without his wife's knowledge. He is cooperating with us to set her up for a stint in prison. That has been difficult. She never does anything but socialises. Maybe that can be an avenue to bring her down. Loose lips. As for the Grabowski's health empire, just who is running that?"

CHAPTER 20

In Moscow four men wearing expensive business suits, walked separately into a side door on the south side of the Kremlin. They showed their passes as they went past the desk where all are supposed to sign the register upon entry. These four men routinely never signed in believing their rank would override the requirement and the clerk received payment to overlook the formality. Not a word was spoken other than thanking the guards checking their credentials. Each walked down a deserted passageway, their footsteps echoing down the hall and then down a set of stairs. One by one they entered a room that has been long unused.

The room held files, thousands of files on citizens of old communist Russia. The old file room was long ago decreed as a museum, a reminder of the government's infliction of harsh rule over its citizens. The KGB record rooms were rarely visited by anyone; maybe a university lecturer doing research on people who lived in certain areas of Russia or some government official getting a file for a customer requesting a birth, or marriage or death certificate of the period. But even they kept their visits to a minimum. It was only when gaps occurred in the transferred files to electronic storage did someone find the need to go through the massive filing draws which were systematically labelled.

Secure in the privacy of this dungeon, the group opened their briefcases, pulled out their laptops and fired them up. As they waited, they greeted each other and lit up cigars. One in the group walked over to a rickety cabinet and pulled out the four half bottles of vodka. He handed each one their labelled bottles. Each took a swig and opened a file.

Dimitri Orlov began with his report. "Things are going a bit off track. My youngest son, Artem has reported the following:

"The British assistant, Gerry Randale has been forced to step down while being investigated for accepting bribes. He accepted a million euros into a Cayman account. We got most of the money back. He and the others don't know we are also signatories. We got about eight hundred thousand euros. He spent the rest.

"In France the assistant is still clear. The same in Germany. In Poland, two prison officials have been stepped down. They are also under investigation. We took back a million euros between them.

"The Novaks. They are in Poland but where is not clear. Our contact there has been cut out of the loop. It appears the two detectives Wojcik and Landski are by-passing all normal protocol.

Do we put them up for elimination or delay a little until we find out exactly what they are doing?"

There was a quick discussion. "We did dispose of one of their men, a forensic accountant, Alan Gorski. I think we delay. Too many cops dying will be bad for business," commented Isaak Buteyko. "It will spark a bigger investigation. The last thing we need is more police." The others nodded.

"The company, Exotic Polish Food Company so far appears to be legitimate. Two of their men are running the East European Flower Company. Since then, the profits have increased by five per cent.

That is up from the time the Nowak's disappeared.

"Just a side note. Ivan has killed two mafia men. The mafia raided a safehouse in Britain. Apparently, Ivan smashed a statue over one man's head and shot another with a pistol. He appears to be a bit of a Houdini. I propose we get the mafia to kidnap him and then we take him off their hands. Brain wash him and rebuild him to be an escape goat. He takes the fall and true operatives do the work."

Lazar Turov drummed his fingers, looked at the others before answering, "We need to find him first. He's good at hiding. I suspect he is in disguise and has changed his name. When caught, we brainwash him or as they say these days, radicalise him. No one wants radicals. It has worked in the past. Young men caught and radicalised to be used as a sacrificial lamb or decoy, whatever the task requires. I am in favour to have Ivan Nowak kidnapped." He looked around the room to see the others nodding agreement.

"Now back to the flower company. Since The Exotic Polish Food Company has taken over The East European Flower Company new men have taken over, Thomas Brennen and Peter Schmidt. They don't know it, but they are trafficking guns and supplies to Iran. Sales have increased. The drugs from Iran have got through the boarders more easily. Both the Food and Flower Companies are acting like puppets to our fund-raising cause," said Isaak.

"But the Food company still has majority ownership of the Flower Company" commented Dimitri.

"A minor matter for now. The people in both companies will slowly be replaced. A few of our people are strategically placed and they will be promoted within that system as time permits. They will be in place within three years. The Food Company people running the place will be bumped off," confirmed Isaak.

"We have had reports from my niece, Thea Mazur. She has managed to get her step-son, Mikal Mazur, out of the house and fully disgraced with his studies. He has failed and had reached the point where the university may never permit him back. Mikal junior was spotted moving into a run-down block of apartments. He has placed himself in a position where he is unguarded and no security. He is ripe to take down slowly by drugs or even put in jail. We can plant drugs and guns in the place and call the police. He would get about three years or do we make him an addict?" asked Lazar Turov.

"A slow demise looks better and more natural. He will be vilified by his shrinking circle," said Dimitri Orlov.

"We have people in place at different levels of the Mazur Constructions ready to step up into the higher ranks. We just need to get rid of Mikal senior and two other directors. Creating a void quickly will force the company to quickly promote people through their system," said Lazar.

"Thea is working on Mikal to change his will, so she becomes the only beneficiary. When that is done and given close to a year, Mikal goes to heaven," said Dimitri.

"We can't have Thea killing Mikal. She will go to prison and the will be declared void. If Mikal junior is still alive, he may inherit the company, but a guardian will be appointed to look after his interests. Then we will have to find someone to do that task. Not as easy as it may sound. We need Thea to be the figure head for control of that company. I suggest we get Anna Duba to do the killing. She is not exactly one of us. She is mafia and is expendable," said Desya Sudakov.

"She did organise the death of her own daughter Sonya. I believe Sonya was about to go to the police and sell her mother out. Anna got to her first. Anna is disposable. Anna is always clocking up gambling debts. She is also an alcoholic. She will soon have very loose lips," stated Lazar.

"Is she in debt now?" asked Dimitri.

"Actually, no. She has been very careful on that front. When the time comes, we will create a gambling debt. We get her to go to an all-expenses paid holiday to Macau in China with gambling chips to $US15,000. We dress the trip up as a promotion. She's greedy. We play on that. We also get one of our men to charm her off her feet to make the holiday one she won't forget. The cost will be about 200,000 euros. Chicken feed in the scope of things," pointed out Desya Sudakov.

The men grinned and nodded approval.

"Now we have the Grabowski problem. That was a stuff-up. What exactly happened there? I am getting conflicting information. Enlighten me," asked Isaak.

Dimitri adjusted himself in his chair before answering. "We knew the Sawicki and the Grabowski were good friends. Their sons went on a skiing trip to the ski resort outside Saint Petersburg. We should have ordered their execution at that location. But the mafia side wanted the whole of the Grabowski family in one go - a sensational crime to divert police attention from what was going on.

The takeover of that company is in full progress. Most of our people have moved through the ranks. We can just about start taking over the processing of vitamins, minerals and dried foods."

"The problem was the Sawicki got themselves invited to the house just before the murders."

Isaak interrupted, "The other company which we are infiltrating?"

"The very same," confirmed Dimitri.

"We took months to plan that murders in the Sawicki's and Grabowski's home: listening devices, a few cameras outside, phone taps on the landline and all their mobiles," commented Isaak as he took a swig of vodka from his bottle.

"All the Grabowski's are dead and so are Levi and Laura Sawicki. Their son Szymon got away. The mafia have been chasing him ever since without success. The mafia placed a bounty on his head because he has over time taken out six of their men. There could be more, but they are not telling. Too embarrassing. Actually, the man has very good survival skills. A damn good sniper," said Isaak.

"Sniper?" asked the others in tandem. Isaak nodded. "He handles rifle just as good as any Russian army sniper. He is supposed to be on the Olympic team for Poland for shooting. He is tipped to be a good contender for a medal. He keeps escaping the area and has reclaimed his parents' stolen cars and one belonging to the mafia. He has successfully disposed of the bodies. I was informed when the police turned up at his house, he saved their skins. Two mafia went down, both dead. Szymon shot the men dead in front of the police he was protecting. He didn't wince. I was told by internal sources, he steals the deceased's wallets and ID's, uses their cash until the account is empty. He lives by his wits. He's making the mafia look foolish. I believe the bounty on him has reached the 1,500,000 euros mark."

Isaak sighed. "We get the mafia to kidnap him and they bring him here, like we do with Ivan. Then we change him. Get him to work for us. We have done that before. Kidnap, brain wash, break them down and rebuild them for our purposes. We don't have to break him down much. He is halfway there. Isolated and a bit twisted." He looked around the room to see others around him considering the suggestion. "Not many twenty something can handle murdering others with a rifle, and he is doing that without training. He could be a more valuable asset than Ivan. When he makes an error, he is disposable."

"Does he have any weaknesses?" asked Desya.

"A long standing girlfriend. She is out of the picture. The mafia kidnapped her and her parents.

The parents were shot and dumped in the Black Forest in Germany. The girlfriend was taken to the backwaters of Iran. She was sold to be a drugged-up sex slave. What I gather, they keep her drugged up to keep her in line. She has tried to escape. I was told she was a fighter. She severely injured one of the mafia men holding her in her fancy cell. I am not sure what sedation they are using. I am not sure if they are mixing drugs. The Iranians don't care as long as the female does as she is told while in the bedroom. If she develops any venereal diseases, then she will be disposed of. Szymon doesn't know where she is. She is his weak point," said Isaak.

"What about the council in Poznan. Have any officials been bribed yet?" asked Lazar.

"No. Not directly with us. They do accept a few kickbacks but not from Mazur Constructions and Sawicki Engineering. Then the 'donations' go to some charities. The Sawicki Company is doing a major pipeline from Lviv through to Gdansk. The mafia who have managed to be drivers of the trucks, have successfully smuggled three Iranian operatives. The operatives are somewhere in Europe, most likely stirring up local mosques," said Desya.

"We need our men in the Sawicki and Mazur mix so they can secretly install valves to divert any oil or gas or water the pipes. We get control of the valve system; we get anything we need to and from anywhere in the east. Poznan will collapse first. They will call new local elections, then our people go in. How many candidates are planning their fake profiles?" asked Isaak.

"We have about two in each seat posing to hold up different agendas to appeal to different popular age groups and streams of thought. Some are playing the independent game and others are in political parties. When we get control of Poznan, then we can start spreading through Poland. It will be easier to bring back Poland under old communist rule," said Dimitri.

Lazar smirked. "Plan B is being formulated. All plans are going as smoothly as expected. Just make sure the president does not catch wind of what is going on. When he is internationally embarrassed, then we can walk in," Lazar's smiled widened. "We were powerful and fearful when the communist rule was absolute. Bring on the good old days." He gave a salute. The others raised their bottles for the toast.

"Shall we get back to our usual tasks? Time is moving on," said Desya.

Dimitri Orlov sighed. "I'm going to Saint Petersburg to have a chat with our dear mafia friends. Give them a boost and new orders regarding Ivan Nowak and Szymon Sawicki. We want them alive, not dead. I may have to give them some ideas on how to catch this Szymon. It will be their job to find Ivan. Also, I need to check up on our moles in France, Germany and Poland. I need to make sure they are happy. It is very important that they get their happy pills."

CHAPTER 21

Eryk and Radoslaw were drawing up teams to investigate the three companies, Mazur Construction, Sawicki Engineering, and The East European Flower Company. Now they added the Polish Vitamin Company following the deaths of their founders and information provided by Szymon. They looked up from their work when Natan and Fabian walked in.

"Where's Oskar?" asked Natan.

"His girlfriend is seriously ill, cancer I believe. She is not expected to live much longer. He's taking time off to be with her," said Radoslaw.

"That's rough. Wasn't she the one he was going to marry?" Fabian enquired.

Eryk nodded as he closed his eyes. "He is refusing to do more trips to the east at this stage."

Although Fabian had frequently looked at the map Oskar added to the wall, he was always surprised by the amount of information Oskar was able to bring back on that one journey. He stared at the map again. "We are missing something. The pipeline that is being built, have we got any details on the route?"

"Partial. Only what passes through Poland," said Natan.

"Get an overlay. I want to see something," ordered Fabian.

Eryk pulled out an A5 sheet of clear plastic and clipped it over the map. Radoslaw dropped what he was doing and googled the information. He read out the pathway that was published on the net.

Fabian drew with black felt pen the known path. He stood back. He stared again. Something was running around in his brain, but it wasn't crystallizing. "Contact Szymon. I want to know what he knows about the pipeline."

Szymon answered his phone. He was in a hairdresser. His long hair was now neatly trimmed and was halfway the time needed for the colour to take hold. "I don't have much details." He looked round the store to make sure the staff were at a distance. He kept his voice soft. "The pipe in Poland is supposed to carry water and at various points, feed towns and or villages."

"Could it carry oil?' asked Fabian.

"It could. But you can't mix the products. You need different pipes for different products. Oil will poison the water and water would damage the quality of the oil. They must be separate. Why what's up?"

"Just running a few ideas. Are there any maps of the pipeline?"

"In dad's office. I doubt if there is anything at home. The house is still being watched. The bastards stole lots of things and I was powerless to stop it."

"Can you go to your father's office and get a map?"

"Difficult in the sense of people drowning me in sympathies or looking at me in disgust for not reporting the murders earlier. There could be resistance from other members of the board to me accessing the maps. It may be easier if I was with one of you."

Fabian nodded. "Okay, I will set up an appointment as soon as possible. How is the transformation going?"

"I barely recognise myself. I also contacted the university to put the rest of my studies on deferment."

"How are you coping, I mean readjusting to everything?" asked Fabian in a fatherly tone.

"Slowly. Lots of night terrors. Counselling is helping. Thank you for arranging that. I have to go." He clicked off.

Szymon walked into the office where his father previously worked. Following behind him was Natan and Radoslaw. Eyes followed their every move. When they went into his father's office, whispers filled the air. Someone contacted Olivier Sawicki to organise a meeting.

Szymon took out plans he knew his father was working on. He spread them across the now empty desk. Just as they began to pour over the plans, Olivier walked in.

Szymon introduced the detectives. But Olivier just stared. When he recovered, he gave Szymon a hug. "Why didn't you tell me?"

"I was scared. If I opened my mouth, I could have been dead and coming to you was out of the question. They would have killed you too. I had to protect myself and others. There was enough death."

Olivier stood back from Szymon. "The experience has made you old before your time. You look about ten years older. Sorry. The strain has aged you. I think the staff noticed it too." Szymon brought the topic back to the maps.

"The detectives need to look at the current big project the company is working on. It may reveal why there was an attack."

Olivier looked puzzled but kept quiet. He straightened the plans across the desk. "What part do you want to know?"

"Just about all of it. Water or oil for starters."

"Two pipes follow near identical pathways. The first pipeline is for water. That is the main one. Most goes to the new township being designed, the new satellite city between Poznan and Warsaw." He pointed to the location. "That is where Mazur Constructions is still designing the layout of the town and shopping area. How are the Mazur family taking this news of Levi and Laura's death? And the Grabowski massacre?"

Natan, who hadn't taken his eyes off the plans and didn't look up. "Very hard. They have their very own unique threat issues to deal with. Before we leave, we need you to make a time to come down to the station."

Szymon butted in, "Not the station. Somewhere more neutral and a bit hidden. There are too many eyes and ears watching and listening."

Olivier was startled by Szymon's comment. "What's wrong with the station?"

"Nothing. Safe and secure but eyes are outside, and ears are listening. Uncle I have trust issues and have become a bit paranoid ever since the murders. Trust no one, forever on guard, always ready to act." Szymon walked around the room as if examining every item. He opened a window and leaned out. He picked up a black looking button. He held it up. "Shh."

Natan swore under his breath, "The building needs to be checked."

Olivier went white with shock. He sat down heavily on the office chair. "And you have been living this out for three or more months?"

Szymon nodded. "Shh".

Szymon pushed the fire emergency button. The staff who had numerous drills in the past, stopped working and filed out of building. Any visitor in the building was led away by the closest staff member.

Natan said as he followed Olivier and Szymon out. "You didn't have to do that. Push the fire alarm."

"Yes. I did. It gives the listeners a headache and sore ears for a few days. When no one is around, it makes it easier for the crew to locate bugs. The people inside who may have bugged the place won't have an opportunity to remove anything. Check the phone system and computers for hacking. Someone here, maybe more than one person knows something. Those who have access to this level, the main hub of planning and decision making, is the main area." He pointed to the office while waiting for the lifts.

Natan was on the phone organising a team to debug the office. By the time the group reached the ground floor, he had also called in the bomb squad. He knew there was no bomb, but he had to hide the search of the building.

Olivier was lost for words. A million questions were forming in his mid. Szymon gave his uncle a hug as they were leaving the lift. He said softly, "I have to go. This will be the last time you see me. I am leaving and will be uncontactable. Give my love to the family."

Olivier asked, "Where are you going?"

"Don't know. I will be told when I get there. If I did know, I still couldn't tell you. I will come back only when it is safe. If you see Julia, let her know I love her. Please give her this." He pulled out the box containing the engagement ring. I have been carrying it around with me for months. I was going to propose to her three months ago when I got back from the skiing holiday. I haven't been able to contact her. Let her decide what to do with it. Accept her decision no matter what it is."

Olivier nodded. He said softly to the detectives, "I will wait for your call for a meeting."

Olivier stood outside with the staff. He watched Szymon leave with the detectives. A tear rolled down his face. He sniffed heavily attracting the attention of another director.

The second director asked quietly, "Where's the fire?"

"None. Bomb threat," said Olivier as he securely held listening devise Szymon had slipped to him earlier. "The police are sending in a bomb squad. We have to get our IT checked. It could be compromised."

While the crowd waited on the footpath, Olivier spotted a dog on a leash. Not really sure that the device was working, he reacted on impulse. The owner of the dog wove her way through the crowd. As the lady approached, Olivier moved slightly out of his way and bent over to pat the dog. While he was doing that, he slipped the listening devise onto the dog's collar. At the same time, he engaged in a short conversation with the owner before she and the dog moved on.

Back at the station, Radoslaw, Eryk and Natan organised for the three friends, Szymon, Ivan /Peter and Mikal to be at the station. Thomas /Stefan joined the group minutes later.

"Now that I have all of you here, I want further information. This is to help us draw a picture as to what is going on. I mean the big picture. The pieces we have are not sitting together that well. We have theories," said Eryk. "For the benefit of Szymon and Mikal, and a reminder to all, please practice addressing Ivan and Stefan with their new names."

Natan put up a fresh white board. He started with Thomas and Peter. As the men spoke a mud map was formed. "Thomas. Your business is flowers. Flowers go across the length of Europe. Can enough flowers hide the odour of drugs?"

"In a nutshell, yes and any other contraband. You can hide lots of things in flowers, including objects of any type and size." Natan drew a line from the flowers to drugs, artefacts, guns plus other objects.

"Mikal, what does your father do?" asked Natan.

"Construction. There is a massive government project in advance planning stages. It's the new city between Poznan and Warsaw."

Natan drew a line from construction to the drug list to add new word, money laundering.

"What did the Grabowski family do?"

"Health products, mostly vitamin and mineral tablets. They also do dried food and freeze-dried food. They ship them mostly to the west. On occasions, they ship dried food towards the Black Sea, but not beyond."

Natan drew a line back to the drugs.

"Szymon, what does your family do?"

Szymon answered, "Aqua-hydraulic engineering. They are system designers for water and sewerage. We will do a few oil lines. The latter is not the main source of income. We work with the council and state authorities. We prefer big contracts like Mikal's family. Our families frequently work together. We sometimes share the infrastructure of transport - like the project between Warsaw and Poznan."

Natan drew a line back to money laundering and added the words power slash control of cities.

"Cities don't function without power and water. Nations go down the tube if those vital services are switched off. Now let's look at the criminal death list and where they are from."

Natan got an A1 size sheet of butcher's paper and pinned it over the top of the existing board. "Sorry about the paper. This job has blown up so much, we have run out boards. This is the leftover from the storeroom when we didn't have whiteboards. We did use the windows one stage, but the cleaners had the idea it was graffiti. They would clean the notes off."

He divided the paper into three columns. On the left side he wrote a list of criminal names and where they died. In the centre he wrote any deaths they were responsible for and in the final column any other crimes he knew about but couldn't get enough evidence to put the person away.

Thomas who hadn't said a word said as he continued to look at the information in front of him. "Only the very top mafia know what is truly going on. The flowers, food and the health company are smoke screens. The construction companies are the vehicles to launder both money and shift people around." He broke off his thoughts. The maps of the pipelines, where do they go?"

Szymon drew his finger on the map. Then Thomas looked at Oskar's map. He focused on the small camping trails. He asked Szymon, "Who is responsible for the pipeline coming in from Bialystok in the north-east?"

"We go to the boarder. Belarus is on the other side. We meet up in no-man's land. It is all water pipes. Oil pipes in the future come in via Zamosc, in the south-east. The family does not have any contracts for that. Dad and my uncle have submitted their tender. It is still under consideration."

Thomas asked, "Just who is financing the pipework in the Belarus and the Ukraine?"

"Russia," chorused Natan and Ivan.

Eryk asked, "Didn't they finance the oil line through Romania, down to Turkey?"

Thomas nodded. He added, "It also leaked out. They went joint venture with the Armenians, and joint venture for a port in Georgia."

"But the president is on record, he is not in any deal with the Ukrainians. That can be taken with a grain of salt," commented Eryk.

Szymon looked at the maps again. "Just suppose the president is telling the truth. Just suppose there are dark elements in his own government doing deals behind his back, then it is a matter of who?"

Mikal continued with the hypo-theoretical, "Okay, if we go along with a renegade group in the Russian government, then they are manipulating the Russian mafia to do their bidding. The mafia gets free access for drugs and whatever they fancy. These mystery men get control of Poland as they are in control of power, water and resources. When the government of Russia is embarrassed, the ghosts walk in and take over Russia. Welcome back communist rule and Poland becomes their first victim." Mikal looked around the room and noticed the expressions on the others. He shook his head. "Too far-fetched?"

Thomas sighed. "I lived through communist rule as a kid. Believe me, you don't want them back. But who do we tell in the city, our state or our country? And how do we tell the Russian president? He won't believe that, but I do think what Mikal says makes sense."

Radoslaw said, "A few weeks ago, I thought all the criminal activity was a smoke screen. I am still not convinced it is a renegade Russian plot."

There was a knock on the door. Fabian was followed by Oskar. Fabian sat on an empty chair and showed his mobile. I have this horrible news. That creepy Anna Duba has invited me and Oskar to another of her dreadful cocktail parties. This time is a going away party. Yipee! Some company wanted her, a socialite to go to China, all-expense paid. When she comes back, she writes an article aimed at the over forty's market what China has in place for that age group."

"Are you going with her?" asked Eryk as he shot a wink at Oskar.

"Heaven forbid it. A solid week with the witch? I would never survive," he retorted.

Oskar sighed. "I won't be back to work for a few more weeks. Lydia is declining at a very fast rate. I must meet with the boys before they take another inland trip. I am collecting their guns and ammo and do up the trucks for the trip east. With luck, I may get to the source of the guns. I have been worming my way in. Puppy," he pointed to himself, "is happy to play message boy and they don't mind. I am being very efficient and effective in their eyes." Oskar looked at the maps and the paper with the listings. He shook his head. "And war hasn't even started." He left the room.

Fabian said when Oskar was well out of earshot, "He loves Lydia so much. He granted her a wish."

"What was that?" asked Natan.

"He married her in the hospital bed. Just the immediate parents and brothers and sisters. He is by her side all the time except for these short bursts of jobs for the mafia. He is doing a good job keeping everyone happy. I just hope he doesn't collapse at the wrong time. Pressure can take its toll."

Eryk looked at his mobile phone. "Szymon say your goodbyes. You are leaving now. Have you got your stuff ready?"

"Yes. Where am I going?"

"To the airport. But from there, I don't know," said Eryk.

Szymon gave his friends a final hug and thanked all in the room. Eryke escorted him out of the building and down to the underground carpark in the station. Both Eryk and Szymon got into the unmarked car and drove off.

On the way to the airport, the driver said, "We have a tail. The blue car three cars back. Get down. I am heading back to the station." The driver u-turned on the freeway and drove as fast as the on-coming traffic would permit. Eryk called the others in the station of the event.

Police cars were dispatched.

The driver zigzagged through the traffic with the blue car in pursuit. The police helicopter circled above giving commentary to those in the police station and those who were now in the chase.

The unmarked police car was now off the motorway but still on the wrong side of the road. It turned into a street and joined the normal traffic flow. Gun fire from tailing car pierced the window - narrowly missing Eryk and the driver. Eryk pushed Szymon's head down further and then stretched himself over Szymon. The car rolled before smashing into a light pole. The driver was dead. Eryk was locked over Szymon. Eryk felt arms pull him out before feeling the butt of a gun across the back of his head. Szymon was yanked out of the car. He screamed and kicked in front of by-standers and the slowing traffic. The unknown men dragging Szymon fired on the bystanders. Their bullets ricocheted off the pavement to fly at random directions. Most bystanders scattered while a couple hit the ground. Szymon was bungled into the tailing car and disappeared down a tunnel entrance. The above helicopter reported the incident and hovered to watch for the kidnapper's car. The blue car never came out. A switch had taken place in the tunnel.

Eryk was whisked away to hospital. Radoslaw and the others who were in the situation room cursed. Radoslaw cursed as he drove to the hospital. His mind was running faster than his car.

CHAPTER 22

Fabian took the others back to their safe house. "Pack. You're all leaving, now!"

There was flurry of activity. Mikal, Ivan and Stephan piled into Fabian's car. He drove west going towards the German border.

They drove for the rest of the day before diverting to the country town of Rzepin, about forty kilometres within the Polish border. They booked into the only bed and breakfast.

In the sanctuary of the shared bedroom, Mikal spoke to Ivan/ Peter, "So this is what you had to do in Britain, France and Germany."

Peter nodded. "Once we didn't even get a chance to pack. There are moles in the system. We escaped with the clothes on our back and anything in our wallets. We had to get new IDs. We will be safe tonight, but where we go from here is anyone's guess."

"Szymon is a big worry. Kidnapped. I thought they only stole kids, not adults," said Mikal.

"Once upon a time. Now anyone could disappear. It's all about money or ideology. No matter which way you look at it, it comes down to greed and power. Get some sleep if you can. Tomorrow will be an interesting day."

Thomas organised a picnic basket at the bed and breakfast. "We will be back later," he said to the clerk. The girl nodded. "I will keep the rooms until seven p.m. If you are not back by then, your belongings will be packed up and stored in the cupboard behind the desk" She pointed to the cupboard.

"Thanks," said Thomas as he paid for the night, they all just had. "I will make sure we get back before then. The clerk watched him disappear through the door. She continued with her work.

Fabian loaded everyone into the car. He was very concerned. "Eryk was badly injured. He will take a while to recover. Head injuries take time. Whoever hit Szymon and Eyrk has major fist power. We are going south east from here just for half a day. We need to get some ideas and that will determine where we go."

In the seclusion of the countryside, Fabian, Peter, Thomas and Mikal discussed what they were going to do. "Then that is settled. Tomorrow we head to Gdansk. Then sail to Saint Petersburg. Hiding under their noses will be interesting. Maybe we should do a tour of Moscow while we are in that direction. Anyone for casing the Kremlin?" Three hands popped up.

Mikal asked, "Does anyone speak Russian? I only know about six words."

Thomas said, "Not much. I am so rusty. I was made to learn it in primary school. My parents were disgusted it was compulsory. I wasn't permitted to practice speaking it at home. I am not sure if they expect tourists to speak Russian."

The next day they were on a small overnight ferry. They were crowded into a four-bunk shoe box size cabin. The weather was cooler than they expected. They bought warm clothes at the only shop on board. Peter commented, "Extortion prices." He slipped on the jacket.

In the early hours of the following morning, the group disembarked at Saint Petersburg. They went through customs without a hitch. They headed directly to the city via the courtesy coach which dropped them off at a fancy motel. They didn't go inside but walked across the road to a park where young adults and children were happy to feed the birds. They found themselves a bench, sat down to plan their next move. "We got to do better than flying by the seat of our pants," said Thomas.

Fabian just sighed. "You'll get used to it. That's what I do most times." He pointed to the large orthodox cathedral. "We might as well play tourist and have a look inside. I believe they are opulent. We can do with some divine intervention."

Having nothing better to do, they walked over to the cathedral where a small crowd had gathered. The doors opened. The priest welcomed the small group of ten people in two different languages, Russian and English. Another priest came forward and repeated the greeting in Latvian which made the other people smile. The tour lasted for twenty minutes. They were invited to stay for private worship. Fabian encouraged the other three to stay. He said softly to avoid the echoing of his voice in the now quiet church, "We need all the help we can. Stay. The big guy upstairs does assist. That old saying, God helps those who ask and tries to help themselves. It's true. So, let's put in a joint effort." From behind the cloisters the two priests watched the small group. They nodded their approval. One elbowed the other. "They are in trouble. Let's give them a hand." The priests began a set of prayers.

When the group left the church, Peter stopped walking as they all passed a patisserie. Peter whispered, "The food in the window looks nice but for some reason, I get a bad vibe from the place. Move away quickly." Thomas looked into the shop. He stood at the door. An assistant greeted him with a smile. He waved back. He turned around. "A cute assistant. Very cute. Yeah, you're right, the vibe is bad."

Fabian lingered before deciding to go in. He looked at the food in the display cabinet. The assistant tried to encourage a sale by explaining the items and giving them a name. Fabian glanced up occasionally. He frowned at what he glimpsed. He played at being fussy but had one eye on the open door behind the counter. It allowed him to see down a narrow passageway. A door open and closed. A heavily tattooed man went from one door to another. Fabian thought he heard crackling sounds of a communication system. Muffled words drifted out; some were in Russian, some in English and one which made him pique his interest. The words were in Polish. He smiled at the assistant and then left.

"Let's get out of here. We are in mafia central. But before we do, line up in front of the shop. I want a photo of this place," said Fabian. The others complied and began to carry on like crazy tourists. Fabian could see through the phone camera, the shop assistant shaking her head. He could read her expression calling them idiots. The tattooed man walked out. His big frame filling the doorway. "Scoot," he said in Russian. The group moved on taking more photos of the shop next door. Fabian made sure the next series of pictures included the statuesque man. They moved to two more shops repeating the same merriment. When the man disappeared into the shop, Fabian sent the photo to Radoslaw with a message.

Look up this guy.

The group found a cheap motel six blocks away. They checked into two share rooms. A seven that night, they met again in the bar next door. Fabian said, "Radoslaw was very quick to get a result. The monster in the patisserie is a mafia. He is red tagged at Interpol. We accidentally found a big fish."

Mikal muttered under his breath, "I want to burn his place down. He has organised our destruction. Now I want to see how he feels when he gets a taste of his own medicine." Fabian and Thomas both said "Shh!" Fabian continued, "You don't want to end up in a Russian jail. If the inmates don't kill you, the cold will. I do understand your sentiments. Now enjoy the evening. We go to Moscow tomorrow."

In the early hours of the morning, Mikal woke Peter up. "Want to create a bit of havoc? Give Mr. Mafia a taste of his own medicine?"

"Sounds like a good idea. But the place would be loaded with security."

"Hmm. Your right. But we can cut the power or have fun with some water. I know how to cut power. I know how to flood the place. I've done it before. No tools needed."

Peter hesitated. "I'm not really in favour. I want to stay low.'

"Come on. This is for Szymon and Antoni."

Slowly Peter dressed. "If we get caught, we are history."

Mikal and Peter approached the patisserie but stopped three shops away. They looked for cameras. "Too many," said Peter. He tugged on Mikal's arm. "Let's go back." They walked back a short distance before Mikal checked again for cameras. None were visible.

"The stormwater. Let's go down the stormwater."

"Not without torches. The place will be crawling with furry creatures and assorted bugs."

"Then keep watch." Mikal went down on his knees and pulled up the heavy grill. He disappeared inside. Peter looked at his watch. He called out, "Twenty minutes and get out."

Mikal's voice echoed a reply. "Okay."

In the dark Mikal used his phone as a torch. He walked comfortably down a few tunnels and guessing which fork would lead him to what he was looking for. He found a platform with some machinery. He went up the steps to check it out. It was exactly what he was looking for - the industrial pump. He moved the torch around to look for switches. He flicked one switch. The overhead light came on. He studied the gauges to look for another switch. He found a large lever in the down position. He moved the lever up. He watched the gauges to see what would happen. Slowly the dials started to move towards zero. The sound of the motor in the pump came to a stop. He wiped his fingerprints off with the bottom of his shirt. He left the motor to retrace his steps back to the manhole.

He started to move faster as he felt the water touching his shoes. The drain was starting to fill. He ran as fast as he could to the opening where he entered, the one Peter was still guarding. He clambered out and shut the grill. Peter stood back a few feet. "Gee you stink."

Mikal smiled. "One pump is switched off. Ideally, we need two to be off. One will flood the area nice and slow. Then the pressure builds up. Bang! Let's get moving. The water is starting to come up the pipes and a nice street fountain will magically appear. The water will go down the slope and hopefully into the patisserie."

The next morning, the council was fixing the stormwater. The shops between the stormwater entrance and the patisserie entrance showed minor flooding. Just ankle deep and enough to cause trade to stop and replacement of some furnishings. The group walked past the patisserie, Thomas asked the cute assistant, "What had happened?"

"Water damage. We had to throw out the food. The water caused a short in the fridges and freezers. The underground pumps failed. The other shops are not too bad. The boss is very angry. He lost his favourite toy. Well, that is what I call it. The lazy bastard sits all day at his electronics and talks to everyone but to his customers. The flooding nearly caused a fire."

"Sorry to hear that. It looks like we don't get any goodies today," said Thomas as he slowly turned to the others.

The men hired a car and headed towards Moscow. Mikal and Peter couldn't wipe the smiles off their faces. Fabian eventually said, "Did you two have a hand at that natural disaster?"

"I confess," said Mikal. "They can have some inconvenience. What a shame the place didn't go up."

Thomas looked at Peter. "What was your role?"

"Watchman on the street," replied Peter then he quickly added, "Divine assistance was granted."

Fabian gasped. "Don't abuse divine help. Were there any cameras?"

Mikal answered, "We did see heaps of cameras and doubled back to the stormwater where there were no cameras. That was when the decision to go underground was made. No cameras. No security. People in their right minds don't go into those places. It is only because they fear of getting lost and sudden gushes of water sweeping them away. No pumps to keep the water flowing means water backs up. Pressure increases and hey, presto! A fountain emerges. Simple."

Just who taught you that stuff?" asked Fabian.

"Uni. Szymon and workers in their company. We needed to go down pipes and make sure all the pipes linked to the right outlets. You can't always be sure from above. Dad would sometimes go down. On house construction, no need to worry as the infrastructure is in place and the pipes are near the surface. But big complexes and tall buildings, it is necessary to do a visual check," explained Mikal.

"You better hope, that there were no other cameras watching you go in and out. That is all I am worried about," said Thomas.

CHAPTER 23

The men parked their car in an underground carpark. They walked two blocks to Red Square. Their eyes wandered over to the Kremlin. Fabian gasped. "This place is massive."

Mikal waved them forward. "Come on. This way to tours."

The group paid their fee and joined the large tour group.

The guide took them to the permitted areas. Cameras beamed down at every angle and at every person. Mikal and Peter studied their locations. Some rotated as if following a person, others were stationery. Fabian and Thomas were transfixed on the interior. The enormity of the building silencing them. The tour ended after an hour. Fabian and Thomas nodded their heads, satisfied at what they saw and learned. Mikal and Peter blew a puff of air. "Incredible. All so controlled. Did you notice, they didn't answer any questions people had unless it related to the artwork?"

Peter confirmed, "Yep. Mentally tiring with so much information. We only saw a drop. The real workings are well-hidden behind closed doors. After we grab a bite to eat, how about a long walk around the outside. It must be at least five kilometres."

"Fabian, Dad, are you two up for a perimeter walk?"

Thomas wiped beads of sweat. "The car would be faster."

"No we need to study the place," said Peter. "We need slower transport and look more like tourists."

"Can we hire bicycles? It would be faster," replied Thomas who was thinking of his age and fitness level.

Mikal looked around the area and walked towards Red Square. There was a booth to hire bikes and electric scooters beside a very busy café. "Over there on the other side of the Square."

The four men hired bikes which were significantly cheaper. It took them an hour to ride slowly around the Kremlin – pedestrians walking without really looking crossed their paths or they would stop and look at the gardens surrounding the building. That was Thomas's request. Most of the time Thomas and Fabian led the way. Peter and Mikal studied the entrances.

They noted there were ten main entrances with varying degrees of importance. Each of these entrances had more official looking driveways or slightly grandiose paths leading to doors. Then there were much smaller side doors which did not always have associated gates or even paths leading to them. They were small and set back – almost unnoticeable to the public. No matter where you looked, security was tight. Peter and Mikal couldn't help themselves making mental notes where each of these doors were.

At their modest motel, Fabian and Thomas groaned at their stiff muscles. After dinner, Fabian and Thomas wanted was bed. Mikal and Peter decided night life was more their style.

Mikal and Peter crossed the road where a bar was full of young people, dancing to loud music and drinking assorted beverages. Mikal struck up a conversation with a local girl, Alena while Peter struck up a conversation with Irina. In spite of the language differences, they made themselves understood to each other. As the night at the venue was coming to closing, both women invited them to their shared home.

Both women walked them to a large rundown house. Mikal and Peter stopped at the gate. For some unknown reason, both hesitated going in. Mikal pulled Peter aside. "This was too easy. Something is not right. We quit while we are ahead."

Peter nodded. "Okay, we give these two something to talk or fume about. Whatever. Ready?"

"Ready for what?" asked Mikal.

"Pretend to be gay." Peter slipped his arm over Mikal's shoulder and both walked away. Mikal glanced over his shoulder. The women were dumbfounded, mouths open and silent.

They let go of each other when they were one block away. The women were now inside. "I want to go back. Something about that place smells. Just outside," said Mikal.

"Yeah. Something is off. A cat den?"

"Maybe."

Mikal and Peter went back to the gates of the house. They stood, watched and listened. Loud voices floated through. Sounds of cries followed. Peter and Mikal hesitated. "I think the girls are getting bashed up. They didn't bring in business. What do we do?"

"Call the cops? We can't make ourselves understood. Wait. Watch."

"We wait under the tree," said Peter.

The noise in the house died down. Irina was first to exit. She was quickly followed by Alena.

The big man from the patisserie from St. Petersburg was blocking the doorway, yelling at the women.

"Oh, fuck," swore Mikal. "That mountain of a man is everywhere with his bad odour."

"Let's get out of here."

Mikal and Peter ran down the dark street. They ran down the steps to a railway station. They jumped the ticket gate and down the platform. They looked over their shoulder to see if anyone was in pursuit. "Railway guards! Run," said Peter. They ran down the nearest deserted platform and back up another set of stairs which took them to another exit. They jumped the exit gate and ran down another street. It was a dead end. Lost. They sat down on the moist grass and laughed.

"I am now geographically embarrassed," laughed Peter as he pulled out his phone to go to the navigator app.

He pointed. "We go back out of this dead end. And turn left." The navigation app started to play up. It started to flash. Then another map formed. "Okay. My battery must be nearly dead. The phone is playing up. It's starting to flicker between one set of maps and another."

"Not possible. There is some big magnetic thing around. Let's go to the end of the street and get another reading," suggested Mikal as he pulled out his own phone which was doing a similar thing.

It was close to three in the morning when Mikal and Peter flopped on their motel beds. They were dead to the world in an instant.

Fabian and Thomas knocked on their door at nine. Fabian called through the door, "Wake up you two. Time to go."

No answer. "Are they inside?"

"I think so. Ivan err I mean Peter generally texts a message if he does an all-nighter. I will get a concierge to open up."

Fifteen minutes later the door was open. Peter and Mikal were fast asleep and not responding too well to being shaken. "Go away," slurred Mikal.

"Big night, eh," said Fabian, "With some girls, no doubt."

Mikal rolled over slurring, "The patisserie hulk was watch dog. Ran so mu…."

Fabian looked up at Thomas. "We give them one more hour and then we force them out."

At eleven Fabian and Thomas were at Peter's and Mikal's door. "Hey, sleeping beauties, rise and shine," called Fabian through the door. "It's eleven o'clock. The world awaits and needs your presence." Mikal stumbled out of bed and wiped his eyes as he opened the door.

Peter sleepily gave a salute. "What did you two do this time?" asked Thomas.

Peter slowly rolled over. "Chatted up a couple of birds, walked them home. Because we didn't go in, the girls were assaulted by that very same bastard who owns the patisserie in St. Petersburg. We ran to a station. Then the guards started chasing us because we jumped the gates. We didn't catch a train. Jumped another exit gate and ran blindly down some streets. We got lost. We tried using the navigation on the phone, but it played up. It was flashing two maps."

"That sounded very eventful," said Thomas.

"My legs ache," complained Mikal.

"Mine too," added Peter as he looked towards his father. "What are we going to do for the rest of the day?"

Fabian said, "I had to return the hire car. You can show us where the gorilla lives and just maybe go to where the phones played up. Flashing maps sounds very interesting."

Peter and Mikal sat up on their separate beds, their attention totally captured. "Yeah that last place was weird. I would like to check that out but not overly keen to go near that house," said Mikal.

Mikal pointed out the house which Irina and Alena led them to. Mikal said, "I am not knocking on that door to see if the girls are alright. They may have that man there expecting the women to do their stuff. I really don't feel like finding out how hard the man hits if we say, not interested in the merchandise." Fabian took a photo of the house and typed in the address. He sent it to Radoslaw.

The group walked to the station. Peter pointed out, "We ran in here and came out…" He bobbed his head around trying to see the other exit to another street. Mikal pointed to the spot. "Over there. Then we ran down that street. Did we turn left or right?"

Peter shrugged. "I can't recall. But we did end up in a dead-end. That was where the maps went berserk."

"Let's go there and see if it happens again - maps going funny," said Fabian.

When they reached the other side of the station, Peter led them to the corner and stopped. "This is where I can't recall which way we went. We'll go left and see if anything looks familiar then come back before we go right."

Mikal looked on. "Funny, I can't recall which direction either. Two of us not recalling is very odd."

Fabian pondered for a while. "I am going to google something. We don't move from here until I get some info." Fifteen minutes later he put the phone away. "Okay. A theory. Not a good one. It's called electro-magnetic field. You two accidently walked into a field. Powerful fields can wipe a person's memory. If subjected to multiple attacks, the memory change is permanent. You two experienced a possible attack. Your memory should come back. Shall we go left to start with?"

Thomas looked around trying to find something which could radiate such a field. There was a communications tower. "Let's go to the tower first and see if anything happens. Some people say the towers emit electro-magnetic fields and causes cancer. That is if you are in the presence of the towers long term."

"I don't recall any towers. Certainly not their big steel legs," replied Peter.

"It was dark. We were panicking and running blind. We could have missed the structure. It's worth a shot," commented Mikal.

The group walked towards the tower. "Sorry," said Peter, "This doesn't seem right. I really can't recall."

Mikal pulled out his phone, "The phone looks normal on navigation." He put the phone in his pocket.

Fabian looked at the area directly under the tower. He frowned as he walked to the other side where there was a distinct clearing of about fifteen metres. He pointed to the dead foliage. "This area is sterile." He walked around the edge where sickly plants were obviously living out their last days. "No bugs. No ants. No form of animal life." He peered deeper into the bushes and waved the others towards what he was looking at. He pulled out his phone and opened the navigation app.

"It's going crazy." The others also went to the app on their own phones. They saw the maps flashing. Then Thomas felt a low humming sound hitting the pit of his stomach. "Let's get out of here while that thing is going on."

They all ran back a distance. Mikal was confused. "I don't recall being in the bushes or hearing that sound."

Then he noticed he and the other three were rubbing their heads. Things were starting to be foggy.

They assisted each other to move back further down the street. "What the hell was that?" asked Thomas.

"Wrong question," said Fabian. "What are the Russians doing and hiding? Towers don't do that. Something is down there or around it. We better not go there unless we feel up to it. If it restarts when we are in very close proximity, then we know it is a deterrent for something the public should not know about."

They sat on the edge of the footpath waiting for the effects of the electro-magnetic field to fade away. Voices coming from behind them made them turn. Two men who looked like they were in their sixties and wearing expensive suits appeared. The group looked at the men who stared back at them. In Russian, one man said as his face turned grim. "Get out of here."

Thomas translated for the group. "They want us to move." He asked the men for direction in broken Russian. "We are lost. Tourists. Lost." The man looked at the group up and down.

"The main road to Red Square is that way." He pointed to the right. The two men continued walking in the direction they were pointing to the group. "Let's follow," said Fabian. "Something is still not right. I thought Red Square was further away and more in that direction." He pointed south west.

The men they were following got into an official car which met them at a bus stop on the main road. As the car drove off slowly in the heavy traffic, Fabian took a picture. He sent it to Radoslaw with a message:

Two men in a government car going to Red Square. Check the car and the men out.

To the others. "Let's have a bite to eat and then we go back. Men dressed like that don't materialise out of bushes."

Back at the tower, the group noted the noise was no longer humming through the air. Their minds were clear. They searched the bushes where the two strangers seemed to have materialised. Mikal called the others to have a look at what appeared to be a very large tree stump. In fact, it was made from resin carefully crafted to look like a stump. It blended in so perfectly, that no one would look twice.

The group gathered around the stump. "There has to be an opening somewhere. Tap, press, pull all parts of it," said Mikal. Nothing happened. Thomas sat down to rest. But when he stood up, he tripped over what appeared to be protruding root. A door opened. A narrow staircase led downwards to an unknown place.

"Let's go," said Peter as if he was reliving a part of his childhood exploring drains in his home area.

He went first. He passed a sensor. Lights went on. The narrow stair well stopped at a train platform.

They all looked in wonder. This was a station built in the forties or fifties going by the structural style. It was pristine and showed no sign of ever being used, except for today.

"Which way do we go?" asked Thomas as his eyes surveyed for cameras.

"The ticket counter is down there. Let's go there and see if there is a map," said Fabian.

The ticket office was open. A yellowed map graced one wall. Their location was clearly indicated with a red arrow. Thomas racked his brain trying to recall the Russian he had learned in school.

"Fascinating," he mumbled. "This was built in the height of the communist rule. It goes around the city in a circle and connects to stations which radiate outwards to different outlying areas. It doesn't say why it was built. We can only conjecture – rapid deployment of soldiers to an uprising or escape routes for the ruling elite should the people rebel. The entry we came through is a new addition. It isn't marked.

Someone is using this system for their own purposes." He pointed to a series of rooms. "Now these rooms look like they all belong to the by-gone era. Shall we look?"

The group walked down the platform; their steps echoing in the quietness. The first door, Thomas read, "Men's room." He went inside and looked around. "Someone has been using it. Paper, soap and a few drops of soap on the porcelain. Excuse me. I might as well use it too."

The next room was a ladies' room. No paper. No evidence of it being used. A thick layer of dust confirmed the room was not in use. They moved on to another room. Fabian turned the old-style knob. Empty. No signs of it being used.

The next room along looked as if was recently used. It smelled of disinfectant. It was scrubbed clean. They wondered who and what it was used for. Fabian suggested it was being prepared for usage. They opened a door to the rear of this room. It contained cleaning products and a wet mop, obviously a cleaner's storeroom. The group moved on.

The next room contained a shower. The floor was wet, and the old curtain showed signs of mildew. There was a cake of soap which was still moist, but the lather had died down. No towels of any description were to be seen. There was a bench just far enough away to keep clothes dry. "Someone had a bath recently," commented Mikal. They continued to the next room.

"Interesting", said Fabian. "It looks like a first aide room. He peered in the basket near a sink. "Someone had some treatment. Bandages with blood." The group went silent. Footsteps were heard coming down the platform. They hid themselves as best as they could in the room. The footsteps continued down the platform. Fabian peeked out.

Two uniformed men carrying a sports bag and a tray of food turned into a locked room further down. When the door was shut, Thomas followed. Thomas peered through a narrow and dusty window, only to see the room empty again. Then the men reappeared. They came out of what appeared to be an alcove. *Another door?* thought Thomas. Thomas scrambled back to the others. "Hide" he said in a loud whisper.

The uniformed men walked past the room in which the group were hiding. When their footsteps could no longer be heard, the group moved out of their hiding positions. Thomas said in a soft voice, "There is another room inside a room down a few doors. I think someone is inside."

Peter said, "We should take look. You don't take food and maybe a bag of clothes into a room and come out almost instantly and not carrying anything. We need to break in. Anyone up for that."

"I am," whispered Mikal.

Fabian pulled them back. "Thomas keep watch when we get inside. We will see what or who is in the second door in that room."

Not knowing what he would need. Mikal took one of two small first aid kits from the first aid room.

When they approached the main exterior door, Mikal gave it a test. The old-style lock with its large keyhole worked to their advantage. A long set of tweezers was used to jiggle the outer door lock. The door opened after several tries. While the others ventured deeper into the room, Thomas took position at the same window, this time peering out. He waved his hand for the others to continue. The others went to the alcove where they found a second locked door. Again, Mikal inserted the tweezers and any other tool which would slide into the lock. The door was more resistant, but it eventually gave way.

The room was dimly lit. It was bare except for a mattress on the floor and a coffee table. The bag the men were carrying earlier was placed on the crude bed and the tray of food was placed on an old coffee table.

Mikal built up the courage. "Anyone in here?" Silence. He turned on his phone to throw more light into the room.

Fabian went further into the shadows. "Anyone in here?" he repeated. Silence.

Peter's ears pricked when he heard the faintest of noises. "We are not going to hurt you. If anything, we will get you out."

Again, there was a soft sound of movement and then a whimper. Huddled in the darkest corner was a teenage boy quietly sobbing. Peter said in a gentler voice, "Hello. We are not going to hurt you. Show yourself." Mikal shone the light of the phone in that direction.

The voice was trembling, and the person tried curling into a smaller ball. In Russian, the voice said, "Go Away. No more. I can't take any more." The person sobbed more.

Fabian walked closer and said with broken Russian, "Shh! It's over. Let's get you out of here. Are there any others?"

The young boy, no older than seventeen, slowly revealed himself. Fabian said to Peter, "Get your father." Thomas came in behind Peter and gasped. "Good Lord. It's a kid. The poor child. What has been done to you?" The boy sobbed. "There is a chair they tie us up to. Then they put headphones on us. There is a noise and vibrations coming through the headphones. It makes us dizzy and sick to the stomach."

"Where are the others?" asked Fabian. Thomas translated.

"There is an older person. They are giving him a much rougher time. I don't know where they are keeping him," whimpered the youth.

"Get dressed. You're getting out and with us. I am Thomas and these are my friends. What exactly is this place?"

"A torture chamber," the boy replied. "My name is Kazmir."

"Kazmir, I am Thomas. This is Peter and a family friend Mikal, and this is Fabian. Fabian is a policeman helping us. We found this place by accident."

Kazmir gave a slight grin. He moved more freely in the room. He headed towards the bag of clothes and he dressed himself.

Kazmir joined the group outside his cell. He saw the platform for the first time without being in a daze. "A station! What station is this?" Kazmir asked.

Fabian replied, "One that is under the underground. A hidden piece of engineering some fifty plus years old. It is not supposed to exist."

"I don't think I exist either. What is the date?"

"The twentieth," said Thomas.

"I have been in that hole for nearly five days, I think," said Kazmir. "Thank you for getting me out."

"We better get moving," said Mikal.

They continued along the platform testing each door in turn. The third door let them in. They checked the room. It was empty and no alcove to a hidden room. They all froze and scurried into the shadows of the room corners. Voices and footsteps were heard coming in their direction. The two men in suits who they met a few hours earlier were back. The men frowned at the door which was opened and shut it. One pulled out a set of keys and locked it. "Lazy staff," he grumbled to the other.

Thomas waited a minute before unlocking the door from the inside. He signalled to the others to follow when he thought it was safe.

Thomas led the group onto the tracks. Hiding behind the platform wall in the pit, they waited until the men reappeared. This time the men walked a short distance along the platform and into a room which was the cleaner's storeroom. The men never reappeared.

The group waited nearly ten minutes before Peter said, "I am going into that room and into the cleaner's room. We obviously missed something." He climbed onto the platform, ran to the outer door, opened it before going into the cleaner's room and disappeared inside. Peter turned on the phone for light and studied the room more carefully. At the left side and half concealed by a set of shelves, was a door. As he opened the door, a sensor light turned on. He went up the stairs to what was another cleaner's storage room. He opened the door. He was on the platform of the railway station which he and Mikal ran the night before. He returned to the others within minutes.

"You're not going to believe this, when you go through that room and into the cleaner's storeroom, on the left is another door which takes you to the underground. It's another entrance."

The others climbed out. Fabian asked Kazmir, "Take us to the room with the chair."

Kazmir shook his head. "Not going back there. Not ever."

Mikal grinned. "How about helping me wreck the equipment?"

"You mean vandalise it?"

Mikal nodded. "Yeah, stuff up the workings on the inside but everything to look normal outside. With luck, it goes up in smoke."

Kazmir smirked and nodded. "But I don't know which room I was in. I was always drugged up and a bag over my head. All know it isn't far from here."

"Then we test each door," said Thomas who was now finding translation becoming easier with memories of school days Russian slowly returning.

The group heard voices again. Quickly they opened the nearest door, a room they had never been in. They hid themselves as best as they could. Peter was observing the outside through the dusty window.

He saw two men wearing white laboratory coats and carrying clip-boards. The men walked into the room next door. It was signed with the words 'customer lounge'. The white coated men were quickly fol-lowed by the two suited men. These men were not the same as the men before. However, they wore equally expensive suits. Seconds later, two uniformed men wearing military police uniforms were seen dragging a semi-unconscious man.

Peter who had his eye peeking over the edge of the dirty glass win-dow ledge, gulped. His eyes popped at what who he saw. "Szymon?" he whispered loudly. He squatted down, spun around to the others and whispered again, "It's Szymon. The bastards are torturing Szymon." The others moved to the window and popped their eyes over the edge and back down again. "What is he doing here?"

Fabian guessed. "Brainwashing him to do their bidding. Disposable soldier. Fall guy. Who knows for sure."

"What can we do to stop the session?" asked Thomas.

"Blow the place up, but with what?" asked Mikal.

"We can go the generator room," suggested Kazmir.

"Show us the way," said Mikal.

When Peter signalled all was clear, Kazmir led the way to the generator. "I saw the generator when I first came. We, my brother and I, accidentally stumbled into this place. My brother tripped on a trees stump which opened a door."

Fabian said, "Thomas tripped over the same stump. That's how we found the place."

Kazmir continued, "We were opening and closing everything. Exploring as you did. In a way it was amusing. We were looking at some plans which I think wasn't very accurate – maybe misleading on purpose. Come this way." He led them back to the rail pit.

Kazmir ran beside the rails all the time bent over. He stopped halfway back from where they came. He pointed. "The ladies toilets have a big mirror. It is a door to the generator room."

How did you know that?" asked Thomas. Kazmir was now find-ing his brain was becoming clearer and a few memories re-emerging. "When my brother and I discovered this place, we opened and closed every door we could. When we were about to leave, there was a vibrat-ing sound. The floor shook a little. The mirror moved like a door.

We looked inside and saw it was the generator room. We ran out and smack into the hands of two soldiers who you saw earlier. One shot my brother. He died instantly." Kazmir started to cry at the remerging memory. He repeated, "They killed my brother. They shot him. I don't know what they did with his body. Someone yelled. I was attacked by someone wearing a white lab coat. He said, I was going to be their test subject. He also was angry at the soldiers for shooting my brother. They kept me to be a test animal. The generator is very odd. It has massive coils and what I think are magnets. Huge magnets which would make your arms stick to it if you wore anything metal. I was given a demo. They put cuffs on me. I flew through the air and stuck to the machinery. I couldn't move. They had to turn it off to release me. They said next time, I would be fed into the machine itself. I wasn't sure if they were bullshitting me or not. I didn't want to find out. They most probably dumped my brother's body and maybe make out I was the killer." Kazmir drew in a deep breath and wiped away tears.

"A magnetron creating electro-magnetic energy," said Mikal who was trying to recall some university physics.

The group entered the generator room. They stared at the size. Mikal said, "No wonder the phones went crazy. Okay let's get to work."

"What do we do to make it fail?" asked Kazmir.

Mikal walked around the room and looked up at the overhead pipes. "I don't know what is in the pipes, but I am making an educated guess. Water or oil. If we puncture the pipes, just small holes, and the water or oil drips slowly out, the drips should go on the copper coils and make them heat up. Steam or instant fire. The pressure should drop. We need to put a second hole in a pipe over here so the exiting water or oil leaks over the electrical box. The breakdown won't occur that quickly, but it will occur and hopefully cause a fire. It will be interesting to see the fire brigade locates the seat of the fire in a place which is not supposed to exist. Unfortunately, Szymon will have to endure another round of torture."

All the men searched the room for a possible tool to jab the pipes. Fabian found a toolbox with very basic tools. He opened the box, "I've found a toolbox loaded with tools," he said rather loudly. Mikal took a large screwdriver out. He walked to where the pipes clustered on one side of the room. He systematically jabbed each one. Instantly water started to flow out. *The cooling system*, thought Mikal. He gave a grin. He ordered the others to start leaving the room and go to the rail pit. Then he went to another set of pipes which were directly over the main magnet. He struggled to punch a hole into the much thicker pipe. A much smaller hole was made and it slowly dripped oil. In the section near the electricity box, he made another hole in the pipe. He didn't know what was going to drip out. He struck oil. Puff! All the lights went out. He ran out of the room to hide with the others.

The emergency lights came on giving an eerie yellow glow. They watched the two military policemen run to the generator room. The two suited men stood on the platform searching for something or someone which shouldn't be there. One lab coated man came out and spoke to the two men. They all went inside.

Szymon was dragged out of a room and dumped on a bench. He was unsupervised. The chair of horrors was pushed out to the platform, squeaking in protest to the two lab coated men. They were making preparation to lift and tie Szymon into the chair when they were called back to the room by the well-suited men. Szymon tried to stand up. He wobbled a few steps and fell. No one paid attention. The military police were occupied trying to put the fire out in the generator room. The lab coated men and the suited men were in the chamber of horrors. What they were trying to do or save was anyone's guess. It was unimportant now, Szymon was.

The group quickly climbed out of their hiding pace and snatched Szymon. He tried putting up a fight until he heard their voices. "Szymon, it's Mikal."

"Szymon. It's Peter or Ivan whatever you remember."

Szymon stop resisting and gave a faint smile before passing out. They dragged him to an empty room which led to the cleaner's storeroom and up the narrow stairwell. In the underground station, they emerged one by one. Szymon was hoisted over Peter's shoulder. Passers-by looked. Fabian shoved an empty beer bottle from a rubbish bin into Szymon's hands giving the appearance the person was well over the consumption limit. Thomas shoved a 50 ruble note into the guard's hand for a supposed journey. The guard looked at the note and signalled them through. They disappeared down the street to a cab rank.

They went directly to the cheap motel where they were still booked in. Fabian phoned Radoslaw to organise a jet to Helsinki, Finland. "We leave the country now," ordered Fabian.

We catch the train to Saint Petersburg and then get a bus into Finland."

"Two big problems," said Thomas. "Szymon and Kazmir don't have passports."

Fabian muttered, "Here goes my career. We smuggle them out. We better not get caught.

On the train trip to Saint Petersburg, Thomas translated the news he heard on the radio.

"The large fire at the station near Red Square was deliberately lit. Five men, one of whom was being carried, were seen coming out of the storeroom, the seat of the fire. The fire has caused the popular railway station to be closed and will remain closed until the police determine the exact cause.

"That's us," said Thomas after translating the news. "They will never disclose the exact cause but use us as patsies."

Kazmir commented, "Good-bye to a nightmare place. I bet the station's existence will never be exposed to the public. It should be."

Thomas thought about his past and the missing homeless people. "It was built by the old communist government swallowing millions of rubles and making people starve. I bet crims or slave labour built the place."

Thomas patted the teen's shoulder and smiled. "I was destitute once and living in the streets. Other homeless people disappeared. I was constantly hiding at night trying to avoid being scooped up. I bet the homeless of that time built that place. When they were too ill or weak, they disappeared forever. It was a horrible time for me. I do not want to talk about it. Life goes on. But you, young man, endured something I didn't, the effects of that machine. And that machine is a new invention, not something from the past."

In Saint Petersburg, they explored the ways of smuggling Kazmir and Szymon into Finland. It drew a blank. They turned their attention to the port where they split up to find a boat which would take them to Kotha, Finland.

The group didn't have any luck until late in the afternoon. Fabian found a small trawler with a shifty skipper who was willing for a small sum of money for each passenger to ferry them to Kotha. He made it clear the people would have to work as deckhands to make their presence look more legitimate. Having not much of a choice, Fabian agreed to the deal - two thousand euros per head. No amount of bargaining was going to sway the man.

Again, Fabian called Radoslaw. After some heated words, Radoslaw organised the money to be transferred into the fisherman's account.

When the boat arrived in Kotha, Szymon and Kazmir were placed in large icy containers. They wore a thick layer of warm clothes. Layers of plastic were wrapped around them to help keep some of the moisture and fish odour off their body. Two straws were inserted in their mouths. Fish were poured over them followed by ice. The others walked through customs.

Szymon's and Kazmir's containers were directed to the depot where fish were left for sorting and dispersing. Szymon's container was earmarked for a town some twenty kilometres away. Kazmir's box was bought by a local restaurant.

The hired fisherman saw Szymon's container being loaded onto the back of a refrigerated truck. He distracted the driver with a mix of conversation and offers of an all-expense paid night out while the others went into the back to rescue Szymon.

Kazmir's box was still waiting for collection. He took a gamble after realising the noise of people and vehicles could no longer be heard. He opened the unlocked box by pushing up on the lid. As he climbed out, he looked around to see a mass of dead fish on the floor. Still wearing thick clothes bound with plastic, he bolted out of the complex towards the gate where he waited behind some industrial bins. While he was waiting, he removed the plastic off his clothes. All he could do was wait for the others to return.

At the local bar where the fisherman booked in to the small but clean rooms for their overnight stay, Szymon sat in the tub soaking up the warm water. Kazmir was in another room, doing a similar thing. Thomas had taken their clothes and put them through the wash twice trying to remove the stubborn odour of fish. At the end he tossed the cloths away and bought each of them fresh clothes from the few local shops which were still open.

The bus trip to Helsinki was uneventful. Szymon was looking much better but evidence of memory loss frustrated him. There were flashes, but incoherent. At times Peter and Thomas were able to fill the gaps. The nightmares continued – torture of the electromagnetic energy entering his brain alternated with shootings of people he once knew and who he killed. Being covered with fish didn't help. That was added to the mix. He was now never sure if he was safe but he knew he was confused.

Kazmir took the event in his stride. He was now becoming his old self but there were still scars. He avoided recliners of any colour or model. The fear of being restrained in such seats still overpowered him. Knowing he was going to Poland, excited him. But it also saddened him that he could never return home. The unknown men would pin his brother's death on him and the fire at the station could also be added. Arson was a serious crime, especially of government property. He resigned to never going back to his family. That was his cross to bear. He thought about using social media to contact his parents but was warned of its danger. The unknown men, most likely from the Kremlin, would have people watching the internet. They would come after him no matter where he hid himself. His family and friends would be watched. That would be a given. He was now isolated with new people who had saved his life. New friends with new connections.

In Helsinki the group caught a taxi to the airport. They were met by the local police and border force, interviewed and then ushered to the waiting jet.

They were met by Radoslaw in a minivan and whisked away to the countryside. In an overcrowded cottage, each gave their version of what had happened. Radoslaw sighed, when he sat down trying to make sense of Szymon's and Kazmir's kidnappings. The rescues, he knew were accidental discoveries. He was satisfied. Peter and Thomas would return to their posts at the Flower Company. Szymon and Kazmir would remain at the cottage to receive medical assistance and all paid for by Thomas who also insisted in reimbursing the cost of the fishing trip.

With Fabian adding new information, the trawler they were in was just another link in the drug trade. The fisherman was too ready to accept their company. They were given free reign of the boat and in that time, Fabian took pictures of the packets of drugs headed for Finland. Details were forwarded to the Finish authorities. They would organise their own watch and seizures.

Mikal was now back at university trying to catch up on ten days of missed lessons. He decided only to do two of what he considered to be lighter subjects. He sat at the computer watching the recorded lessons. His concentration was poor; distracted as too many events ran through his head. He was always on guard for his own safety. He could be kidnapped just like Szymon. With difficulty, he pieced together an assignment which added to 15 per cent of his marks. He felt it wasn't his best work but knew it would suffice. He knew it would be a pass but not to the standard he would normally submit. He then phoned his father at his office to see what was going on.

CHAPTER 24

Mikal met his father two days later. They embraced before sitting down to a meal in a small tucked away restaurant in a suburb well away from the home.

Mikal explained his recent trip to Russia. "I will never be able to go back. I am sure I will be wanted. Dad, I want to help someone who assisted us to save Szymon. Like me, he cannot return to Russia. The invisible men will make the murder of his brother and the fire at the station be all his fault. The experiences of the torture in that machine, has given him mental problems which Thomas, I mean Stefan is paying for the therapy. I also need some too after what I have been through. I would like Kazmir to stay with us and rebuild his life and get him some education."

Mikal senior looked thoughtfully at Mikal and smiled. "Now you are being a philanthropist. Not a bad thing." He shook a finger. "Just don't get over generous to your own detriment."

They ate in silence for a few minutes. Mikal Senior was struggling with what he had to say next.

"Julia's parents' bodies were found in the Black Forest in Germany. Some hikers found the bodies. Shot and dumped. There is no word about Julia. Is Szymon capable of handling that news?"

Mikal shook his head. "I am not sure. Half his memory is erased. I think we may have to keep that bit quiet for a while. Anything can set him back. It is much easier if he recalls himself, well at least recalling who Julia was to him. Then it will be time to tell him. Now tell me about Thea."

Mikal senior threw back his head and gave a short laugh. "I showed her the will she wants. Not ratified or registered under the law. The will wasn't signed either. I had my fingers on the spot. She doesn't know the difference or procedures. The will which you inherit everything was ratified and registered two days later. It was drawn up at the same time by the family's lawyer. Your copy of the will is kept at the lawyer's office as a safeguard. The registration had to be delayed by two days as a minimum precaution in case the one for Thea magically appeared with a false signature. It is always the last will which overrides anything else.

"The one she believes is for her also has small print which she did not read, and I did not point out. It says, if I am found dead, she goes to jail and the recording is evidence of that. If she doesn't kill me herself, she still goes for conspiracy. She goes to jail no matter what. Our lawyer has a copy of the recording and the original is in a custody box in our bank in Poznan." He slipped a copy of the bank details and passwords to Mikal. "Hide it," he ordered. "Don't try committing it to memory, you have too much stuff going on in your head."

"The papers for the divorce are being drawn up. They will be ready next week. She gets all the jewellery she bought with my money. She gets the apartment on the third floor in the apartment building which we own. There is a clause which states she can live there free until the council gives us consent to redevelop the site. The entire building will be knocked down. She will be forced to move out. All the owners of the apartments have taken one of the two offers we have provided them. Take the money and run or use their current apartment as a deposit for the new. They get a slightly larger apartment and in the same position they are now living. Only ten of the thirty people have taken that offer. There is no such offer for Thea with her apartment. The apartment is still in the company's name when she moves in and she has no recourse to action by accepting the apartment. She won't have anywhere to go but she will find another sucker. People like that always survive."

"How long will the apartment redevelopment take place?" asked Mikal.

"It has been lodged. You know all the steps and the slow process. I give it two years," replied Mikal senior.

"Have you had the office debugged and checked for other spy stuff?"

"Yes. A few cameras with voice recording were found. One in the men's room where people wash their hands. One in the staff room and one in my office. No one has hacked into the computer systems, but checks are being done on a monthly basis. Are you sure about the Russian involvement in all this pipe construction stuff?"

"More so now than ever. When I saw what they had done to Szymon, I was very angry. He's a mess. I think we got to him in time before he was totally irretrievable. What the purpose of the brain wiping, is only conjecture – train to go against his own country, an assassin. Who knows? Szymon was training to join the Olympic team for all styles of rifle shooting.

"He was very good. We had a feral animal permit. The government had issued them one summer to help rangers remove feral pigs, goats, cats and dogs out of the national park. On one camping trip, the camp was just set up. It was early evening and we just put on a pot of water for the dehydrated packaged meals. We heard the cat meow. The animal was black with one white patch no bigger than the palm of your hand. Szymon just picked up the rifle and without taking time to aim like I would do, shot the thing. Bang. Plop. The dead creature fell out of the tree above us and straight down just missing the campfire by centimetres."

Mikal senior suggested, "They want a sniper for some purpose. Being from another country, he would be expendable. They were starting to break him down, wipe his memory and then retrain him for some nasty event. Just how did you know he was there?"

"We didn't. Ivan or I should say Peter and I hit the local pub. I told you before."

Mikal leaned back on his seat, "You created an explosion which destroyed over half of the station. What did you do?"

"I just punched holes in different pipes and let nature do the rest. I was expecting a localised fire not for it to spread into the station above or explode. They didn't mention on the Russian news of the explosion, just fire. They are trying to pin the fire and explosion on all of us. The real culprits, those men if ever found, have some explaining to do."

"You have a knack for sabotaging. I just hope those people don't see your talent and kidnap you."

"I am a bit edgy." Mikal's junior phone rang. "Radoslaw has sent a car for me. It's downstairs. I better go. Keep in touch." Both Mikals stood up to leave the restaurant. Mikal senior gave his son a quick hug and watched him be driven away.

Mikal senior slowly walked to his car. He cursed. Someone slashed his tyres. He called the police and took photos. He looked around. He moved back into the bar area in the restaurant which had a view to the street. He stayed there until he saw the police arrive. Cautiously he ventured outside. He gave a sigh of relief when he saw Oskar with the uniformed man. His own car was towed away, and Mikal senior was driven home.

When they reached Mikal's home, Oskar saw the front door was slightly ajar. He ordered the uniformed policeman to call in for back up. He ordered Mikal to stay in his car. Oskar drew out his gun before pushing the door open. Thea came charging out holding a knife. Oskar fired. Shooting her in the stomach.

She fell in a heap. From the ground she stared at Oskar. "No. No. Wrong person." She dropped the knife she was holding. She gave a sardonic look and said in a soft voice, "I fucked that up, didn't I?"

Mikal ran to Thea while the officer in the car called the ambulance. Oskar pushed Mikal back. "Sorry," said Oskar. Mikal stood looking at Thea. He noted how dishevelled she appeared. She saw him look at her uncharacteristically grimy hands. She looked at him with a blank expression. He pulled out his phone, pushed the record button before questioning her. She admitted she had followed him to the restaurant, saw him with Mikal junior and then slashed his tyres. She didn't expect to see anyone but Mikal to come through the door.

Oskar bent over and read her rights. She looked at Mikal. "Those divorce papers won't get rid of me. Bastard. You and your precious son, bastards. I will see you both in hell. I am going to get everything." Oskar pointed to the CCT which had sound recording and showed her Mikal's phone. He nodded. "You are definitely going to get everything the system will throw at you."

Oskar added, "I am also charging you with conspiracy to murder. I advise you to keep your mouth shut until you find a lawyer. Good luck finding one."

The ambulance loaded her in the back. Both Oskar and Mikal just looked at the vehicle driving her away. At the same time, they both whispered, "Bitch."

"How much time will she get?" asked Mikal.

"We will throw everything at her. Conspiracy two times and an attempted murder of you and me. We will look deeper into her background and see what else we can find. At this stage, it is watertight recorded threats, threats in front of a witness and the vandalising of your car. Maybe five to ten years. Five if she gets a good lawyer. The CCT and your recording will make it very difficult for her to deny her actions and threats. "

"I wasn't expecting the divorce papers to be served on her for another few days. I must thank my lawyer for his expediency," said Mikal. "Hang around just in case there are more surprises."

The men walked into each room. Everything was in order except the safe was open and the fake will was on the coffee table. The divorce papers were on top of the will. "She had a bit of a read," said Mikal.

"She didn't like the fine print." He noted the fine print regarding the tenancy of the apartment had been circled in black pen. "Serves her right. I really thought I had a strong happy marriage. The only problem I could see was planted faults with Mikal. Mikal just didn't like her. I should have listened instead of putting it down to child-like jealousy. My son was right. I stuffed up as a father. He is a better person than me. Smarter too." Mikal looked at Oskar, "Thank you for everything. I could have died tonight."

Oskar nodded. "Take care of yourself. Lock up well and get the locks changed even the ones on the windows. This is not over."

Mikal looked ashen. "Not over? Isn't this enough?"

"She is one piece of a massive puzzle," said Oskar.

CHAPTER 25

Norbert Zielinski screamed in anger and shock when he heard on the radio news his favourite cousin had been shot by a police officer when she tried to murder her husband. When he left the car to go into a convenience store, he felt sick. Like salt being rubbed into wounds, seeing her face splashed across all the newspapers, angered him more. He wanted desperately to see her in hospital but knew he couldn't. She would be under guard. He knew Artem would call him as soon as he heard the news. He was bracing himself for that.

While sitting in his car, he read in the newspaper the details of the motive and threats were verbalised and her attempt to kill Mikal senior but attacked a police officer instead. The attempt and the threats were recorded on CCT. There was no escaping the fact she would go to jail. He slammed his hand down on the dashboard of the car over and over to relieve his frustration. He allowed himself a few tears, but the tears slowly turned to revenge. He pulled out of the car bay and drove full speed down the street.

He drove to Mikal's senior house where he knew Mikal would be the sole occupant of his large home. He studied the property. He would formulate a plan. *Thea didn't deserve to be shot,* he thought. He saw from his observation from across the road, Mikal was already in his car and coming out of his garage. Mikal was slowly approaching the heavy barred gates. The gates slowly opened giving Norbert time to jump out and approach Mika with a pistol at the ready.

He aimed his gun at the windscreen directly at Mikal's head and fired. He swore loudly. Mikal's windscreen was bullet proof. The bullet ricocheted to disappear somewhere on the grass. Mikal bent down for cover. Norbert was now at the side window ready to shoot Mikal at close range. Just before he could press his finger on the trigger, he screamed with fear, anger and horror. Mikal activated a flame thrower. Norbert stepped away; his legs were alight. He dropped his gun and fell to the ground. Mikal pulled out the fire blanket and got out of the car. He covered Norbert to douse the flames. Then he called both the police and ambulance. He contacted Radoslaw Lanski and explained what had happened.

Radoslaw was the last of the people to arrive at the scene. He walked quickly to the other police and the ambulance before going to Mikal. Radoslaw ordered the staff to follow the ambulance. Norbert would also be placed under guard at the hospital. Radoslaw his gave full attention to Mikal.

Mikal led Radoslaw back to the house and offered to make Radoslaw a coffee or tea. "Sorry to pull you out of bed. It has been quite eventful around here. Shall I make you a breakfast while you get details?"

"If it is not too much. Toast will be fine." replied Radoslaw

"It certainly didn't take long for the media to advertise the incident. And I guess, they will be broadcasting today's attack. It was somewhat prudent to have bullet-proof windows and that flame thrower. Is it legal?"

Mikal looked squarely at Radoslaw. "Bullet proof yes. Flame thrower, I am not sure. I worked in South Africa for a while. It was normal for Mercedes cars to have flame throwers as standard equipment. Cars, especially the upper end cars, were subject to carjacking when a person was about to get in or leave or waiting for lights to change. Over a ten-year period, it basically stopped carjacking of Mercedes. The thieves focused on other cars but soon found other brands soon copied. It was an extra for me and in three years of having the car, it was the very first time I ever used it. It was for me to have a greater piece of mind rather than a tool I would ever use. No one said, flame throwers were illegal in this country."

Radoslaw nodded. "Like an air bag, you know it is there and hope it will never be deployed."

Mikal grinned and pointed at Radoslaw. "Exactly. And what do you want on the toast?"

"Just plain a scaping of butter on the toast and thank you," replied Radoslaw.

As the men ate, Radoslaw said, "We are still checking Thea's background. We will do the same for this Norbert Zielinski. Norbert was released from jail just under two years ago. From what we can see, he has been keeping clean but still not in the right company. Last year, his best cell friend Wikto Duba died and not long before that Duba's brother died in Britain. I believe Ivan Nowak killed him."

"Ivan? Killed?"

Ivan and his father are in witness protection. There was a leak. The safe house was attacked. Ivan had a gun pointed to his head and was ordered out of the room which Stefan and the two minders were in. Ivan faked tripping and gabbed a statue and slammed it over the man's head. He took the gun and shot the other invader. The second man died in hospital days later." Radoslaw's phone rang. He nodded and put the phone away. "Thea and Norbert are cousins. Norbert was on a revenge kill for Thea's injuries. He had a lot to be angry about; a best friend and a brother dropping off and a cousin hospitalised."

"I know of Norbert but never met the man. Thea spoke frequently to Norbert. The pest called her nearly every day," commented Mikal.

"More bad news. Can you handle it?" asked Radoslaw.

Mikal went white. "What could be worse?"

"We know Wikto Duba and the Zielinski men were part of the Russian mafia. Thea was sent in as a part of the plot to gain control of your company. They needed it for money laundering and for shifting drugs and other illegal stuff around."

Mikal spluttered on his coffee. He wiped himself and the surrounds. "I am putting this place on the market. They will be coming after me like they are doing with the Nowaks."

Radoslaw nodded. "They have a much bigger agenda. We have theories and no evidence. There is something much deeper going on. We just don't know what just yet."

Mikal looked into Radoslaw's eyes. "General destruction always has greed and power written over it. Those people have no idea how much hard work goes into planning a business and nurturing it through highs and lows. They think a simple take over will solve their problems. That's naive."

"Mikal, the mafia are slowly becoming more sophisticated. They have their children become university graduates working their way through industries. Rightful qualification in the right jobs. I need to get access to your office and employee records. We need to do background checks. Bumping you off, Mikal off and any other board member is a method to create vacancies to promote employees - their people up the system for eventual takeover. We have found a few plants in both the Sawicki's and the Grabwoski's companies." Mikal splattered his coffee a second time and then poured it down the sink.

"Am I under witness protection as well?"

"Yes. I will send a man called Natan Byko to assist you." Radoslaw stood up taking the last half of his slice of toast with him. "Start cancelling today. Don't speak to any media. Keep low as possible. I will assign a uniformed officer here until Natan arrives.

Two days later, Mikal was in the same building as his son and the Nowaks. Mikal junior said, "Dad you have to get used to using their new names, Peter Schmidt and Thomas Brennen."

"Is it that bad? Having to change your names?"

All the others nodded. "Gees," said Mikal senior as he slowly sat down in an armchair.

To Thomas he asked, "Tell me your story and later I want to hear Iv...no Peter's story. I have all day."

Radoslaw was in his office when Oskar walked in carrying a heavy backpack, sleeping bag and another bag of goods for a teenage girl. "I have to get moving with the Boss. He gave me time off with Lydia and her funeral. Also, I have to keep up appearances with the tribe and the smugglers."

He handed Radoslaw a piece of paper. "That's my new phone number." The new phone has a better range and a few other bells and whistles which the old one didn't have."

"Good," said Radoslaw. "Keep your eyes and ears open for pipelines of any description, trafficking details and anything else. You know the drill. We must have evidence or knowledge of how and what is happening out there. We need the links with the nightmare happening around us. Take care and come back in one piece."

Oskar smiled. "I have every intention of doing that."

CHAPTER 26

The mafia convoy took the same inland road as before to arrive at Odessa, the coastal city of the Ukraine one week later. They went through customs with ease when Boss slipped the officer five hundred Euros. They were polished moves of give, take and conceal. Boss pointed to the four-wheel drives waiting on the other side of the gates. The convoy of vans and four-wheel drives drove to a secluded place outside Odessa. The vans were emptied, and all contents transferred to the four wheel drives.

They drove to the outskirts of Odessa, along a bumpy road which had seen much better days. They met the truck drivers who guided them on foot to a clearing where the trucks carrying the shipping containers were stored. Boss opened one container and peered briefly inside. Then opened the next and called out. "This needs a clean-up. Grumpy, you and your team clean this mess up. We will meet you in Constanta."

Oskar desperately want to look inside, but Boss had already shut and locked the doors. Grumpy and his team emptied out their four-wheel vehicle and placed whatever they had on the ground. Grumpy threw the SUV keys to the unknown truck drivers. Everyone departed. Grumpy's four-wheel drive went first but turned to go north along the road which they all had come. The other vehicles including the one Puppy was in, went south followed by two of the three trucks and four-wheel drives.

They drove along the coastal road. Boss frequently looked into the rear-view mirror checking the others following behind in assorted vehicles. At next checkpoint, Constanta in Romania, Boss slipped the officer more cash. He and the others were waved through after their passport books were stamped. They checked into a cheap motel. All was going to plan.

In his own room, Oskar sought the opportunity to check in with a text message and an email with a collection of photos. He deleted everything. He joined the other men downstairs in their nightly ritual of drinking and chatting up any females. Some of the men took the females upstairs to their bedrooms for the night. Oskar just had a few drinks and left as soon as the other men began pairing off. Memories of Lydia were still too fresh, and he just didn't think there was local talent.

The next day they were on pier twenty. The cargo they were carrying was now secured into a half-size shipping container. They watched as the containers were hoisted aboard and carefully loaded on the cargo deck with a mix of half and full-size containers. Their containers totally blended in with the other legitimate cargo.

The team boarded the ship where they were directed to small stuffy cabins. The cabins had four bunks. The only storage space was below the lower bunks where there were two sets of drawers. There was a musty smell of the rooms mixed with the odours coming from the engine room. Not wanting to stay in the stuffy rooms, the men stowed their belongings and everything else where space permitted before exiting to the upper decks.

When the small ship left its moorings, Oskar walked around the deck snapping photos with a hidden button-size camera. He aimed for the shipping container numbers, the crew and other visible identifying markings for later reference. He sent the information to Radoslaw and then wiped everything. When he was finished, he joined Boss and two others in the group in the dining room. He watched them play some gambling game which resembled poker. They invited him to join the game but declined explaining he was unfamiliar with the game and would watch for a while. He watched three rounds before joining in. They taught him the rules, played a few coaching games before leaving him to his own play moves.

Late in the afternoon the next day, the smugglers and their cargo disembarked at Batumi, Georgia. The cargo, still in the shipping containers, were loaded onto three small semi-trailers driven by local unknown men. The rest of the group were to travel in three hired vans which would hold personal luggage and other equipment of the rest of the group. Boss gave orders, "Next stop Baku, Azerbaijan then be ready for a very long trip."

"Exactly where," asked Puppy.

"I don't get that information until we get there. Security. And if there is a problem, then we can change at the last minute," replied Boss.

As they drove, Oskar tried to memorize what he was seeing. What dominated Oskar's view were huge pipelines under construction. The conditions for the workers appeared to be rough – exposure to the elements and tents for accommodation. Puppy wanted to take photos but that was too dangerous. He pointed and asked Boss, "What is all this for?"

"One is for oil. Crude oil. The other is for water. Well that is what I was told. It's a big project. Some international governments can get their act together and cooperate." Puppy left it at that. Any more questions would make it obvious.

The convoy stopped at Ardabil in Iran. To Puppy it was a hole of a place - primitive by most people's standards. Where they stopped was, in Oskar's eyes, a glorified shed. But there was a runway, a *small airport*, thought Oskar. They were able to get out of the vehicles and stretch their legs at this rundown building which was a mix of steel and glass walls, mostly broken seats, no kiosk and no air-conditioning. He shook his head. Only men's toilets available. Women were expected to hang on or were always left at home, not entitled to have a holiday. The building was staffed by three people who each received a tip from Boss. They waited around without saying a word to each other.

Boss took his attention outside. Three trucks, with the half-sized shipping containers pulled up outside. Each now displayed new magnetic signs stating U.N. aide. Boss opened the back of one truck and closed it almost immediately. This time Oskar was able to get a glimpse of what was inside. Puppy was shocked to see four women were inside. Western women drugged up for a trip to hell. He desperately wanted a photo of each woman. He had to be smart about that. The button camera on his shirt was almost reaching full capacity with photos.

Oskar noted that one man got into the back of the truck, he asked the person from Trouble's team,

"Do you want company in there?"

"If you want to share this sweatbox, you are welcome." The man handed Oskar a bag containing drugs. "You can help me feed them and give them a shot." Oskar climbed in. The doors closed. The man switched on a light to reveal the women. Oskar tried to hide his shock, but the man picked up on it. "You'll get used to it. They are worth a few Eruos." He handed Oskar a bowl and poured some cool water in it. He nodded for him to start giving the women a drink. The truck moved on with Oskar and the other man inside.

Oskar slowly helped the women to have a drink. He empathised in the women's transport; no windows, heat and drugs making disorientation greater than it should be. The steel cocoon was almost soundproof with thick walls blocking out most exterior sounds. The women were in hell. But he made every effort to memorize the women and their faces, faces which were thin and drawn like ghosts in some horror movie. He was sharing their personal hell.

He tried to concentrate on the movement of the trucks form inside the container. Rough road, smooth road, turn left, and turn right, going slowly and going faster.

The heat in the containers got worse as the day went on. Sweat filled the confined space. The men who were outside faired a little better. They sat in the truck's air-conditioned cabins or in air-conditioned vehicles. The air-conditioners struggled to keep the heat at bay. The stark landscape looked the same in all directions – miles of nothing but sky and sand with sharp protruding pebbles. They were going deeper into the desert.

The trucks and the hired vehicles travelled smoothly indicating, to Oskar the road was well cared for. The vibration of passing traffic confirmed they were on a wider road, maybe a highway of sorts. Then the truck he was in slowed down and made a turn. It had turned onto a minor road and kept going slow to minimize bouncing and any suspension damage. The bouncing continued for ten minutes before it came to a stop. The doors opened. The hot desert air rushed in. It was a relief as the truck was starting to boil. Oskar and the other man got out first and jabbed the women with a drug as each was removed from the back of the truck. The women were put in a camp fold away chairs and left in the sun.

Puppy looked around. A few crumpled buildings which had seen much better days, a near dead tree of some description, a few palm trees struggling against the elements and not much more. "Where are we?" Puppy asked one of the men.

"In a shit hole, ten minutes away from a bigger one called Manji. People here don't like strangers. Keep your mouth shut unless spoken to. Try to be invisible. Let Boss do the work." Puppy said nothing until he saw movement in the distance. A dust trail was filling the skyline in the west. The men stood to attention placing themselves around the vehicles and the women.

Three trucks of similar set up came to a dusty halt less than ten metres away from their vehicles, the convoy Puppy was in. Boss walked forward. He spoke with the man who got out of the first vehicle. He was a tall lean man sporting a long greying beard. He wore typical Arab clothing. The man immediately walked over to the Boss's trucks and climbed inside. He examined the contents and then walked over to the women. He examined them as if they were some form of livestock. He nodded. Boss inspected their delivery and nodded.

Hardly a word was spoken between the two camps. All the cargo was swapped from one vehicle to another except the one containing the women. The women were reloaded into the truck they came out of. The truck and its signage were simply swapped. The Iranians drove off with their supplies and women and Boss and his crew drove off with assorted drugs.

The journey back to Baku wasn't pleasant. The air-conditioning was on, but the air couldn't circulate.

Oskar noted the road back to Baku was largely deserted. Travelling in the early afternoon heat kept people off the road. Oskar wondered if the rare trucks he saw going to Manji were also carrying contraband or were going to distribute goods they delivered not more than one hour ago.

When they reached the outskirts of Baku, Boss used his mobile to contact a person. Puppy wanted to know who the person was but Boss was careful with names. He just said yes, okay and then clicked off. He told the others in the cabin, "No plane flight back. It is overland." Everyone groaned.

Puppy said, "When we get out of the city area, pull up. I'm riding on top of the container.'

Boss laughed. "I didn't know you could truck-surf. It's dangerous up there."

"At least I get oxygen," retorted Puppy.

"No. You don't. The police will pull us up or worse still you will get shot. I can't allow that."

"Yes you can. You won't get caught. I will see to that," replied Oskar now feeling a little uncertain.

Outside Baku, the truck pulled over. Puppy climbed up. He spread a towel down and laid down on it. He held the edge near the cabin with gloved hands. Only his head was visible from the front. He couldn't be seen by anyone coming from the rear of the truck. He tapped his foot to indicate he was ready. The truck drove off slowly at first and then just under the speed limit. From the top, Puppy noticed the pipelines running parallel to the road some forty meters away.

At night, the group pulled into a camp area. Puppy climbed down from his position and assisted the others setting up camp.

The pipeline which followed the road was running very close alongside to the camp. Puppy walked over and checked it out. The pipes were suspended above ground with huge concrete pylons. Puppy looked at their construction. He bobbed his head around to see where the others were. Too risky. No photos. Then he walked back to the main camp and asked if someone could take his picture of him beside the pipelines. One man offered but was joined by another. Puppy pulled him into the picture. Boss called out, "You're not on a tour. Stop playing tourists."

Puppy yelled back, "I know. I am just fascinated by the work here. Lots of money on water movement."

"We didn't hear you complain about using it," said Boss. The others walked away when the photo was taken.

Now away from the others, Puppy listened to the sounds of liquid going through the pipes. Squirt. Hiss. Thump. Hiss. Squirt. He noticed a small pipe which branched off the main pipe. The gravity fed the water down to a tank which the group used. He looked for a valve, only a tap. He puzzled over the control of the water. There had to be a control box somewhere to regulate the flow. He didn't see any. He re-joined the group. Water was being syphoned into the camp, legally or illegally could not be determined.

The next afternoon they were back in Batumi. They boarded the same small container ship. The cargo was buried with the other containers. Puppy again walked around the containers. He saw one of the men watching. Puppy signalled the man over. He had a causal conversation about the weather and the clouds forming in the sky. Puppy pointed to something that resembled an early stage water spout. He angled the camera to include the container he was interested in.

The storm began to increase. A waterspout was now fully formed. "Let's get out of here," he almost yelled as the rain came down almost sideways, assisted by the growing wind strength. By the time the men reached the door, the distant waterspout was just meters away. The ship was buffeted by the spout and the sea made the small ship roll. The storm lasted for four hours. Puppy was in his bed with a bucket beside him. When the ship arrived at Constanta, he was relieved.

The cargo was unloaded onto the trucks. They drove to a farm. The cargo was unloaded into vans. The trucks driven into the barns and waited for the next trip.

They were heading back to Lviv. Puppy knew he was two days away from Poland. He gave a sigh of relief. The home stretch looked good. This time they didn't stay overnight at Lviv. They went directly to the camp where he was supposed to have married Preshka. *Fun and games*, he thought.

When they arrived at the usual spot it was close to two a.m. Boss ordered for the tents to be set up and sleep before company came.

It was close to ten a.m., many of the men were sleeping in their separate tents. Puppy jumped when he felt someone sliding in beside him. Preshka laughed and apologised. "Sorry. You've been away for so long."

Puppy nodded. "Oskar." He reminded her.

"No puppy. It suits you," she laughed.

"As you wish. I need more sleep." He rolled over. She snuggled into him and stroked his hair. She watched him sleep before drifting off herself.

It was mid-afternoon before he stirred. He pulled his second backpack over and rummaged through it. She stirred with his movements. "I have some things for you. I hope you like them," he said in broken Ukraine. She looked at him. "Hmm. Ukraine. Have you had some lessons?"

"A few." He handed her two parcels. "Go on open them." Her face lit up. One was a dainty nine carat gold chain. She was so excited, she fumbled with the clip. Oskar helped her. "There. Very nice. Just right."

She planted a kiss on him. Then she tore open the much larger bag with the enthusiasm of a child on Christmas Day. She squealed her delight as she held up a matching snow parker and trousers outfit.

She quickly put them on despite the temperature being close to twenty degrees Celsius. The garments were one size too big. It didn't matter too her. "I feel like a million euros. I have seen these in magazines and never thought one day I would own such an outfit. Thank you." She planted another kiss on him as sweat from being distinctively overdressed started to pour down her forehead. She changed back to her clothes. She was about to take the chain off when Oskar said, "No. Wear that." She gently toyed with the chain again. "I better get up," he said. He looked at his watch. "It's later than I thought.

He stepped outside first. Preshka followed. She was grinning from ear to ear. She held his hand and led him to the makeshift eating area. Preshka's father, Rostik, looked at them as they approached. "About time you two joined the rest of us." He gave a wink to his wife, Darina. "Sit." He ushered Oskar and Preshka to an area slightly away from the others. "I want a private conversation with you. Preshka," he ordered, "I want a few words with Puppy. Now go and show off that gold chain to your mother and friends."

Preshka's father slipped an arm around Puppy's shoulder. "Listen here, I know you didn't have sex with my daughter. The blood trick didn't quite work. I saw the bandage around your arm. What's wrong with her?"

Puppy gulped. "Nothing. Too young. There are laws regarding sex with under aged females. And if she did get pregnant, that could cause medical problems. Her body is not mature enough. Give her a couple of years. She may not like an old man like me by then."

"Hmm. I know you are no fucking saint because you hang around with these men. Trafficking drugs. Not a good life. I want you to stay. We need more men here. We are getting picked off by Russians chasing us off our traditional homeland. They are being assisted by the Ukrainian army. They want to build something here, but I don't know what. They tried bribing us and now they are picking us off. Look around. Old men and very few young ones. The girls need protection as well. Some have been raped and others both raped and murdered. You respect women more than the others I see in this group. I am not asking but begging you to stay. I need someone to lead and protect. I can't keep this up forever. Since you have been away, I have had three bullet grazes. I'm slowing down. The next time I may not be so lucky. My wife, Darina, over there is also in agreement for you to lead us. She also knows you didn't and still didn't fuck my daughter just now. She looked inside and found you both sleeping like babies. Preshka is a bad sleeper ever since the raids have been increasing in number and intensity. For her to sleep for so long and soundly, tells me you are the one for her and to lead us."

Oskar was stunned. "I…I don't know what to say other than I'm not Moses." Rostik burst out laughing and slapped his thigh. "You're close enough." Oskar felt embarrassed and tried to change the subject. "I think I know what is going to be built across your land."

"What is it?"

"Pipes. There are three pipes going to be built here. Not all the places have three pipes. One is for oil. One is for water. They are standard size as I understand. The one that puzzles me looks like prefabricated tunnels. It is large enough for trucks to drive through. The tunnels are not in all places I have been to. There are gaps in construction. I don't know if that is by design or some other reason. They could be built later. That jumbo pipeline is still a mystery." He pulled out his phone and showed the picture of the pipes and himself with a couple of the smuggler's team in Armenia. "As for staying, I am not sure. Give me time to think and talk it over with Boss." Rostik nodded and slapped his thighs. "You have one day. Now eat your food." He looked over to Preshka and his wife and called them over.

Puppy watched the others drive away. He would be picked up by another team who would come through next week. That was the best compromise Puppy could work out between the two groups.

Puppy slipped back into his tent and called Radoslaw to give him an update. He sent pictures of the massive pipes which had almost crossed all of the land between the Black and Caspian Seas. He closed off at mid-sentence when he saw a shadow outside the tent. Preshka came in. "Dad wants to speak with you." Without a word he followed Preshka to the large tent.

"Sit. We have a lot to do." He rolled out a map with the boundaries of his land. "I know every inch of this land. You must know it as well. The pipes as you believe, are going to go across my land from here to here." He drew a feint pencil line across the land. "I have seen many strangers taking measurements all along here."

He pointed to an area going from Ternopil outside of Lviv and up to Ludin. "The area under survey is well away from the towns as if they are hiding the route. I don't know which way north or south the pipeline goes from these places. It doesn't matter. What matters is they cut through our land and the government says suck it up. As for compensation they offered was an insult. Just two Euros per square kilometre. Because we said no, they have waged war. Our government is killing us with the aid of the Russians. Not right. They pick one of us off. We give them two of theirs to collect. Three or four if we are lucky. They keep sending soldiers and we keep giving them back. But we are small in numbers. I want you protect the families here. The women, in particular, need protection. Now I am going to leave you with this map for you to come up with some fresh ideas." He walked out of the tent.

Puppy poured over the map and took photos. He called Radoslaw again to ask for advice. Thirty minutes later, Puppy left the tent and looked at the surrounding hills. Preshka walked over. "What are you looking for?"

He turned around. "I'm trying to get ideas. Are there any caves?"

"Plenty. Some are just up there overlooking this camp. Some are much larger and deeper. Some are high up while others are almost at ground level."

"Can you show me some of the caves?"

One hour later, Puppy was prepared for the hike up the mountains. Preshka was going to be his guide. Her father met them at the crude path which led to the first mountain. "Look after each other. Preshka, if you hear any shooting, keep away. I don't want you running back here. Go to the office in the cave. There are supplies of food and water there." To Preshka he ordered, "If we are attacked, stay in the mountains and let Puppy take you where it is safe, even if it is back to Poland. I will see you both tomorrow." Preshka gave her father a hug.

They walked in silence up the mountain. Preshka purposefully zigzagged. She was taught to move up the mountains in this manner. She studied the ground. If a known path looked obvious, she would detour. She puffed. "We take different paths up so not to wear the vegetation down and make a clear path."

"How long has that strategy been in place? It's a good one."

"Nearly two years. The well-worn previous path has almost disappeared now." She stopped and looked back at the campsite below. "Dad was never a person to worry. He never used to trade with the men before. But now he does. We need ammunition and food. They move on and no one says a word." Oskar glanced back at the camp below.

"What exactly did your parent's do before all of this?" Preshka went suddenly quiet and slightly agitated. "Tribal war-lord," she said in an unconvincing manner. Oskar picked up on the cue.

"I know you people don't live here on a permanent basis. I know you move around. Is there somewhere that was semi-permanent or permanent?"

Preshka looked down. "Yes. We were not always nomadic. We lived in houses just like everyone else. Then the houses were taken away from us. The army took them as a base to control the area. The president is a bastard. He puts his interests first and doesn't care who he squashes. We are insects. Come. The first cave is not far away."

They walked into the first cave. Oskar asked, "How far does this go?"

"I'm not sure. I have never been beyond where light disappears."

"Then we better find out." He pulled a torch out. They walked for ten minutes. The cave twisted and turned. There were no branches for them to decide left or right. Eventually light appeared. They hurried towards it. Preshka smiled. "We are on the other side of the mountain. Definitely, a short cut. The sun is setting, we better make camp."

The next morning, Preshka led Oskar not down the mountain but first going sideways to another cave. "This is a cave I don't like being in. Too many tunnels and sudden drops. We really need mountain climbing gear. We don't have that. Let's go down that way." She pointed to the left. "Another cave that is a good one."

"Why is it good?"

"You'll see."

The cave opened to a large chamber. Stalactites and stalagmites decorated one side. The sound of dripping water echoed across the cavity. The rest of the area was dry with a mix of dust and sand. The floor gently sloped towards the limestone structures. Oskar smiled. "This is a good place for people to hide. A continuous supple of water is important. Is there a creek nearby?"

Preshka shook her head. "I think the big drops go to an underground water supply. I am not going to find out. Too scary."

"Your parents know of this cave?"

" Of course. Dad keeps quiet about lots of things these days. He is sheltering us from the problems we face."

"He mentioned a cave office. What is it and where is that?"

"On the next mountain there is a cave at near ground level. Boulders to the front conceal it from view. A little twisting path behind the boulders gets you there. The entrance requires one to crawl through the first two meters and then one can stand up. Dad uses the office to hide stuff. He's been using it for the last two years since we were evicted from our homes."

"Where are the homes?"

"On the other side of the same mountain. It is good farming land and the well water is so nice to drink. Dad used to work in the city and this farm was his retreat. He called it his happy place."

"What did he do for work in the city?"

Preshka bit her lip and hesitated and then decided to lie, "A greengrocer. That is what he would say."

Oskar picked up on the lie but didn't push it. The truth would eventually come out. "Have you been to this office cave?"

"Not for many years. I must have been about five when I last went inside. He told me I was never to go inside unless instructed and it had to be an emergency."

Oskar looked thoughtfully. "I think an emergency is coming. Lead me to this cave. Does your father have a phone?"

Preshka nodded. "We have to go outside. No reception in this place."

The walk to the next mountain took just under an hour. The sun was coming down and reflected off the surrounding rocks to increase the temperature. Oskar and Preshka sat on a rock sharing the last of their food. From a distance, they could hear vehicles. Oskar quickly phoned Rostik and gave details of what was heading their way. He pulled out a small set of binoculars and gave Rostik a description. Oskar could hear the growing panic in Rostik's voice.

From their position, Oskar and Preshka kept low and observed the mini convoy. Oskar took photos with his phone. He wished he had a proper camera with a zoom lens. The vehicles rushing by carried armed soldiers, four in each jeep. Oskar swore, "We got to get into the cave. Now!" Without hesitation, Preshka led him up the small path and crawled through a mini tunnel.

Preshka led Oskar directly to the cavern. Oskar gulped at what he saw.

Hell, he thought, a command centre. He looked around amazed at the information decorating the walls on makeshift hessian curtains. One curtain was labelled with dates and times the smugglers had arrived at the camp. But he looked carefully to note there was more than one camp. There were four in all and these were rotated or used as safety required.

On another were photographs of all the smugglers and their names written across their shoulders.

He flipped one over. On the back was information. But the information was patchy – bits missing.

He saw his own face decorating an area near the base of the curtain. He flipped it over and starred in disbelief. On the back was his real full name, undercover name, given nick name and nationality.

On the next curtain were pictures of the clan. Members who had died over the last five years. Old men and women – names and their natural causes. A few young people from accidents. As his eyes slowly went down the curtain, young men, teens and a handful of women deceased - shot over the last two years. Oskar groaned, *too many lost lives,* he thought. "Are any of these deceased people related to you?" he asked Preshka who was standing beside him. His voice snapped her out of her thoughts. She brushed a tear away. "Most are relatives. About a quarter are long-time family friends." She pointed to a teenager. "My brother." Oskar could see she was becoming distressed. Ghosts on the curtain were tugging at her. He pulled her close and gave her a hug. "I can see why your father didn't want you in this place. It is a mix of shrine and war room. Go outside. I will continue to look around."

"No. I want to see what is in here. It doesn't really make sense to me. All these photos. And these women over here. Who and why are they here?" She pointed to the next curtain which was dripping with photos of women. The curtain was covered on both sides. Most were nameless. Oskar gasped and went pale. He recognised a face. He pointed to one about halfway down the second side.

"This girl. This girl," his hands shook as he pointed. "She was reported missing. He boyfriend was kidnapped and taken to Russia. He was tortured with some machinery designed to wipe his memory. Her name is Julia Tomszcowski. Your father must have seen her. She was smuggled out this way and to Iran. Oh my God!" Preshka stared at Oskar. "How come you know that?" Oskar didn't reply as he was piecing the information together. Preshka pulled away and walked back from him. "Are you a cop?"

Subconsciously, Oskar gave a slight nod. "And I think your father is one too. Look around you. Why would he be creating what is called a situation room. Why did he not want anyone here unless it was an emergency? Cops can sometime smell another cop under cover. Your father sniffed me. That is why he gave me the task to protect you and the others. There was no one else he could trust."

"Is Oskar your real name?"

"No. My undercover name. Sorry, I can't tell you my real name. Safety reasons. It's Puppy or Oskar to you."

"Fuckin' hell. No wonder you kept your paws off me." She suddenly looked shy. "Thanks. Much appreciated."

"You've got some growing up to do and you won't want to be stuck with an old man like me."

"You're not that old, are you?"

"Nearly twice your age. I prefer to regard you as a kid sister. Can we settle on that? Just for the record, we are not married. Your father pulls a nice bluff on the young ones. I suppose he thinks it is some form of protection."

Preshka nodded. She diverted her attention to another curtain.

There were photos of Russian and Ukrainian soldiers and policemen killed in skirmishes. Oskar recognised the Russian police that were killed on his first trip here. He pointed to the two Russians. "These two were cops. The group I was with killed them. I stole their horses and gold. Why they were carrying gold is still not clear – bribery or fossicking. I won't know for a long while."

"We better get back to the camp," said Preshka. "What do you want to do with all of this?"

"It best left here. We can come back for it. And it can be passed on to police," he said looking concerned.

"The Polish police can have it. I don't know who to go to and trust in the Ukrainian police force."

Preshka and Oskar left the cave. They walked slowly towards the other side of the mountain where they could go directly to the camp. Oskar pulled Preshka back and pulled her down. A plume of smoke was seen coming from the camp. "Not good. Not good at all," said Oskar.

Preshka gasped. "They were attacked. No! No!" Oskar grabbed Preshka to restrain her. She fought back giving him a harder time than he expected. Eventually she calmed down. "We wait and see who is around. We go back to the first mountain and watch."

After determining the camp was safe to approach, Oskar and Preshka walked slowly into the now smouldering camp. As they neared the first tent now blowing semi-anchored in the breeze, Oskar lifted the covers. No one was inside. They approached the next tent. A dead soldier wearing a Ukrainian uniform was inside. Oskar took his gun and any ammunition on the soldier's body.

He checked the gun for ammunition and inserted a round. He waved Preshka on.

Preshka stopped and gave a cry outside the main tent where she and her parents lived. Her sister was dead, but her parents were gone. She ran to her dead sister and held her tightly as she rocked and cried. Oskar felt helpless for the first time since Lydia died. *This is so wrong. No one needs to die like this,* he thought. It puzzled him greatly. All he could think of was that *Rostik was undercover like him. He was trying to protect his ancestral land from being overtaken by the Ukrainian government at the so-called promises of greater wealth for the Ukrainians and thanks to the Russian government. Rostik was still in the police force but found he couldn't trust a sole. He just kept collecting information and storing it in the cave. And along come me, a cop from Poland who he somehow instantly trusted.* Why? Still puzzled him. The camp was in disarray. He left Preshka to grieve for her sister as he explored the camp in more detail.

Three more soldiers were found. He dragged the four soldiers to one side of the camp. He stripped them of any equipment he could find. He tore one side off a tent and placed the equipment on it ready for their removal.

He gathered the few remaining pieces of food, mostly raw vegetables and fruit. In one tent he found a container of Ukrainian sweets. He added that to the small pile of food. Preshka was still in the tent. He called his office in Poznan and explained what had happened. Radoslaw told him to hide in the caves and collect all the information inside. They would organise an airlift. He and Preshka would be brought back to Poland. The issue of no passport for Preshka was a matter of concern but there were ways around that.

CHAPTER 27

Oskar knocked on his parent's door. He introduced Preshka to his family and quickly gave some background information. "How long will she be here?" asked his mother.

"I don't know. A month for sure." He turned to Preshka. "It is school for you young lady. You have missed so much."

"I know. It won't be as exciting," she replied.

"I think you have had enough excitement. School," he ordered.

She gave him a salute and giggled. "Yes, captain."

"She is all yours," he said to his parents and handed them a Ukrainian-Polish dictionary.

He disappeared before anyone could say a word.

At the station, Oskar assisted the others with the photos he had taken from the office cave.

Two file boxes were carefully emptied. Oskar had created divisions between each group by wrapping them in cut tent fabric. He had pre-labelled the groups with a permanent marker. In a smaller box was a collection of passports of deceased soldiers, missing women, deceased friends and family of Preshka's family. Oskar displayed all the photos of the pipelines and located known path on a new map. He added the pipeline that would traverse through parts of Ukraine and signs of construction in other countries.

While he was away, satellite images of the pipelines were added. Two normal size tubes and the giant-sized rectangular structure beside them snaked their way from Baku, Azerbaijan to Batumi, Georgia. From there it was clear, the link through the northern parts of Turkey which followed the curve of the Black Sea to the outer most edges of Sakarya. There, the pipelines stopped and turned south towards to Yalova to re-emerge on the other side of the expanse of water at the town of Tekirdag. It followed the border to the town of Burgas in Bulgaria, then north by north-west to Dorbrik. Then it followed the Romanian border before swinging up Calarasi in the far north. They crossed the border into Maldova near the town of Balti. Then the pipe travelled to Lviv. They stopped there where Preshka's family was in dispute. Rostik had provided the proposed link between Lviv and the next two destinations. One branch enters Poland and stops at Zamosi. The other travels along the Belause border, travelling north before crossing the border again into Russia. The pipelines going from the border to Moscow were clearly completed. When the pipelines crossed the borders, and within other countries, the work was patchy. Radoslaw couldn't determine if the countries were struggling to pay for such a piece of infrastructure or were waiting for more Russian funding. That was something the Sawicki family might be able to assist us with.

Oskar pointed out an odd feature of the pipeline. "Two pipes are the typical cylinder shape and the other is a rectangular. The rectangular one is attached to the normal cylinder one. Every so often the rectangular one has vents and in places cut outs under, I suppose you can call it a sunshade. That, I think, is to keep some of the weather out. I am not sure if it has a screen to keep small animals out.

"I have a hunch. The rectangular pipe is a tunnel for one-way vehicle travel." He squinted at the pictures. "The pipes branch off or stop at isolated locations not far from each town. Natural features add protection to the entries and exits. A vehicle can get out or go in unnoticed. Can this picture be magnified?" He pointed to the town of Yalova, Turkey.

"Do you know who is building these pipes?" asked Natan.

"I am guessing. I think each country is contributing to these pipes and each will get some oil and or water. But the contribution would at best only be enough for one pipe. I would say the Russians are financing the rest."

Radoslaw tossed the idea around in his head before coming up with an idea. "Suppose the Russian government did commission and assist with legitimate pipeline development. They got one set of plans and the rogue element is going ahead with that but attaching their own touches.

While you were away the Russian president was genuinely upset with the fire at the station, the one that Fabian and friends caused. We could see he was genuinely disturbed by the findings. He knew of the tunnel system but was unaware of the use of an electro-megatron, let alone someone or group was using it for brainwashing purposes."

Natan nodded. "Okay, I am going to say something that could sound totally outlandish." The others looked at him waiting for the idea.

"Just suppose all the events are linked but made to look like isolated incidences. The mafia are disposable foot soldiers and are rewarded by officials turning a blind eye to their criminal activities."

"Moles are in the system to ensure the mafia can do as they please. The moles also give information to get rid of people in both the mafia's way and to allow the faceless men to skirt around any system or organisation. The faceless Russian men are organising wars or take overs of countries, whether by stealth as they are trying to do here or by open conflict. Stealth would be better, more subtle and less noticeable, less resistance from the populous."

"That does not explain why they have set their eyes on three Polish companies and the kidnapping of Szymon," said Fabian.

"Szymon was to be the fall guy for anything that needs to be cleaned up. Break him down, retrain him, remodel him and dispose of him if things get sticky. He takes the wrap and they walk free.

Just suppose these faceless people do succeed and the Russian president is internationally embarrassed or decried for his so-called actions. Anger from Poland and other countries and some from within Russia itself – a perfect scenario for upset people to want to have a go to get rid of the president. Szymon was going to be the assassin trained by the men wanting a coup d'état. Szymon goes to prison or is executed for treason, Poland is then shamed. Poland falls under Russian rule again. Poland is strategically placed in Eastern Europe, handy to everywhere. The supply of water and oil to the countries can be switched off. No country operates or can function without water and oil. The square pipe can conceal the deployment of troops if any uprising occurs. Specially trained soldiers can be transported faster and unnoticed through the rectangular pipe. War is being planned and not by the president. He will be a causality," said Natan.

Radoslaw drummed his fingers. "How do we warn our president and the Russian president? Who do we trust in the existing government knowing there are moles at every level in any place? We can just keep fighting these faked individual incidences and achieve little and the problem remains."

Oskar sat back in his chair, rotating it from side to side. He was deep in thought. "Okay, how does this sound. It could be considered corny."

The others looked at him waiting for a possible solution. "Just suppose we by-pass all channels of diplomacy. We get to the president first. Show him proof and hope to God that he believes it. Denial can be an issue."

"Spit it out," ordered Radoslaw.

"Moscow is hosting the Olympic Committee in two weeks. They are wanting another go at the winter Olympics. That will be an ideal time to slip someone in and personally deliver a note."

"Not possible. The man will always be surrounded by guards. We can't trust his guards as they too could be behind this."

Oskar grinned. "Guess who got the contract to decorate the banquet with flowers? Yours truly Stefan."

Radoslaw protested. "We can't send an amateur in. He is doing enough now."

"Who said amateur? One of us goes as a part of the work team. I'm free to go."

"Aren't you going back with that smuggler's group and staying behind in no-man's land to find Preshka's family?"

"Nope. I got a call that they are suspending things for a month - a bit too hot. They didn't like what happened. Everyone disappearing and the mess that was left behind didn't sit well. They were surprised I escaped. I made up a story, well half true. I was in the mountains being a look out for Rostik, err that's Preshka's father. I was able to tell them it was a raid by the two armies. It's cool off time. They will tell me when the next trip is going ahead. Do I or someone else join Stefan and company?"

Radoslaw nodded. "Go with Stefan but a few changes - hair, coloured contacts, eyebrows and nose."

CHAPTER 28

It was twelve hours before the banquet was to begin. The Kremlin staff were checking the place settings. They were wearing white gloves and each of the two hundred places were being measured.

Ivan, Stefan, Oskar and two staff from the flower company were told to wait with their flowers until measuring task was done.

When they were given the signal, each of the people from The East European Flower Company was accompanied by a Kremlin staffer and a security person. Each arrangement was carefully examined and then placed in an exact position at equal distant from one arrangement to the next as directed by the staffers attending to the place settings. The arrangements were adjusted if they were greater than one centimetre off centre. The task took close to an hour. When the final tables were being set with flowers, the president's wife, Karina Gurin, popped her head through the door to watch the proceedings.

Oskar took the opportunity to distract the lady. He called Stefan over and introduced him as the mastermind of the floral display. Stefan presented her with a corsage for the evening. "For you. It is optional for you to wear the corsage." He nodded his head and turned sharply to continue working.

The Karina smiled at the gift. She looked at Oskar. "I have never been presented with a corsage from any company before. A truly wonderful gesture."

Oskar gave a slight grin, just enough for his lips to make a slight curve. It was almost flirtatious. "There is more, for you. Compliments of the company. This is for your husband, the President, Georgy Gurin". He presented her with an envelope upon which was a tiepin in a gift box. The box was made of solid timber with a see-through panel.

Karina smiled and commented, "It is truly beautiful." Playfully she added, "I just might keep this for myself."

"The company can send you a brooch of the same design," offered Oskar.

She laughed. "No. No. This is enough. More than enough. I tell you what, if he doesn't like it, then I will use it. Deal?"

"And if he likes it?"

"I will wear it when he doesn't," she gave Oskar a playful wink.

"And the envelope?" she asked.

"Papers of authenticity by the manufacturer and stone dealer. Just make sure he reads the details. He needs to register the ownership with the manufacturer. That is very important as it acts like an insurance. If anything happens like lost or stolen and the tiepin ends up on the black market or in some shady street stall, the company will give the police all specifications and photographs. It is a valuable gift from the company and is only offered for hosts at events as these. A piece of appreciation and unashamedly P.R." Oskar politely nodded his head and went to the door to follow the others out of the room.

Karina walked back to her living quarters. She had already pulled out her husband's suit he wanted to wear that night. He hadn't selected a tie. She placed five of his ties on the bed along with the gift and the envelope. She looked at the envelope wanting to fill in the form inside in a bid to save time for her husband. She picked it up and placed it down again. *No*, she thought, *he can read it tomorrow.* She left the envelope where she initially placed it.

It was close to an hour before the banquet was about to start. Karina was ready and waiting. Her husband, Georgy quickly walked in taking layers of clothes off as he went. The clothes left a trail through the private apartment. Immediately he showered and started to dress. He picked out one of the five ties and then stopped. "What's this?" he asked.

"A P.R. gift from The East European Flower Company. They did the floral arrangements for the banquet," she replied. She handed him his gift.

"It looks expensive," he commented.

"Expensive enough to require papers of authenticity drawn up. The papers need to be registered and sent for insurance purposes."

"Unusual." He opened the letter and turned white. He sat down on the edge of the bed.

"What is it?" she asked when she saw the change of colour in his face.

"Who gave you this?"

"One of the workers. Why?"

"It was someone who was working undercover. It is a warning from the Polish police and a few photos to back up their claims. There is a nasty plot to discredit me and for my assassinations." He placed the letter in his jacket. The letter played on his mind. He stripped the top half of his clothes, placed a thin bullet vest on and redressed. He wriggled to adjust his body into the extra layer.

"Now we shall leave. Keep your eyes open." He gave his wife a kiss on her forehead. "Smile the best you can. Act. Pretend as if everything is in order," he whispered to her before placing an affectionate kiss on her lips. She wiped away a small smear of lipstick from his lips. "Let's go."

The next morning in his office, Georgy Gurin re-read the letter. He pondered. He picked up the phone, not once or twice but six times. Hesitating. He stood up and walked to the window. He looked across the gardens and to the nearest edge of Red Square. He picked up the phone and called security. "I want every room checked including the basements for bugs. I want all registers of people entering and going through every door brought to my room. I want all recordings from all security cameras. I want a brand-new computer. I want to unpack the computer myself. I want everything like yesterday."

Two hours later, Georgy was given a new computer. He placed the 'do not disturb' sign up. In the past he made it clear to the staff, if the sign goes up, he must not be disturbed unless there was a nuclear bomb on the way. If he wanted anything, he would make a request. Only the person making that delivery would be permitted to disturb him.

He removed the computer from its box, downloaded a couple of programs, set up a new email. He placed the first of many SMD cards inside. These cards showed recordings of people entering each door of the Kremlin. He studied the tour groups and the mass of individual faces. Looking for someone was taking a long time and searching for the person looking everywhere but at the tour guide was tedious.

Nothing. He studied the ministers and the staff going to different entrances. Again nothing. He picked up the phone and called for more SMD cards going back five more months.

Again, he studied the faces pausing at ministers or military personnel who appeared at the entrances. Again, nothing seemed to be out of order. Yet something was niggling at the far reaches of his mind. It hadn't crystallised. *What am I missing?* He closed his eyes. Nothing.

He walked down the passageway to the small internal gym, the one he had installed not only for himself and Karina, but for ministers who seem to have growing waistlines. He chuckled to himself when he made it mandatory for all ministers to go to this gym or any other and do thirty minutes of exercise. As a joke, he placed a small treadmill in parliament. The speaker liked the idea. Instead of asking the minister to leave, he ordered them ten minutes on the treadmill. Georgy smirked when he recalled ministers ran out of breath and could barely speak. At times there were more than one acid-tongued politician forced to line up for their time on the treadmill. They could not leave the area until they did their time. He smirked again as he thought some considered the treadmill akin to some medieval torture. It didn't matter what they thought; civility had returned to parliament.

On the tread mill he pounded the imaginary pavement breaking into a sweat. He stopped to take a pulse rate. Too high. He rested until his pulse when back to normal. He was on the mill again going at a slower pace for the next fifteen minutes. Suddenly, he rushed out of the room down the hall and back to his office.

He looked again for faces that shouldn't be in certain locations. Faces going into doors leading to unknown internal locations. The face or faces that just don't fit into the zone of work. There was a pattern. Four of his more senior ministers were entering the southern door. Once a month the four men walked in separately. Georgy immediately knew they were brewing something. He looked at the letter that came with the tie pin. He re-read it. There was an element of truth in the letter smuggled to him. He looked at the smuggled letter again and pondered just who in the Russian police force or in the top security agency, he could trust. He shut down the computer and stowed it at the bottom of a cupboard.

He walked to the south corner entrance. He had to see for himself. The genuine register and the personnel he had never previously spoken to.

He approached the clerk at the desk and read the name, Ipati Falin. Ipati's mouth dropped open. He stood to attention and saluted. He stammered, "S-Sir."

Georgy nodded. "Where is the supervisor?"

Ipati pointed to the door behind his desk. Ipati walked over to the door and knocked as Georgy entered the clerk's room.

A middle-aged man wearing a neatly trimmed beard, opened the door to see the president filling the space. The supervisor gave a slight bow of the head and held out his hand. The president shook it as the man introduced himself, "Kolzak Shubin at your service. I am honoured by your presence. How may I assist you?"

Georgy looked around the small office before answering. "I want to examine the register of all people entering this section. The last six months will suffice."

Caught off guard, Kolzak immediately went to the shelves lining one side of the room. He pulled out the monthly registers for the requested time period. He put them on the table.

Georgy then told Kolzak to leave the room while he searched the registers.

Georgy eyes skimmed down the pages and stopped when he noticed the four minister's names were missing. He referred to the dates and time he saw on the CCT. He double checked entries on the dates. Each month the four names did not appear. When he was satisfied, he called Kolzak back. "Thank you. You can return these to the shelves. I want to go back six more months. I want the SDM cards going back six more months and then the books which match." Kolzak did as requested. He placed the SDM cards in the computer on his desk and let the president do as he wanted. Again, the faces appeared on the CCT but still there was no names in the register. He closed the books up and called Kolzak in again.

"I want to look at the staff rosters for these dates and times." Georgy handed the list over to Kolzak.

By this time, Kolzak was beginning to worry what was going on. Kolzak didn't voice his concern. Georgy sensed the man was beginning to be unnerved.

Kolzak handed the roster of the people working at the desk on those days. Two names consistently appeared, Ipati Falin and Makar Bobin. Georgy ordered, "I want these two men in here now."

Ipati is just outside and Makar is in the lunchroom. I will get them now."

"Send Ipati in first."

Georgy was pacing the room when Ipati knocked and walked in.

"Sir, you wanted to see me?"

"Yes. Keep standing. This won't take long."

Immediately Ipati felt uncomfortable. He braced himself.

"Do you like this job?" asked Georgy.

"Yes Sir," replied Ipati not knowing what the question or questions would lead to.

"How long have you worked here?"

"Three years."

"Is the pay good enough? You are being paid slightly over the normal clerk's wage plus there are other social benefits like free hospital, free dental, sick pay and a pension."

Ipati gulped. "The pay is excellent."

"Good. I was going through your records of service. Very punctual."

Ipati gave a sigh of relief. Then he almost choked.

"How much have Dimitri Orlov, Desya Sudakov, Isaak Buteyko and Lazar Turov been tipping you?"

"Sir, I have not accepted any bribes."

"Really? Just sworn to secrecy, eh?"

Ipati nodded. Georgy's calm demeanour changed. Anger flashed across his face. Ipati could have sworn fire flashed out of the President's eyes when he felt a vice like grip around his neck. The President let go. "Are the bribes worth the job loss?"

Shocked and humbled, and still gasping for air, a weak squeaky voice said, "Maybe not."

"How long has this been going on?" asked Georgy through gritted teeth.

"Not long."

"Define not long," said Georgy who was edging his way closer to Ipati.

"Six months, maybe a year," whimpered Ipati.

"Try longer," snarled Georgy.

"I really don't know. I have only been here for three years. It was going on before that."

Georgy stood back thinking, *that was when the elections were on. They formed their little party in case I won. Bastards.* "How were you paid? Cash? Gifts"

Ipati said, "Electronic transfer directly into my account."

"I hope it was worth it," spat Georgy.

"Good. Some honesty. After this shift of work, hand in all your passes, you get one-month severance pay, forfeit the pension you have earned since starting with us. No reference. Go." Ipati left the room with tears rolling down his face. It was an immediate sign to Makar what was going to happen.

Kolzak was confused and concern. He had never seen any male reduced to tears. Something seriously happened in there. Kolzak waited outside as directed by Georgy. He pressed his ears to the crack of the door hoping sounds of their voices would drift through.

Georgy went through the same process. When Makar left the office, Kolzac was stunned to see Makar holding back tears and going directly to the staff change rooms. Kolzac was called in. He braced himself. He stared, at loss for words when he was told of what two staff members were doing. He was given the orders to ensure all their passes were handed back, and what he had to do for the payrolls. He was now down staff, almost a punishment in itself.

He asked permission to find replacements. "Not just yet," replied Georgy, "Just add extra time to the existing staff. I will tell you within a week about extra staff. Thank you for your time and the inconvenience I have caused you. I will be back before the end of the day with other security staff."

With that Georgy strode out of the room, gave a quick sideways glance at a puffy faced, subdued Ipati and out of the front door. He u-turned and walked back to Ipati. "Where did these ministers go?"

Ipati didn't want to answer, but he forced himself, "Down the passageway to the right. At the end is a set of stairs. I don't know where they went after that."

"Thank you," replied Georgy.

Kolzak sat on his office chair feeling stunned at what had transpired. He had only heard rumours about Georgy Gurin's efficiency in stamping out corruption. It was something that had endeared him to the citizens but created enemies within his own ranks. Many heads rolled and today two of his own staff fell to the Gurin axe.

He looked at his mobile phone when it buzzed. A text was coming through. Georgy was coming back with security. The man said he was coming back but he wasn't expecting it so soon.

CHAPTER 29

Trusting no one, the President with two security men carrying unmarked boxes moved down the steps Ipati had indicated earlier. They opened each door to examine each room. Only one room piqued Georgy's interest. In the old KGB file room, now the least used room in the entire complex, four chairs were placed in a cleared area. The room was stale with cigar smells. No ventilation. Georgy and the men examined the shelves for disturbances. Nothing. Georgy opened an old cabinet and smiled. Four vodka bottles with letters in felt pen drawn on the label. D.O., I.B., l.T and D.S. He took out his phone and took a photo of each bottle and a group photo. He closed the cabinet. Before leaving the room, he ordered the two security men to immediately install equipment they were carrying.

It took twenty minutes for the room to have four carefully placed hidden cameras which also had voice recording facilities. A link was then made back to the new computer installed in his office and to his phone. Now it was a matter of time when the tell-tale ping would alert Georgy of a meeting in progress.

One week later, Dimitri Orlov, Isaak Buteyko, Lazar Turov and Desya Sudakov entered the basement. Immediately Georgy received the alarm to his phone. He cursed under his breath. It occurred in the middle of an important meeting with his Defence Minister. He excused himself and requested a new time to continue the meeting. He went to his office, hit the record button and watched and listened to the meeting going on in the south end basement.

Dimitri spoke first, "The cause of the pipeline delays in the Ukraine has been eliminated. That pesky Rostik and his wife Darina, family and friends were captured and shot. Our soldiers and police in the area should have no more issues. The surveyors should be able to progress without further incidences."

"Where have the rebels been buried?" asked Desya.

"Under the pipeline running outside Lviv. They won't be easily found. The land is now free of its owner and our soldiers won't be picked off as they have been. Our police in the area who have been patrolling, haven't unearthed further resistance to the pipelines. They haven't had the need to bribe the locals. Just as well. It was becoming an issue to get gold in nuggets and dust."

"Now that fire and subsequent explosion at the railway station. Just how did that happen?" asked Isaak.

"The fire brigade said it was cause by burst water and oil pipes. The leaks dripped on the electro-megatron. Hushing that up cost us a fair bit of money. We all know someone sabotaged it and the equipment leading to the chair. Our two escape goats were rescued by the same party. The footage at the railway station showed four unknown people with our two. Their faces were beamed across the world. They are fugitives now. I made sure of that," said Dimitri.

"Where's the original full-length footage?" asked Lazar.

There was no verbal answer but a nod towards the thousands of paper files cramming the shelves in the room.

"We need to find another candidate. Another foreigner to take the fall. We need to find one quickly," said Dimitri. "Or we find this Szymon character and bring him back."

"One advantage is that he has displayed an ability to kill without remorse. Taking out some mafia members at his age is better than some of the most seasoned men. He is in hiding," commented Isaak.

"Yes. Someone is hiding him. Keeping him safe until he recovers. That would be a long time before he fully recovers. Mind you he fought us very well. A resilience that is truly admirable," said Dimitri.

"Now the plans in Poland. The Exotic Polish Food Company is now controlling The East European Flower Company. Thomas Brennen is doing a brilliant job. I think we need to convert him, make him one of us. The same with Peter Schmidt, his marketing person. Excellent workers and on the ball. But we need to stop their other worker, Oskar Byko from going on more trips with the mafia. He needs to go. Who is the best hit man in Poland?"

"It was Thea Sorkin or the newly ex-Mrs. Mazur. She got greedy about taking over her husband's company and got caught trying to kill him. She lunged a knife at a cop who opened the front door of the house. She got a bullet for her effort. Any other women? Hardly anyone suspects women to kill," said Isaak.

"Anna Duba is available but her drinking and gambling has made her unstable. I had my son, Artem, give her a trip to Macau, China. All expenses paid and enough chips to make her go into debt, a debt she can only cancel if she killed someone. She was being primed to kill Mazur but that was thwarted by Thea. She still owes us." said Dimitri.

"We get her to go after this Oskar," said Lazar.

"A bit of a problem. She likes Oskar's father, Fabian. She thinks the sun shines out of his bum. No, she won't agree to that," said Dimitri.

"How about Roza Zielinski, Norbert's daughter?" asked Isaak.

"No. She is the best person to use as a lure. She gets people into position for a takedown….like that Ivan Nowak. She set him up to get to Stefan. It screwed up the family's reputation and that flowed on to the business. The East European Flower Company and the execution of one driver and a few attacks on the franchisee, caused the company's value to dive. Now the Exotic Polish Food Company has taken over. Now, we are in a position for our people to move in. We need to convert Schmidt and Brennen. That is a priority to get our people in the right places. Roza works perfectly to get the ball rolling. She is the bait or catalyst," said Dimitri.

"Another car accident or poisoning" suggested Desya.

"A car accident may look more natural and less suspicious. The men who travel with Oskar on the drug routes can do the job. We will ask one of them to follow Oskar, follow his patterns and then put him down. He knows enough of the drug routes and may have cottoned on to what was happening in the Ukraine. He and one of Rostik's daughters were missing from the head count. We get Oskar first," said Lazar.

"No a better idea," said Desya, "Lure this missing girl to get Oskar. Oskar bites the dust and then the girl goes east to join the others. I believe a girl at her age and untouched is desirable."

"Dimitri looked around the room, "Agreed. But Duba is still an issue."

"Just have her kidnapped and shot. She has no value," suggested Lazar.

All the men stood up and left the room.

The president who was watching and listening ordered their immediate arrests. The news of the arrests spread around the world. There were screams of the president being a tyrannical bastard, a throw-back to the communist era. The screams cooled down when sections of the tapes were played: the illegal use of the station for holding innocent and captive foreigners and covering up the explosion that followed. The rescuers without instruction blew up the area to ensure the venue was never used again. He released the news of the murders in the Ukraine but kept the snippets of the murder plots under wraps for the courts. Public unrest on the domestic front immediately settled but the battles with the immediate neighbours regarding the over budget pipelines and the deaths would continue to play out on the international arena.

Secret meetings between the nations, diplomacy in overdrive, openness and accountability was restructured and heads rolled. New ones emerged taking on a task which was now very much in public view.

Over a few months, crises with the neighbours had virtually come to an end with minor loose ends in the process of being tidied up.

The president and his wife decided to take a few days of rest. The stresses of the last few months had pushed their limits. They were chauffer driven to the presidential retreat, a place he had only visited once after the election.

As soon as he had arrived, Georgy went to the office to make a call. He put the network scrambler on before dialling The East European Flower Company using his private mobile phone. The installed specialised network scrambler blocked all incoming signals and possible exterior listening devices.

Any listener would get an initial loud whistle followed by dead silence. No matter what they did, they could not intercept any communications. No incoming communications could enter the premises either unless the president flicked a secondary switch to permit incoming calls.

Georgy dialled the number which connected to a private mobile phone, to a somewhat shocked Thomas Brennen. After a short introduction and a quick exchange of pleasantries, Thomas gave the president the mobile number of Detective Radoslaw Lanski.

The president invited Radoslaw, Thomas Brennen and Oskar to the retreat. Not to draw attention to the meeting, the trio flew to Moscow and were met by a chauffeur in a hired limousine. The limousine drove to them a pre-designated point not far from the Kremlin. The trio were then directed to walk to another location just fifty metres away where they met another chauffeur who escorted them to a very ordinary white four-wheel drive. The chauffeur drove them drove them to the presidential retreat.

The president not only wanted to thank them personally for their assistance but wanted background information as to how his once trusted advisors and members of his parliament, had instigated the kidnapping of a foreign national. Radoslaw, Oskar and Thomas spoke at length but at the same time protected what they felt was sensitive information still being investigated. Each gave information of their activities. Their stories were interrupted with recordings and photographs of events the president wanted more, if any, information. He wanted details of what was obviously hidden from him.

Thomas went first. He made it clear, all this started when bribed prison officials refused to listen to the advice of the police. He spoke of the initial character assignation of his son to draw himself and his company into disrepute. That was followed by personal attacks while in witness protection. That was then followed by attacks on the board of directors, and on innocent workers – the truck driver and franchisees. Thomas told of the attacks on two other companies in Poland. He mentioned the execution murders of two families where Szymon was the only one to escape. He briefly listed the fear Szymon lived with and how he did his best to protect his own property, all well before being kidnapped. Thomas omitted the shootings on that property. To Georgy, this filled some of the missing pieces as to why a foreign national was kidnapped.

The problematic Russian mafia was a thorn in the president's side. Taking over such companies would hide the smell of drugs and the people smuggling racket he realised by listening to the covert meeting. His ministers were in cohorts with the mafia. He felt sick to the core.

Georgy played more recordings. Some were news clips. Some were clippings not released to the public.

Radoslaw spoke of the attack on Eryk who after months in hospital, is slowly recovering with a busy schedule of different therapies. He spoke of the murder of the police accountant and others in Britain. Then the arson attacks in France. He spoke of the kidnapping of Szymon and notified the president, one of their own, a teenage boy named Kazmir. The discoveries of Szymon and Kazmir in the sub-underground station were accidents and the men enacted improvised a rescue. The fire was to burn the electro-megatron to deflect attention away from the kidnapping. Only those in the inner circle would know of the truth. No one was expecting an explosion.

Georgy stopped Radoslaw. "It wasn't just a fire at the railway station, but a major explosion which ripped a hole so deep, it was frightening. You say there was a station under the existing underground!"

Thomas took over. "I was homeless in my late teens-early twenties. Homeless people disappeared in Poland. I have to guess, taken to build this vast underground railway system. What happened to them after the complex was completed, will remain a mystery. They are still missing, most probably dead. The map on the wall of the main ticket office showed the lines run in rings around the city, almost following the circular road system you have here and from certain points radiating outwards. I heard the news of the fire, most of us just heard fire." Georgy nodded and then gave a grin. "Our underground needs expanding. If this system already exists, then it comes out of mothballs. It will only need upgrading or modernization. That will save several millions on the economy. Are there any other exists you know of?"

Thomas shook his head. "You may have to rip out some of the new construction on the rebuild of the railway. Maybe some workmen saw what was there. Who knows? There were two entrances close together. That is something you will have to investigate. No doubt, there are hidden exists and entries at existing stations."

Georgy nodded. "As you saw from one of the recordings, there was mention of large sums of money paid to the fire department to keep the cause of the explosion and the mothballed train lines secret.

No doubt builders were paid hush money. It would account for the extraordinary rebuild costs. The contractors will have their contracts revoked and criminal charges will be laid."

Oskar built up the courage and asked, "Sir, the pipeline going through the different countries, were they authorised by you or the previous president?"

"The previous president."

"Sir, was the authorization for two pipes or three?"

"Only two. One for water and one for oil. Why?"

In many parts of the fully constructed pipelines, there are three. Two that you know about and the third is rectangular, wide and tall enough for vehicles to travel through. I can show you some pictures," said Oskar. Oskar showed him a few pictures on his phone.

The president was silent and shocked. He returned the phone. "That would explain the budget blow out. That would also explain the ire I have been getting from the affected countries. They have been furious that the project was so expensive and where the countries were to receive the oil and water benefits, it has not occurred. They were right to complain. The pumping stations and their access is limited or severely restricted or non-existent. More heads will roll. Oskar, exactly what did you see and do out there?"

Oskar told his story. At the end the president made it clear. "You know too much. They are after you. You saw and heard that. I am going to start cleaning out my cupboards and you people, I already see, have already started cleaning out yours. Moles and deception always lead to destruction. In the last few hours, I have heard more going on behind the scenes than I ever imagined." He was silent for a while longer and then spoke firmly and in a softer voice, "I want you to do something very special for me. I feel can trust you. I will give the same instructions to my lawyer just as a backup."

There was a soft knock on door. Karina smiled as she entered. "You men must be hungry. Dinner is served." She led them to the formal dining room where five settings were provided. A chef walked in holding a large ornate serving soup pot. Everyone was silent as the man scooped out each serving. When he disappeared, Oskar noted the tie pin he had given to Georgy months ago.

Karina picked up on Oskar looking at the tie pin. Before she could say a word, Georgy commented, "She has claimed it."

Oskar offered, "I can get another."

Georgy stopped eating and laughed. "No you don't. She has a habit of claiming every tie pin given to me. It is me who has to ask to wear any."

Karina retorted in a friendly manner, "He can only wear one tie pin at a time. I can figure out ways to wear two at a time. And this one is one of the nicest ones we have ever received. What also makes it special is that it was given out of kindness, not with a diplomatic attachment. It has come from kind people with a good heart and that genuine goodwill attaches itself to the item. It speaks of kindness and love."

Georgy sighed. "Jewellery is one of her pet subjects. She used to be a designer and has a good eye for quality as well. She says some of the tie pins were one step better than tourist junk. But this one was definitely up there with a handful of the best."

The next day, Georgy and Karina were at the retreat all by themselves. They had dismissed all the staff. They wanted time with no one around. Georgy needed time to consider all he learned. No disturbances. He formulated plans in his mind. Russia had to move forward and fit in with a fast-changing world. The isolationist policies which permeated through old Russia and the controlling few who governed with an iron fists were gone. In his eyes, that was gone forever. Russia could no long function in its old ways. The new world structures just wouldn't allow it.

When the President returned to Moscow and parliament, he demanded a major review of the contracts between each country through which the pipeline was or still being constructed. He demanded the account books to examine the expenditure. The parliament was in uproar with accusations and counter accusations. Tempers raised, threats aired, and looks of hate spread across the room. The President walked out of the room screaming orders in a way he didn't want to do.

He retreated to his private office and stared at the cluttered desk. He drummed his fingers and slowly picked up the phone, calling the first president in a long list of presidents going from Lithuania to the Caspian Sea. He made appointments to meet each president. He was going to visit the sites and remedy the situation. Good international relations were important to him and Russia. There were not going to be any more standover tactics of the past. The same tactics which never endeared Russia to any other government or to its own people. Visits needed to be planned in secrecy.

He phoned parliamentary members whom he thought he could trust. He wasn't confident any more as to whom he could and could not trust. It worried him greatly. He set up the meeting at the retreat but this time he had miniature cameras and voice recorders installed everywhere but, in the bathroom, where only a sound recorder was installed and nothing in their bedroom. Karina pointed out to Georgy; she had never seen him so stressed. In her eyes, he had aged.

He prepared himself for heated discussions and the intended cessation of construction of the pipelines. It was not going to be a popular move, but such matters never were. He wondered just how his new precarious position within the party was. That would slowly reveal itself over the next few weeks and would show up in the meetings with the other presidents.

The men gathered in the smallest meeting room in the retreat. The President presented his findings for the review of the pipelines. He questioned under whose authority altered the plans. Evasive answers made the President angrier. The anger slowly built up. He called a break when he reached exploding point. The day continued with more discussions which seemed to run in circles. At five in the afternoon, Georgy called it a day and for the group to return in two days with answers or solutions.

The meeting was over but, the air was thick with silent anger which could be cut with a knife. It was obvious to Georgy; he had ruffled many feathers. He couldn't tell if all were honest, lazy and dismissive or if an undiscovered mole who was more loyal to old and defunct communist Russia than to press ahead with modernisation was present.

The ministers packed their brief cases in verbal silence, but the briefcase clips were slammed into position before being locked. Each nodded their head to each other and to Georgy as they left. Angry silence diminished as each left the retreat in their own vehicles. Georgy didn't watch them go. He shut the door and walked back to the meeting room where the aggressive atmosphere still lingered. He looked around the room and noted one brief case was left behind. He carried it to the front hall table in the hallway leading to the front door. He left the bag there as he was certain, the owner would shortly return. But no one did.

An hour passed when Georgy and Karina decided to go out. They had already dismissed the staff and wanted a night on their own. They were warmly dressed for the cool evening which was expected to become cooler. Georgy picked up his car and house keys which were on the same hall table as the briefcase. He adjusted his tie in front of the mirror directly above the hall table. Karina assured him he looked perfect and pecked him on the cheek.

There was a knock on the door. "Someone has finally remembered the briefcase," he said to Karina as he picked it up. He walked to the door holding the briefcase. The chauffeur for the Minister of Defence, gave a slight smile; his lips curled up slightly at the sides. He extended his left hand to take the briefcase.

"Sorry, for the inconvenience," he said as he quickly drew out a gun with his right hand from the pocket of the overcoat and shot Georgy at point blank. The bullet passed through Georgy's body to hit the floor behind him. On the way down to the ground, Georgy pushed a remote control he now always carried in a pocket to activate the transfer of events being recorded on his hidden cameras. Karina received a bullet to the head mid-scream. Silenced forever.

Following the chauffeur was the Minister for Defence. Both stepped over the bodies, went to the security room and pulled the CCT and every other older CCT recording going back three years being stored on shelves in the security room. The recordings were stowed in three large extra strong garbage bags. The place was wiped clean of prints, especially in the meeting room. When satisfied all was done, they walked out of the front door and stuffed the boot of the car with the recordings and equipment. The Minister of Defence walked back inside the house and dragged the two bodies together and placed the briefcase on top. He set the timer for two hours later. He walked out to the car and climbed inside. "Go. Thank you for your assistance."

The Minister of Defence was unaware of the additional mini recording devices which all information was beamed to Radoslaw's computer and to Georgy's lawyer's office. Radoslaw witnessed the ransacking of the standard CCT and he saw who the culprits were and who not only shot the president and his wife and removing the equipment. Shocked at what he saw, he immediately contacted the Russian police to inform them of what had happened and advised of a possible bomb and the need of an ambulance service. He then sent a copy of the assassination to the Russian police before making several copies. The Russian police received another feed, this time coming for Georgy Gurin's lawyer. They had no option but to act.

The two assassins drove away in silence to a recycling depot for plastics and electronic equipment. Both men drove through the gates with no questions asked by the bribed guard on night duty. Minutes later the sound of the crusher turned on. All the evidence was dumped in the machine to be converted into near dust sized particles. Everything looked normal. Evidence gone. The machine was turned off.

They drove through the gate saluting the guard and slipped him a thick wad of money. The car drove off. The guard went to the control room some ten metres away and wiped that part of the CCT. The footage wouldn't be missed as there was no reason to believe anything happened at night.

The Minister of Defence directed the driver to a night club. "Join me with a celebratory drink," he said with calmness and sincerity.

The chauffeur followed the Minister of Defence where they sat down at an alcove in the near empty venue. The barman walked over to take their orders. Minutes later he returned with their requests. The minister paid for the drinks. The men sat in silence. Minutes later the chauffeur was dead. He had swallowed cyanide hidden in his drink. Men hidden in the shadows of the bar picked the chauffeur up by throwing him over one man's shoulder and both men disappeared through the back door.

The guard at the recycle centre didn't arrive home. His car crashed on a sharp narrow bend. Those supervising the crash walked over to make sure he was dead. The wad of money was removed. They poured alcohol over his body and some into his mouth and left the bottle in his hand. It looked like he was drunk at the wheel. The alcohol odour was strong. It was enough to warrant no further investigation; just another statistic of drink-driving.

One day later, the murder of Karina Gurin and the attempted assassination were announced to the world. The police only had the household staff and their reports who attended the meeting. There were two bullets, one for each person. Karina was pronounced dead at the scene. Georgy was rushed to hospital; he was barely alive.

The Russian people rose up in anger and vetted their shock and dismay at the walls of the Kremlin. The politicians were huddle inside fearing for their existence. Then everything went silent.

A news feeds coming out of Poland and one from Moscow itself filled the outdoor screens. The feeds were streamed to all radio and television stations and to anyone operating a mobile. The feeds showed the chauffeur shooting the president and his wife. He was accompanied by the Minister of Defence. They saw the bomb being set in the briefcase. The intended bombing failed when police removed the briefcase and tossed it away. The bomb exploded in the air. No escaping the captured evidence, both men were guilty.

The people rioting outside the Kremlin, bayed for the Minister of Defence. Politicians standing near him were shocked and slowly moved away from him. The murderer was there in their presence. The Minister of Defence suddenly looked small. He held up his hands in surrender.

From somewhere in the back of the internal crowd. A gunshot was heard. The Minister of Defence fell where he stood while the other politicians ducked for cover. A lone young man dressed as a security guard walked forward to look at the body at his feet. He dropped his revolver and placed his hands out to be cuffed. He didn't say a word.

The top security officer flanked by four armed senior guards ran into parliament. Their guns aimed at the assassin. The assassin said in broken Russian, "My name is Szymon Chzov. I am a Polish national who was the only survivor of the mass execution of the Grabowski and Sawicki families in Poland. I was kidnapped by your Minister of Defence and his friends and tortured to wipe all memories of the past. I was accidentally discovered by other Polish nationals on holidays. They smuggled me back to Poland where I have been receiving treatment. I consider myself sane except when it comes to the mafia. The Minister of Defence and the other minister jailed earlier, Desya Sudakov, Dimitri Orlov, Lazar Turov and Isaak Buteyko were not just

Ministers of Parliament who wanted Russia to return to a communist dictatorship but are also the head of the Russian mafia. Russia was going to be ruled by the mafia."

Gasps were audible around the room. Szymon held out his hands again to be cuffed. "I am willing to go to jail for this assassination. Further police investigations will prove I have told you all the truth." With that ending, Szymon knelt and placed his hands behind his back in preparation to be taken away.

The security men moved forward but looked around when they heard clapping coming from the gallery. Standing in the lofty position in the above gallery, was a sickly man in a wheelchair with an attending nurse. It was the President who had barely survived the assassination and intended bomb to destroy the presidential retreat. Gasps and shocked murmurs filled the air.

With the aid of a load speaker, the president in his wheelchair said, "He speaks the truth. He needs a medal not a jail cell. Bring him here." The guards escorted Szymon to the gallery. Szymon was beckoned. The president said, "That was the most impressive and boldest thing I had ever witnessed. I was informed of what was going on by the Polish police. It seems the Polish people know more of what is going on inside Russia than the Russian politicians do. Just how did you get into this place without alarms going off?"

"Sir, under buildings are service tunnels and with the extra railway station under the city, it was a simple matter of navigation."

Georgy tried to laugh, but he grabbed his chest when pain shot through. He nodded. "Szymon, give my regards to Thomas Brennen and the Polish police. Unfortunately, you will still be arrested. If I had my way, you would walk free. But, under law and this circumstance, it will be a very light penalty." Szymon nodded as the guards took him away.

Georgy signalled to be wheeled back to his quarters. He sat in silence knowing a possible injustice may be imposed by the courts. Who was clean and honest and who was dirty and wanted a promotion in the mafia chain of command, played on his mind. All he knew he had to recover and be a witness in the courts.

When the people heard the Minister of Defence was shot by a guard, many were shocked. They demanded to see the man who had the courage to dispense a politician in parliament house. They never did see who it was. His identity hidden. The people reacted with protests and riots for demands of the truth. That night they got their answer. Szymon's identity was concealed, but his speech and the voice of the president were broadcasted over the media, not only in Russia but around the world. Back in Poland, Radoslaw and the others sat shocked and numb. Their brains trying to comprehend the information across the media. Radoslaw's face went white when he picked up the phone. Szymon was missing from the hospital from where he was receiving treatment. Radoslaw was initially too stunned for words. The others looked at him questioning what had happened. He stuttered, "I …I think I know who killed the Russian Minister of Defence."

"Who?" asked Fabian.

"Szymon Sawicki. He escaped from the hospital. He must have killed the Minister. We need to organise a very smart and expensive lawyer."

"Well it was the Ministers of Parliament who organised his kidnapping and brainwashing. They twisted him to make him a killer. They got what they trained him to do, kill without remorse. They got what they paid for – a foreigner to take the fall for an assassination. It may not have been the right person he was being trained to assassinate, but he did do as trained and instructed," said Fabian. Oskar looked worried. "We have not informed our own president about what is happening. How can he send diplomats to Szymon without details?"

"We will work out a way to get the man's attention and have a long meeting to show him what facts and evidence we have collected. He won't believe the number of deaths which have occurred in this trail of destruction."

CHAPTER 30

The events in Russia spilled over to the hall of the Polish government. The President of Poland, Kacper Dudek, had received threats of his own. Politicians throughout Poland crawled out of their holes to sprout fear, unrest and incompetent aspects of the government, and they took opportunity to refocus on the overpriced pipelines.

The president of Poland, Kacper Dudek and his Treasurer, Adam Ovinko received a hand delivered letter from the Poznan police. Initially, they dismissed the letter, but the recollection of the Russian president's speech made them think twice. With their interest piqued, a secret meeting was arranged in Warsaw. Radoslaw and his team accompanied by Ivan/Peter, Stefan/Thomas and the two Mikal Mazurs met at parliament house. The group were escorted to a meeting room which suddenly shrunk in size due to the number of occupants. Radoslaw introduced his team and their roles before introducing the others.

Immediately, Radoslaw began with the release of hard core criminals from the jail system against police advice. Then he allowed each victim turned collaborator to state their story. These were aided with photos. Then the criminal events were mentioned in their chronological order- murders, attacks, attempted murders, white collar criminals working their way up Polish corporations, assassinations in Russia and assassinations and attempted assassinations of innocent business people., thefts, drug, gun and artefact smuggling operations, and people smuggling. Kacper and Adam hardly spoke a word.

Their faces went ghostly white when they heard, the Russian mafia were under the direction of the assassinated and jailed Russian politicians, had planted mafia cum Russian puppets in various electoral seats. Radoslaw was quick to mention the candidates were presently faceless and proof of their allegiance was not yet evident. He commented, "It is a work in progress. But a little help would be appreciated with new laws such as the person must show proof of birth in Poland or naturalization. The candidates to declare all social, political, and club associations and investments in this country, the surrounding and EU countries."

Adam sighed. "That is a very big order to scrutinise candidates like this. I can hear the screams of foul and invasion of privacy coming from every direction."

"We hear that too, but we can't have the mafia working for Russia running this country. It is the lesser of the two evils. We can start this on a covert basis and if we find dirt, bring it out and let that intended politician defend the muck. Let them hang themselves with it."

Kacper said, "We go covert. The Warsaw police will be ordered to do the checks. Meeting closed."

"Not quite. We still have the issue of Szymon Sawicki also known as Szymon Chzov who is now sitting in a Russian prison. He needs to be repatriated back and be placed into therapy."

"Good Lord," said Kacper, "Is he one of our people?"

There was a chorus, "Yes."

Radoslaw added, "It was on the news. He declared his citizenship."

Adam looked firmly. "I thought he was making it up. How did a Polish person get into a Russian parliament and shoot a minister? Our special forces couldn't achieve that!"

"A desperate person can do anything. He's a patriot who didn't want Russia in Poland. He had his personal motives which were broadcasted to the world. Above all, he is a patriot and should not be rotting in foreign prisons," replied Nathan.

Ivan added, "Listen to the mini-speech he gave after shooting the Minister of Defence. He said he was Polish. Mikal and I went to school with him. Before he escaped the massacre and the brainwashing, he was very sane and was a candidate to represent Poland in shooting in the next Olympic Games. He, above all has been the person who has suffered the greatest infliction."

"He has valuable information about the mafia," lied Radoslaw. "Although he is a civilian, he did some valuable work for us. He has indicated he has collected more information. We need him out of Russia."

"I'm lost here," said Kacper. "You said he needs medical help, but you accept his work. How can you rely on a twisted person?"

"Simple. He is only twisted about the mafia and wants them out of action. After all they did kidnap him and torched him. They trafficked his girlfriend whom he was going to marry, they killed her parents and his, bugged his father's company and infiltrated it to ensure money laundering looked very legitimate. He only has motive to put the animals away. Otherwise, he is saner than most of us. But don't let the Russian know that. He is playing the mentally disturbed roll in prison so other prisoners will not go near him. But he could turn if he stays in that place for much longer. He is more skilled than all of us put together. You don't want him on the streets if he turns. He is salvageable at this stage."

Adam and Kacper stood up. "We will need to think this over. I will give a reply in a couple of days," said Kacper.

The Poznan group left the meeting room not feeling they had achieved anything. "We can only wait," said Fabian.

Oskar's phone rang. His mother sounded distressed, "The school where Preshka was going said students heard her scream and saw her being pushed into a cream and brown van. Come home quickly."

"Fuck….sorry mum. I know where they will take her. I got to go and try to beat them there. See you in a few days."

Radoslaw asked, "What has happened?"

"Preshka has been kidnapped. I need to get into north Iran, like yesterday."

"How are you going to cross the border"

"Corruption is rife. Bribes are always good passports. I know who is on the take."

"It's too dangerous. I won't allow it," ordered Radoslaw. We don't need another diplomatic incident. She's Ukrainian. We notify the Ukrainian government."

"What? They are just as corrupt as the Iranians. No! I will go alone. I am not asking anyone to come with me."

Ivan looked at Oskar. "You are into her, I see."

"No. A promise to her parents and to her. No more."

Ivan shot a glance to Stefan. "I go with you as far as Constanta and wait for you there. I will wait a week and then return."

Stefan shouted, "No you don't. You are in retirement and back to normal life, whatever normal is these days."

"Just this trip and then no more. Promise."

"And what do I say to your immediate staff?

"They get an extra two days holiday. Anyway, they will be relieved not to have me around. And I get a break from them, especially Lucia."

Oskar joked, "That sexy number who purrs better than most kittens is into you? I'll be."

"She's all yours. Claws and all," said Ivan knowing Lucia was not only attractive and efficient but he just wasn't interested. The chemistry just wasn't there.

In Constanta, Peter/Ivan and Oskar checked into a motel near the water's edge. Oskar immediately went to the airport to catch a flight to Batumi in Georgia. From there he caught a six-seater to fly to Baku, Azerbaijan. It took him a couple of days to find a place where he could hire a four-wheel drive and buy food and camping equipment, binoculars and a gun with a small store of ammunition.

He crossed the border into Iran after slipping a familiar faced guard a few extra euros. He topped up the car with fuel and bought twenty litre tanks for refuelling. As he continued to drive south, he tried to recall the feel of the road he had experienced while in the back of the truck with the drugged-up women. He made a detour onto a side road and drove along that for ten minutes then stopped. He studied the landscape for a while and went back along the same track to the main road. There was another side-track which was equally as bouncy. After ten minutes he stopped again to survey the landscape. He knew for sure he was in the right place. He drove the car to the only tree which was almost dead. It was the only thing that offered any form of cover and walked the short distance to the known point of exchange. He dug a shallow trench and waited.

It was two days when the cream and brown mafia van arrived. It was accompanied by two four-wheel drive cars and a small truck. All the men climbed out of their vehicles first. Six men this time instead of the usual ten. Oskar liked the reduced number. The women were pulled out of the truck and placed again in the sun.

Oskar took aim and downed two men. The rest ran for cover behind their vehicles. Oskar slid on the ground to change his position. He fired again killing another and injuring one more he recognised as Trouble. He moved around again, sliding as if he were some snake. He took aim again, injuring another who he also recognised as Grumpy. The other person managed to run under the truck. Oskar took aim at the truck. Purposefully he shot out two tyres and then went for the fuel tank. Fumes leaked out. The man scrambled out and ran to one of the vans. Oskar shot him in the back of the head. *Definitely dead*, thought Oskar.

The other injured men tried to shoot at Oskar. One bullet just missed Oskar by centimetres. He felt the dirt sting an arm and his face. He wriggled again back towards his first hole which he laid in for two days. From here he had a clear view of one of the men. Oskar shot him through the chest. The other man realised he was now alone called out, "I'm giving up!"

Oskar didn't reply. He recognised the voice, it was Boss. The man yelled again, "I'm giving up. I'm tossing my gun." Boss threw the gun just slightly out of arm's reach. He struggled to stand up. Oskar shot him again. Oskar walked over knowing Boss was still alive. He wanted Boss to know who shot him. Oskar looked down at Boss and nudged his legs. Boss's vision was now becoming blurry. He could barely make out the person towering over him. "Puppy? Puppy you did this?" Oskar clicked the gun and cursed. He was out of bullets. He gave Boss another nudge to distract him from any attempt to attack. Oskar reloaded, "I'm taking over this operation. Orders from above." Oskar looked at the sky. Boss tried to laugh as blood trickled out of his mouth. He tried to say something, but his last breath beat him.

Oskar walked over to the three females. Preshka was totally tripping out. The older two women were in a slightly better state. One by one he loaded them into his four-wheel drive. He left the area as fast as he could. He just hit the main road when he saw the trucks which were used for swaps kicking up dirt in the distance. He drove back to Ardabil to refuel his car and to give the women food and drink. He found a shop selling scarves and khimars. He bought three of each. When he went back to the car and he said, "Put these on. It's for your safety." The two older women did as instructed and then helped Preshka; she was slowly coming out of her drug stupor. When they had their new clothes on, he was then able to let them out of the car. "I think the toilets are that way." He pointed to a sign which had a symbol of a man. "I'll escort you just in case someone takes offence."

As they neared the toilets, Oskar told them to wait. There were no toilets for women. He entered the men's toilets as one man was coming out. Oskar looked back at the man to ensure he kept walking. The man turned to Oskar and gave a grin. He said something in Arabic which Oskar didn't understand but took a guess, that a man with three women was lucky. No man was inside. Oskar ushered the women in as he stood guard. One man tried to enter while the women were inside, but Oskar held him back. The man was just starting to become agitated when the women trooped out.

Oskar guessed the man apologised in Arabic.

Back in Constanta, Ivan counted the days. In that time, he played tourist and lazed around on the beachfront cafes or took walks to the local shops. It was on his third day while he was sitting in a coffee shop, when a voice addressed him, "Hello, Ivan. Long-time no see." He swung around to see Marlena pushing a toddler in a pram. He stared. Of all the places, miles away from anywhere, here she was. He gulped at the ambush. He stuttered, "Hello." He gave her a hug. Both looked at each other grinning from ear to ear. Eventually, Ivan said, "Sit. Join me if you have time."

"Just a few minutes. My parents and Lavinia are heading this way. Lavinia is trying to con dad into buying a piece of jewellery. I came ahead to get a couple of tables which we could slide together. This place can get crowded about this time." Ivan pulled three tables to join his.

"How is Leon going?" Ivan bent down to take a closer look at the child.

"Good. He makes his needs known," she said in a somewhat motherly manner.

Ivan managed a grin. "Things are almost back to normal now. Less complicated."

Marlena nodded. "Less complicated? I am not sure. Did you hear the political turmoil back home? Some election candidates have been arrested for having ties with the mafia and others have been shown to be Russian plants. The country is going to pot."

Ivan didn't say a word, he let her speak. She only stopped when she saw the rest of the family coming. When they approached, they gave a questioning look before Lavinia realised Marlena was talking to Ivan.

After the meal, Ivan was invited back to their holiday apartment. There was more catch up history, more coming from Marlena's family than from Ivan. The next three days he was frequently in their company until he got a call from Oskar. Ivan knew he had to make excuses to leave. He held the phone up as he said, "My holiday is over. I have just been summoned to work."

"Make sure you don't be a stranger anymore." said Marlena as she gave a parting hug.

Ivan spent the day purchasing tickets for five people to go back to Poland.

Back in Poland, Preshka took more time off from school to recover. The other women were met by their families at the police station. Oskar stayed back to fill in a report and account for the long list of expenses. He gave his parents another call and said he would go directly home and would see them tomorrow for lunch.

Oskar, his parents and Preshka were sitting at the dining room table. Oskar looked at Preshka and joking said, "When you go to school next week, I will make sure you are delivered in an armoured truck and it goes right to the doors of the administration building."

She retorted, "Only after my unofficial big brother signs autographs for my friends. You are a bit of a hero. It was…." Nothing more was said. A blast ripped through the home killing all inside.

Radoslaw heard the police sirens from his office not realising one more member of his team was affected. He swore when he heard the news and tears rolled down his face. "They just never stop. The holes in the Russian hierarchy and in Polish politics has just allowed a set of promotions to continue the battle." When Radoslaw went to Oskar's parent's home, to examine the destruction, he shook his head. The damage was so complete that neighbouring houses were impacted. He returned to his car to discover a note under the windscreen. He looked around at the people going back and forth wondering who had time to place a note. He opened the note and he screamed. A uniformed officer came running to his aid. Radoslaw shook as he handed the note over.

This goes a long way to even the six men killed in Iran.
You kill us. We kill you. A promise.

CHAPTER 31

Two Years Later.

Ivan married Marlena. Taking on a child who wasn't his didn't faze Ivan and elevated Ivan in his parents-in-laws eyes, particularly her father, Dominik. Maja, Marlena's mother, played the happy and proud hostess, kissing all on their cheek and hugging each person she met. Dominik, seemed to be glowing and somewhat gushy whenever Ivan was mentioned – an ultra-warm welcome, a very happy occasion. Nothing went wrong. Perfect.

Ivan was a bit overwhelmed but did his best to cope with the event. If he and Marlena had their way, it would have been a group of twenty friends or what was left of them. They never told any member either side of their family where they were going for their honeymoon. All they knew was little Leon was going with them. Maja didn't get her way to look after Leon for the two weeks. She eventually relented with a display of the sulks.

After the honeymoon, Ivan and Malena slowly settled into married life. Everything was going perfectly. Stefan would visit once a month to spend an entire day. Dominik and Maja wanted to occupy every weekend with the couple. But Marlena and Ivan stood firm, one weekend per month and two nights a week a family meal. Maja disliked the feeling her grip on her daughter had loosened but Dominik secretly approved. To him he saw Ivan was the man of his house. That suited his old-fashioned values.

It was close to six months when they announced another child was on the way. Maja grew cluckier. Dominik accepted the news like other expectant grandfathers; proud and looking forward to the addition. There was a barbeque organised for the immediate families and friends. It was on this day, things changed.

All but two guests had left, and they were in the process of leaving when Dominik asked Ivan into his home office. He closed the door and hung a 'do not disturb sign' on the knob. The women knew when the sign was up, he was never to be interrupted unless he requested something and that came via phone. He ordered Ivan, "Sit. We are going to have a very long discussion." For some reason, Ivan expected the worse. Scenarios ran through his mind but not what he was about to hear.

"What I am about to say, stays in this room. Do I make myself very clear?"

Ivan nodded and braced himself. The tone didn't sound things were good.

"Good. I want you to listen carefully. Call me a little old fashion, if you desire. I will accept that."

"I have noted some old-fashioned traits. Then when I am your age, I would think Leon and the new brother or sister will think the same."

Ivan just looked at Dominik who gave a broad grin. "That is a perceptive thought but it's not like that," he said as if reading Ivan's earlier thoughts. Dominik sat in his office chair and lit up his third cigar of the day. Ivan coughed as the smoke drifted in his direction. "Sorry," said Dominik, "These things are the death of me. Smart of you not to smoke." He pulled out a cigar clipper and chopped the lit end off. It fell into a small dish full of cigar endings and ash. He put the cigar away. "I brought you in here as I have some important things to say." Ivan wriggled in his seat to adjust himself.

"I am very happy you are my son-in-law. I have never seen Marlena so happy, really happy."

"Thank you. It works both ways." Dominik held up his hand to stop Ivan from speaking.

"Keep looking after her the way you are, and I will be happy for the rest of my life which will be short. I have cancer, lung cancer from those cigars. I have about two years to live. I will tell the girls in about six months. But for now, they need not know. Maja would kill me with concern. You know what I mean." Ivan nodded.

"I will make it clear and now, I have appointed a couple of people, faceless to you, well not exactly faceless, you have met them over the last two years but I have given them a task. If anything between you and the girls turns south, they will straighten the issue out. They will hear two sides of the story and then make a judgement. That is just insurance."

Ivan gasped. "Then they or anyone else shouldn't give me cause."

Dominik laughed. "I have already tested you on one point well before you met Marlena in Constanta."

"W-What? How?" asked Ivan. He was blown away.

"That secretary, Lucia is one of my people who was cultivated in the new direction I was steering everyone who wanted to go that way. She was there to tempt you and compromise you. She is a genuine secretary. She lodged complaints about you which only endeared me more towards you. She failed. You won. Impressive. Damned impressive. Most men would have fallen, but you just threw more work at her to keep her occupied. The more she tried, the more work you threw at her." Dominik chuckled. "Very clever."

"I just wasn't interested in her or any other woman. I figured if she had time to flirt with me, she didn't have enough work to do."

Dominik laughed louder. "Brilliant. I must remember that. Lucia complained to me that she was so loaded with work, it ruined her social life. She gave you some unfavourable descriptions which only endeared me to you even more. Now back to the main subject."

"I want to tell you a very long story about your father and me."

Ivan frowned. "The two of you? I didn't even know you two had history."

"Not a direct history. I really wanted to be friends with your father, but life forbade that."

Ivan gulped and wondered where all of this was leading to. He had noted the two men were friendly whenever they were together, but he always considered it a mutual respect due to their children being married.

"I first saw your father in the courts defending himself against accusations of being a member of the gang who broke in, robbed and murdered the two store owners. Hell, I was impressed by his ability to fend off the most bitter of questioning I had ever witnessed. I was always taken to court when so called friends and relatives were in trouble. My parents made me sit through everything on school holidays or if I didn't want to attend school. I was there. They said I had to learn the processes and procedures but above all defend myself." Dominik waved a finger at Ivan. "Nothing compared to what I saw your father do, never wavering on any detail, sticking to the truth and choosing his words carefully to make it difficult for the prosecutor or his lawyer to challenge him on any other issue not relevant to the court case. When the prosecutor or his lawyer tried to steer away from the actual event and dig up irrelevancies, your father steered them back. I was in awe of him. It was also the defining moment in my life.

"I no longer wanted the life my parents were carving out for me. I wanted to be like your father, being honest and having no fear. It was a long time after the court case when I saw your father again. He was homeless. It was a time when mud sticks like glue. He lost everything. When I saw him, he took shelter in a shed at the bottom of an aunt's home. In the winter she would allow only one homeless person take shelter. She would chase away others as a crowd would have drawn attention. Many other people did the same. She would only allow a person stay Monday to Friday and when their week was up, the first to show up on Monday would have the privilege. She would serve them a bowl of soup with some bread each night. I asked her why she did it. Her reply was, 'to be forgiven for the sins of the family she was born into.'

"One night, your father was there. I recognised him from the kitchen window. I wanted to speak to him and give him his meal, but my aunt said no. It was too dangerous for me to go. A fight could break out. So, I watched him from the window thinking how cruel it was when an honest man is brought down in such a manner. From then on, I kept a distant watch. I became impressed how he pulled himself out of the situation. Hell, he had all the ingredients to go bad; no home, no job and family rejection, nothing to lose. He didn't. That just raised my admiration for him. When he went into business, I watched it grow. Never once did he put a foot wrong. I noticed just how loved your father was. There was a two-way respect between him and his employees. I compared that to what I was groomed for. I wanted what your father had achieved. That was another turning point. I wanted out of a life of deceit, drugs, guns, and everything else. I was tired of going to courts and funerals."

Ivan looked surprised at what he heard. He almost felt blown away by the information. "Exactly, what has all of this got to do the worst three years of dad's and our lives, the years before I married Marlena"

Dominik leaned forward. "I learned from some men in the family, that some prison officers were on the take and some people on the review board were bribed, huge bribes to let Norbert Zielinski and Wikto Duba out. I sent an anonymous message to the police citing evidence, the two had been recruited to the Russian mafia while in prison and were planning a series of crimes. They took it seriously, more so when things did check out. Unfortunately, they failed. Evidence rejected as hearsay.

"So that is when the three newspaper articles splashed me across town, me proposing to three different women. Each paper had a different woman with two pictures which were photo shopped."

Dominik twiddled with a pen. He was itching for that cigar sitting on his desk. "I did my best to stop the three false articles. But some people don't listen. I had no cause to discredit you or your father. I had lost power. My power base had diminished and the mafia family I was raised in split into two under my leadership years before. I was on the minority side, with minority everything."

"What exactly happened?"

"As I said, I was watching your father from a distance. I wanted everything he had but couldn't do so under the circumstances I was living. After I heard your mother died in a car accident and then discovered the car was tampered with to cause that accident. It was the last straw for me. I had inherited control of the family, as the Italians say, I was the Don. I was furious that older men were taking advantage of my age and lack of authority. They did what they pleased whenever they pleased. It was a growing mess. Out of frustration, I decided to give everyone a vote at a very rare compulsory meeting. I made it clear, it was for any person, male or female, over the age of eighteen to attend and vote. There was a debate between me and Gregori Zielinski, the man who you killed in Britain."

Ivan gasped and his eyes widened. "Only the police knew that. I was never charged. It was self- defence. They said it was reasonable force."

"I was given a copy of the report. Phones take good pictures. The majority went with Zielinski and over the years, their numbers went down due to deaths and on occasion, I would drop an anonymous tip to the cops. Some were put away for a long time. The cops never knew the source and the others never found out. I sat back and watched their fights go public and splashed across the newspapers and T.V. They killed their own and were in total self-destruct mode. The result was their numbers declined and had no one to guide them anywhere. That is when the Russians walked in offering false gifts. They were so drunk by the offerings. They couldn't see their own final demise.

"For fifteen years, those who were loyal to me and saw the vision of where I was going, prospered and lived very healthy and comfortable lives. They felt secure and free. The others who chose to go down the old path became jealous. They would attack family members who chose the new path.

"That was when I purchased the run-down school, spent thousands restoring parts, added new buildings which were as best as funds would allow, be sensitive to the original architecture. Genuine teachers were brought in and every other personnel. All were ignorant of the purpose of the school except for the founding families. When the wheels were in motion, the school became self-funding.

"The school was to protect all the children from the break-away group such as mine and keep track on what other wealthy mafia groups were doing. There were spaces, about twenty percent of the enrolment, for non-related families such as yours, the Grabwoskis, Sawickis, and Hartoviskis to name a few. They were permitted in as we needed genuine injection of new blood, new ideas and new money. I wanted to watch the families to see which students would best fit in to our new group."

Ivan interrupted, "Bastard. You were grooming innocent people to join your personal wars. I feel sick, no disgusted."

"I was expecting that reaction. No. It was to make sure our kids went to a safe school and I could have eyes on the enemy. Grooming with or without parental permission, was a side effect. Kids, such as yourself, were not trained in killing, deception or destruction but to be captains of industry with sharpened survival skills." Dominik leaned back in his chair and said in a smug manner, "It worked. The students came out confident, went to university or took on apprenticeships of different types and became upstanding members of the community. They didn't want to follow their parent's murky past although many were aware of family matters. Some may regress in the future, but they were given tools to survive when the chips were down. They know there is an alternative to resorting to crime when things went crappy. They had a network of friends who could pull them through."

Ivan was still annoyed. "And families which had zero links?"

Dominik waved his hand around while holding the pen as if it were a cigar, "A good education. Leadership."

Ivan wasn't quite convinced. "That war and undermining of the so-called other side, killed the Grabowski's and their company struggle to yet recover from incorrect consumer presumptions. Sawicki Engineering has nearly gone broke due to lost contracts. The Mazur Constructions is trying to rebuild itself. This is not to mention dad's company, The East European Flower Company and the initial fake Exotic Polish Food Company suffered. Even Lavinia was affected. I knew Antoni was intending to marry Lavinia. Now he's dead and she has been badly affected."

Dominik leaned forward extending himself across his desk. "And you not only survived but steered them through success against all odds. You are your father's son, well and truly. Together, we will make amends to the Sawicki family and their business. Together we will fix the mess for the others."

"How? You only have two years at the best. No maybe less when you're wired up to machines and just maybe vomiting up everything you eat."

"True. While I am still composed and with your father at your side, you can do anything. This conversation just isn't about us fixing a wrong. It is about succession."

"Succession to what?" asked Ivan who wasn't sure if he was confused or not or was going to dislike more of what he was going to hear. "Corporate crime disguised as welfare?"

"No. But if you to go down that path, then watch your back and everyone around you. The stress will kill you before reach forty-five."

Dominik stood up and walked over to a mini bar on the other side of the room. He looked at Ivan trying to work out what Ivan would say or even do. "Do you want a drink?"

Ivan thought about it. Sure, he wanted one after he felt like he was peppered with one hand-grenade after another, but he wanted to be clear minded against a crafty man. "No thanks."

"I have questions, they may not come in logical order, but I want them answered with truth not side-stepped etc."

Dominik filled his glass up, gave a gesture for cheers. "Okay. It is only fair. You listened to me. And I see you're a bit shell-shocked."

"That's putting it politely," said Ivan not sure if his father-in-law was harbouring more secrets and tactics than whatever he could imagine. What he said already floored him a couple of times. He wondered if anything more could resemble a kick. "Why did you pick me for succession? Others who are loyal to you should have been asked and given the opportunity."

"They were asked. They are so comfortable in their new life; they didn't want any specks of dust from the past to annoy them. They all turned down the job and many nominated you without any prompting or hesitation. It has always been a tradition; the son of the 'Don' takes over. But I have no sons and you have proved your worth and had passed many tests while I did organise your protection from the other side."

"Exactly, what do you mean protection from the other side?"

"You were watched by myside and the other side. There was a bounty on your head put on by the Russians and a bigger one on your father. It cost me a lot of time, effort and a bit of money to get the bounty lifted." Ivan swallowed hard at the revelation of a bounty being lifted. "That means, I didn't exactly survive on my own."

"What it means was I paid half the bounty on your father's head for them to piss off. I had minders in the background watching you in case you were kidnapped. There were two attempts and the kidnappers went to jail. Landski was fed the information. He knew any anonymous tip about the growing case was going to be accurate. Every time there was an attempt, the cops took them away."

Ivan's mind went blank as he heard Dominik continue, "Ivan Nowak, Ivan Kowalski, and Peter Schmidt. Stefan Nowak, Stefan Wozniak, Thomas Brennan. All the scum knew except the Russian Ministers." Ivan just whispered and went ghostly white. "Fuck."

"Why did this monstrous family feud, have to kill the Grabowski, their domestic staff and Szymon's parents?"

"As I said I had limited people. Sometimes things slip through. I wasn't aware their lives were going to be cut short. The Russians controlled the remainders and like stupid puppets, they did what they were told. The sweetener was to get rid of half or more of the family and take over the manufacturing. The legitimate supplements were going to be created as normal. A new plant was going to be built where drugs disguised as supplements would be created and trafficked. Szymon, unknowingly delayed that action and disposed of their men who were going to raid the headquarters and kill many innocent workers. And for his trouble, the rogue Russian ministers saw his potential and kidnapped him. You know the rest to that bit."

"And Sawicki Engineering, how does that fit in to the scheme of things?"

"That wasn't us Poles at all. It was the same Russian rogue ministers wanting access and control of all water and oil in East Europe. No country operates without those vital products. I didn't know the Russian government old guard was going after Szymon or his family. I just didn't know. Sorry. It was that trip to Russia when you and the others fled that brought that out in the open. The assassination of the Defence Minister was bold and brilliant. I have heard, Szymon only spent a month in jail. He was brought back to Poland and is undergoing treatment. The treatment is free for him at one of my facilities."

Ivan frowned. "Free? Your facilities?"

"Over the years, I built small clinics around the country. I am just the financier, a job for you to learn."

"Szymon has weekend passes. He goes to another minder family where they help to integrate him back to normal society, whatever normal is these days." Dominik loaded up a second drink.

"What I gather from the clinic and the minders, is he is quite sane on many levels, a bit forgetful but snaps. He goes like a killer on steroids at the mention of mafia or Russians."

"Yeah, I figured that out months ago," said Ivan. "I went to visit before he escaped to Russia and shot the Minister. Why was the Mazur family targeted?"

"The mafia wanted them for money laundering. Buy places with the excess cash. But most of what they were buying was Russian controlled and with Russian money. The Polish government is nullifying the purchases - eyes on the inside. The land will come back on the market. We buy that land for another private school. This school will be for anyone who can afford the fees. The fees will be a bit cheaper and the classes slightly larger. I have already made preliminary enquiries with the different levels of government. They like the idea."

Ivan thought about the answers. Then he thought about Oskar. "Why was Oskar, his family and that Ukrainian girl murdered?"

"That was another gap in the limited eyes I have. It was an order from the gang of four Russian ministers. Oskar was one of us. So were his parents. My people. He never accepted a cent from us as that would have caught attention from the people above. There is a mole in the police force in Poznan. I just haven't found him. Someone who knew exactly where to find you and your father in Britain, and in Germany and France. There is a network of them, maybe inspector rank and up. Another job to be cleared before I go. The witness protection program will continue to fail. Any mafia from any country want the witnesses buried. Those on the take must get good pay, and maybe under a pseudo name."

"Why would they want to kill Preshka?" asked Ivan.

She was the last surviving person from the clan who owned a large tract of land which was suspected to have minerals in the mountains. And the pipeline was designed to go through the middle. In many countries if an heir is not located, the land returns to the government. She stood to inherit a massive fortune. She was a loose end which needed to be put away so evil untold plans can go ahead."

Ivan recalled what Oskar had said about the cave with the water and stalagmites and stalactites. It could be a tourist mecca. He kept the thought to himself.

Ivan looked at Dominik not sure what to think other than this father-in-law confession confused his view of man, and then he wasn't sure if he was a saint or the devil incarnate. Ruthless, yes. Protective, yes. Ivan sat quietly for a while. Thinking what he married into. He spent years lying to others, lying to himself only to discover, he was caught in a family feud. He could live without this.

"Just exactly, what do you mean by specks of dust?" asked Ivan.

"Unfinished business and the remaining family members who are still on the dark-side. Then there are the Russians who may get a bit toey. That gorilla who runs the patisserie in St. Petersburg that was one you and Mikal flushed out. We knew someone was there but who and where, was unknown to us. Over time, the police will flush him and others out. It's their job. We will just supply anonymous information to shove things along. A part of your job description is to keep the family safe and going in the new direction. As I said before, no illegal rubbish like drugs, guns and robberies. Now we will remove the rubbish by anonymous tips to the cops and let them sweep up the mess. The mess goes in one of two boxes: coffins of their own making or jail nudged along by us.

No direct revenge killings by us. We keep squeaky clean. That is what this succession is about. No more family feuds and internal wars. Those days are over."

"Let's back track one more time," said Ivan. Dominik studied Ivan with careful eyes wondering what else he needed to explain.

"When I met up with Malena and the rest of you in Constanta, why were you there? I know now it wasn't an accident."

Dominik gave a genuine smile. "When Oskar went on his trips with the mob, he would inform me. It was information gathering on my behalf and ensuring Oskar would have help if he required. When he told me he wiped out two Russians and four of the family still on the dark side, I wanted to give him support if the shit hit the fan. It didn't at that point of time. I knew you were there in a similar capacity.

"I tried pumping you for information, but you were guarded and very tight lipped. That impressed me as well. Another test you passed. You have no idea how hard I tried to squeeze you, but you didn't fall into any traps. Then I realised why Malena gave Leon, Ivan as a second name. She was carrying a torch for you. Ahh, dumb of me. Lucia failed as you were carrying a torch for Malena. Why didn't I see that before?"

"Simple. We men are always guilty of being blind. Hell, I didn't wake up until I was in France and when I laid eyes on her when she was sleeping in the hospital. I broke all the rules to do that and I got punished for the effort. Our paths crossed in France. We swapped notes and kept in touch by using false names on Facebook when it was safe for me to do so and what I said was very limited."

Dominik raised an eyebrow at the revelation. "I didn't know Marlena could keep secrets. I wonder if she knows about any of this stuff we have been talking about?"

"Bits. She opened up to me about some things over the last two years and you just confirmed them."

Dominik brushed his hair back. "She is smarter than I gave her credit for."

The men sat quietly looking at each other; both absorbing new information and reassessing each other. Dominik gave a slight grin. "Taking on this job, a job you were voted in to by the others, will be both rewarding and frustrating. They will support you and help you like they have done with me. "Consider them as your guardians watching out for snakes in the grass. Some will pop up even in the business world. I know you are already aware of that."

Ivan adjusted himself in his seat as thoughts ran through his mind. "As for the final dregs in the family, ninety per cent are gone, to jail, in coffins, or gone to the Russians. It is just the remaining few where I will coach you to get rid of to jail. I will say this once, snakes have toxins and if bitten, the toxin never leaves. I am still having some reminders, like scary skeletons in the cupboard.

"I will go down two ways in the family history. Those who continued with the old ways, will consider me a ruthless bastard. Yes, I am ruthless. The cupboard needed cleaning big time. Those who followed me may remember me as a tyrannical reformer who brought in peace and prosperity. Your job is to consolidate, merge, and expand the family business, a new type of Don. What do you say to that?"

Ivan was still mute when Dominik extended his hand for Ivan to shake. Out of habit he shook Dominik's hand. Dominik said in jest, "Welcome to the new Polish business mafia." The second he shook Dominik's hand, he realised what that action meant.

Ivan thought, *fuck*.

www.ingramcontent.com/pod-product-compliance
Lightning Source LLC
Chambersburg PA
CBHW071229210726
48293CB00002B/638